Mel Massey

Earth's Magick

Book Two
~Water~

Cover Art:
Select-O-Grafix

Publisher's Note:

This is a work of fiction. All names, characters, places, and
events are the work of the author's imagination.

Any resemblance to real persons, places, or events is
coincidental.

Solstice Publishing - www.solsticepublishing.com

THE EARTH'S MAGICK SERIES:

Earth's Magick, Book 1 ~Earth~

Decker: The first companion novel to the series

Earth's Magick, Book 2 ~Water~

Coming soon:

Vasha: The second companion novel to the series

Chapter 1

Mela rolled over in bed and almost cried out in pain. Every muscle in her body screamed when she tried to reach for her cell phone to turn the alarm off. After a few unsuccessful attempts, she finally managed to reach it and hit the right button.

"Oww," Mela groaned. Sitting up was harder than it should have been. Every muscle in her body, including her hands, burned with the slightest of movement.

It was Saturday. Normally, she'd sleep late, enjoy a lazy morning sipping coffee, and watch television. Her life wasn't normal anymore.

"Hey….you up yet, Poppet? Time to get to work. Time to bleed!" Decker laughed as he gave her bedroom door a few hard thumps with his fist.

"I'm up, I'm up. Stop it. Shit!" Swinging her legs onto the floor was difficult to do since Mela was trying very hard not to use her abdominal muscles. She shuffled like an old woman to the bathroom and closed the door behind her. Every morning for the past two weeks was the same. Decker made her train before work and after work. She was exhausted.

Since it was Saturday, they would be training off and on all day. Decker made her run as well. Mela hated to run. He forced her to do sit-ups, pull-ups, pushups, yoga, and finally combat training. She thought it would be more fun than it really was. The people in movies made learning new stuff look way too easy. This was not easy.

After an obscene amount of exercise, Decker would toss her a wooden sword and make her slowly go through drills. Her muscles were so sore the practice sword felt like lead in her hands. With painfully slow movements, Decker would stand directly in front of Mela and she was to

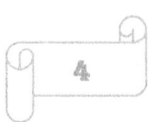

duplicate his every move. She thought she would never look as graceful as he did when he sliced his sword through the air.

Like a cat, he would bend and stretch his body and he looked so damn strong while he did it. She watched his muscles flex in his arms and his back. His power and grace were hard to watch and not get lost in. His balance was the only thing Mela seemed to be able to mirror with little difficulty. There were times when he would shift his weight from one foot to the next and she was thankful she could follow him.

It wasn't simply the workouts or the sword play that hurt her. It was what happened after all of that. When Decker took her sword and turned to face her with his mischievous grin, she knew he was about to hit her. The first time he hit her, it hurt like hell. It caught her off guard and she fell flat on her ass. Learning to block was her first lesson and that was why her arms were so sore. His punches, although he denied it, were full of power. If that was a light punch, then she never wanted to be at the receiving end of real one.

Mela washed her face and picked up dirty clothes from the floor. She sniffed them and decided they weren't rank enough to wash yet, so she put them on. A bit of dirt, and what looked like dried blood was on the front of the t-shirt, but other than that, it would work. She looked at herself in the mirror and, despite being exhausted, she saw she'd dropped a few pounds and a healthy glow was in her cheeks. As she brushed her teeth, Mela found something to tie her hair back with. The last time she forgot to do that, Decker grabbed a fistful of her brown locks and took her to the ground. Pulling hair really is an effective tactic in a fight.

She felt somewhat ready as she made her way into the living room and started turning on lights.

Decker sat on the kitchen counter eating something that resembled a sandwich. But it dripped with too much sauce and he made a mess. Decker recently became aware of hot sauce and now he drowned everything he ate in it. He hopped off the counter when he saw Mela and shoved the remnants of the sandwich in his mouth.

"You ready?" his words were muffled but she nodded to him. Together, they walked outside into the early morning. The sun wasn't really up yet. The sky was gray and a slight morning chill was in the air. Mela inhaled the smell of fall and memories of her childhood flooded her mind. This was the time of year children were going back to school, she thought. She remembered this early morning smell of fall as she walked to the bus stop. Everything was so calm and normal to her back then.

"Oy...catch," Decker tossed her a wooden sword and she deftly caught it in her right hand. Despite being sore, she really enjoyed these lessons with him. Vasha would make his way out to watch as well, after he slept late and ate a big breakfast, of course. Surprised, Mela thought they wouldn't be fighting this early, but she took her stance and bent her knees, readying herself for the fight. Decker gave her a look and shook his head. "Not yet," he said as he stretched his muscular arms across his chest. She relaxed and stood, wary, wondering if this was some sort of test. Or worse, if he'd attack her with no warning.

Mela began stretching, keeping a close eye on him as she did. After a few moments, she heard footsteps crunching on the freshly fallen leaves. Theo and Bear walked casually together towards them. For a moment, it seemed as though they were having a silent conversation. However, since she was keeping one eye on Decker, she couldn't tell before Bear and Theo parted ways.

Theo crouched down just outside of the designated fighting area. Bear galloped to Mela and leaned his large form against her in greeting. She rubbed his head and looked at Decker questioning him.

"Time for a bit of a change up. As my brother has pointed out, if I'm to train you, I've got to train your familiar as well," Bear watched Decker, his bright brown eyes attentive and ready. Mela frowned and bit her bottom lip.

"You won't hurt him, will you?" Mela asked.

Decker threw his hands in the air in frustration. "No, no more than I hurt you. But he's gotta learn, Mela. He's your familiar and Theo's been teaching him a few things as well. That right, brother?" Mela turned and Theo nodded his head.

"All is well. He understands much and is eager to fight by your side." Theo's soft voice made her feel a lot more secure. She knew Decker wouldn't hurt her, per se, but she trusted Bear's life to Theo over anyone else.

She turned and took her fighting position with Bear by her side. Decker smiled and made a feint toward her. Mela stepped back deftly, wooden sword at the ready, when he did. Bear took two steps back and circled behind Decker. Mela smiled, seeing the plan, and decided to go on the offensive. She made a swift strike that barely missed Decker's chest and he hopped back, laughter in his eyes.

"You can't get me....Ouch!" Bear had Decker's leg in his jaws. His bite wasn't hard enough to break the skin but tight enough that he could toss his head back and forth and let loose a low growl as he did. That was all Mela needed.

She slid on the ground toward him, as he'd often told her to do, and gave his shins a solid whack with the side of the sword. Bear let go of Decker and Mela was once again on her feet. Decker was rubbing both of his shins and cursing up a storm. She smiled, knowing she'd regret the smugness later, but she couldn't help it. It was the first time she'd been able to gain the upper hand against him.

It felt good.

Chapter 2

The sound of thunder woke Mela from a deep sleep. From her bed she watched the dark sky brighten with streaks of blue light. She felt each rumble of the thunder as the skies opened up and rain began to fall. She stayed in bed and watched the rain slide down the window, and snuggling deeper into the covers, she felt content. The sounds of the rain and rolling thunder made her feel calm, soothing her back to sleep.

When she opened her eyes again, the sun was struggling to shine through the gray clouds. September always brought on strong storms in the south. Southerners took it all in stride and carried on with their business as if nothing was amiss. The only real danger to Mela, or her home, was the possibility of floods on the old country roads. However, since it was Sunday, she was happy to stretch her sore muscles and lazily make her way into the kitchen to make coffee without worrying about driving in the storm.

Pleased at the amount of rain and lightning, Mela figured her training was cancelled for the day. As she sipped her piping hot cup of coffee, she heard footsteps on the back porch and her excitement for deferring training for the day waned. Decker let himself into the kitchen and, shaking his head like a dog, splattered water all over the laundry room floor.

"Gah….I hate getting wet," he complained. Mela pulled another mug down from the cabinet and poured him a cup. With thanks, he took the coffee and slurped his first taste of it. Mela waited for him to bring up the subject of training--she didn't want to sound too eager to skip it. She watched him over the rim of her cup and slid into a chair at the table. He followed her and sat.

"You know, you can sleep in the extra room in the house. No sense in getting rained on all night." She said.

He waved off her words and slurped from his cup again. "I slept in the shed with Vasha. We were up late anyway, so I crashed out before the storm hit."

"Oh? What were you guys up to all night?"

Decker met her eyes for a brief moment and looked away. He looked away and made a production out of blowing on his coffee.

Narrowing her eyes, she asked again. "What were you doing all night?"

"Just....talking," he said before he hopped out of his chair and placed his half empty cup in the sink. "No need to train today." He gestured at the window. "Won't get much done in this mess."

"You okay?"

"Oh sure. Right as rain." He laughed at his joke and absently waved to her as he went back out the door and into the rain once again.

"Well, that was odd," she said to herself. She really couldn't remember the last time she had a day to herself with no one else in the house and no training to do. She sat and listened to the sound of the rain hit the roof of the house in peace. The sound and the feel of the spectacular display calmed her and soon, Mela was happily sweeping the floors and tidying up the kitchen. She'd been quite a bit better at keeping a cleaner house of late. With so many people traipsing in and out, she found she was embarrassed by the stack of dishes and ever present mountain of laundry.

Breakfast was a healthy serving of fruit and organic granola in yogurt. Feeling quite pleased and excited for a day of freedom, Mela thought of what she should do next. She looked out of the window and watched as a black crow flew to her front porch and sat at the window seeking refuge from the storm. This newcomer excited Kat and he sat on the edge of the couch, tail swooshing from side to side, watching the intruder with interest. Bear, moving slowly and wagging his tail, greeted Mela with his wet nose, and then went in search of his breakfast. Feeling that all was right in the world, Mela made a plan to cuddle up with a book of no consequence and take a day all for herself. She couldn't remember the last time she did that. Excited, she placed her dirty dishes in the sink, rinsed them, then went to peruse her book collection.

While trying to decide between a classic or a trashy romance, her phone chirped from the other room. She fought the urge to ignore it but assumed it was either Wyatt or Todd, and it was best to go ahead and answer it. Sure enough, it was a text from Todd asking if she wanted to spend the afternoon together. She smiled and sent him her reply, thrilled to have some quiet time with him later in the day to look forward to. His work schedule had shifted of late. He spent many evenings and late nights working in the small, local hospital. That alone had kept them from spending as much time together as they would have liked but adding in Mela's training, and the exhaustion that followed, meant they had far less time for casual dates than they would have liked.

She spent the rest of the morning reading a trashy romance novel in blissful silence. All was right in her world, so when she went to stand on the rain-drenched patio to have a cigarette, she inhaled the smell of the damp earth. Rain was a beautiful thing but what came afterwards was always her favorite. Everything was so clean, the trees seemed a bit greener, and she sensed the deep, refreshing breath the forest took. Wet footsteps brought her back to the present and she smiled as Theo and Decker approached her, presumably from Vasha's shed.

"I hope you are enjoying your day, Mela. I too love the rain." Theo spread his impressive wings as he spoke and shook them free of the droplets. Decker walked past Mela and wiped the rain water from the seat.

"Have a seat," he said to her, motioning to his chair. Mela frowned. Both of them stood still, staring at her. A deep sense of foreboding hit her and she sank into the chair, scared of what was to come.

"Do not worry, my dearest friend. We mean only to discuss some matters with you. Some important things..." Theo's voice trailed off as Decker caught his eye and shook his head.

"What? What's going on?" she asked. Decker settled himself against the rail on the porch and folded his hands in front of him His calm demeanor worried her deeply. What were they up to?

"I don't really know how best to say this so I'm gonna go ahead and just say it, Theo and me have to leave for a little bit." Mela felt his words like a blow to her gut. She sat in Decker's chair, stunned and silent. "I know you're wanting to know what this is about and we'll tell you, just not yet. This is something we've got to do."

"I...what...why?" Mela felt the familiar icy fingers of panic tickle her insides. If they left her, she'd be alone. She wasn't afraid of The Hag but she was afraid of losing them. "Will you be back?" she hadn't meant it to sound as pathetic as it did but as the words came out, tears stung her eyes and she fought to blink them away.

"Aye. We'll be back. Don't worry about that."

"When?"

"Can't rightly say. As soon as we can." Mela looked at Theo who was watching her intently. For his sake and her own, she took a few deep breaths to control the ache that seemed to hollow her out from the inside. Without them here, not having either of them close would leave her feeling lost and alone. Sure, she had Wyatt, who had always been her best friend, but he wasn't them. He wasn't...other.

"We will return as soon as we're able, Mela. We love you and do not wish to be parted. But this we must do. Sooner rather than later." Theo said.

What could she say or do except nod her head in silent agreement? So she did and watched as Decker jumped off the porch, smiling as he grabbed a small rucksack she hadn't noticed before from the ground and tossed it over his shoulder. He seemed excited at the idea of leaving and for some reason this made her hurt more. Was it so horrible here? Was he so unhappy that he was anxious to leave? Where were they going?

"Wait," she called to them. "Are you going to stay together? I just don't want anything to happen…" she couldn't make the words come out and she blinked furiously as Theo approached her.

"We will be together and we will be safe." He placed a soft, furry kiss on her cheek and turned to follow his brother towards the trees.

"Decker," she called to him. His avoidance of saying goodbye hurt her deeply. He turned and stared at her from across the yard. "I'll miss you. Hurry back." He smiled, extended his arms to either side of him, and bowed toward her. She was reminded of the first time they met, when he did the exact same thing. They both smiled.

"Don't wait up!" he said, laughing loudly as he and Theo disappeared into the trees. Sighing heavily, Mela stood motionless. Did they know how happy she had been alone this morning? Had she done something to cause them to want to leave? She already missed them and her mind worked overtime as she tried to figure out what they were up to and why they had to leave right away.

"Are you well?" Sammuele's voice cut into her silent monologue and she jumped. Laughing at herself, she turned to face him, the lost Angel, forced to stay with her until they completed their task.

"I'm all right. Just…the boys, Decker and Theo, they left." She hated saying the words. She hated to think of them off out there and what could happen to them knowing the dangers they faced. She hated not having them here to protect her when she slept. She hated all of it but the simple truth was, she would miss her friends.

"They've been whispering for days. I'd inquired about the subject, however…Decker felt it was a family matter." Sammuele's voice gave no hint of emotion but he frowned when he spoke. Mela realized she wasn't the only one who felt alone here in her big backyard.

"Well, nothing we can do about it. They didn't tell me what they were up to either, so don't feel bad."

"I don't." Mela let out a small laugh. "However, I do think it's time we made some progress in something other than your training. It behooves us to cast the spell, to find the next key before the hour grows too late." Mela nodded absently and chewed on her bottom lip. Theo wouldn't be here to help her set up, chattering away about the trees as she gathered dead wood for a fire. Decker wouldn't be here to heckle Sammuele, which although mean, had become a constant in their daily lives.

"Sure, why not?" she said as she tossed her cigarette into the barren fire pit.

"Good. Shall we meet her in an hour then?" he said. Something in his voice made her look into his eyes and she saw something there that was different. She couldn't put her finger on it, but it was definitely new. She smiled at him and nodded before turning to go inside. As she thought about what she might need, the rain began to fall again. The Green Book was an obvious necessity but she wondered about casting more protection prior to the spell and she sat down to thumb through the book for ideas. As the rain splattered against the window, a black shape caught her eye. The black crow was back, settled in against the window for protection from the rain.

Mela found she couldn't concentrate after all on the book and shut it with a bit more force than was necessary. Since finding an umbrella seemed impossible, she pulled the black, ruby studded cloak from her closet. Vasha had made it for her and it was gorgeous. So gorgeous she thought she shouldn't wear it. The material was so soft and heavy, it felt like water in her hands. Slipping it over her shoulders, there was a clasp, studded with rubies, that fastened with a metallic *CLICK*. The hood was large and loose when she pulled it up over her head. She felt like a proper witch. The thought made her laugh and she tucked the Green Book under her arm and headed for the back door. The beep of her phone going off stopped her in her tracks.

"Oh no." She smacked her forehead and let out a sigh. She'd completely forgotten about her plans with Todd. Checking her phone, she saw she would be late if she didn't leave right away. The message was from him, asking is she wanted to have an early dinner together. "Oh man," she sighed and sank onto the couch, placing the Green Book beside her. Absently flipping her phone in her hands, she weighed her options. Spend an evening with Todd or find the next key? Logic told her the obvious answer would be to do the magick she needed to do but she so wanted to spend some time with him.

"Does something vex you?" Sammuele broke into her thoughts. She looked up surprised he was inside. He never came inside.

"Yes. Something vexes me. What are you doing in here? And how many times have I asked you to announce yourself before you just start blabbering?" She was angry, not at him, of course--at herself and the way the day had taken such a bad turn.

"Yes, you have told me. I apologize. I only thought you would want to know Vashanu is without and asks permission to witness the spell. I do not trust that…creature."

"He doesn't trust you. He's not a creature…he's a…he's Vasha."

"I apologize I interrupted your thoughts. You are sad because Decktrios and Theothane have gone away?" Sammuele asked. Mela looked up at him as he stood, so tall and out of place in her little living room, and checked to see if he was poking fun at her. His face showed genuine confusion and interest.

"Yes. I'm sad because Theo and Decker aren't here. I'm going to miss them and worry about them until they come back."

"I believe they will survive whatever misadventures they have set upon. You needn't worry." His hand twitched as he reached out but jerked back to his side. She wasn't sure what had gotten into him but her phone chiming signaling another text message from Todd made her groan. Reading his message over again, she replied as quick as she dared that something came up and they would have to reschedule. She hit send and tossed the phone on the couch, grabbed the Green Book in her arms and headed out the door. All the while she had a nagging feeling that she would regret pushing send.

When she walked outside, followed by Sammuele, Vasha turned to greet her.

"Hello, Little Witch. Since my brothers are gone, it is up to me to assist you and watch over you."

"You wouldn't be able to tell me where they went, would you?" she asked. His yellow eyes narrowed, one hand caressing her shoulder while the other held broken tree limbs.

"No, pretty one, I wouldn't," he smiled and winked at her as he dropped the wood into the fire pit and settled back on his hind legs. Mela gave him a shake of the head and opened the Green Book to the page that showed the

Seal she needed to draw. Handing it to Vasha, she took a long stick and began to recreate the ancient symbols into the dirt, as she did, she could feel Vasha's eyes on her. Tilting her head this way and that and looking to Sammuele for confirmation, they decided it was an accurate depiction, so she lit the fire. She didn't need the fire really, but she felt better having it near. The warmth wasn't required but she enjoyed the smell and the crackling wood as the fire consumed it.

"What words do you say?" Vasha asked as he eyed The Green Book in fascination.

"I just ask for the Key. Nothing special really." She said lamely. Vasha gave her a sideways look and chuckled.

"Do you not use rhymes in your spell work? Has that practice gone away?"

"No…I mean yes. I use them. I just don't really need to with this…" she said and felt even more like a child as he watched her fidget. "Do you think I should rhyme this spell? Why?" Vasha indulged her with a smile and folded his arms, all four of them, across his chest.

"To rhyme your words adds power. Why do you think they call it spelling, Little Witch? This is such an elementary concept, I'm surprised you do not know this." He looked over to Sammuele, who was silent, and then back to Mela.

"Alright….rhyme my words. Sure. I can do that," she exhaled loudly and approached the seal on the ground. "I'm searching for the second Key, make the Key's location known to me." She smiled and looked up to Vasha for approval. He nodded his head and smiled. Movement caught her eye as the symbols on the ground began to shift and reshape into words:

Annabelle Martello

"Annabelle Martello…" Mela read aloud and noted the direction she had to look. "That's the symbol for Earth."

"Then your Key lies to the North, yes?" Vasha asked without looking away from the words in the ground.

"Yes, we go North,"

"Where are we going?" Wyatt's sing song voice carried from the back porch and Mela waved him over to them. He looked every bit the male model as he smiled at her. He ran his hand through his hair and greeted Sammuele with a nod, Mela with a side hug, and Vasha embraced him like a lost lover. "Seriously," he said, still in Vasha's arms, "Where are we off to now?"

"Somewhere north of here. Time to put some detective skills to work."

"I'm on it," Wyatt extracted himself from Vasha's embrace with a good-natured smile. "I can start tonight and call you as soon as I figure something out. Hey," he smoothed his pant legs and the front of his shirt as he spoke, "I thought you were going out with Todd tonight. What happened?" Mela didn't meet his eyes. She felt the guilt roar inside her because she knew that not only did she disappoint Todd but Wyatt as well.

"I had to reschedule," she said. He frowned and crossed his arms. "As much as I like him, I do have other priorities."

"This is true," Sammuele chimed in.

"Well, Cupcake, you'd better do some damn good damage control." Feeling low, she cleared the writing from the ground and watched as Vasha and Wyatt walked off together. Feeling a bit left out, she walked past Sammuele to go inside.

"Will you need anything else?" he asked. She stopped and frowned as she looked at him. He was acting so weird.

"No. I'll let you know if we come up with something tomorrow." Mela turned to go inside, leaving Sammuele alone in the backyard.

She really didn't want to check her phone, afraid of what she'd see. What she saw, when she checked it, was nothing. He hadn't responded. That was worse than anything he could have said.

Chapter Three

Monday morning dawned to another gray day that threatened rain as she drove to work in the wee hours. Turning on the windshield wipers, Mela made a mental checklist for the day. She planned on getting some time on the treadmill in before she started work. This new habit shocked many of her coworkers. Although Claudia, Mela's forever impeccably dressed boss, was keen on the idea, she spent a lot of time watching Mela.

Claudia made it a point to pretend she didn't know things in Mela's life were different but Mela could feel her eyes on her constantly. It wasn't a week prior that Claudia casually asked about the bruises on Mela's arms. Laughing, she explained she was working on her property and it was hard physical labor, often resulting in the many scrapes and bruises. Whether or not Claudia bought this explanation was anyone's guess. That woman had perfected the art of plastering on a smile, all the while hiding a calculating mind which was cataloging everything she saw. At some point, Mela knew she would have to come up with a better explanation or face some serious inquiries from her boss.

InStep was the only health club in Trinity Hills and Mela had worked in the offices since she left high school. As she walked in the doors, the gym floor was empty except for a few scattered older folks who came to walk on the treadmills before the crowds arrived. Waving as she passed, Mela unlocked her office door and turned on the lights. Her desk was neat and organized, despite being small and crammed with papers. She turned on her computer and began stretching before her early morning run.

Slowly, she reached down to touch her toes and felt the muscles in her lower back ache as she did. Straightening up slowly, feeling every vertebrae roll into place, she remembered Vasha telling her about the necessity for a healthy body in order to do proper magick.

"The blood flows, as do the hormones in your body, like a machine, Baby Witch. Your body, every luscious curve, should be used to increase your powers. Your mind is but one important part of the enigma that is a Witch. Your physical body should be cared for in the same manner. You are a creature of nature and it is imperative you treat your body as it should be treated. The right fuel, clean and healthy food, will give you the energy you need. Be mindful of how much alcohol and tobacco you take in." Mela remembered laughing at the hypocrisy of the statement as Vasha puffed on his Hookah and sipped wine.

She did start phasing meat from her diet and eating better – cleaner – food. Her energy was astounding once she did this. The smokes and booze…She wasn't ready to phase those out yet. She did feel the effects of both when she ran, however. One day, she knew, she'd have to put out her last cigarette and face a lifetime of missing them. But this wasn't the time.

Jogging at a comfortable rate, Mela was able to mentally check out. It was a glorious feeling. All she felt were her muscles working and the only sound was her breath and heartbeat. The primal rhythm to her life, *thump, thump, thump, breathe, thump thump thump, breathe…*

"Morning!" Mela was startled and slowed down her pace to see her boss, Claudia, in the building far earlier than normal.

"Morning. Sorry…just getting a bit of a jog in before work." Mela stumbled and stepped off the treadmill. Smiling, Claudia came closer.

"Make sure when you're running, you don't lean forward so much. It cuts off your air and makes taking deep breaths harder. And crank up the incline," she said over her shoulder as she turned to walk away. "The increase is better for training." Stunned, Mela grabbed a towel and wiped the sweat from her face. Training? What did Claudia think she was training for?

With no time to start down the what-if road, Mela was in her chair at her desk quick as can be to start her day. The endless calls that came in kept her busy for most of the morning. Claudia was going over the promotional photos Wyatt sent to her on her email and she kept asking Mela's advice on which one she preferred. Mela had a hard time deciding because, frankly, they all looked the same.

She was looking forward to lunchtime so she could spend some uninterrupted time doing research for Annabelle Martello. Wyatt's voice outside of her office made her smile. She could always count on the fact that one could hear Wyatt coming before seeing him. Beaming his bright smile to someone behind him, Wyatt let himself into Mela's office and stepped aside to allow his companion in. It was Todd, wearing a sheepish smile and looking to Wyatt, then at Mela.

"Hello, you two." Mela said, forcing herself to smile. The previous night's cold shoulder from Todd made her uneasy.

"Hi," Todd said with a smile and he stepped closer to Mela as Wyatt elegantly plopped into the chair opposite her desk. Awkwardly, Todd leaned in to plant a kiss on Mela's lips. She turned and offered her cheek, thinking it was bad manners to be locking lips at work. He frowned and stepped back a bit. "Sorry to drop in on you like this but Wyatt and I were going to lunch and we thought we'd come by to see you. Maybe if you want to come…if you have time, that is." His brown eyes were full of some emotion but Mela was too uncomfortable to try and delve into the depths she saw there. This was her work, a job she loved, and she tried hard to leave her personal life at home.

"We're going to Tita's for lunch. They have the best TexMex food and they're fast. Can you come?" Wyatt asked. Glancing at her schedule book, Mela went over what she needed to do for the day. Of course, work could wait until she got back. But she needed the time to research Annabelle…

"Do I have to beg?" Todd asked with a sad smile. Her heart clinched in her chest and the guilt came pouring over her.

"Oh, Snickerdoodle, I found that person we were looking for. You know….who we were talking about last night?" Wyatt said.

"Oh?"

"Yep," he reached into his pocket, pulled out a folded piece of paper, and passed it to her. "I think Sammuele might want to know it. But I think," he made it a point to lean forward, raising his eyebrows as he continued. "It can wait until tonight." Todd watched the exchange with a placid look but his eyes darted between Mela and Wyatt's faces. Nodding, Mela took the paper and tucked into her purse.

"I hear you," she said and gathered her things. "Well, let's go." She said and made a dramatic show of waiting for the men to hurry up. Laughing, all three walked from her office. Passing Tracey at the front desk, Mela and Todd ignored her but Wyatt stopped with a dramatic deep breath.

"Oh sweet nibblets, are you sick?" Mela looked over her shoulder and saw Tracey indeed looked like she was ill. Her hair was pulled back into a ponytail contrary to her usual flashy locks. Her face was pale and dull. "You should see a doctor about whatever that is," Wyatt quipped as he ushered Mela out of the door. Todd groaned and Mela stifled a laugh.

"Was that necessary?" Todd asked, half-smiling.

"Absolutely." Wyatt said firmly and walked to his car, unlocking the doors without another word. Mela shook her head and fought off the urge to scold him. He was never the one to let a slight against himself or his friends slip, even if that meant reminding the person constantly that they had once wounded him. Mela wondered how much forgiveness was really in her dearest friend.

Lunch was a rowdy and fun time. It was over too quickly and before the hour was out Mela was back to work at her desk. Tracey turned her back to Mela as she went around taking inventory. Mela frowned, wondering briefly what had Tracey looking so…sad.

Shrugging off whatever empathy she had for her coworker, she got back to work and enjoyed the rest of the day in silence. Late afternoon brought on dark clouds and the promise of the rain from earlier started to fall. As the thunder rolled in the skies, Mela saw many members leave early to avoid the worst of the rain that was coming. It felt like night as Mela watched the lights turn on in the parking lot and the rain fall in sheets. With her work completed for the day, there really wasn't much to do other than man the phones. So, Mela reached into her purse and found the folded piece of paper Wyatt had given her. It was a computer printout, with Annabelle's name at the top, and under it an address.

"North Texas Juvenile Mental Health Facility," she read aloud. She read the hospital's address and then some scribbled handwriting from Wyatt that told her this was the only Annabelle Martello in all of Texas. Followed up by a big, sad emoticon. "I need to tell Sammuele," she said to herself.

"Tell me what?" Mela jumped from her chair and yelped. Standing directly behind her was Sammuele.

"What the hell are you doing here?" she asked, clutching her chest. Sammuele shrugged his shoulders.

"You said we were to never be alone. I am ensuring your safety while here in your place of employment. Is that not what you said?" he asked, searching her face for an explanation. Calming down a little, Mela made sure no one was watching and sat back down.

"Yes, I said that. But I didn't think... I just didn't know you were here.... Are you here often and I don't know?" she asked.

"I am here often, yes. No one can see me, only you."

"So, right now it looks like I'm talking to myself?"

"Most likely. What was it you needed to show me?" Still a bit miffed that she was essentially being spied upon, Mela handed him the paper and he read it over quickly.

"What do you think? Can you go there and see?" she asked. Sammuele handed the paper back to her and nodded.

"I will go straightaway. I will know when I see her if she is indeed the Key."

"Good. Come back and tell me what you find, if you would," Sammuele nodded but she reached out to grab his arm. "And make yourself visible to me. I really, really don't like someone hanging around that I can't see. I'd rather see you."

"As you wish," Sammuele said and held Mela's gaze before nodding and turning to disappear. Feeling uneasy, Mela tried to focus on organizing work for the following day. Sammuele had been acting strange lately and she decided she would try to get him to talk about his odd behavior the next time she had the chance. With Theo and Decker gone to who knows where, she didn't want to miss anything that might be a danger to them. She trusted Sammuele, she knew she did, but his idea of help had never been what she would call helpful. She preferred Theo's honesty.

She missed the evenings with Decker when he would tell her stories about his life as they sparred. She knew Wyatt had spent several nights with Decker and wrote his stories down. She was dead curious to read them. However, Wyatt said he was typing them up before he handed them to her. He hinted at Decker's painful past and many times urged her to patience when she was frustrated with him. "He's never had a real family before, Doll Face. Be patient with our boy." She could still see the pain in his eyes as he said it.

"I've picked out the photos from the ones Wyatt sent me," Claudia's burst into Mela's office and set down a stack of folders on her desk. "I like the one we both picked out, the one with the staff in the background." She said as she flipped through the papers in the first file folder.

"Will these be on the new flyers?" Mela asked. Claudia nodded and licked her fingers to get a better grasp on the papers she was counting. Mela nodded and turned to her computer screen. When she did, she came face to face with Sammuele who was standing right over her. Letting out another unintended yelp that stopped Claudia's counting, Mela put her hand on her forehead.

"What?" Claudia asked, slightly irritated. Mela looked at Sammuele briefly, then back to Claudia.

"Noth…nothing. Sorry. I saw a…spider. I hate spiders." Claudia eyed her for a moment longer before resuming her counting. Mela exhaled and gave Sammuele a piercing look.

"It is the Key. This one might be complicated." He said. Mela looked at him then glanced in Claudia's direction. Nodding silently, she hoped he would simply go away.

"Can you make sure these are given to all employees please?" Claudia handed her the file folder she'd been looking at. "

"Sure."

"We need to put protection in place for Annabelle quickly. She is very young--"

"And don't let anyone put their lunches in the cooler for clients to see. Next time I see that, I'm going to start throwing them away." Claudia said as she opened the other file folders.

"Okay," Mela said to Claudia but looked at Sammuele for a moment.

"What's wrong? You look like you've seen a ghost."

"Nope, no ghosts here." Mela said in an effort to sound nonchalant. It came out squeaky and tense.

"I will go and keep watch on the Key. We will speak this evening about it." Relieved, Mela nodded.

"Good idea," she said, then cringed.

"What's a good idea?" Claudia asked looking more and more concerned for her employee.

"No...I mean...It's a good idea to throw them away. The lunches...I mean." Mela wished for the floor to open up and suck her through it. Claudia frowned, gathered her folders in her arms and announced she was leaving early.

"I don't want to get stuck on the road in a flash flood," she said, turning to leave. She stopped halfway out of the door and turned to look at Mela. "You sure you're doing all right, hun?" Touched, Mela smiled and nodded to her boss.

"Yes. Sorry, I'm just a bit scattered getting the schedule done for the week. I'm okay though. Thanks." Mela tried to look confident but the guilt of lying to her boss hit her hard. What else could she have said? "Oh yes, Boss, it was just Sammuele, an invisible angel, who startled me. I can see him but you can't." No sooner than the words would be out of her mouth, she'd be carted away to a mental health facility of her very own.

The rain was falling heavily outside as Mela ran to her car. Jumping in the front seat, she heard her phone chirping that she had a call. She answered it while she started the air defroster and tried to defog the windows.

"Hello?"

"Hey, it's me. Todd."

"Hi. I'm just leaving work and had to run to my car. The roads look like a river right now."

"Yeah, I know. Well, if you didn't want to drive all the way home, I could come get you. Take you to my place…" Mela felt the butterflies jump around in her chest and a warmth crept through her.

"That's sweet, Todd. But I'll be fine. I don't mind driving in it, really. I just have to be careful is all." A long silence followed her words and she squeezed her eyes shut. She always managed to say the wrong things to him. She didn't want to be seen as needing to be rescued. She was a strong woman and didn't need that. But it came across all wrong.

"Well…I'm glad we got lunch today. It was good to see you. Even if it was Wyatt that got you out." His words sliced her heart.

"What does that mean?" She could hear him sigh heavily on the other end of the phone.

"You're avoiding me. The only reason you went to lunch today was because Wyatt was there. I know it. I'm not trying to sound like I'm complaining--"

"Yet you are."

"Yeah. I think I have a right to complain a little. I know you have some….weird things in your life--"

"Whoa…weird things? Those weird things are people, Todd."

"People? Seriously?" Mela's anger boiled over at the sarcastic tone in his voice.

"I know it isn't cookie cutter perfect. I know it isn't totally normal. But they're my friends. More like my family really-"

"Not even human but they get more of your attention than I do. Do I need to remind you I came running too when you needed help? I just want to be considered important to you too."

"So you insult the people closest to me?"

"I'm sorry. Really. They're...fine. I just want-"

"I know what you want, Todd. But you have to remember there's a lot going on that I haven't told you. *Weird stuff.* Stuff I can't tell you and that stuff has to take priority over--"

"Over me. Just say it, Mela. They all take priority over me. I'm just...waiting in the wings for you to make time for me. Which you don't do often."

"This is really unfair."

"It really is. I've been telling myself that a lot. I've volunteered at the hospital tonight. It has really been busy and they need me. Unless you're free? If you're free to spend time together, I'll cancel..." Mela closed her eyes and counted to five. She needed to talk to Wyatt and Sammuele about making plans to visit the Key, Annabelle. She needed to find out what Sammuele meant when he said this one was going to be "complicated."

"Well..."

"I'll take that as a no. Have a good night, Mela." And then he hung up. Mela exhaled and tossed her phone in the passenger seat. Her hands shaking, she drove home in silence.

Chapter Four

When Mela got home, she looked hopefully for signs of Theo and Decker's return. With a heavy heart, she opened the door and was welcomed by Bear.

"At least I have you," she said as she sat on the floor, and wrapped her arms around his neck. Happy for the attention, Bear rolled on his back and begged her for belly rubs. Mela heard her phone going off in her purse but she ignored it. She was enjoying a few moments alone with Bear, something she didn't get often anymore. The threat of tears stung her eyes. She was at the precipice of getting control over her emotions and going on, or letting go and letting the tears flow.

Bear, sensing her sadness, wiggled on the floor, his big pink tongue lolling. His face looked dopey upside down and his face stretched to mimic a huge smile. Mela smiled in return. As soon as he saw her smile, he jumped up and ran around the room, much as he did when he was a puppy. Laughing, Mela pretended to chase him and that's what she was doing when Sammuele appeared.

"Hello. Are you well?" he asked. Bear skidded to a stop to sniff Sammuele and then he trotted to stand beside Mela.

"Sammuele," she said as she scratched Bear's head. Their eyes met for a moment and then they looked back at the angel. Stepping over her purse on the floor, he approached Mela.

"We need to speak of the Key."

"Annabelle."

"Yes."

"Use her name. She isn't a thing, Sammuele. She's a person." Mela sank into the cushions on the couch and patted the seat next to her. Cautiously, Sammuele followed her and rigidly perched on the seat beside her.

"Tell me about Annabelle."

"She is a child. A child of no more than ten," Mela groaned and wondered at the state of Annabelle's mind. "She is a ward of this hospital."

"Her parents? Where are they?"

"I do not know. She is alone, with the exception of the hospital staff. However, the child is…unique," he turned his dark eyes to Mela and she saw the first real flicker of emotion in them.

"What is it?"

"She has the ability to speak with the dead. I felt them there, all around her. She is surrounded by the spirits of those who have passed before her. The lost souls who do not know they are dead or who do not wish to move on. Those are her companions. Her mind, although not as addled as the other K--" Mela narrowed her eyes. "--not as badly damaged as Sandra Jones, is different."

"Different. She's just a kid, Sammuele. What are we going to do?"

"You will have to meet with her, as you did the other. We must find a way." Mela chewed on her bottom lip as she tried to work out how to accomplish a visit with an unknown minor in a mental hospital.

"I'll work on it. Maybe I'll ask Wyatt to help out. He's good at this sort of thing," she said. Sammuele nodded. A few moments went by and neither one spoke. Mela sat back against the cushions and exhaled. When he turned to look at her, their eyes met for a moment, and she was struck at how human he seemed. Uncomfortable with the silence, Mela stood, stretching as she spoke.

"I'd better get changed. Even though Decker isn't here, I have to keep up training. I'm going to see if Vasha wants to play," she said, smiling. She walked past him and quickly went down the hallway. Sammuele's weirdness was starting to get uncomfortable. Whatever was going on in his angel brain was creeping her out.

Mela changed into proper workout clothes and headed out to see where Vasha was. Happily, she saw Sammuele was no longer sitting on the couch, so Mela and Bear headed out to the back yard. The rain was dripping slowly from the trees, not enough to dissuade her from being outside. A quick glance around showed her Vasha must be in the shed, but she could tell Bear was anxious to run. So they did. She ran in her bare feet, into the grass and she tried to keep up with her four legged friend. There was no chance of it, but he seemed to enjoy her trying. Turning around the old oak tree, Mela cut back toward the house. She wasn't sure if she could manage a proper sword workout on her own, but she thought she should grab the wooden swords from the shed anyway.

She approached the doors and hesitated. It was her shed, but it was Vasha's home now, wasn't it? She raised her hand and knocked on the thin, wooden door.

"*Entre vous,*" Vasha's sultry voice called to her. No matter what he said, no matter what he did, she had to smile and laugh. What else could she do? Poking her head inside, she saw Vasha snuggled deeply beneath pillows and fringed blankets. He motioned for her to come in and she opened the door wider. Bear, pushing past her, bounced into the room, claiming one of the corner pillows as if he did it all the time. She wondered if he did.

"Sorry to bother you, Vasha, but I..." she didn't know what to say. He didn't seem the fighting type to her. Would he help her train? she wondered.

"You are normally getting hot and sweaty with my brother but he is not here....so you came to me. Finally, alone at last," he said, smiling his secretive smile as he spoke. Mela let out a short laugh and rolled her eyes. She was becoming accustomed to the sexual innuendos by now.

"Yeah, since they left me high and dry," she said. It came out a bit more bitchy than she'd intended.

"Tsk tsk…Come sit, little one. I will help you train. But," he said as he leaned in toward her, tracing a blue finger up her arm as he spoke, "I would like to teach you some of what I know." Vasha smiled.

"No," Mela said and made to leave. She adored Vasha but getting freaky with him in the shed was not what she had in mind. He grabbed her arm and pulled her back down.

"Such a randy little thing to think I want to devour you. I do, mind you, I would enjoy watching your toes curl and your back arch in pure bliss. But, that is not what I mean to teach you this night. Unless," he smiled, "you're open to the idea?" Mela shook her head firmly. "Very well. Will you listen to me? Will you learn from me? I'm not as exciting as my brothers are, but I can be helpful, in many ways…."

Mela settled back onto a large, purple pillow and wrapped her arms around her knees. Vasha readjusted himself so that he was laying on his side, facing her, with one arm holding his head while another held a metal pipe. He saw her eyeing his long pipe and smiled.

"Do you like it? It is a treasure from long forgotten days. I keep it so that I may remember….I like to remember. Unlike my brothers who wish to forget. I like my memories, the happy ones and the painful ones. You see," he took a puff from his pipe and exhaled it. "I know a bit of magick myself. Not like you, of course." One of his hands batted the words away in dismissal. "But I was taught a little. It is different, but powerful."

"Who taught you?" Mela's curiosity was piqued.

"Mages, from long ago. They rescued me…but that is a story for another time. What I wish to tell you about is how beauty can be useful. Seduction is also a powerful tool, but I think we'll wait for that lesson." He smiled when he saw the worried look on her face. "Come closer, Mela, come closer to me. I want you to see," Mela scooted closer and Vasha made room for her on his pile of pillows.

"What am I looking at?" she asked. Being alone with Vasha, no matter how benign the reason, made her very self-conscious.

"Look at my skin. Beautiful, is it not?" His skin really was a gorgeous shade of blue. "Look closely, tell me what you see." Mela leaned closer and after a moment, she saw them. Markings on his skin. Some were ragged lines, others swirls. They were scars.

"Scars?" Mela flinched when her eyes adjusted to the contours of his skin. Welts of varying sizes and shapes covered his entire body.

"Yes. Some, some were given in malice. Wounds inflicted upon me for…well…I thought I deserved them at the time. However, the ones I want to bring your attention to are these." He lifted Mela's hand and made her trace the swirled scars with her finger on his chest. These were more uniform, spaced out by inches, and they covered his entire torso, front and back.

"What are these? There are others mixed in…what do they mean? Who did these?" Mela, no longer worried about touching Vasha, began to inspect the scars as he spoke.

"These, the ones that look like that, those were given to me by the Mages I spoke of. They are for protection, Little Witch. At times, when I mean to look my best and most fierce, I trace them in paint to make them stand out. However, the Mages gave me a permanent gift of protection. They taught me how to paint the ancient symbols and what they mean."

"What do they protect you from?"

"From dark magick, Mela. I am forever protected from dark magicks by these. I can never be lied to again. Never again will I be tricked… but they also protect from certain magick that could harm, not simply fool me."

"If I did that, would I have the scars as well?"

"We could, to make them more permanent. Perhaps one day you will think it best. But I have another plan. We shall draw them on you."

"Draw them? With what?"

'With this," he reached behind his back and pulled out a small, glass jar filled with a black liquid. In his other hand he held a long, dark blue feather. "It is ink. *Mehndi* or henna, as you would know it."

"I've heard of that. I've seen pictures of people who use it to draw on their hands and arms." Vasha nodded and pulled the stopper from the top of the jar.

"Yes, beauty…within beauty there is power. The symbols have meaning, depending on what is drawn. The lotus flower, the geometric shapes…all together are beautiful. The designs you see on me, although crude because they were meant to be forever, are no less powerful. And thusly, are beautiful to me."

"So….you want to draw on me? Right?"

"Just so. I will show you how beauty can be a tool, Mela. You are so conservative with yourself. With your beauty and your sexuality. It is a wonder you are from this century at all."

Mela laughed. "I'm really not a prude."

Vasha sat up and smiled. "Very well then, take off your shirt."

"Wait, what?"

"I do not intend on painting your hands as you have seen the adornments on others. No. These are not for that purpose. I need the smooth skin of your back." Mela narrowed her eyes at him, then shrugged her shoulders.

"What the hell." She grabbed her shirt and pulled it over her head. Aware of his gaze on her, she turned to the side.

"I will need your underthings gone as well." Throwing him a look of warning, Mela unhooked her bra and covered her breasts with her hands. Vasha motioned for her to lay down on the pillows, smiling all the while.

Mela hugged the pillows to her chest as she felt Vasha settle in next to her. She felt his hands caress her skin, running his long blue fingers over every curve as he did. His hands were warm and she found herself oddly relaxed. His warmth contrasted to the cool fabric beneath her breasts. Being alone with him made her think of Pan. It had been a long time since she saw him last and being in this close of quarters to Vasha made her miss him.

"Now, it will feel very warm to you, the ink. I will be heating it on an open flame."

"You're drawing it with your finger or the feather?" she asked.

"Although my hands are quite skilled at many things, this is something a delicate feather can accomplish with far better results. Now, just relax." When the warmth touched her skin, she was able to let go. She hadn't realized how tense she was until she released her grip on the pillows beneath her.

Turning her head to the side, Mela relaxed a bit more and studied the room. It was no longer a dingy shed. She realized that he had made it into his home. The pillows and blankets that littered the room weren't the only signs of someone living here. Trunks with intricately painted designs on them told her he had brought all of his worldly possessions and was now living cramped in her utility shed. She felt the all too familiar squeeze of guilt when she thought of where he must have come from and where he was now.

"Vasha?"

"Hmm?" No longer talkative, he worked diligently on the blank canvas before him.

"Where were you before you came here? What were you doing when Theo brought you?"

He completed the portion he was working on before he spoke. "I was living in the wild when Theo found me. I was, shall we say, homeless. I had not called anywhere home in a long, long time. I believe, the trees told Theo where I was." Mela let that sink in and she felt a little better. This, at least, was better than being homeless.

"Now tell *me* something. Why have you not bedded the handsome Doctor? He is nice to look at. Good, strong body. He admires you, that much I can see. Do you not desire him?" Mela considered his question.

"Honestly, Vasha, I don't know. I'm not the type to just...you know..."

"Fuck. Call it what it is, beloved."

"Fine. I don't know why I haven't fucked him. There, happy now?" She heard him chuckle as he continued working on her back. "I just... I like him. I do. A lot. But he's so...so...normal."

"What is normal? What do you mean by this?"

"I mean he's the dream guy for almost any girl in Trinity Hills. He's smart and has a great job. He's really nice to me...most of the time. I just think we're...we're really different though. He's Mister Trinity Hills and I'm..."

"The most powerful witch around."

"Yeah. Something like that. I think he wants me to be more like him. More normal. Less...witchy. I can't do that. If I'm going to sleep with anyone, it'll be because he accepts all of me. Not just tolerates us."

"Us?" Vasha asked, pausing.

Mela chewed her lip and thought about her slip of the tongue. "Yeah...he kind of let it slip he finds this...you guys...a little unnerving."

Vasha was silent for a long time. Mela thought about what she just said and allowed the truth of her own words hit home. Vasha, Theo, Decker, and even Sammuele were a part of her now. If he couldn't accept them completely, she couldn't be with him.

"There have been many people in my life I have loved. I have loved both men and women, so I know them both well. I have learned many things about love. What I know for a certainty is this : you must trust your instincts when it comes to affairs of the heart. If it feels wrong, that is your inner self trying to warn you. If your body screams for him, then you must have him or else you will never be satisfied. Do you understand what I am saying to you? Listen to your inner self and follow that voice, above all others, at all times. People, lovers, friends, they will all have motives when telling you to do a thing. Your inner voice is the only voice that is completely true to you, and you alone."

She felt the weight of his words and they continued on in silence for some time. She let what he said settle in her mind and finally allowed herself to relax fully in his presence. She accepted the warm tickling of the ink on her back. Vasha would occasionally hum to himself, but otherwise, he worked in uncharacteristic silence. An hour or more passed before he patted her rump and exclaimed, "We are finished."

Feeling as though she was waking from a nap, Mela stretched and wondered what her back looked like now that he was done with it. "Would you like to see it? Here, I can help you to see," Vasha turned and rummaged through one of the bigger boxes against the wall, pulling things out while he searched. Sitting up, cupping her breasts in her hands, Mela watched the most bizarre items fall to the floor in his search. Bells, swatches of cloth, trinkets made from bronze and silver clattered to the floor. His four arms worked feverishly, sifting through the contents, until from the bottom he pulled a thick square, wrapped in brown material from the box. "Here we are," he exclaimed.

"What's that?"

"A mirror, Little Witch." He carefully unwrapped the square and Mela saw it was indeed a mirror. However, this was unlike any mirror she'd ever seen. The edges were lined in gold. On the face of the mirror, intricate drawings of people lined the edges, carefully crafted in gold. Knowing Vasha, she figured it was real gold, not something meant to simply appear gaudy. He handed Mela a smaller mirror that sat against the stack of boxes. This one was plain, no adornments and held together by a simple wooden frame. "Turn your back to me," he commanded. She did as he told her and held the mirror up to her face. In the reflection, she watched Vasha move closer and hold the mirror up so that her back showed in sharp contrast to the golden images on the glass. Adjusting her mirror just so, she held her breath. Her back was once as plain as the mirror she held. Now, after the careful attention of Vasha's talent, she gazed at a foreign stretch of flesh. The contours of her back were highlighted with elegant brush strokes of ink. Flowers, shapes and seemingly random dabs of ink that created an exotic image in the glass. Letting her eyes adjust, she allowed herself to admire not only the art, but her own image. She didn't feel plain, standing in Vasha's shed at this moment. In the reflection of the golden mirror, she saw beauty. The delicate, golden renditions of naked people framed her curves in the mirror. It was an image she'd never forget.

"This is…amazing," she said softly.

"As are you, Mela." She turned and met Vasha's gaze. No longer concerned about concealing her nudity, she smiled. She felt beautiful, here in his shed, surrounded by images of naked men and women, it seemed perfectly natural to be without concealment.

"I love it," she said. "Thank you." Vasha bowed slightly and smiled, carefully placing the mirror to the side.

"You will need to keep it dry until tomorrow at the earliest. The stain should set and remain for weeks. I will occasionally touch it up to ensure it stays for as long as you need it to. This is the protection I can offer you. Among other things." His sly smile made her laugh as she reached for her clothes.

"It's getting late and I'm hungry. Want to eat with me?"

"I would like nothing more," he said and busied himself with placing the discarded items back in the large box. "Please allow me to put things in order here, then I will join you outside." She nodded and picked up her clothes, carrying them outside. She only remembered her nudity when the cool evening air caressed her skin.

Knowing she was beautiful but not wanting to expose herself to others, she decided to dress. She didn't want to smudge the newly applied ink with her bra, so she gently pulled her t-shirt over her head and covered herself once more. Feelings relaxed and a bit rebellious, Mela considered what she and Vasha would eat for diner. He didn't seem to be the type to prefer sandwiches, like Decker did. Snagging the fresh vegetables from the drawer and a wedge of cheese, Mela placed the items on the counter to start chopping. The alert on her phone told her she had messages and she sighed. Placing the knife on the cutting board, she went to find her phone, still in her purse from hours ago. Four missed calls and eight text messages waited for her. Something wasn't right...

Checking the messages, she saw they were all from Todd, as were the missed calls. More than a little worried, she opened the messages and they all said the same thing, *'Please call me. Emergency.'* He left both his office number and a few other numbers she recognized as hospital numbers. This was not good. Their conversation from earlier made her wary to return the call-- it was the "please" that caught her attention. If he were angry with her, he wouldn't sound so…desperate.

Dialing the first of the given numbers, she heard the phone ring on the other end, then a woman's voice answered,

"Trinity Hills Memorial Hospital, how may I direct your call?"

"Yes, I need to speak with Doctor Morgan please."

"One moment." With a click of a button, Mela was put on hold and an odd classical rendition of a pop tune played in her ear. She was trying to remember the original song's name when she heard Todd's voice come on the line,

"This is Doctor Morgan." He sounded brisk and irritated.

"Todd, it's me. Sorry I miss--"

"Oh thank God, it's you," she heard him exhale loudly and he lowered his voice when he spoke next. "I need you to know something…I don't know if it has anything to do with your…the stuff happening to you but…" he hesitated to go on.

"What is it?" She felt a tickle of annoyance that he would infer something happening there might be her fault, but she bit her tongue.

"We've been busy here, lots of patients coming in, both local and more from neighboring counties who don't have the facilities for them. I haven't said anything to you because I couldn't, but tonight… they're acting the same and it's the damndest thing I have ever seen. I've never seen anything like this, Mela. They're all saying--"

"Who is they?" she asked.

"My patients."

"What are they saying? And what does it have to do with me?" She couldn't fight the annoyance in her voice. Either he didn't notice or he ignored it when he answered.

"The patients, all of them, are psychiatric patients, Mela. They all have to be restrained or they hurt themselves. I'm telling you because they all started saying the same thing tonight. Maybe they said it before but it was the first time I really put it together. It has to have something to do with you. It's the only thing that makes sense." Mela closed her eyes and felt the anger rise up. Gritting her teeth, she spoke,

"What makes you think that?"

"They keep saying the same thing over and over again. They're scared of something and tonight I got it. They keep trying to warn me about the monsters with the big black eyes. That mean anything to you?" Mela felt her anger extinguish into an icy pool of dread.

"Yes. I think I do. I need to see them."

"Yeah, I figured as much. Wait until the graveyard shift comes in. There's less people I have to explain to." Then he hung up. Mela didn't have time to be petty about her shaky relationship with her boyfriend. The Black-Eyed creatures had come to Trinity Hills.

Chapter Five

Mela stepped outside and almost collided with Vasha on the porch. She was so intent on her thoughts, she missed the large, blue man-cat standing right in front of her.

"Vasha, we have trouble," she said quickly. His smile faded and his eyebrows raised in question. "Todd called, said something about his patients at the hospital seeing black-eyed monsters."

"You cannot go alone," he stated firmly.

"I know. Get your things, you're coming with me." He smiled and leaped from the porch faster than she'd ever seen him move. His body was a bright blue blur as he crossed the backyard and disappeared into the shed. Moments later, he returned with a bundle held by his lower arms. The other two arms fitted an odd restraint around his upper chest that glittered with jewels.

"I was keeping this for a more appropriate time. This seems appropriate, however." He handed her the bundle. Mela took it and unfolded the material. It was the same as that of her cloak he made for her birthday. The fluid, black material felt heavy in her hands as she shook out the small swatch. "Do you like it?" Confused, Mela held it up and examined it. Two large triangles held together by thin strips of fabric and two longer strips trailed down.

"What is it?" she asked. He laughed and stepped closer, taking the material from her. As he spoke, he pulled her t-shirt over her head like a child.

"This is to complete the set, Little Witch. I will show you." Once again half-naked, Mela stood and watched the flurry of blue hands place the black garment against her skin and artfully wrap and tie it snuggly closed. The two triangles covered her breasts, and that was about all it covered. Her back was fully exposed, however, and she enjoyed the thought of what she must look like in Vasha's golden mirror.

"Wow," was all she could say.

"You should see yourself, Mela. A true Goddess." He smiled again, more seductively this time, as he unfolded the other bundle. It looked like a long skirt. He showed her it was, in fact, very loose fitting pants. Without another thought, she stripped her shorts off and stepped into the black pants, guided by Vasha's eager hands. He turned her around to fasten the top tightly against her skin with the same sort of long cloth. The pants didn't go much higher than her hip bones. So much of her was exposed, yet artfully displayed, she couldn't help but feel the power Vasha spoke of earlier. She felt seductive. She felt powerful.

"I like it. The cloak then?" she asked, slipping her shoes back on and Vasha nodded as he busied himself with the leather contraption around his chest. Mela went inside and caught a glimpse of herself in the bathroom mirror. She stopped and stared. The black material was deep and shimmered when the light hit it just right. She saw the familiar sparkle of red stones woven into the fabric. Gently touching one, she knew immediately Vasha would only use real rubies as he did with her cloak. Shaking herself back to the present, she rushed to her room to find the black cloak that completed the look Vasha created for her. Doubling back to her closet, she snatched the leather belt that held the sword Decker gave her. She'd only worn it a few times and handled the sword itself even less. But this wasn't a time for wooden swords. If she didn't need it, fine. If she did, she did not want to be without it.

"You are a vision. A fierce woman to behold," Vasha said as she stepped outside. Bear tried to follow, but she shooed him back inside.

"Stay," she commanded him. His loving brown eyes looked to her in question and his tail drooped down. Sighing, she cupped his furry face in her hands and kissed his wet nose. "I'll be back soon, my Bear. Be a good boy." She ruffled his head and he wagged his tail once more before she shut the door.

"What's all that?" she asked when she saw the intricately woven leather straps crisscrossing his chest.

"All in good time, my eager child. Do you have a weapon?"

"Other than my hands? Yes," she smiled.

"Good. It is not always acceptable to draw attention to yourself, Mela. Even in battle. Reserve the use of fire. Especially around humans. They will not understand and will panic. We do not want that." Mela nodded and adjusted the leather belt that held her sword. For a brief moment, she felt silly. Like a child playing dress-up, she wondered if she made a serious mistake. The hoot from an owl overhead made her jump. There, sitting calmly, was a white owl. Was it the same one? There was no real way to tell. It ruffled its feathers and twisted its head this way and that, focusing on the creatures below it.

"Do you like it?" Mela asked, holding her hands to her sides. The owl let out a soft '*Hoo*' that made her laugh. Other birds in the trees screeched and both Mela and Vasha turned to see black crows lined the branch opposite of the white owl.

"That is curious," Vasha said softly.

"Is it?" she asked. They were birds in a tree, not very curious at all, really. Crows were always round this time of year. The cooler weather and the sound of their cries from the sky were what she always thought of when she recalled the fall season in Texas.

"Crows…many of them. Curious," he said, then shifted his attention back to Mela. "We will travel to this place where your lover works. A hospital?" Mela nodded her head and wondered just how they would fit him in her car. "Give me your hand," he commanded and she obeyed. He pulled her close and motioned for her to his back. There, on his long, cat-like body, was a small leather saddle. Mela shook head.

"No way. I'm not riding you like a…like a…"

"Beast?" he laughed and nudged her closer. "Mela, my darling Little Witch, that is exactly what I am. I do not deny it. In fact, I relish it." With one last push, he coaxed her leg over his back and she sat astride just as she would a horse. He stood taller, and Mela found herself almost as high as she would if she were on an actual horse. His skin, so unlike that of human skin, was soft beneath her hands. The small leather saddle was only large enough to cover her backside. Not knowing where to put her hands made her uncomfortable. As Vasha fiddled with the leather straps, making them tighter here and there, she admired his long, flowing black hair. He braided pieces here and there and the effect was astonishingly beautiful. Tiny jewels glittered from the raven backdrop in which they lay hidden until the light captured their beauty.

"Here." He handed her what looked like braided leather reins. "Something to hold onto. I will guide us. But you must hold on. Tightly with both your legs and onto these. Keep low and close to my body. Turn as I do, lean when I do. Before long, you will ride me with ease." Mela snorted and Vasha let out a wonderfully excited laugh.

"Let's go then," she said. Mela pointed the way and they were off. At first, she felt awkward and heavy sitting upon such an elegant creature like Vasha. He stayed in the dark shadows of the trees and Mela was at once happy for the dark clothing she wore. Maybe it was a good idea after all. At times he ran so fast, the cool night air made it hard to breathe. She clung to the reins and averted her face from the wind. No matter what, she was thankful she wasn't flying. Mela hated heights and nothing in the world scared her more than the thought of flying. She'd take running at incredible speeds any day.

With Mela's directions, they were able to approach the hospital that sat nestled against a hill, with trees forming a backdrop. Still in the shadows, they crept closer until there were no more trees left to shelter them. Mela slid off Vasha's back and stood beside him, wondering how next to proceed.

"I'll go in and find Todd," she said. Vasha held her back and put a finger to his lips. From a pouch at his waist, he pulled out a leather strap and placed something inside it. He started swinging it over his head, round and round until it was a blur. He grunted as he flung whatever was inside and she saw the nearest street lamp explode into sparks. Together they crept through the shadows between cars and he repeated the process until they were flush against the side of the building, hidden by darkness and shadows.

"This is where I leave you. I will watch the windows for a sign. Open the window when you get to a safe place and I will join you." Mela nodded and nervously stepped from his side. "Mela," he whispered before she reached the door. "You look delicious," he said with a smile. Laughing under her breath, Mela shook her head and opened the door they carefully chose. It was a side door, dimly lit, as it was mostly used for the comings and goings of staff. Mela walked down the hallway and became cautious of anyone seeing her. She desperately wanted to go unnoticed so she pulled the hood of her cloak over her head and made her way to the stairway doors.

The heavy, metal doors creaked and groaned when she opened them, but she managed to slip into the stairwell without being seen. She knew Todd was on the next floor up. When she reached the door with the number two painted on it in fading blue paint, she opened it a crack and peeped out. She saw shadows down the hall to the right where it looked as though the staff had lowered the lights for their patients. Light streamed in from the other side but she couldn't see down that corridor. She assumed that was where the nurse's station was. With her heart thudding in her chest, Mela opened the door a little wider. She saw, just across the hall, a broom closet that was open a crack. Stepping from the stairway door, she rushed into the closet and closed the door behind her. Her breathing was raspy and her heart was thudding madly in her chest. She didn't want to be seen and she tried not to laugh at herself when she decided she would never have made a very good spy. The cloak and dagger business wasn't for her. Then she put a hand over her mouth to stifle her laugh. The fact that she wore a cloak and carried a dagger made her burst with giggles.

She opened the closet door and peeked out so she could see the nurse's station clearly. There, standing at the counter, was Todd. He was writing something and clearly wasn't paying any attention to what was going on around him. Mela could tell there was a nurse behind the counter but, unless she stood, she'd never see Mela if she stepped out. So she did. As quietly as possible and slowly so as not to catch anyone's eye, she stepped from the closet and stood still in the hallway. She watched Todd scribble away on the paper in front of him, checking his watch on occasion as he did. He looked up at one point, looking over his shoulder opposite of where Mela stood. Shaking his head, he went back to writing in his folder. He really was handsome, and seeing him completely in his element, Mela felt an unfamiliar stirring, a desire for him that took her by surprise. With a half-smile, she shook the thought from her mind. Now wasn't the time.

Tired of waiting for him to see her, she pulled the cloak back from her face a little and whispered his name.

She saw the moment he heard her. His body went stiff and his hand froze. Looking first at the nurse, then to his right again, he finally turned to Mela's direction. His mouth hung open for a moment, then he closed the folder he was writing in. He said something quietly to the nurse and approached Mela in the hallway.

"What are you doing? What are you wearing? Get in here." He opened a door and ushered her inside. He clicked the light on and stared at Mela. "My God."

"I don't have time to argue with you about my clothes. Where are the patients you told me about?" She saw his jaw clinch and he peeked out of the tiny window in the door.

"I'll get you to the room next door. There's a guy there who's not as bad off as the others. You might get something from him. His meds aren't as high of a dose as all the rest." He looked her up and down and she saw a flicker of something in his eyes. He opened the door and stepped out, holding his arm out for her to follow him. Two steps across and they were inside another room.

This room was even dimmer than the hallway. Only one light beside the patient's head cast an eerie glow around the room. But it wasn't the man lying in the bed that held Mela frozen where she stood in fear.

It was the monster beside his bed.

Stunned, Mela grabbed Todd's arm and whispered in his ear, "Do you see it?"

Startled, he looked at her, then again at the man in the bed.

"I see Mr. Albright. He came in sometime last week if I remember," Todd absentmindedly grabbed the chart from the foot of the bed and started flipping through papers. Shocked, Mela stepped closer to Todd and realized she was the only one who could see the monster in the room.

It was small, no larger than a child. Its skin was gray and leathery and its arms looked too long for its body. Its body was like that of a human but absurdly thin. The gray skin wrinkled in places, making it look even more like aged leather. The head was enormous compared to the thin, frail body. It bobbed up and down as if the weight of it was almost too much.

It was squatting on the head of the bed, with a hand clutching the neck of the patient, Mr. Albright. It turned to look at the intruders, then turned its attention back to its prey. The head was large, way too large for its body. The neck was so thin, she wondered how it could possibly hold such a bulbous weight. She watched as it leaned in close to Mr. Albright and appeared to whisper into his ear.

Mela pushed the edges of her cloak back to free her sword should she need it. She had a sinking feeling she would. Stepping closer to the man on the bed, Mela stayed on the opposite side from the creature that dug his claws into the man's neck.

"Mela, what is that?" Without looking away from the creature, she spoke,

"Do you see it?" Dropping the chart on the bed, Todd grabbed her arm and turned her to face him.

"A sword, Mela? Really? This isn't some fantasy game. This is a hospital. I can't let you have that here," Anger welled inside her so quickly, she forced herself not to hit him.

"Try to take it from me." Her voice was low and she glared at him with every ounce of rage she could manage. Shocked at what he saw in her eyes, he dropped her arm and stepped away from her.

"You need to go now," he said, as he straightened his white coat. Mela shook her head slowly and pointed toward the creature.

"You don't see it? You really don't?"

He looked where she was pointing, and then back at her, shaking his head.

"Get off of him," she demanded, looking directly at the creature. Slowly, the thing on the bed ceased its whispers in the man's ear and looked up to meet Mela's eyes.

All she could so was gasp. The creature's eyes were solid black. There was no life in them, no warmth, no anger – just a massive void of nothingness. As she looked into its large eyes, she had the feeling that she was falling from somewhere high and she forced herself to look away.

"Run," the man in the bed whispered. Both Mela and Todd looked at the pitiful man who lay lost under the white sheets. "Run," his hoarse voice whispered. Todd tried to approach but Mela shoved him away.

"Maybe you should've listened to your patients a long time ago, Doctor. You need to get back." She pulled her sword from the sheath and pointed it at the creature. "Get away from him," she said through clenched teeth.

The creature opened its mouth and let loose a loud cry that chilled her to her core. It reminded her of nails slowly dragging down a chalkboard. She saw rows of tiny, sharp teeth poking from black gums and knew it meant to use them. The creature stood up on the bed and took a step toward her. "Watch the door and stay where you are," she said as she backed away. She didn't check to see if Todd was listening. She was too busy watching the creature take small, jerking steps in her direction. Mela raised her sword.

"What's going on?" Todd asked softly, obviously stunned by the turn of events. Mela saw the creature bend its legs, preparing to leap in her direction. She raised her sword higher, placing her left foot behind her to brace for the coming attack.

The creature moved so fast, she barely saw it coming, even though she was prepared for it. A gray blur flew at her face, sharp teeth flashing and screeching, as it reached for her face with long claws. Her reflexes made her drop low. As she did, she positioned the sword to impale the creature upon impact.

It was quicker than she was.

Just before it made impact with her body, the creature brought its feet up and slammed them into her chest, bouncing off her like a rubber ball. She felt the impact and let out an "Oh," as the blade sliced the creature just enough to draw oozing, thick, black blood. Mela stumbled back against the wall, eyes searching the darkness for the creature.

"Todd, open the window," she said softly. "Todd." She turned to look and saw him, arms raised and a look of absolute terror on his face. The creature attached itself to his back, legs wrapped around his waist, long claws held his throat, and the rows of sharp teeth hovered over the tender flesh of his neck.

"Mela…" Todd begged her for his life in one single whisper of her name. Frozen with horror, he was incapable of moving and she was certain he saw the invisible guest now. She held her free hand up and took slow, measured steps toward the window.

"It wants me to take him out of this room. Mela, what do I do?" He sounded so small, and so afraid.

Mela spoke in a soft, calm voice just as she would to a frightened child. "It's okay…everything is okay. I'm opening the window…" she felt the latches that locked the window in place and, with one hand, raised it open. Still holding her sword, she backed away from it and waited. If her plan worked, she would have backup soon. "Through that window is the only way you'll leave." Mela said to the creature. It let out a hiss in reply but she saw it shifted its attention to look at the opening that was now available.

"What is it? What's on me?" Todd whimpered.

Mela held her finger to her lips, shushing him. mouth telling him to stay quiet. She watched the creature as it crawled down Todd's back and she heard the soft *THUD* when its feet hit the floor. Slowly, the creature and Mela each took steps toward their respective goals. Mela wanted to reach Todd and the creature apparently wanted to reach the window. Fine with her. She watched it step and shift its body from side to side, ready to pounce in any direction at a moment's notice.

Mela was nearing Todd, and as she did, she reached out for him, grabbed his arm and pulled him behind her. She raised her sword and motioned to the window, hoping it would understand her. One of the long, spidery arms reached for the ledge beneath the window, but it hesitated. It turned back to the man in the bed and looked as though it was deciding between him, or its escape.

Mela stepped forward, making it hiss at her and swipe at the air in her direction. She saw, as it scrambled to perch on the ledge, the black blood that oozed from a ragged line down its belly. Black drops of the oily substance splattered to the floor every time it moved. She positioned herself between both Todd and the patient in the bed, wondering which one the creature would leap for if it tried again.

A shadow moved at the window and Mela barely had time to register her relief before the creature was snatched by the neck, and dragged from its perch by a large, blue hand. She heard the muffled sounds of a struggle outside the window, and then there was silence.

"My God…" Todd whispered.

Mela snorted and turned to face him. "That   thing has nothing to do with God." She glanced at the man in the bed, staring at her with wide, still terrified eyes. She tried a smile, but she couldn't manage one, so it looked like she had a twitch in her cheek. Sounds from the window made everyone tense until she saw Vasha's head and torso start to squeeze through.

"You okay?" she asked, going over to assist him as he squeezed his oversized body through the small window.

"I am well. This one is not." He held up something with one of his hands. He held the creature whose neck was obviously broken. Black ooze dripped from its mouth and the long, spidery legs and arms trailed the ground as Vasha finally managed to get all of his body inside with much difficulty.

"Oh my God…" Todd said again as he looked back and forth between the door and the others in the room.

"This thing," Vasha said as he tossed the dead body at Todd's feet, "has met its God. If it has one, which I fervently believe it does not." He turned to Mela and gently caressed her face. "Are you injured?"

She shook her head. "No. I'm fine. I wasn't expecting…that," she said and motioned toward the crumpled body that Todd was carefully inspecting.

"It's not human," Todd said to himself.

"Most assuredly it is not," Vasha said and wiped the black ooze from his body with his hands. "I do not like this tactile experience. I need a cloth to clean myself…it is very sticky…" He shook his hands and black ooze splattered the floor.

Todd rushed to one of the cabinets and tossed Vasha a large towel.

"Many thanks," Vasha said as he attempted to clean the creature's blood from his hands.

Mela sheathed her sword, wondering what they would do with the body when a pitiful sound interrupted her thoughts.

Everyone turned to look at the patient, almost forgotten in the foray. He hadn't moved, and lay there whimpering. Mela approached him, Todd on her heels, until they both stood over him. Mela finally had the chance to see Mr. Albright and what she saw was a pathetic sight.

His hands and ankles were in restraints. He was thin and perhaps the same age as her father. His skin was prematurely wrinkled and he hadn't shaved for days. A mix of gray and brown hair sprouted from his face and from the top of his head. His eyes were crystal blue, and Mela smiled, thinking this man was once quite handsome before time and a hard life robbed him of his youth. His upper body shook with his sobs but his eyes never left Mela's face.

"It's all over now, Mr. Albright. Everything is okay," Todd spoke as he reached into his coat pocket. She saw him pull a syringe out and reached for the I.V. line in his patient's arm.

"What is that? What are you giving him?" she asked. Todd glanced up at her then back to his patient who continued to sob uncontrollably.

"We call it a cocktail. A mix of Ativan, Haldol, and Benadryl. It will knock him out...give him some rest. Maybe he'll even forget about all this, or think it was just a dream of something." Shocked, Mela reached across the bed and grabbed Todd's wrist.

"No. Not yet. I need to talk to him first."

"Make it quick. He's obviously upset. He gets violent." Todd stepped back and Mela leaned forward so Mr. Albright could see her face clearly.

"Mr. Albright... can you understand me? Shhh." She gently stroked his cheek and felt the rough bristles that grew there. He quieted down and took a few deep breaths before he nodded. "I saw it. I saw what was in the room with you." His eyes got wider and tears leaked from the corners of his eyes. He fought to keep his mouth closed, squeezing his lips together as he nodded. "It's dead, Mr. Albright. We killed it. Do you want to see?" Wide eyes looked back and forth between Mela and his doctor, waiting for someone to decide for him.

"I don't know if that is a good idea," Todd whispered. Mela stared hard at him but spoke as calmly as she could manage.

"He needs to see. Please." She willed him to understand and, after a silent fight with himself, he nodded. Reaching his hands under his patients head and neck, he raised him up. Mr. Albright seemed to panic at the sight of Vasha, but Mela cooed in his ear that it was safe.

"This wasn't a good idea," Todd said, but Mela hushed him.

"He needs to see…don't you, Mr. Albright?" The patient nodded his head. Vasha reached down, lifted the dead creature by one of its arms, and held it out for the man to see.

"Do not be frightened, dear, tortured soul. I have killed the thing that haunts you." Mr. Albright started sobbing again. Mela and Todd gently laid him back down. Todd motioned to Mela and they spoke quietly at the foot of the bed.

"I need to go check in with the staff. You have a few minutes with him. Don't excite him. He's obviously been through a lot-"

"That's not my fault," she broke in and he gave her a skeptical look.

"I'll be back in a few minutes," Without another word, Todd walked out of the room. Meeting Vasha's gaze for a moment and shaking her head, she turned once more to the man tied to the bed. She stepped closer and carefully sat on the edge of the mattress and studied the man as he struggled to make sense of his surroundings.

"Mr. Albright, I don't want you to forget. No matter what happens, no matter what anyone tells you, everything you saw was real. A bad thing came and was hurting you. That wasn't your imagination," she said quietly. Fresh tears fell from his eyes as he nodded. "Don't give up. Be strong. Can you do that for me?" she asked. Mr. Albright's hand shook as he lifted it as high as the restraints would let him and reached for her. Carefully, she placed her hand in his and he held on to it tightly.

"I...I," he cleared his throat and took a deep, ragged breath. "I tried to warn you...could have hurt you. It was telling me..." More tears fell from his eyes and pooled onto the pillow beside his face. Mela reached out and brushed them from his face.

"What did it tell you?"

"It...it said," he licked his dry lips before he continued. "It told me all the bad things I ever did. It said I killed people...told me I'd hurt more one day. It knew things...about me. It got in my head...mushed up everything in there. I don't know what's true and what's not...It made me see things that other people couldn't...dead bodies....kids." He closed his eyes and fought off the sobs that threatened to choke him. "But I don't know if they were real or not..." He began to sob again and Mela stroked his face with her free hand.

"I'm real. Vasha is real. The thing was real. That's all you need to remember. That and that we killed it. You don't have to be afraid anymore," she said. His eyes popped open wide and he shook his head frantically from side to side.

"No....I see them...they're everywhere. They can hide real good..." Mela's heart thudded in her chest and a nagging question bounced around in her head. She checked to see if Todd was coming back before she spoke again.

"Are there more here? Here in the hospital?" she asked. Mr. Albright nodded his head and his grip on her hand tightened.

"They're everywhere. I told you to run...I tried to warn you... why didn't you run?"

Mela smiled and leaned forward and placed a gentle kiss on the man's forehead. "Because I don't run from bad things, Mr. Albright," she whispered. "They run from me." She stood and squeezed his hand briefly. "Don't forget me. My name is Mela. Mela Malone." He nodded and squeezed her hand before letting it go.

Mela turned as the door opened again and Todd entered. Nodding to Vasha, he came to stand next to Mela and looked down at his patient.

"Everything okay?" he asked. Mela nodded and Mr. Albright lay in the bed, wide eyed but resolute.

"Fine, everything is fine. Todd," she leaned in to whisper the question that had been nagging her since he left the room, "How many patients like Mr. Albright are here right now?" Todd met her gaze and his confusion gave way to horror as he looked from Mela to Vasha, and then back to his patient on the bed. "Todd, how many are there?" she asked again.

"Including Mr. Albright, eight…There're eight of them. All with the same symptoms."

Chapter Six

"Eight?" she said to herself. Vasha straightened the leather straps on his chest and smiled.

"It seems we have a long night ahead of us, Little Witch. Shall we?" His eyes twinkled when he smiled and she couldn't help but do the same.

"Wait...you can't...I mean...we have to be careful..." Todd stammered. Mela chewed on her bottom lip for a moment and considered what they had in store for them with seven more patients on this floor and an unknown number of black-eyed creatures roaming around.

"We might need a little help," she mused out loud.

"I can't help you...I'm not sure I could..." Todd said and Mela waved him off.

"Not you. I need Sammuele. Vasha, could you?" Vasha nodded.

"What should I do?" Todd asked nervously. Mela watched her would-be lover nervously fidget and straighten his white lab coat.

"You might want to take that off," she said as she turned his shoulder to look at his back and wrinkled her nose at the large black stain that was there. Moving quickly, Todd shrugged off the lab coat, turning it in his hands until he saw the stain. Disgusted, he rolled it into a ball and tossed it in the nearest biological waste bin. He moved to the door, his hand lingering over the knob as he spoke,

"Try not to make a mess," he said, and he was out of the room in a flash. Mela fumed but knew she had little time for petty outbursts. She stood staring at the door for a few minutes in silence. Vasha was whispering to himself, calling Sammuele to them. It sounded oddly like a prayer to Mela; however, she didn't have time to consider what that meant before Sammuele appeared from nothing and stood at her side.

"Good evening, Mela. You saw the creature?" Frowning at the formal salutation, she turned to face him and nodded.

"Yeah. Saw it, fought it, and really didn't like it. Vasha killed it though,"

"Only after you mortally wounded it, my dear," Vasha said from across the room. The trio turned to face Mr. Albright and Sammuele stepped forward.

"Why is he tied to the bed in that manner?" Sammuele asked and pointed to the restraints at the man's ankles and wrists.

"Well, from what I understand, he got a little...ah...violent," she said the last bit softly so only Sammuele and Vasha could hear. The former stepped closer to the man, his long blue robes stood in stark contrast next to the sterile white background and the pale man in the sheets. Sammuele reached out his hand, resting it gently against the man's forehead. Mr. Albright's eyes were wide but he stayed silent and completely still. Mela tried to catch his eye, to try to tell him everything as okay, but he never looked away from Sammuele.

Watching Sammuele close his eyes and move his lips silently, reminded Mela what he really was. He wasn't just her friend and companion, he was a creature of prayer, in servitude to his God. When he opened his eyes, she saw the pain in his eyes. The reflection of Mr. Albright's agony showed in Sammuele's face, as he stood straight once again, and backed away from the bed. Mela stepped close to Sammuele and looked up at him. Slowly, she reached out and placed a hand on his back.

He turned to look at her, tears glistening in his eyes, and she pulled him close. She felt his lean body against her and he awkwardly returned the half hug. Vasha clearing his throat behind them made Mela jump.

"We have much to do and I do not think our precious Doctor Todd will have much patience for us. The man here, tied to the bed, what is his name?" He stepped forward, larger than life, and peered down at Mr. Albright.

"His name is Mr. Albright...I don't know his first name," Mela said, reaching for the chart at the foot of the bed.

"His name is Matthew," Sammuele said softly. Mela turned to him with a questioning look. "His name is Matthew and he should be treated with more dignity than this," he said and gestured to the bed.

"It matters not," Vasha said in an uncharacteristically brisk tone. He leaned forward on the bed, all four, lovely blue hands rested on the thin sheets that covered the man's legs. "The danger to you has passed for now. We must go--" he motioned to his friends-- "and rid this place of the other foul creatures that are haunting the others. You know this, do you not?" Vasha asked, raising his delicate eyebrows.

Mr. Albright nodded his head and bit his lower lip in an attempt to ward off the tears. Vasha nodded in approval and stood up straight. "Then rest easy and fear not."

He turned to the others and spoke as he moved toward the door. "Very well, we shall go and spill more black blood this night," Mela stepped away from the bed, following Vasha to the door, but looked back. Sammuele stood over Mr. Albright, still lost in sadness.

"Sammuele," Mela said softly. "We need you now," He looked up, nodded his head and followed.

"I will go first," Sammuele said. "I will alert you if anyone is in the hall." Both agreed and Sammuele faded from view. Mela stood close to Vasha as they waited. She could smell the mix of perfumes that followed every move he made. His muscles were taunt with anticipation but she had little time to consider his obvious delight at the fight before Sammuele's face appeared at the window in the door.

Opening the door, Mela stepped out into the hallway first. She pulled the hood over her head on the off chance they were seen. Vasha followed close behind her. He was entirely too enormous to hide and she was terrified someone would come walking around the corner as they debated which direction to go. She inched closer to the next door and peeked in the window. Sure enough, there lay a patient just as Mr. Albright had and, next to the bed, was one of the creatures. She felt ill immediately and turned to them, nodding her head. She felt Vasha standing very close as she opened the door to slip inside the room. He followed and they waited for Sammuele to enter. However, he apparently had no intention of entering because he stood with his back to the door and appeared to keep watch. Shrugging her shoulders, Mela drew her sword and together they approached the bed.

A man lay in the bed, restrained much the same way Mr. Albright was next door, but he slept. His face occasionally contorted into a grimace, so his slumber was not a peaceful one. Mela carefully looked the creature over and saw at once that it was an exact replica of the other one. The gray, leather skin stretched tight over the thin, gangly body. The terrifyingly large head leaned in close to the man on the bed. She watched as it opened its mouth showing row after row of sharp teeth inside. Vasha moved faster than she could and caught the thing before it could clamp its jaws down on the sleeping man.

With a movement so fast she almost missed it, he pulled the creature back by an arm and threw it against the wall with a loud *thud*. The creature slid down the wall and lay in a crumpled heap on the floor. Mela approached the thing, sword pointed at its chest, and felt as if she should make sure it was dead. Should she simply stick it with her sword to be sure? Or had Vasha killed it already? While she considered her next move, she saw the thing's long fingers clinch into tight fists. It was still alive.

"Kill it, Mela. It must be you this time. I will be here to make sure it cannot get away," Vasha said.

Mela nodded and made to stab the creature. It must have been watching her, or heard her coming, because when she made a move toward it, it jumped onto all fours and hissed like a deranged animal. Positioning herself just so, Mela took a wild swing, missing it completely. "Focus, Mela. See how it moves....watch it move....do you see?"

She did see. The thing had such long legs and arms, it could easily get around on all fours just as easily as two. It was quick, but all she had to do was wait for the right moment.

The thing jumped onto the bed and she was afraid it would wake the patient. Luckily, the patient was either fast asleep, or more likely, too drugged up to wake no matter what happened around him. Mela feinted right but quickly shifted her weight to the left and caught it easily in the side with the tip of her sword. She felt the blade pierce its side and the weight of the creature's body brought the tip of her sword down with it. The creature let out was a fearful screech. All she wanted to do was shut it up. She jerked the sword lose from its body.

Vasha backed away, giving her plenty of room in which to confront the creature that now crawled pitifully across the floor, leaving a trail of black ooze in its wake. Mela stepped in front of it and brought the sword, point down, through its back. The creature's long limbs flailed at its sides for a moment and then it was still. She shook from head to toe, feeling the adrenaline course through her entire body. She made her first kill. For some reason, she missed Decker more in that moment than she had since they left.

As if he heard her thoughts, Vasha spoke. "My brother would be proud of you. I cannot wait to tell him of it. Come." He pulled her back and in doing so, her sword came out of the creature with a wet noise. "I will dispose of this one and off we go to find another. The next one is mine!" He sounded as merry as though they were making plans to go to a party. Dragging the creature behind him, he opened the window with one hand and lazily tossed the dead body from the window.

They went to the door, after checking on the sleeping man who was still lost in his medicated slumber. Sammuele stood vigil and turned to them when Mela cracked open the door.

"All clear?" she whispered. Sammuele looked down the hall and frowned.

"There are people there…We must pass them to get to the other rooms." He was right. They were in the last patient room next to the door to the stairway. They would have to pass the nurse's station in order to reach the long hallway where the other patients slept. Frustrated, Mela swore under her breath and Vasha looked anxious to get moving.

"Can you do something, Sammuele? Make them look the other way long enough to get by?" she asked.

Sammuele actually looked a bit excited. "I can create a diversion. Be ready," he said, and then disappeared. She felt Vasha crowd close to her, although, his closeness didn't seem to bother her anymore.

"He has changed much. Have you noticed?"

Mela nodded.

"Yeah, I have. It's weird…I didn't think he--" Her words were cut short by an extremely loud crash that sounded like metal pans falling to the floor. Mela turned to look at Vasha and he smiled. Waiting until she was certain all of the nurses were running toward the sound, they crept from the room and ran, bent as low as they could, past the nurse's station and into the opposite hall.

She could hear people talking loudly, asking each other what happened and what caused something to fall. Mela stifled a fit of giggles as she cracked open the first door she came to. The vision of Sammuele randomly knocking over stuff in order to make noise amused her. Her amusement was short-lived. Nothing was inside the first room, no patient and no monsters, so they crept to the next door and peeked inside. Mela knew they had to find six more patients and, she assumed, as many creatures with them. Nothing was in the second room either and she was starting to get anxious. Vasha growled in frustration behind her as they crept along to the next door.

At one point Mela froze when she heard voices getting closer from behind and she had a moment of panic. Before she could turn around to take cover in the last empty room they checked, she heard another louder crash from somewhere far away. The voices that were headed their way changed direction and she heard the sound of running feet getting further and further away.

"Thanks, Sammuele," she whispered. They continued to creep along to a set of double doors. She looked and saw that there were a set on either side of the hallway. Using hand gestures, she asked Vasha which one they should go through and he motioned for her to enter the one that was closest on the left. The swinging door was blessedly silent.

They crept inside, thankful for shadows in which they could hide. It took a moment for her eyes to adjust to the darkness. The room was enormous compared to the smaller, private, rooms that were on the other end of the hall. This room was lined with beds. Mela counted five on either side of the room. Each one was separated by a partially drawn curtain. She saw the first two patients as they lay tied to the beds in restraints and she saw each one had a creature of his very own. Vasha looked down at her and smiled.

"I lay claim to this side. Those there you may kill." He gestured to his right and she thought it was a good plan. Exhaling a deep breath, she pulled out her sword and stepped toward the bed nearest to her. The creature paid no attention to her, and she thought, as long as she didn't look right at it, it wouldn't even know she saw it. So she approached the bed and stood within feet of the creature's side. It was using its long fingers to grasp the throat of the young man in the bed. She watched as the creature choked the man briefly and watched him gasp for air when the creature released its grip. It could have killed him easily, she realized. It enjoyed torturing him. Anger flared deep inside her. A newly awakened, primal, part of her felt alive for the first time. She let the feeling wash over her. Mela smiled, knowing the creature would be dead soon.

Getting a firm grip on the hilt of the sword, she stepped back with her right foot and brought the sword over her right shoulder. She took in a breath and released it as she swung the sword, slicing the air – and the creature's neck – in one blow. The bulbous head fell first onto the bed, but then rolled and hit the floor with a wet *splat*. Black blood poured thickly from both the hole where the head once sat and the head itself. She pulled the body from the bed and let it fall to the floor. She felt no remorse.

Feeling emboldened by her swing, she left the young man's bedside and reached for the thin curtain that separated him from the next bed. Slowly, she pulled the material to the side to reveal another man, this one about the same age as Mr. Albright, restrained but very much awake. The creature that tormented this man sat on his chest, digging its claws down his throat, choking him while he stared, wide-eyed, at his would-be killer.

Just as the last, this one never looked in her direction when she stepped closer. Mela, not wanting to give the game away, stared into the terrified, wide eyes of the man in bed. His arms were stiff, fingers splayed out, unable to defend himself from the attack. She smiled at the man and placed her finger to her lips to tell him to be quiet. She griped her sword in both hands and brought it up level to her right shoulder, pointed at the creature. As she did, it looked up from the man's face and his empty black eyes stared right at her as she lunged forward and sank her sword into the its chest. The blade was so deep, it protruded from the creature's back, dripping with black blood. It frantically tried to remove the sword from her hands but Mela pushed until the hilt of the sword rested on the creature's unnatural, gray skin.

"Die," she whispered when her face was as close as she dared. The large head began to droop and finally it went limp, falling forward against her. Disgusted at the feel of its flesh, she pushed it back and removed her sword, letting the body fall to the floor. The thick, black blood pooled beneath the creature, whose arms and legs lay completely still. Satisfied it was dead, Mela looked once more at the man in bed. He was older than she previously thought and very much awake. She put her finger to her lips once more and he nodded. He raised his hand from the bed as far as he could in the restraints and pointed in the direction of the next bed. Letting him know she understood, she nodded and stepped over the dead body at her feet to the curtain that separated the beds. As she reached out to draw the curtain back, she heard movement behind it. Mela froze.

Something behind the curtain threw itself at her, knocking her backwards and snarling her up in the material. The creature hit her square in the chest, ripping the fabric down, and now there was only the thin curtain between it and her. She felt the creature on her, pawing at the material in order to reach her. Breathing heavily, she squirmed until she was able to bring one of her knees up to her chest and kept the creature at a safe distance by pushing against it. Feeling the thing's fingers raking at the material on her face, she clumsily pushed the creature back using all the force she could. It didn't do much, but she was able to rip the curtain from her face and roll away from it. She wasn't fast enough. The thing leaped in the air, mouth open, claws reaching, and came straight on her. Whether due to her training with Decker, or pure instinct, Mela braced her hands on the floor and kicked straight out at it. Her foot made solid contact with the creature before it reached her. It fell back onto the floor and let out an irritated cry before scrambling to all fours again.

Now able to stand, she rose, breathing heavily. When she fell, she dropped her sword and couldn't find it in the blackness she now found herself in. Unable to search for it, she frantically tried to decide what to do next. The creature made a move to the right and she stepped in its way. For good or for ill, she wasn't going to let it past her. She stepped back on her right foot, ready to break the thing's neck if she had to in a hand to hand fight. That step gave her the greatest relief she had ever known. Her foot touched the blade of her sword. Relief filled her and she move a little more until she knew she was standing right over it.

The creature watched her and made a new noise when it found itself cornered. The cry was different from the one before--it was deeper, although no less painful to hear. It twisted its enormous head from side to side and repeated the call. The realization hit her that the creature was calling for help. Unsure of where Vasha was and if he was busy facing his own opponent, Mela spoke to it.

"Your friends are all dead," she said softly, coldly. She bent her knees, reached down without looking away from the thing, grabbed her sword. When she felt the weight of it in her hands once more, she immediately felt her confidence soar. Standing tall once again, she stepped closer to the creature and it cowered from her. Her body vibrated with righteous anger. With every inch of her soul, she wanted the thing before her dead.

A part of her wanted to feel what it was like to kill it with her bare hands. She looked down at her sword and then back at the thing cowering on the floor partway beneath the bed. She stepped closer and the thing let out a pitiful scream as it tried to crawl past her. Almost enjoying herself, Mela brought the tip of her sword down and felt the skin pop as the blade sank into its belly. The long arms reached out to something unknown as Mela pulled the sword from it and stepped behind it. Holding the wound in its middle, unable to stop the black ooze from falling, the creature pushed itself up and made to stand once more. Unable to, it sank back to the floor and tried to stop the flow of blood from the hole in its body.

Seeing her opportunity, Mela spread her legs and brought the sword across her body to the right and used every muscle in her to swing the blade. The creature's tiny neck was easy to cut. The large head fell forward and rolled a few feet before it came to a stop. She took a moment to look at the fearsome, black eyes. They were blank with no hint of seeing. Curious how the thing's eyes looked the same in life as it did in death. The mouth hung open showing the now familiar tiny sharp teeth. Footsteps behind her made her turn, sword at the ready.

"It is I," Vasha's voice tickled the shadows before he stepped into the dim light from the nearest bed. "You did well. I watched from across the room."

"Oh thanks. You couldn't have come to give me hand? I dropped my sword and that thing was on me," Mela said in a fierce whisper.

"I would have intervened if you were truly in danger. You were frightful to see, Mela my love. I wish you could see yourself...a true force of nature." She couldn't help but feel satisfied with his words of praise.

Eyeing the black blood on her sword, she didn't want to put it back into the sheath. She didn't want to get the goo all over the leather any more than it already was.

"How many were over there?" she asked as they dragged the bodies to the front doors.

"Two. There were only two on my side," he said as he tossed both severed heads onto the pile of gray, bloody, bodies. She noticed the bodies he brought from the other side of the room seemed to be missing the arms and legs from the torso.

"That means there's one more patient somewhere." She looked around and whispered once more. "You sure we got them all from in here?" Vasha nodded his head.

Biting her lip, she peeked from the sliver of a window and saw the double doors across the hall. From where she stood, it appeared to have a faint light coming from somewhere in the large room across the way. Mela beckoned for Vasha to look and pointed across the hall. He peered through the window and nodded his head.

She looked behind her at the pile of bodies and then to Vasha in question. It was obvious that whatever black magick animated these creatures protected them from being seen by almost everyone. But apparently, once they were dead, anyone could see them. She didn't have time to work out the details of how Todd saw the creature before it died. Vasha was already opening the swinging doors and stepping cautiously into the dim hallway. Mela followed, sword by her side.

Darting quickly across the wide hall, they entered the room exactly like the one they just left. This one, however, had empty beds along the entire right side. On the left, only one bed had curtains drawn around it and that is where both Vasha and Mela went. Quietly, they approached the second bed, putting room between themselves in case of another attack from behind the curtain. It wouldn't do to hurt each other by standing too close.

Vasha reached out and gently grasped the edge of the curtain and met her gaze. Silently they nodded to each other in readiness and he slid the white curtain to the side. What they saw made Mela freeze in terror.

A woman lay in the bed, restrained as the others were. All around her swarmed gray creatures. Mela counted four that were each busy tormenting her in turn. They stood beside the bed and whispered in her ears. The woman was painfully awake and lay as still as possible, eyes full of tears, mouth open in a silent scream. One creature sat astride her middle dragging its long claws across her bare chest. Her hospital gown gapped open, exposing her breasts for all the world to see. Filled with a deep disgust and rage for the woman, Mela glanced at Vasha who seemed to be soaking it all in.

The last creature used its teeth on her leg, biting down and tasting her blood as it did. A long, black tongue flicked out from its mouth and dug into the wound it caused. Spasms shook the woman and it reacted with delight at her pain. Mela wanted to kill that one first.

It was too close to the woman for her to remove its head so she readied herself to skewer the creature as it prepared to stick a finger in the wound it created. Raising her sword, Mela saw from the corner of her eyes, Vasha extend all four of his arms to the side and a fearsome expression changed his face so much so that she finally saw the beast inside him.

Releasing her breath and exhaling as she struck, as Decker taught her to do, she caught the creature under the arms and she felt the blade wedge itself in bone. It looked up in surprise and let out an awful cry. It fell back, taking her with it. She had to steady herself and pull hard to release her blade from the twitching body at her feet. Black blood pooled on the floor and she stepped over it towards the next creature.

As she did this, Vasha grabbed the creature nearest to him and, with all four hands, grasped the neck, arm and both legs, holding it high in the air. With a growl that sounded anything but human, his muscles grew taunt and he pulled. The creature's mouth was open, but it was unable to free itself from Vasha's death grip. Before she reached the next creature, she heard a ripping noise and pop, followed by a spray of black ooze that covered the white bed and floor. Vasha easily dismembered the creature in a matter of moments. Tossing the pieces aside like bits of a broken toy, Vasha reach out in a flash of blue and golden jewels to grab another, just as Mela pounced on the next.

It felt more satisfying than anything she'd ever experienced to watch the creature's surprise and shock as the blade of her sword pushed into its repulsive gray skin. It fought with the sword, scrapping and clawing at the metal as Mela forced it down to the ground. Rage filled her as she pushed the blade down until she felt the stone of the floor meet the tip. The thing twitched and opened its mouth to let loose a cry. Pulling the blade quickly from the hole in its chest, she brought it savagely across the creature's neck, partially severing the head. Another slice and the bulbous head lobbed to the side, the mouth frozen open.

As she straightened, Mela heard the sound of the last creature being ripped apart by Vasha. She looked up and saw the final moments as the limbs went completely limp in his arms and watched as the headless torso fell with a *thud* to the floor.

Everything was covered in the black oozing blood. It dripped like dirty oil from the sheets on the bed and pooled on the floor beneath the pile of dismembered bodies. While Vasha busied himself with piling the bodies together, Mela approached the woman in the bed.

The lady was middle-aged, weathered by a hard life or by her experiences, she couldn't tell. She lay panting, her face covered in the black, sticky ooze. Placing her sword on the bed, Mela reached up to draw the woman's gown closed and covered her breasts. On a stand beside the table, Mela found paper towels and she grabbed a handful. Slowly and carefully, she wiped the sticky substance from the woman's face. The woman silently watched, helpless to everything happening around her.

"It's alright. Everything is going to be okay. They're gone now. All dead," Mela whispered as she tidied the woman up. The woman said nothing, only stared wide-eyed as tears fell on the pillow. Mela felt lost, unable to help her any more than she already had, so she made to go.

"Thank you," the woman whispered, and Mela turned around to look at her. Mela felt guilty leaving the helpless woman tied to her bed in terror and in pain. Her eyes found the wound on the woman's leg and it bled a little from the torture she endured. Mela hoped a nurse or even Todd would see it soon and take care of her.

"We must remove the bodies now," Vasha said in a whisper. Turning to him, she saw he carried the four bodies plus a few of the severed appendages. Sighing heavily, Mela sheathed her sword and gathered up the remaining limbs under her arms. The heads were difficult to carry but she managed not to drop any.

Peeking through the window, Vasha nodded to her and she followed him out into the hall. He inclined his head down the hall, back to one of the empty rooms they had first passed before finding the double doors. She nodded and quickly followed him, crossing the hall as fast as possible and finally stepping inside. Vasha dumped the bodies at his feet and went back to the door.

"See the window opened and drop these to the ground below. We must get them all outside as quick as possible. Make sure to leave nothing behind." Nodding Mela went to the window and unlatched it. Leave nothing behind....panic seized her for a moment because they'd left plenty behind. The black blood that was next to impossible to wipe away was everywhere they had been tonight. There wasn't anything she could do about it. She hoped Todd found a reasonable excuse for it all, possibly an oil leak somewhere? She shrugged and hefted the first headless body up and pushed it out the window. Sticking her head out, she watched it fall with a crash to the hedges that lined the boarder of the building. Feeling good about the cover, she reached for the next one and then the next.

Vasha entering once more with the remaining bodies under his arms interrupted her. He tossed them into the pile and joined her, which made the process go quicker. Before long, they had every oozing body part out of the room and they stood staring at one another.

"I don't know about you, but when the heat of battle has passed, I find myself in need of passionate release. Do you, by chance feel the same way?" Mela covered her mouth, doubling over in laughter. She laughed harder than was necessary and, before long, Vasha joined her.

Wrapping his arms around her, he reached down and held her face in his other two hands. Gently he kissed her on the lips. It wasn't a sleazy opportunistic kiss. She felt the friendship in his touch and the lack of his tongue in her mouth told her a lot. She kissed him back and then pulled away from him, smiling.

"It has been a good night," he said softly. She nodded and pulled the hood over her head.

"But I think we'd better skedaddle before Todd sees the mess we've made."

"Very well. How will you leave? The same way you came in?" Vasha asked climbing out of the window.

Mela chewed on her lip for a moment and considered her options. It was too high to jump from the window, no way in hell that was happening. "I'll go the way I came in. Meet me outside," she said and he nodded as he attempted the difficult task of squeezing through the window. Mela turned and peered out the long window on the door. No one was there, so she crept out and closed the door gently behind her. With every step, she listened for voices or for the sound of people approaching. A figure down the hall, where she wanted to go, appeared so suddenly her heart thudded in her chest. It was Sammuele.

She waved to him and pointed her finger questioning if there were people there. Sammuele held his hand up, telling her to wait, then disappeared once again. In moments she heard the familiar sound of metal pans crashing to the floor from somewhere nearby. Mela heard the nurses curse and go running, shouting orders to one another as they did. Stifling her laughter, Mela ducked and ran down the hall, past the nurses stationed and reached the door to the stairway without being seen. With her hand on the handle, she thought about Mr. Albright and his warnings to her. Checking over her shoulder, she left the stairway and headed for his room.

She peeked inside and saw him alone and in a seemingly peaceful sleep. She debated on whether she should go in or not. Would she upset him if she appeared again? Had he been drugged after all? If he had been, her coming into his room would go unnoticed.

Mind made up, Mela crept inside and softly closed the door behind her. The moment the door was closed with a click, Mr. Albright's eyes popped open. She smiled and put her finger to her lips as she went to his side. Gently sitting on the bed beside him, she leaned close and whispered in his ear.

"We got them all. They're all dead, Mr. Albright. You rest easy now. Nothing's left to hurt you or anyone else." She pulled back and saw the first glimmer of a smile brighten his face. He reached for her hand and she obliged, immensely happy with his reaction. "If anything like this happens again, you see anything like those things again, you tell Doctor Morgan. Okay? He'll get me and I'll come running back," she said. He nodded and squeezed her hand.

"You're a good girl," he said in a hoarse voice. She smiled and kissed his cheek in farewell.

She crept from the room and quickly made her way to the stairway, down the flight of stairs, and through the door that would take her outside. When she looked down the hallway, she saw two nurses walking together, too busy chatting to notice her. They continued to walk in the opposite direction so Mela left the safety of the stairway and rushed down the hall to the door.

The cool night air rushed at her and she breathed it in happily. She looked across the parking lot and searched the shadows for signs of Vasha.

"I am here," she heard him say from her left. He was standing as still as a statue in the dark, and she walked right past him. Relieved, she joined him in the shadows and they walked together across the parking lot the way they'd come in. When they reached the edge of the trees, Vasha motioned for her to get on his back. This time she swung her leg over his back without a second thought.

Vasha was her friend. He was her teacher and her source of much embarrassment and joy. But Vasha was also a beast. That was clear to her now.

Chapter Seven

The trip home was slower than the one they made to get to the hospital. Vasha took his time and Mela was fine with it. The night air was cool, but not cold, yet. Texas really only has two seasons – blazing hot summers and freezing, wet winters. This was the short-lived pleasant time of year where the days were warm but not oppressively so. The nights were cooler, and by chance, the mosquitos were fewer because of it.

They neared the woods that surrounded Mela's home but Vasha made a turn that took them deeper into the woods. Looking behind her, she saw they were leaving the shadows near the road and headed in the wrong direction.

"Where are we going?" She wasn't concerned really. But she was looking forward to getting cleaned up and eventually going to bed soon. The adrenaline had long since left her; she was weak, and her muscles ached beyond belief.

"Patience, little one," was all he said as they made their way slowly through the brush. Dried leaves covered the forest floor so every step they made announced their movements. She hoped they weren't trying to sneak unnoticed anywhere.

"Vasha, what did you do with the bodies? Of the Black-Eyed creatures, I mean. What do you think they are? What were they doing there?" Vasha's deep, throaty chuckle echoed in the night.

"Questions. So many questions," he laughed and continued on, moving branches and thorny bushes from his way. "As to the creature's remains, I did not give them a burial. I left them in the woods to be scavenged by animals or to rot away into the earth. Either way I care not what happens to them. But--" he ducked beneath a branch and she did the same--"no one will find them."

"That's good," she said.

"I am pleased you approve. Now, as to other questions," he stepped over a fallen tree. Mela watched a raccoon eye them as they passed. "I do not know what they are. I can only make conjectures as to what we are dealing with. Tell me, little Witch, what did you feel when you were near them?"

Mela thought about it and tried to remember everything she could about the night's events. "I guess....I felt...nothing. That's as close as I can get. Not nothing...but a...a....void. An emptiness. Does that make sense?"

"It does. What do you know of The Darkness? Have my brothers told you much of the man we met so long ago? The one who tainted our love for our sisters and for one another?"

"Not a lot, no. Why?"

"When we, my brothers and I, when we would met with the man...I remember feeling the same emptiness, as you call it. I remembered the feeling only tonight when I looked into the eyes of the creature. It was from The Darkness, that much I know," he said firmly.

Mela let his words sink in and she felt a shudder of fear tickle her back. "This is going to get bad, isn't it?" she asked softly.

Vasha stepped out into an open pasture and pointed to a creek that ran right through it. The water wasn't very high, but it bubbled along merrily from the woods, across the pasture, and into the night.

"We are indeed facing dark times. However, in the darkness, we are free to choose with no one watching, our own direction." Mela nodded, not entirely sure what he meant but she had a pretty good idea. "Come, let us go wash ourselves in the water from the Earth. I prefer to bathe in this water." With that, he ran full speed ahead and Mela clung to him, laughing, until they skidded to a stop at the muddy edge of the creek.

She swung her leg over his back and slid to the ground. She looked down at her running shoes and sighed. They were covered in black, monster blood, and she knew it would never come out. She pulled them from her feet and felt the soft, cool, mud between her toes. She held out her hand to Vasha and they entered the water together, still wearing their clothes. The water was still warm although the air was cool. It had a relaxing feel to it. The water never really cooled off in Texas until a deep freeze set in.

Vasha walked into the deepest part of the water, and immersed himself as deeply as he could. He cupped the water in his hands and poured it over his chest and stomach. Mela copied him and felt the warmth through her elegant wardrobe.

"Will the water ruin my clothes?" she was concerned about ruining that which he made for her with such obvious care.

"No. They will be the better for it." Vasha said as he grabbed handfuls of mud, covered the black stains on his body, and rubbed it in. Raising her eyebrows, Mela copied him and found that the mud was an excellent solution to the sticky mess that was all over her hands and chest. Rinsing the mud from her skin, it felt fresh and new. She smiled and went to help Vasha with the bits he couldn't reach.

Slowly, they were able to rid themselves of the tar-like substance. She inspected her shoes and saw black blood stuck in every crease, even on the inside. She knew she'd never wear them again. She would have to buy another pair soon. Dripping with water but completely satisfied with the night's events, Mela tossed her shoes into the water and watched them sink and tumble away with the water.

Mela smiled and dug her toes a little deeper into the ground beneath her. "There was no saving them. Sometimes, if something is ruined beyond repair, it's best to just let it go." She smiled and looked to her friend. He returned her smile and reached for her hand.

"Such a wise little Witch," he said as they turned to walk home.

* * *

She slept in late the next morning. It was Saturday and she refused to get up early and train. If Decker wanted to get angry about it, he would have to be there to do it, she thought. She rolled over and snuggled deeper into her covers. The sun was shining through the window blinds. Rolling over, she reached for her phone to check the time. It was late morning, far later than she'd slept in for as long as she could remember. But she also saw there were messages. A lot of them.

Groaning, she pulled herself out of bed and visited the bathroom. Whatever crisis that was waiting for her would have wait until she had coffee in hand. Black-Eyed monsters be damned. She took her phone and fresh cup of coffee to sit on the patio, still avoiding sitting in the chair Decker reserved for himself. A flash of anger surprised her. She was angry and hurt he left the way he did. Why did he leave? What was so important that he had to leave her and take Theo with him without so much as a proper goodbye?

Lighting a cigarette, Mela started sifting through the messages. A few were from Todd. They weren't nice either. Apparently, he had to clean up all of the mess they left behind and he wasn't very happy about it. She hit delete without another thought. She'd deal with him later after he calmed down. There was another message from Connie that delighted her. She was planning a trip to Texas to take care of some business and she hoped to see Mela while she was nearby. Mela felt lighter and happier after reading it and made a mental note to call her. The last was from Wyatt, ordering her to call him back immediately because they *'had shit to do today.'* She laughed and messaged him back that she was awake and to come over when he was ready. Mela and Bear enjoyed the morning together in silence.

She took her time sipping coffee and smoking until she felt awake enough to start the day. The sun was already high in the sky by this time, so her shower was short and cool. Before she got dressed, she tried to check out her back in the mirror to see how the henna art survived the night's events, the dip in the creek, and now the shower. She didn't see anything wonky, so she dressed as carefully as possible, her usual t-shirt and jeans, and spent the time waiting for Wyatt brushing her hair and applying a bit of makeup.

Less than an hour after speaking to him, Wyatt showed up, dressed to kill, flashing her his million-dollar smile.

"Morning, Pop Tart. You look good," he said and helped himself to a glass and juice.

"Thanks," she said with a smile, and joined him in the kitchen. "What's the important shit we have to do today?" she asked. Frowning, Wyatt tilted his head and stared at her.

"You look different. Why?" he demanded. She laughed and shrugged her shoulders

"I put on some makeup, that's about it."

"Hmm… Well, I'm glad you have me around. I didn't forget what we had to do today. Today we're going to see a patient at North West Psychiatric Hospital. Little Miss Annabelle Martello."

Mela smacked her forehead and sighed heavily. "Oh my God, I can't believe I forgot. Shit. Last night has me all messed up," she said.

"Oh? What happened last night?" He leaned across the counter and wiggled his eyebrows. "Did you see Todd?"

"Oh I saw him alright. But it wasn't for any good reasons,"

"Oh no…"

"Yeah. It gets worse. He called and told me about what was happening at work, some seriously crazy shit." Mela told him the whole story from beginning to end and, after he stopped screeching, he dropped down into a chair at the table.

"Those things…they're out there?" He waved his hands in the air. "And can attack people but we can't see them?" He asked with a panicked look.

Mela nodded and joined him at the table. "Yeah but I can see them. Vasha can too. I guess Decker and Theo can as well but…"

"But they're not here," he said, eyeing her from across the table.

"No. No they're not." She said a bit too harshly and got up to put her mug in the sink. Wyatt sipped his drink in silence and pulled out his phone. After pushing a few buttons, he read to her from the screen,

"Visiting hours are from noon to five on Saturdays only. So, Cupcake, we have to go if we want to meet this little girl today." Mela nodded and went to grabbed her purse, scratched Kat's head and gave Bear kisses before they walked out the door. Wyatt wanted to drive so they loaded into his new, flashy, sports car for the ride.

The trip north wasn't terribly long. Most freeways run north/south or east/west in Texas. I-45 took them as far north as they needed and they left the freeway to the back roads that would take them to the facility. Open fields filled with the occasional cluster of cows was all she could see for a long time. It wasn't anything special but it was a dazzling display of the color green. Even in fall, Texas stayed green for as long as possible, until the freeze set in.

Up ahead, Mela saw the huge building that would under different circumstances, be quite beautiful. It was a tall, three story stone building surrounded by lush green grass that was immaculately tended. She could see a sign up ahead and they followed the directions to the visitor parking lot and parked beneath a tree.

Getting out and stretching, Mela heard a huge flock of crows screeching to one another. It seemed everywhere she looked they lined the trees and telephone wires that ran the length of the road. Occasionally, one would fly overhead, calling out to his friends and they would answer in kind.

As they walked to the large glass doors, Wyatt told her the plan.

"I spoke with one of the nurses yesterday. Since Annabelle is a ward of the State, they have to approve visitors. I told her I knew the parents, who are dead by the way, and I only just learned where Annabelle was."

"Good plan," she said as they entered the building.

"So just let me do all the talking, okay?" he said as they approached the front desk that was tall and made from a fancy, dark wood. Mela slowly paced around the waiting room, looking at the artwork on the walls. There were very pretty paintings done of the building by a number of the patients. The sofa that sat against the wall was plush and made of a soft, light blue material. Vasha would love it.

A woman appeared at the desk from a back room and greeted them with a smile. She was a red headed lady, possibly in her late thirties or forties, but she was quite beautiful. She reminded Mela of a porcelain doll she once saw as a child. Her skin was so fair that her bright red hair stood out in stark contrast. Her eyes were artfully made up and her lips were a bright shade of red.

"Hello, may I help you?" she asked. Her voice was deep and thick with the country twang of a Texas woman. Nevertheless, Mela could immediately tell this woman was no fool.

"I'm looking for Renee," Wyatt said. "I spoke with her on the phone yesterday about…"

"About Annabelle? I'm Renee." She reached over the desk to shake Wyatt's hand and then respectfully smiled in Mela's direction. "I didn't find any record of your name in her file but, truth be told, no one comes around asking for her. I spoke with her a little this morning to see how she felt about a visitor and she seemed tickled pink at the idea. She doesn't have much to be happy about….not here," Nurse Renee cleared her throat and slid a clipboard toward Wyatt. "Just sign in here, darlin' and I'll take you to her. Is your friend going too?" Wyatt smiled and nodded.

"Yes, I wanted her to come along so Annabelle wasn't nervous. Plus, it's a long ride from Trinity Hills," he said as he signed his name in the appropriate place.

"I see. If you could also sign in…ah…"

"Mela," she answered and joined Wyatt at the desk. After they finished the required paperwork, Renee walked around to the front of the desk, pulled out a set of keys, and unlocked a large door that would take them out of the comfy waiting area. Wyatt and Mela followed behind like little ducks in a row, taking in everything they passed along the way. People roamed the halls, some in hospital gowns, and others in medical scrubs. Either way, this was a busy place.

Mela caught herself more than once searching the dark corners for any sign of the Black-Eyed monsters but saw no sign of them. They passed through a large recreational room where some patients played ping pong or board games. One young man smiled and waved as they passed. Renee knew them all by name and greeted them kindly as they went along. So far, she was very impressed with the redheaded nurse and the hospital.

After taking turns down hallways and down long corridors, they were in a much quieter wing of the hospital. It seemed duller and less welcoming than the area they left. No one roamed the halls and the rooms they passed were all empty.

"Excuse me? Renee?" Mela called out to their guide.

"Yes?" she half turned as they continued to walk at a brisk pace.

"Where are we going? It seems really far and we passed all those people..." Renee was already nodding, preparing her answer.

"Yes, that was the north wing, where the older patients live. Those patients have more freedom to come and go with their escorts and validated trips off property. Here however," they turned a corner and entered another communal area. "Is where the children under ten are placed." The room was empty.

"Where are they?" Mela asked with a frown. Renee stopped walking and turned to face the duo with a serious expression.

"Annabelle is the only child in this facility under the age of ten. She'll turn ten this year, so she still has another year or more before she can be moved to the north wing. It's hospital and State policy to keep the patients segregated by age. For obvious safety reasons, of course." She waved them on to follow and Mela met Wyatt's open-mouthed stare with the same shock and disbelief.

"Renee, who takes care of Annabelle?" Wyatt asked.

She let out a half laugh-half sigh.

"I do, mostly. At night, one of the staff is supposed to look in on her, but I spend half my day walking back and forth between the north wing and the children's wing. I even stop in on my days off to make sure she's eating and properly dressed. We're not allowed to hire another nurse for this wing unless we meet the minimum requirements. And that's five patients to a wing. Since we only have one, they figure we can handle that. Little do they know...." She let her words trail off as she approached a door that had tiny color cut-outs of hearts tapped all over it.

"This is her room. Don't be surprised if she doesn't talk to you. Annabelle only really speaks when I'm around or... well, she talks to herself a lot. Sometimes the doctors will come in and we'll try to get her to chat but she's just..." Renee shook her head and knocked on the door before opening it.

Mela and Wyatt followed her inside, both still stunned at what they were seeing. Wyatt closed the door behind them and they stood behind nurse Renee to take it all in. The room was average size, but only had a small bed and dresser in one corner and a chair by the door. Pictures from magazines of smiling faces, families holding hands, or children running and laughing plastered the walls of the gloomy hospital room. Wyatt met Mela's stunned look with one of his own. She didn't have a good feeling about this.

From beside the bed, a little girl stood and stared at the visitors. She was a frail looking thing. In Mela's opinion, too skinny for her age. Her hair was brown and pulled back in a tight braid that ran down her back. Mela suspected Renee did that for her because, apparently, no one else was around to help the poor child. She wore a faded red outfit that was a few sizes too small. The dress didn't cover her knees and the sleeves were inches from her wrists. Annabelle Martello was a pitiful sight.

"Annabelle, these are the friends I told you would come to visit with you today. Will you say hello to them?"

Renee spoke in a soft, gentle tone to the child as she opened up the curtains to the nearest window.

Mela and Wyatt stepped forward and smiled. Mela was always uncomfortable around children. She never knew what to say to them and they always seemed to cry a lot. Wyatt however, took the reins, knelt on one knee before the little girl, and smiled his most charming smile.

"Hello, Annabelle. I'm Wyatt. This is my best friend, Mela. We came to visit you," he said.

The little girl raised her eyes to the visitor and Mela could see she was sizing him up. She was a pretty girl, other than the ill-fitting clothes and bleak surroundings. Her eyes were a dark brown and she had a delicate sprinkling of freckles across the bridge of her nose. Wyatt extended his hand to her and her small little hand reached out to him. They shook hands, Wyatt beaming all the while.

"Well, I've got to get back to the front desk and check in. You two have a little time and I'll come check in on you before dinner." The child looked up at the nurse. "Be on your best behavior." Renee said softly before letting herself out of the room. The door closed and the silence immediately made Mela uncomfortable. She had to keep reminding herself why they were there.

"I like all of your pictures, Annabelle. It's so colorful and pretty in here. I'm a photographer, you know. I like taking pictures and looking at pictures too." He stood up and went over to the nearest collage of smiling, happy faces. Annabelle looked to Mela, then back at Wyatt. Slowly, she turned and joined him in looking at the clippings on her wall. Wyatt didn't say a word. He just crossed his arms and studied the images she'd taped up. On occasion, Annabelle would look up at Wyatt and then back at the wall of art.

Mela busied herself with trying to stay out of the way. She really wished Sammuele was with them. She was in a mental hospital so she should probably keep the conversations with the invisible angel to a minimum. There was a small, wooden chair set against the wall and Mela sat down on it and waited. She had enough faith in Wyatt that he knew what he was doing and she was perfectly willing to let him take lead on this one.

"I like this one the best, I think," Wyatt said to Annabelle, and pointed to a picture of a little girl flying a kite. Mela watched Annabelle who was watching Wyatt, still sizing him up. Slowly, the little girl lifted her small hand and pointed to another image on the wall.

The image was of a family at a picnic, laughing and enjoying the sunshine. Wyatt stepped close to the picture and studied it before he spoke.

"This is nice. Good color, nice use of shadows," he looked down at Annabelle and smiled. "You have a good eye for this. Maybe you should be a photographer too."

Annabelle smiled. Her smile was short lived, however. She turned and went to sit on the edge of her bed and placed her hands in her lap. Mela watched as the sad little girl stared silently at her hands. Wyatt, catching Mela's eye, nodded to her to speak. Licking her lips before she spoke, Mela desperately looked around for inspiration on what to say.

"Annabelle," Mela said and the little girl looked up from her hands and watched her. "Do you know why we're here, Annabelle?" Mela asked softly. The little girl slowly nodded her head. Mela smiled.

"They said you were coming..." Her tiny voice whispered from across the room. Mela and Wyatt exchanged a look.

"Who said I was coming?" Mela asked.

Terrified, Annabelle's eyes filled with tears and she went back to studying her hands. Wyatt approached and knelt on the floor in front of her.

"It's okay, sweetheart," he said as he reached out to wipe the tears away from her cheeks. "My friend Mela here, she's got...special powers and she's here to help you." Annabelle looked up with so much hope in her eyes that Mela's heart broke.

"Powers?" Annabelle asked quietly.

"Yes," Wyatt said shifting to sit on the bed next to her. "Mela here, she's a Witch." Annabelle's eyes grew large and she looked to Mela, then back at Wyatt. He smiled. "Not the bad kind of Witch, Princess. But the kind that helps little girls."

"Like the fairies in the stories?" she asked him.

"Yes. But much cooler," he said.

"I'm here to help you do something, Annabelle. Do you know what that is?" Mela asked gently.

Annabelle nodded.

"They told me to be brave and to wait. The others that are here aren't nice at all." Her delicate voice carried in the room.

"Who told you to be brave?" Mela asked. What Annabelle was saying was very close to what Sandra told her when they first met. But she was curious who 'they' were.

"The ones who talk to me when I'm sleeping. They're real nice. They're my friends. But the bad ones...sometimes they scare me. They're not in my dreams. They're real. I don't like them," she said.

"What do they look like? The bad ones?" Mela was terrified the little girl had been enduring a torment she'd never wish on anyone locked alone in a mental hospital.

"They're some of the people who died. A long time ago. They come into my room and say mean things to me. They're not my friends. There was a little boy who would come to play with me, but he doesn't come anymore," she said, and looked to the visitors to gauge their reactions.

Mela stood and went to sit with them on the bed. Silently she called to Sammuele to come. She had a feeling he would know what to say about this because neither Mela nor Wyatt had any experience with ghosts or spirits.

When Sammuele appeared, all three looked up at him. Wyatt put his arm around Annabelle's shoulders to comfort her.

"It's okay, Princess. This is Sammuele. He's our friend. He likes to help too."

"Hello, Annabelle Martello." Sammuele said calmly. He stood still and folded his hands innocently in front of him as he spoke. Mela smiled weakly and nodded him in encouragement.

"I saw you," Annabelle said. All three looked down at her in question.

"What do you mean, honey?" Wyatt asked.

"Him," she pointed to Sammuele. "He came a couple of days ago and watched everything for a little while. Then he left. He didn't say anything to me. I don't talk to the ones who just watch." She said. Mela looked back at Sammuele who's eyebrows were raised and a curious expression on his face.

"You saw me watching you, child?" Annabelle nodded. "How interesting. Do you know your duty, Annabelle?" She nodded again.

"That is good," he said and that made Annabelle smile.

"You're very important, Annabelle. We're going to keep you safe until the time comes when you'll have to come with me." Mela said softly. Annabelle nodded. Wyatt stroked the little girl's head and it seemed as though he couldn't tear his eyes from her sweet, innocent face.

"Annabelle...do you ever see anything else? Any other kind of...things around?" Mela asked carefully. The little girl looked into Mela's eyes and nodded. "What do they look like?"

"I call them the bug monsters. They have real long arms and legs like a spider," she reached up and cupped her hands beside each of her eyes to make them appear large. "and their eyes are really, really big like this," she said. Mela looked up to Sammuele then back at Annabelle.

"Do they ever come near you? The ones with the big eyes?" Annabelle shook her head and smiled. "Why is that?" Mela was getting more and more curious about the little girl.

"My friends...the nice ones, they told me to pretend I don't see them and they'll leave me alone. So I do. Sometimes, Dottie tells me when they're coming and I go run and hide." A million questions ran through Mela's head, and she looked to Sammuele who appeared to be digesting what he heard. Wyatt, in the meantime, continued to stare at the little girl with sad eyes.

"Who's Dottie?" Mela asked. Annabelle's little legs swung from the edge of the bed as she spoke.

"She's a lady who comes to take care of me. She used to work here a long, long, long time ago. She said she liked her job so much, she never wanted to leave it. So she decided to stay." Confused, Wyatt looked up at Mela.

"Annabelle...is Dottie a ghost?" Mela asked.

"They don't like being called ghosts. They have names like people do. She's just Dottie. She's real nice and helped teach me to tie my shoes." Wyatt covered his mouth with his hand and Mela blinked back tears. The aura of sadness was heavy around the little girl and it was hard to stay positive hearing her speak of the things she experienced as though they were normal.

Mela patted the little girl's hand and smiled. "Okay. I won't call them ghosts. You tell Dottie hi for me and thank her for taking such good care of you." Annabelle beamed at Mela. "You know that someday soon, you're going to have to come with us, right? To do what you're supposed to? Have your friends told you that part?" Mela asked. Annabelle nodded vigorously.

"Yes. They said I'd have the other three with me and that we'll sing songs and make magic!" She seemed very excited at the prospect and her enthusiasm made Mela laugh. Mela got an idea and stood, holding her hand out to the little girl who took it eagerly. Mela walked her to the window and opened it as far as it would go. Which wasn't very far.

"Watch," Mela held out her hand, palm up, and a small, dancing ball of flame appeared in her hand. Annabelle gasped and clapped her hands jumping up and down. She looked back to Wyatt and then to Sammuele to see if they too shared her joy. Sammuele smiled indulgently and Wyatt came to stand by her side. "Now this," Mela closed her hand around the flame and opened it again to reveal a bubble of water shimmering in her hand.

"Wow!" Annabelle exclaimed and clapped her hands again in praise. "Will I be able to do that?" she asked Mela. Mela placed her hand out of the window and a gust of wind carried the ball of water from her hand. She turned to Annabelle and smiled.

"Your magick is going to be even better," Mela said. Pleased, Annabelle looked to Wyatt, who smiled at her and placed his hand on her shoulder. She took a big breath and smiled. She seemed to visibly relax in the company of her new friends.

A knock at the door startled all of them. Renee poked her head inside and smiled.

"How are we doing?" she asked. Annabelle smiled and grabbed Wyatt's hand to drag him to Renee like a show and tell exhibit.

"Ms. Renee, Wyatt is a photographer and he likes my pictures." She said with excitement in her voice for the first time. Her face was animated and happy. Just as a child's face should be. Renee made a big deal about how impressed she was with the news and gave Wyatt a wink when Annabelle wasn't looking. "And Mela….she does magic!" Mela and Wyatt laughed nervously but Renee seemed completely at ease with the declaration. She nodded and pretended to be extremely impressed with Mela for Annabelle's sake. Mela liked her a lot.

"It seems like you've had an exciting afternoon," Renee said. "Dinner will be served soon, Annabelle,"

"Can they stay to eat with me?" she asked the smile still lighting up her face. Mela looked, saw Renee's face, and knew Annabelle wouldn't like the answer. Renee stepped close and placed an arm around the girl's shoulders.

"Now, Annabelle, you know the rules. We can't have dinner guests, I'm sorry. But if you want, you can come eat with me in my office?" she said, smiling. Annabelle's face fell and she jerked away from Renee's embrace.

"I want them to stay!" she said through her tears. Mela looked away, it was hard listening to the desperate plea without feeling like hell.

"We can come back, Princess. What do you think about that? Mela and me, we can come back next Saturday and stay for a long time next time." He knelt before her and took her hands in his. She dropped her head and her shoulders shook as she cried silently. Mela looked to Renee for guidance but the nurse's expression mirrored Mela's own pain. No one was happy.

"I'll be right outside the door, let you say your goodbyes," Renee said and Mela thought she saw the nurse wipe away a tear of her own as she closed the door behind her. Wyatt was talking softly to the little girl, so Mela went to stand beside Sammuele who watched everything with interest.

"I feel so bad," Mela whispered to him. Sammuele nodded. "I wish there was something we could do."

"I will come and stay with her as much as time allows," Sammuele said looking down at Mela. "Will that do to make you happy?" he asked.

Confused, Mela nodded and studied Sammuele. "It would make her happy and that would make me happy," she said in response.

"Very well, then it is settled." He turned his attention back to the child and watched as Wyatt tried to make her happy with promises of their next visit. He stood, still holding Annabelle's hand and went to Mela and Sammuele.

"We're coming back next weekend, isn't that right, Annabelle? We'll have almost all day together next time." Annabelle stared at her shoes in silence.

"And I will come to visit you often and this time, I will talk to you." Annabelle looked up at Sammuele and nodded. She was trying hard not to cry, squeezing her lips together. Wyatt excused himself from the room to speak with Renee and Mela knelt down in front of Annabelle.

"Like Wyatt said, we'll be back soon. While you're hanging out with Sammuele, play games with him. He likes games," Mela said with a mischievous grin. The little girl looked up at Sammuele for confirmation and Mela raised her eyebrows to him, warning him he better agree.

"Of course, I do not know any games. You will need to teach me," he said with a twinkle in his eye. Mela smiled in approval, Annabelle attempted to smile but failed, and she simply nodded.

"We'll see you real soon, Annabelle," Mela gave the little girl a quick hug, then stood, wiping a tear that fell from her eye. Wyatt opened the door and he entered again with Renee in tow.

"Well, Princess, we've got to go."

Annabelle broke down in tears and threw herself in his arms. Wyatt closed his eyes and stroked the back of her head. "It's alright, pretty girl. I'll be back real soon." He let go of her and stood up, eyes red and in pain. Renee stood in the doorway as Mela and Wyatt walked out.

"Please don't go!" Annabelle cried out. "I'll be good, I'll play games with you. I won't be bad…please…please don't leave me…" She broke down in tears and Renee gathered the girl in her arms, waving them off, telling them to leave.

Mela and Wyatt walked slowly back to the north wing, hand in hand. There wasn't anything left to say that their tears weren't already saying. As they stepped outside, the evening air was full of the sounds of crows calling to one another in the distance. They rode home hardly saying a word. As they passed a lake sitting in the middle of a green pasture, Mela desperately wished she could stop and jump in. She needed the comfort it would give. She'd do anything to wash away the pain and guilt in her heart.

Chapter Eight

Mela and Wyatt sat up late into the night with Vasha, drinking wine, and telling him all about little Annabelle Martello and her sad story. Wyatt was unusually quiet and decided to sleep in the spare room after finishing a bottle of wine all by himself. Mela stayed up late with Vasha, listening to him tell her stories of the Zodiac and where the corresponding constellation could be found.

Sunday was a quiet day. Mela and Bear trained in the afternoon and she made plans with Vasha to start to help her with her sword fighting on Monday. He seemed excited at the idea but the trio, plus Bear, enjoyed a lazy day smoking from the hookah (which Wyatt still refused to do) drinking wine, and nibbling on food from the garden. Vasha made a request for hummus, and Mela told him she'd find him some the next time she went shopping. Her grocery bill was a lot smaller now that Decker and Theo were gone. But she missed them. No matter how much they ate and drank from her kitchen, she'd buy them anything to have the backyard gang whole again.

* * *

Sammuele hadn't been around since they left him at the hospital with Annabelle. Mela understood completely and was grateful to him for staying with the girl. As she pulled out of her driveway early Monday morning, she was amazed at the number of black crows were around. Every tree she passed was speckled with the birds. This was an abundance of crows even for Texas in the fall.

Setting aside the unusual phenomenon, Mela went to work. Nothing was unusual, no invisible visitors, no tacky comments from Tracy, and no angry messages from Todd. All in all, it was a good day. Anxious to get home, Mela made a beeline for the door right at quitting time. She was anxious to get home to Vasha. He wasn't like Decker, making her run drills and punching her all the time. Vasha explained things. He knew so much more about magick than his brothers did, so they had plenty to talk about.

Once home, she quickly grabbed herself a bite to eat and changed clothes. The dirty laundry and the clean laundry piles were beginning to converge and she groaned at the prospect of having to do it. Nothing was more irritating that putting away clean laundry. It seemed perfectly reasonable to leave it all out. However, Wyatt disagreed. Often.

She chose a tank top and shorts that barely smelled and happily made her way outside with Bear to collect Vasha. Knocking on the door, she heard him call for her to enter.

"Back from your duties?" he said as he placed a pile of odds and ends into one of the intricately designed trunks. Mela casually sat on a large royal blue pillow and leaned against the wall.

"Yep. All done with my duties,"

"Tell me, what do you do all day? I'm curious as to what keeps you away for so long," he said over his shoulder.

"Well, I answer phones, take care of clients, I update the website...it's all pretty boring stuff," she said, picking at her fingernails.

"If this bores you, why do you do it?" He closed the trunk and faced her.

"Because," she laughed, "that's how I make money. If I don't work, I don't eat. We don't eat."

"I see." He held a bundle of something in his right arms and inclined his head for her to follow. He took her to the clearing where she normally trained with Decker, and placed the long bundle at his feet. "Come see," he said.

Mela went to kneel beside him and gasped. The bundle held a set of four gold swords, each studded with jewels. The hilts were inlaid with large emeralds, surrounded by a delicate pattern of diamonds that wrapped around the entire hilts. The sheaths were as fantastic as the swords themselves, boasting diamonds, rubies, and flecks of emeralds to match the hilt. She was surprised when he pulled the blade free that it was only about a foot and a half long. The silver blade had engraving on both sides but she couldn't decipher any of it.

"Oh, they're beautiful," she breathed.

"Indeed. These are called *Shamshir-e Zomorrodnegar* or the Emerald-Studded Swords. Legend tells that these blades were forged to kill monsters. But now," he grasped the hilt of all four and held them out for her to see. "A monster is their master." Mela smiled.

"I couldn't imagine you with anything less amazing, Vasha," Her words pleased him and he stood up straight and tall.

"I am rather lovely, am I not?" Mela laughed and nodded. "Before the sun sets, shall we spar a bit, you and I? It has been a long time. I would like to become familiar with them once more,"

"But when I train with Decker, we use the wooden swords. I'm not as fast as you are…"

He smiled and relaxed his arms.

"I would not hurt you, Mela. These are old swords and alas," he looked down at the blades as he spoke. "They have not been sharpened in a long time. I do not think I could cut anything as they are."

Satisfied, Mela said, "I forgot to grab mine," and she moved to go. Vasha stopped her.

"No…you will have no blade tonight. You have weapons of your own and you need to use them more. My beloved brother has taught you well, make no mistake. But you must strive for balance in all things. This includes battle. Now, tell me little Witch, what happened when you dropped your sword the other night at the hospital?"

"I dropped it and…I didn't know what to do," she conceded.

Vasha nodded. "Correct. You became scared and distracted."

"But you told me not to use fire when we were there!" she cried.

His elegant eyebrows raised a bit and he looked down at her. "Do you or do you not command all of the elements, not just fire?"

Dejected, Mela nodded and chewed on her bottom lip. The crows overhead began singing a raucous song and both Vasha and Mela looked up at them. He pointed one of the blades at the birds.

"Those are not normal birds."

Mela had to agree. The birds were all fluttering wings and loud caws in every tree she could see. "I do not like these birds," he said finally. Mela nodded and watched the birds flap and caw around them. The noise was aggravating Bear as well. He cocked his head from side to side and trotted up to the nearest tree, lifted his leg, and urinated on it.

She was about to laugh when they heard a new noise. Along with the caws of the crows, a noise she'd never heard before quickly filled the air. Deep and throaty, the noise carried and she spun in circles, searching the sky for the source. It reminded Mela of the sound of a lion chuffing, short bursts accompanied by a low growl.

"No," Vasha dropped the swords and turned, searching the skies for something. "No," he said again. Panicked, Mela stood beside him, heart racing and tapping her thigh with her hand, a nervous habit she'd had since she was a child.

"What? What is it?" He didn't answer but keep whispering, "No" over and over again. The call grew louder, forcing Mela to cower and crouch down close to Bear, who liked the noise even less than she did. His whines and nervous pacing freaked her out. The crows added their voices to the mysterious call. It was all Mela could do to not scream. She crouched down and looked to the skies, waiting.

"There," Vasha pointed to a spot in the sky. She saw nothing. "They come," Standing, having no clue what was happening, she did the only thing she knew how to do – readied herself for a fight.

Vasha could obviously see what was coming, but Mela still couldn't get him to say anything more. He wrung his hands together and paced back and forth, eyes glued to a fixed point in the sky. Looking away from the sky, she watched him and realized he was not preparing for a fight. He was terrified.

"Vasha, please, what's happening?" Her shaking voice was all but drowned out by the clamor around them. He answered her by pointing to the sky once more. She looked and saw, for the first time, a black shape in the distance. The sun was setting behind the trees and the colorful explosion of orange and blue made focusing on the dark shape difficult. Holding a hand over her eyes to shield the light, she was finally able to see what approached them.

It could have been the shape of a man, but it wasn't. It was Theo. In his arms, he carried what looked like a body. Covering her mouth with her hands, all desire to fight melted away. Closer and closer he flew until she could make out the limp form of Decker in his arms.

He landed directly in front of them and Mela let out an involuntary cry. Theo placed him on the ground at Vasha's feet and she was finally able to see Decker clearly. Mela ran to him, kneeling on the ground at his side, and placed a hand on his chest to check if he was breathing.

Theo and Vasha spoke to one another over her, but their words were background noise.

Decker was bleeding from large gashes on his arms, face, and torso. His pants were ripped, caked in dirt and blood. One eye was so swollen, the skin seemed ready to tear apart. So discolored was his eye, half of his face looked as though he painted it with purple, blue and red paint. His one good eye remained closed. His mouth was hanging open, but he was breathing.

Still hovering over his limp form, Mela looked up at Theo, silently asking him what happened. It was then she saw the slow drips of blood coming from a wound on his shoulder. The hair all over his body masked most of the wound itself, but she saw a portion of angry red flesh that appeared to have been ripped open. His eyes never left his brother's body. Mela turned to Vasha who was reaching for Decker. Two arms cradled his head and shoulders while the other two took his legs. He lovingly tucked Decker tight against his chest and sped off to the shed.

Shocked, Mela got up and ran with Bear and Theo to follow him. Bursting through the door, she watched Vasha strip his brother of his tattered pants. He spoke in a foreign language, but whatever he was saying, he sounded incredibly angry. Theo answered back meekly, finally resting against the wall of the shed with his eyes closed.

Bear sniffed the unconscious form of Decker, looking to Mela and Theo with concern. Getting no attention from his mistress, he trotted over to Theo and sat at his feet and stared. Theo reached out and placed a gentle hand on Bear's head, stroking the soft fur between his ears. Comforted somewhat by Theo's attention, he settled down and watched.

Mela sat back, helpless, as Vasha continued to rant in the unknown language all while opening trunks and boxes, collecting jars of herbs from inside.

Without looking to Mela, he spoke, "Go fetch me water and some clean cloth." His command was brisk. Mela frantically ran to the house. Her shaking hands found a large pitcher and placed it in the sink to fill with water from the tap. Anxious, she ran to the closet for towels and grabbed all the clean ones she could carry.

Pitcher and towels in her arms, she made her way back to the shed as quickly as she could. Theo met her at the door, taking the water from her as she stepped inside. She followed behind with the stack of towels, handing them to Vasha who held out a hand without a word. She watched him rip her towels in half, dip them in water, and began cleaning the wounds on Decker's body. She counted four evenly spaced tears in his flesh that started at his neck, going horizontally across his body, ending at his hip. Vaguely, she thought they looked like scratches from an animal.

"I need you, Mela," Vasha said and she rushed to his side. "Hold the cloth over the wounds and press down a little. That will stem the blood flow. I need to prepare a solvent for the wounds." He turned to the side and his four arms frantically began grabbing jars and pouring them into a large, bronze bowl. Mela felt tears sting her eyes that she tried to blink back. Desperate for answers, she turned to Theo.

"What happened Theo? What did this?" As soon as the words came from her lips, the tears she fought to keep at bay began to fall. "Someone tell me what is going on!" she cried.

"Tell her, brother, tell her what you have been up to. Tell her why you abandoned us here when we needed you and what fool's errand you set out to accomplish!" Vasha said with such venom that even she flinched.

"We did not think it was foolish," Theo said softly.

"You are fools, both of you. You should have listened to my council. It was folly, seeking him out,"

Vasha spat from where he grounded herbs in the large bowl. Theo hung his head.

"Decker and I, we went to find our eldest brother in hopes we could either win him to our cause or…" Vasha interrupted with a low growl and slammed the tool he was using down hard with a bang.

"The ignorance," he said under his breath as he turned to tend to Decker. Shocked, Mela's mouth hung open and everything she'd ever been told about Azul ran through her mind.

"Why? Why would you do that?" she whispered both to Theo and to Decker's unconscious face.

"Because my brothers have unrealistic hope when it comes to our eldest brother. He is lost and should be left to his anger and misery until we part this world. I warned you." He looked up to Theo with a piercing, accusing glare. "I warned you this was a lost cause. A dangerous game Decker wanted to play. Neither of you would listen to reason. And this," he wiped a hand through the air over Decker's body. "You did not heed my warning and this is the result."

"Theo, why would you and Decker go to him? You've all told me how dangerous he is. We needed you here." Her voice cracked and more tears began to fall. "I had to fight them. Me and Vasha. The Black-Eyed creatures are here and you left us to find…to find that monster," She wiped away the tears and snot that covered her face and glared at Decker's face. "You're so stupid. He doesn't need you, but we did."

"Azul agreed, Vashanu," Theo said softly. Vasha's hands froze in place for a moment at the words but quickly went back to rubbing herbs in the open wounds.

"He agreed to what? Come on," she spat. "What the fuck are you two not telling me?" Vasha worked on and refused to meet her eyes. He didn't owe her an explanation. Theo did.

"We sought Azul with a hope that he might join us here….to be a family once again…"

"Obviously didn't go the way you planned," Mela spat.

"No…he is quite different now… no longer under dark magick, we believe. He was seeking out all things dark and…he was devouring them," Theo said softly. Mela moved out of Vasha's way as he tended the next rip in Decker's flesh. She covered the wound on his chest and waited for Theo to continue. "He refused to come…he refused many things. He wanted no part in our endeavors. However--" he stepped forward and kneeled so that he was nearer to Mela, intensely holding her gaze. "--he agreed to not kill you, Mela. That was the other reason Dektrios and I left. To protect you. We have much to fight and worse things will come before we see the end of this madness. We did not think it was wise to ignore his existence. Now, he knows that we are with you." He handed her a clean strip of towel to replace the one she was holding. "He knows and will not try to kill you."

"But why this?" she inclined her head to his gaping wounds. Theo looked down, winced, and nodded.

"Dektrios angered him…I was standing beside him and his blow merely grazed me. He took the brunt of it."

"What angered him so? If he agreed to leave us in peace, then what was it that made our dear, loving, elder brother try to eviscerate you?" Vasha demanded.

"He…he threatened to kill Mela if we went back to find him. He said, if we interrupt his quest, he shall interrupt ours. Dektrios did not take kindly to the threat. He called him a snake with legs…the words flew and then, so did his claws." Mela felt weak and deflated. This was for her sake. One of her dearest friends was bleeding and in pain because he tried to spare her from his own brother. The guilt almost choked her. Theo placed a gentle hand on her shoulder as she squeezed her eyes shut.

"No. My brothers and I, we would die to protect you. To protect our sisters' secrets as well. Do not fret, Vasha will tend to his wounds and then all will be well again."

"Your wounds as well," Vasha said as he wrapped a strip of colored cloth around Decker's body to cover the herbs. "Come and sit, Theo. I shall tend to you now," Theo went to Vasha's side and sat, one hand on Decker's bare leg and the other he reached out for Vasha's hand. Vasha stopped what he was doing and stared at the contrast of black on blue.

"I am sorry he was hurt, but we were successful." Vasha nodded. "Do not be cross with us. Please. We tried."

Vasha nodded again and held Theo's hand. "I know this. But he is lost, Theothane. No, listen to me." He pulled gently on Theo's hand to make him look at him. "Azul is gone. Lost in madness and revenge. Let him wallow in his anger and misery. We have pressing matters to see to here," he said softly. Theo nodded and allowed Vasha to clean and dress his wound. Once dressed, Vasha handed him a concoction that looked like black tea and ordered him to drink it up. His work completed, Vasha turned to Mela. "Let us go. They need rest and I--," he stood and went to the door "--need release."

Quickly, Mela followed him but looked over her shoulder at the two recovering brothers. One slept in a pain induced sleep and the other could not sleep for the pain he felt in his heart. Turning, she rushed to catch up to Vasha who was collecting his emerald studded swords from the dirt.

"Let us begin," he said.

***

"Do it again," Vasha said to her with the first hint of a smile on his beautiful face. Mela was afraid, at first, to attempt to fight him with no weapon. However, after a few days, she learned quickly that even without a sword, she could not only defend, but also attack.

"Just don't look like you enjoy it so much," she said with a smirk. Vasha had a strange reaction to pain. It brought him pleasure. The first time she managed to send a jet of water from her hands a few days ago, and it hit him so hard his head flew back, he looked as though she'd kissed him. She knew now that he enjoyed pain. In the kinky way she'd only read about. But that never stopped him from trying to inflict pain on her. He tried, and succeeded, in decorating her arms and thighs with fresh, purple bruises.

The idea for her newest form of attack came from Decker. He spent days sitting in his chair and watching Mela and Vasha spar. He didn't say much. In truth, he hadn't said much of anything to Mela since he hobbled from the shed to plop in his chair two days ago. He pouted with as much ferocity as he fought. Once, while Mela was dodging Vasha's blows, Decker made the snide remark that if he fought like that, he'd want the ground to open up and swallow him. So that's exactly what she did.

Except that she made the ground swallow Vasha. Only in part. But it was enough to make him fall with little grace flat onto the dirt and lose his grip on the swords as he tried to catch himself. At first, Mela felt ashamed and instantly guilty.

"I'm sorry!" she cried and went to help him from the hole she created. As she held two of his blue hands and pulled him from the hole she created, he was laughing.

"Glorious! Yes! That was just as you should have done. Beautifully executed," he said, with laughter in his eyes.

Ever since then, she managed to counter his attack with her magick. Keeping her bare feet on the ground and channeling her energy down to her feet, all she had to do was lightly step on the earth and a hole opened before her. She learned she could control it if she visualized the size she needed to make. She was communicating with the Earth and it felt even better than swinging a sword.

What Vasha wanted her to do again was, once he fell in the hole again, to fill it with water. The first time she did it, he struggled for quite some time before he pulled himself from up. Plenty of time for Mela to either run for safety, if it were a real attack, or execute him easily. As she stepped back and considered how she could change it up, she saw Decker stand and slowly hobble back to the shed without saying a word.

"Really, is he going to be okay? He hasn't said a word to me since he got back," she said.

"He is angry, my beloved brother. He is angry he was bested by, perhaps, the only living soul capable of besting him. He's angry for so many reasons. However, it is his pride that ails him now."

"Hmm. It seems like he should feel lucky to escape his brother. Not pout about it," she said with her hands on her hips, staring at the shed.

Vasha came to her side and wrung water from his hair. "Oh, it is not the fight with Azul that has wounded him so. He knows he cannot best our eldest brother. It is because he cannot teach you what I am teaching you. Or rather, that I am teaching you at all. He prides himself on all matters of war, and forgets that I too have lived through wars. Not the ones he lived through, but I have fought battles and learned many things." Mela stared at Vasha as he rearranged the golden bracelets on his arms. It made sense, that Decker was upset about her training with Vasha. But his avoidance of her since the day he left kept her from feeling too bad about it.

Mela went to work early the next morning, feeling a strange sense of control over herself. Todd hadn't called again, probably due to the fact that she never returned his angry phone calls. She had no idea if he would forgive her but, as she drove in to work, she thought he was in the wrong for being mad at her. In all honesty, maybe it was him that owed her an apology. She did come when he needed the help, despite his attitude toward her and her friends. She saved his patients from a painful torment and what did she get in return? Angry phone calls.

Shrugging her shoulders and feeling strangely composed about it all, Mela went to work and carried out her morning as if nothing was amiss. Answering phone calls and ordering supplies kept her brain dead from her other problems. Sammuele didn't show up in her office and she assumed he was still with Annabelle. It was so very, very quiet.

"Do me a favor," Claudia swept into her office and plopped her clunky, expensive purse on Mela's desk. "I have an appointment that I got to get to. Call your friend, Wyatt, and tell him I'm referring some folks to him. The Carters. They want family photos done, and I told them Wyatt was the best. Which he is," she smiled and dug through the many dark crevices of her purse. "I can't find it…there it is." She pulled out a business card. "They own the restaurant on the square, you know the one, Mamma Rays? Anyway." She waved her hand in the air and pulled the oversized bag to her shoulder. "Could you fill him in? Have him give them a quote and tell him I referred them to him."

Mela looked at the card and nodded. "Sure thing," She reached out to take it from Claudia but the iron grip of perfectly manicured nails grabbed her wrist.

"What in the ever loving hell is this?" She pulled Mela's arm and turned it over to reveal the long, purple and green bruises on her forearms. Vasha's blade wasn't sharp, but his blow was incredibly strong. Mela tried to smile and pull her hand back. But Claudia kept her grip and stared hard at Mela.

"It's not anything bad, Claudia. I promise. I've been working on my house, the shed and the yard. Lots of old wood laying around and I'm clearing it up. I've been moving boxes around…they're heavy." She swallowed hard.

"Working in the yard did all this?" she asked, artfully waxed eyebrows raised in suspicion.

"Well," Mela took her arm back and smiled meekly. "That and I've been working out a lot--"

"I noticed," Claudia said sharply.

"Well, at home, I'm learning how to fight. You know, like martial arts? I get together with some friends who have been…professional fighters. They're teaching me some basics. Like self defense and stuff like that."

"Not that I think taking self defense is a bad idea, but honey, you need to quit looking like you fought a wild hog and lost. Either that or wear long sleeves." With that, she turned and left Mela in the office alone.

Exhaling, Mela rubbed her arms nervously and tried to remember what she was doing before Claudia came in. Five minutes later, she interrupted again.

"This was at the front desk," Tracy said from the doorway. Mela looked at the unwelcome visitor and really saw her for the first time. Tracy was still pale and wore more makeup in an effort to cover it up. Mela strongly suspected she was either doing drugs, or suffered from some horrible virus. Tracy stood, one hand on her hip, and the other holding a paper out lazily. When Mela reached for it, Tracy snatched it back. "Your boyfriend is out on the floor. Seems he *really* likes talking to Natalie Baker. Did you know they were friends? Of course," she smiled a cruel smile, "they certainly seem to be awfully flirty with each other. My guess is they're more than just friends."

Inside, Mela felt like she was doused in ice water and a knife was digging into her chest. On the outside, her face showed no reaction at all. Mela had perfected the art of being humiliated in public with no reaction at all. Some switch, deep down inside of her, clicked into place when her tormentors attacked.

"Still bothers you, doesn't it? Todd going out with me?" Mela hissed. The fury in Tracy's eyes flared and her lips tightened. She slammed the paper down on Mela's desk and turned to leave.

"Well, if he was my boyfriend, he wouldn't have to go looking for attention from Natalie," she said before she reached the door. She stopped and leaned back against the doorway, arms crossed over her voluptuous breasts and smiled. Mela could tell Tracy was watching something out on the floor that amused her. "They look cute together, working out and laughing like that. It's a shame you can't even keep a lame guy like Todd happy."

Mela wasn't aware of her actions as she did them. Slowly, she stood up and walked from behind her desk. She resisted the urge to look out on the floor and see what made Tracy so happy. Instead of coming back with a lame retort, Mela reached out and grabbed Tracy by the shirt and turned, shoving her into the wall behind the door. Tracy's smile quickly faded as her body slammed into the wall. The look of shock on her painted face made Mela smile. Using every muscle at her command, she grasped Tracy by the throat and stepped close to her so that her perfume filled Mela's nose. Tracy clawed at Mela's hands weakly and made wet, choking noises.

"You leave me and Todd alone. Stay away from me, Tracy. If you don't, I promise you'll regret it," she released her grip and Tracy stood still, breathing heavily. "Get out of my office. Now." Tracy sidestepped her and ran from her office.

Mela fought the urge to go out on the floor to confront Todd. Of course, that would be stupid, but it didn't make it any less of a desire. She spent the better part of the next hour cussing Tracy in every way she could come up with. The urge to use magick against her was so strong that she spent a few minutes trying to decide if she could get away with it. But she couldn't, not here anyway. However, if Mela ever ran into Tracy outside of work that would be a different story. It was bad enough she just assaulted her coworker in her office. She really needed to get a grip on her anger.

She tried not to notice who walked in and out of the building, but her office gave a clear view of the front desk and the doors. So, later, it was even more horrible to witness Todd leaving, without saying a word to her, with Natalie right beside him.

Chapter Nine

She fought off the desire to send Todd a scathing text message. By the time she left work, the desire to drink a few glasses of wine and fight someone was overwhelming. Passing Tracy, she held her head high and made a beeline for her car. Once she was inside, she pulled out her phone and tried to call Wyatt. It rang and rang but there was no answer.

"Shit," she hissed and tossed her phone in the seat next to her. She put it in reverse and started home. Fuming as she drove, Mela couldn't wait to get there. She was in the perfect mood to confront Decker about his pouting. She felt like she had been plenty understanding and his irrational pity party needed to stop. Vasha, apparently, had filled him in on the hospital incident and it seemed to set him off even more. Lighting a cigarette, she rehearsed what she would say to Decker and that helped her pass the time.

Pulling into the driveway, she saw Bear and Theo walking from the back to the front of the house to greet her. She grabbed her things from the front seat and opened the door. Stepping from the car and slamming it shut, she passed them both.

"Come back here with me. Where's Decker?" she said a bit loudly. Her heart thumped in her ears and she let the anger wash over her. Following close by, both Theo and Bear knew she was in a malicious mood, so they followed in silence. "Decker?" she yelled. She tossed her purse on the back porch and stood there with her hands on her hips.

"He is with Vasha," Theo said softly.

"Then go get him," she ordered. Digging through her purse for her pack of cigarettes, she saw her cell phone and reached for that as well. Lighting a cigarette, she placed her phone on the railing and took a drag while she waited. She felt them approach before she saw them. For some reason, her senses were heightened to a remarkable degree. They approached her, side by side, but when they saw her, they stopped.

"We need to talk. Now," she said. She glanced at them but waited until they came closer before she would address them. She faced the trees in the distance and let the anger wash over her. Slowly, they came into view. Theo walked, head hung low, ready for whatever came. Vasha was next, smiling and seeming inexplicably pleased at his summons. Decker lagged behind but stared hard at Mela as he approached. She waited until they were side by side before she spoke.

"You wanted us?" Vasha asked. As Decker took his place beside his brother, Mela finally focused on them and uncrossed her arms.

"I'm angry," she began.

"Yes...we see it all over your pretty face, Little Witch," Vasha teased.

Frowning, Mela stepped closer. "This has been a horrible fucking day. But instead of being able to come home to relax with my friends, I'm coming home to this," she said and flung her arms out. Bear approached her, cautiously, until she reached out her hand and called him to her. He came, tail wagging, and took his rightful place by her side. "The past few weeks, Vasha, you've been an incredible help to me. But you kept secrets from me. You knew they went to find Azul and should have told me. At least, we could've been mad together!" she said, fighting back tears. She turned to Theo and stared at him until he looked up from studying her feet. "Theo, stop it. Just stop pouting. You act like you're scared of me or something," she hissed. It irritated her how he met her eyes only briefly before looking down again, over and over.

"I am a little frightened. I have never seen this before," he said softly.

"You've seen me mad,"

"Although we may be accustomed to your outbursts on occasion, it is your appearance my brother is referring to." Vasha said, folding both sets of hands together.

"My appearance? Really? You're going to get on to me about how I look?" Vasha held up his hand to tell her to stop but she just couldn't let his arrogant smiles and witty quips calm her down. "No, I'm not done. You," she said pointing at Decker's face. "You owe me an apology. I needed you! We needed you! You left and didn't even tell me goodbye…nothing! You just waved like you were happy to be going and…" Her voice cracked and she called to that deep place inside of her to find the anger again. Visions of Todd walking away with Natalie and Tracy's smug face brought a new wave of anger over her. "I get it, you went to find your fuck-face brother. He doesn't want anything to do with us! Look at what he did to you!" she held out her hands, pleading for him to understand. "I do, though. I need you and want you to be here and need you to help me. To be my friend. And all you've done since you got back is pout. You're angry with me and I don't know why." Angry tears fell from her eyes and they felt warm on her cheeks.

Decker said nothing. He stared hard at Mela in apparent wonder then looked to his brothers.

"You know about this?" he said, pointing in her direction. Confused she wiped the tears away.

"I saw it when we battled the creatures at the hospital. Truly an amazing sight, is it not?" Even more confused, she was ready to scream. Instead, she stomped her foot like a petulant child.

"What the hell are you talking about?" she demanded. They looked at one another and then back at her.

"Your eyes. You got fire coming out of your eyes." Stunned, she looked to Vasha for confirmation and he smiled as he nodded. She put her hands to her eyes and covered them. She felt nothing and she could see as normally as she always did.

"I will fetch the mirror," Vasha said before he sped off to the shed. The wooden door banged on the outside of the wall as he burst out again, carrying her favorite mirror. Holding the gorgeous, golden framed mirror up, she saw herself in all of her fury.

Where her normal brown eyes once sat, two living flames danced in her skull, and licked the corners of her sockets. Gasping, she stepped back, staring at her friends.

"I think it is a fearsome look. I rather like it," Vasha said as he lowered the mirror.

"Fucking brilliant is what it is," Decker said.

"It frightens me. Does it happen when she fights?" Theo asked Vasha.

"No, only when she is really and truly angry. Such a lovely thing to see," he purred, stepping closer to her and caressing her cheeks.

"That ought to scare the shite right outta those bastards," Decker said. Vasha and Mela looked at one another then, together, looked to Decker.

"I can't believe this…" she said softly. Vasha wrapped a protective arm around her and chuckled. He turned her so that they were both facing Decker and Theo.

"You do know I was against your quest. Not only was it ill advised to leave Mela alone, but it was a doomed endeavor from the start. You owe her an apology, brother," Vasha said.

Decker, now staring at his feet, was kicking a stick from side to side. He looked up and nodded.

"Aye. I do. I didn't want to leave but I was anxious to see, you know? To see if we could... Ah," he kicked the stick hard and it went flying into the yard. "Aye, I'm sorry, mate. I just knew you'd worry and I didn't want you to worry. Thought you'd get some big bright idea to come with and we didn't want that. But we did it to try and help. You know that, right?" He stepped closer to her and she looked up at him. He wasn't as tall as his brothers, around six feet, but his bright yellow eyes and razor sharp teeth could be a bit off-putting to the wrong people.

Mela heard her phone going off but she ignored it. "I know. I know that now. But I thought we were a team. We shouldn't be keeping secrets like this. They get you killed. That's what you said."

He slumped his shoulders. "Aye. I made a right mess out of everything. I know." He hung his head but sneaked a peek at her. The boyish gesture made her laugh. Decker snorted and shook his head, then reached out and gathered Mela in his large, muscular arms. He hugged her tight and placed a sloppy kiss on her forehead.

"Bravo!" Vasha called and Theo beamed. Mela heard her phone buzzing again and she made to pull away from Decker.

"Wait, not yet. Here, Vasha—catch!" He scooped up Mela in his arms and tossed her to Vasha. He caught her deftly while she squealed and he hugged her tightly against him.

"We did not quarrel but I will make up all the same," Vasha said. Laughing, she kicked and tried to release herself from his incredibly strong embrace. "Not yet, kitten," She felt him tense and then she was tossed over to Theo who caught her gently.

His embrace was no less affectionate but far less sensual. He held her close as if she would break and purred from somewhere deep in his chest. Mela smiled and wrapped her arms around his neck and felt the softness of his fur. Bear barked joyfully around them, wanting in on the game.

"Oh, you want to play too, do ya?" Decker called and went for Bear. Tucking his rear end, Bear ran in circles around them all, stopping only to dare Decker to come at him again. Which he did.

"I too am sorry for not including you in our decision. It is only because we love you that we had to leave," Theo said to her softly. She reached up, petting the soft, black fur that covered his face.

"I know, Theo. I love you too."

"Are you frightened of yourself?" he asked.

Stunned, Mela thought for a moment about what he meant. Yes, she was frightened of herself. Up until a few minutes ago, she had no idea her eyes turned to flames when she was angry. She wondered how she would control such a thing out in public. She wondered if she would ever be normal again, or would she continue to change. Slowly, she looked up into his bright, yellow eyes and nodded.

"I scare myself sometimes as well. I suppose that is a good thing. The day you do not fear what you might be, is the day when you should fear what you are," Frowning a bit as she tried to work out what he meant, she smiled and squeezed him once more around the neck.

Theo bent down to carefully place Mela's feet on the ground. She smiled up at him but turned away because her phone rang again.

"Oy, who's got some booze? We should drink a bit. You know? Just to seal the deal is all," Decker said as Vasha turned to scold him. Mela smiled and reached for her phone. Wyatt obviously needed to speak to her because he called three times in the past five minutes. He left a voice mail, so she dialed her inbox to listen. Sticking her finger in her ear to drown out the loud argument over whether they should or shouldn't get drunk tonight, Mela caught only pieces of his message.

"Oh God..." he whispered into the phone. "Oh please come, Mela...the things...Oh God, no!!!" he screamed and the phone went dead. Shock washed over her and her hands shook as she hit the buttons so she could listen again. She waved her arms frantically to the three to get their attention.

She cradled the phone to her ear, desperate to hear more than she did the last time. Shaking, she heard Wyatt's voice again pleading for her to come, somewhere, and help him. His last cry made her feel cold inside. Tears fell from her eyes as she looked to the now frozen trio for guidance.

"What is it?" Vasha said calmly. Mela hit the speaker button and she held the phone out so they could hear. All hell broke loose. Decker screamed in rage, Vasha dashed off to the shed, and Theo stood beside Mela with a hand on her shoulder.

"You should call to Sammuele. He will be useful to know what is going on. Do you know where Wyatt is tonight?" Shaking her head, she couldn't think....was he home? Home alone and someone or something had him? She couldn't remember what day it was anymore.

"Sammuele. Sammuele, please come now. Wyatt is in trouble," she said in a shaking voice. Decker and Vasha shoved something in her hands and she looked down to see it was her sword, wrapped in the black garments Vasha made for her. She looked at the bundle in her arms and had no idea of what to do with them.

"Dress now. We go to fight together this time." Vasha said and helped her undress right there on the back porch. It didn't register that she was baring all for them to see. She didn't care. Her hands fumbled with the clothes when she tried to put them on. Vasha came to her rescue and dressed her, tying the long black ties snuggly around her back. She stepped into the flowing pair of paints just as Sammuele appeared.

"What has happened?" he asked, eyeing her as she lifted her arms to reach for her sword and leather belt.

"It was Wyatt. He called and said...there's something wrong. He was scared and he kept saying 'Please help me.' I don't know where he is...." She took a deep breath, trying to calm her nerves. All around her, Decker, Theo and Vasha hustled, handing one another swords, daggers, and various articles of clothing.

"I will find him," Sammuele said, and he was gone. Relieved they were doing something, Mela fastened the belt around her waist and rearranged it until the sword fell comfortably on her hip. Bear pranced around nervously, anxious at the sudden commotion. She pulled him close and wrapped her arm around his neck, burying her face in his coat.

"He is at the church," Sammuele reappeared, speaking rapidly. "We must go immediately. They have several people." Mela stood and was joined by the others. Vasha fastened her cloak around her shoulders as she stood still like a frighten child.

"Who's got Wyatt?" Decker demanded.

"Creatures...like the ones from the hospital. They have Wyatt and others at the church. They are in grave danger. We must go," Sammuele seemed anxious and she felt terror creep deeper into her. She couldn't allow it to get too close. She couldn't let herself think of Wyatt hurt or worse...

"Tonight is the Bible study group," Mela said softly, finally able to remember where he would normally be. Mrs. Wesley, Wyatt, and others she'd known all her life were there. Those weren't unknown patients in a bed-- these were her people!

"We can run," Vasha said.

"We will not get there in time," Sammuele said.

"I will fly," Theo said.

"No…I will take Mela. I travel faster than all of you," Sammuele said. He turned to Mela and opened his arms to her. Hesitating for a moment, she turned to the trio.

"Meet us there? It's the same way as the hospital, just off a long dirt road. Big white church…." She stepped into Sammuele's waiting arms and felt him bring her close.

"We're on our way already," Decker said and she saw Theo shoot into the sky and Decker swung a leg over Vasha's back. Mela wrapped her arms around Sammuele's waist, looking up at him as she did.

"Do not be afraid," he said. "Close your eyes." And she did. Resting her head on his chest, she clung to his robes and tried to breathe normally. She inhaled the smell of Sammuele and likened it to the scent of a coming rain. It was oddly calming to breathe in his fragrance and to feel him so close. "We are here," he said softly.

She opened her eyes to see they were standing in the trees, directly beside the white church. A long dirt road led right into a path of dying grass where cars were parked in disarray. The church itself must have been built ages ago because the paint peeled and the wood looked aged. The only modern upgrade was the large, illuminated sign that boasted, 'God always leaves a light on for you!' and the hours of services.

Pulling the hood over her head, Mela quietly made her way to the large, white double doors. She hadn't realized she was barefoot until she felt the cool wood on her flesh. The boards groaned softly under her bare feet as she approached. There was no noise from inside and the silence terrified her even more. Sammuele stood by her side and they listened for any sounds on the other side.

She knew there was a small foyer that led to another set of wooden doors. Those doors opened up into the sanctuary and that, Mela thought, was where they would be. She was frozen with indecision. Should she burst in, swords drawn and ready to fight? Should they creep in, through a side door and take them by surprise?

Sammuele broke into her thoughts when he placed a hand on her shoulder. She looked up at him and he nodded to the darkness. Mela turned as Theo approached. She saw his eyes in the darkness first, then his form materialized from the shadows and there he stood.

"Sammuele and I will go in-- you guys stay out here," Mela whispered. She wasn't sure when she made that plan, it just sounded like the right thing to do. Theo nodded and stepped back into the shadows. A blue blur came from the tree line and stopped in the same place where Theo had been standing just a moment before. Decker jumped from Vasha's back, wincing a bit from the pain in his leg, and approached the stairs. She told them the same thing she told Theo. Decker hesitated, but Vasha agreed with a smile.

"We will only frighten them more, brother. Come, we will collect any stragglers and dispatch them as we see fit," he said gleefully. Giving her a lingering look, Decker finally nodded and she watched as they took positions in the shadows, watching for their chance.

Turning to the doors again, she twisted the aged knob and, with a metallic click, the doors opened. Mela thought they were the noisiest doors she'd ever heard in her life. She opened them enough to peek through and, seeing the foyer empty, she stepped through with Sammuele close behind.

She saw the table where the church put flyers and cookies every Sunday morning. Her parents brought her almost every week when she was a child but many of her memories had long ago faded. So she thought. Once she was inside, she smelled the old wood, and remembered running through here as a little girl, dressed in her favorite dress, chasing her sister as they raced for the car.

The sanctuary doors were closed and she thought she heard muted voices from inside. Sammuele stepped close and whispered in her ear.

"I will be with you. They will not see me, but I am here and will help as I can." Resigned, she knew it was too late to change her plan. Honestly, she'd rather walk into a room full of the Black-Eyed creatures with Vasha or Decker by her side. Not an invisible angel. Taking a deep breath, Mela put a hand on the handle of the door to pull it open.

That's when she heard a scream.

Chapter 10

It was a man screaming. She was sure of it. Fear took hold of her heart and made her hands shake. She took deep breaths but nothing she did could calm the spread of fear that seemingly took complete and utter control.

Sammuele stood flush against her back and leaned close to her ear and whispered, "Your fear will not serve you or your friends. Find your anger, Mela. Dig down deep and grasp onto anger as though your life depends upon it. Because, surely, their lives depend on you."

Mela closed her eyes, trying to forget her shaking hands and racing heart. What were they feeling right now? Certainly, the people inside the sanctuary were far more terrified than she was. Her Wyatt was inside. She replayed his message in her mind and focused on his face. Wyatt, the dearest, most important person in her life was facing the Black-Eyed creatures on the other side of the door. How dare they? How dare those vile things harass and threaten the one closest to the Elementai?

Anger. Rage. The all-consuming emotions flooded her belly with its warm embrace. She felt the fire deep within her, extinguished the frigid paralyzing fear, allowed it to take control, and still her shaking hands. One breath….then another….she felt the control that rage gave her. Death lay in the other side of the door. Not her death, but theirs.

Firmly grasping both door handles and stepping back, Mela pulled and opened both doors at once. There was no reason to skulk and sneak into the room. She was the Elementai and these were her people. Sammuele opened the doors wider behind her and she stood in the doorway, cloak over her head, and a hand on the hilt of the sword. She knew the flames were dancing in her eyes. With her face hidden in the shadows of the hood, her entrance would strike fear into any who saw her.

She took a slow step forward, relishing the energy she brought with her. Anger. Rage. Death. The pews were empty. She passed one after another, coming closer and closer to her prey. The podium, where Pastor Rod spoke every Sunday morning, was moved back against the wall. The table, normally brought out to hold communion, sat covered in papers and upturned Bibles. The cross that hung on the wall lay broken on the ground.

A huddled mass of people sat on the floor, terror etched onto their faces, as a Black-Eyed creature stood over them. As she slowly approached, Mela scanned their faces until she found the one she needed to see. Wyatt was alive. He had his arms around Mrs. Wesley. Mrs. Wesley was the one responsible for organizing this Bible study. Her diagnosis of terminal cancer didn't alter her desire to gather her beloved church members and pray for those less fortunate, rally the community to support those in need, and include anyone who was willing to join them. Mrs. Wesley was paler than the last time Mela saw her. Whether it was because of fear, or the disease that ate away at her, but her skin was almost transparent.

Searching the others, Mela saw a man she'd known since childhood, Marcus DeWight. She wasn't sure what he did for a living, but she knew he was as faithful to the congregation of this church as anyone could ever hope to be. Others she saw, cowering in each other's arms, were familiar faces, Sara Buchanan, Mrs. Nortel, Old Mr. Simpson, and another she'd only seen in passing. These were *her* people.

As she approached the front of the sanctuary, Mela saw another group to the left. Two other Black-Eyed creatures held Pastor Rod in a painful grip. His hands were twisted behind his back; one creature had a handful of his white, thinning hair, stretching his head back as far as it could go. It was Pastor Rod who had screamed. Mela was sure of it.

Silence met her entry and no one moved. No human or creature could take their eyes away from the fearsome image standing before them. Meeting Wyatt's eyes, Mela gave him a nod. So much was intended for him in that nod. *I'm glad you're alive. I'm here to help. Help me help these people. Don't be afraid…*

The Black-Eyed creatures, true to their nature, were torturing kind Pastor Rod. Blood dripped from a number of wounds on his face, neck and chest. The creatures turned to face her now that she was close. Amused, she smiled, knowing they would be dead soon.

"Let him go," she said softly. There was no need for her to speak any louder. The room was as quiet as a death chamber. That was, in fact, what it would be soon enough. Hissing, the lone creature took a step towards her, mouthful of sharp teeth showing, and talons poised to attack. She remembered the speed with which these creatures moved. She stood as still as her rage allowed. Her fingers delicately sat on the hilt of her sword as she waited. No one knew what was concealed beneath her black cloak.

She saw the creature's long, gray legs contract and prepare to jump. She smiled and waited until it fully committed to flight before she pulled her sword from her hip. The large head was thrown back as it let out a terrible screech. She saw the terrified onlookers cover their ears and heard a few begin to cry. The creature leaped toward her, claws outstretched in flight, intent on mauling her upon collision.

It was almost too easy. Stepping back, sword in hand, Mela grabbed the hilt in two hands and swung. The blade caught the spindly body of the creature and showered the red carpet with black blood. It was dead before it hit the floor, Mela's strike almost cleaving it in two. The creature lay in a growing pool of black fluid that passed for blood. Mela stepped over the body and addressed the one who held the Pastor.

"These people are mine," she pointed to the group on the floor with her bloodstained sword. "This one," she pointed to Pastor Rod, "is mine as well. Let him go," she said softly. She felt all eyes on her. From behind her, she sensed Sammuele standing close. His scent filed her nose and his presence brought her comfort.

"Be gone, Mage," one of the creatures growled. Slightly taken aback, Mela tried to figure out which one was addressing her. Neither one moved their mouth to speak. Tilting her head to the side, she looked deep into the frightened eyes of Pastor Rod. *I will save you…*

"You can talk. The others I killed, they didn't talk. They cowered on the floor and died screaming," she said with a hint of a smile. She needed to goad them into leaving the Pastor's side. Why they had singled him out, why it was him they were torturing in front of a crowd, was a question better left for later.

"You dare…we will have this one…we rule all…we do not like you here. We tell you to leave," it hissed. She still wasn't sure which one was speaking. However, one had stepped a foot closer and stared hard at her with its black empty eyes.

"I'm not leaving and you can't have him. I told you, he is mine," she said, stepping closer. Her words were met with low growls and a hiss.

"We have claimed them….we will do as we please…we do not want you here…" they said again.

"You can't claim what already belongs to me. They have my protection and if you want me to leave," she said, pushing back the hood from her head and standing tall. "You will have to kill me," she said, daring them to attack.

The creatures turned to one another briefly, then faced her again. "We will give you a slow death...we see you are only one....we will not be defeated by you..." one of them hissed, and they dropped the pastor's hands, making him fall forward to the floor. The creatures stepped away from him and began to stalk Mela from two directions.

She turned sideways, keeping them both in her line of sight. Mela heard Wyatt cry out something from the other side of the room but she couldn't look away from the two creatures stalking her. From behind, a bright white light grew so intense, the creatures stopped their approach and hissed. They could see Sammuele.

"The Elementai is not alone," Sammuele's voice boomed from beside her. Mela glanced quickly at him and saw he held a long sword made of glittering silver. The onlookers gasped again at the newcomer and the creatures halted their attack.

"One for each of us," Mela said softly to Sammuele.

"Let it begin," he said, and they stepped forward together, each approaching a creature. Mela considered the attack she could use. She didn't want to tear down the church to save it, so fire and earth were out of the question. While she thought, the creature took a step and she countered its movement. The large head tilted this way and that before it opened its mouth and shrieked. She watched it prepare to jump and she steadied herself for the fight. When it moved, however, she realized she was wrong. It didn't jump for her but for the group of people to her right.

As it stood upright, she was sure it was mocking her. It darted to the group and reached toward them. Screams from everyone filled her ears but she saw the creature grab a man's arm and pull. Marcus Dewight fell forward, fighting hard to pull away from the creature's grip. Mela rushed the creature but not before it reached out with its other hand and pushed its long, gray fingers into

Marcus's chest. She watched him convulse in pain and clutch his heart before he staggered backward, hitting the floor.

Mela didn't want to swing her sword so close to the terrified people but it was a wasted thought. The creature jumped again, sliding across the table and sending papers and Bibles in all directions. It crouched on all fours and hissed at her, safely out of her reach again.

"We will kill them all…You will watch us kill them and be helpless…" She saw Wyatt crawl towards Marcus who now lay unconscious on the floor. She didn't have time to turn to see how Sammuele was faring. She rashly made for the table, aiming her sword for the plastic top. She was too slow. Her sword cracked the plastic and missed the creature entirely. It leapt into the air and landed directly beside Wyatt.

Wyatt looked up from trying to resuscitate Marcus and stared, open-mouthed, into the creature's eyes. Mela knew he was looking into a void that would keep him frozen in fear. She couldn't move forward fast enough as the creature reached for Wyatt with a slow, deliberate growl.

"No!" Mela heard someone scream. All eyes turned to Mrs. Wesley who jumped forward in between the creature and Wyatt, and landed hard on her weak knees. Wyatt fell onto his back, and watched in horror as the creature grasped Mrs. Wesley's throat. It squeezed. Her arms flew out to her sides as her body shook

The rest of the people pulled Wyatt back to safety as he screamed for Mrs. Wesley. Mela reached the creature and slammed into it, both of them going down. She purposefully dropped her sword and wrestled the creature until her hands touched its face.

"You can't have them," she said as she lit its face on fire. Terrible screams filled the room from the creature and the people who watched. Still clenching the cold, leathery skin, Mela turned until she straddled the struggling creature and felt the body go still. She burned it until it was nothing more than black goo in her hands. Her rage wanted to tear it apart. She wanted to feel the flesh rip under her fingers and drag everything inside it out to rot.

Breathing hard, she stood as Sammuele approached her. His glittering silver sword was now tainted with black blood.

"It is done," he said. Mela nodded. She turned to Wyatt and they held each other's gaze until he nodded. *I'm okay. We're okay. You did it…*

"I will see to this one," Sammuele said, gesturing to Pastor Rod. Mela nodded without looking at him. She was drawn to the limp form of Mrs. Wesley laying on the floor. Stopping to place her sword in the sheath, she slowly approached the small group of survivors. Wyatt was busy barking orders for someone to call for an ambulance. Another was cradling Marcus's head, holding his hand. His eyes fluttered open and then closed. He was alive. Beside him, lay poor Mrs. Wesley.

Her predictable flower print dress had been pushed above her knees, exposing white legs and pale knee-high stockings. Mela knelt beside her and pulled her dress down to cover her. She would've been mortified to have everyone see her that way. One arm was out to the side and the other was over her head. Mela carefully put her arms down, straightening the top of her dress after she did. She was always a pale woman with even paler hair. Mela softly touched her plump cheek. Mrs. Wesley's face was serene in death.

"She's gone…I think she's gone, Mela," Wyatt's voice broke into her sadness and Mela nodded. "I can't believe you came and Sammuele too. I was so scared." Wyatt's voice cracked and she reached for him. Holding her dearest friend in her arms, she finally felt relief. He was alive. Mela would've slaughtered a host of Black-Eyed creatures to save him.

"You okay?" she asked, cupping his face in her hands. He nodded but closed his eyes.

"She saved me…" he said, reaching out to hold Mrs. Wesley's hand. "I…" His voice broke. Rocking back on his heels, he covered his face and sobbed.

Standing, Mela surveyed the mess and then the faces of those left. Every single one of them regarded her with fear. She couldn't look at them. She didn't want to see it. Turning away, she found Sammuele speaking softly to Pastor Rodd.

"You may say so to her yourself," Sammuele said.

Pastor Rod tried to look strong and serious despite his bleeding face, disheveled hair, and torn shirt. "Mela Malone, I…" he looked down then back to Sammuele, who nodded patiently. "I don't know how to thank you. Those things…they…well…I don't rightly know what to say, but God bless you for coming when you did," he said.

"It's what I do," Mela replied. She was uncomfortable under the gaze of so many now that the threat was over. "Sammuele, we should go soon."

"I agree," he said.

Pastor Rod opened his mouth and gaped.

"Go! What if they come back? What about…." He finally looked around and surveyed his church. Black blood was everywhere. Not to mention the dead bodies on the floor. The table was cracked down the middle and the large wooden cross lay toppled and broken. His church was a mess. But Mela wasn't aware, as he walked toward his congregation, that his eyes were on the lifeless body of Mrs. Wesley. "Oh, God have mercy…" He fell to his knees and dropped his head in prayer.

Feeling incredibly uncomfortable now, Mela thought now was a good time to start dragging bodies from the room. Thankfully, they were mostly in one piece. She quickly found the side entrance to the sanctuary and opened the door. She stuck her head out and called out.

"Vasha, Theo, Decker. Here," Moments later, they approached and she wordlessly slid the first body out of the door. "Dump this," she said and motioned for them to wait. As the group huddled around the fallen, Mela rushed about to gather the other bodies. Decker stood in the doorway and took one from her and she dragged the other out behind him.

"I watched you through the colored glass. That was fucking brilliant!" he exclaimed with a smile and a hearty pat on the back. Mela laughed, breathed in the crisp, night air, and closed her eyes briefly. The sound of crows cawing made her eyes pop open. Crows at night? She stepped further away from the door into the night and searched the blackness.

"Mela?" Wyatt's hoarse voice called to her from the church door. He waved her back in and she followed, looking over her shoulder once more, unsure about what else was lurking in the dark.

She followed him back into the somber sanctuary where she was once again face to face with the solemn study group. Pastor Rod stood in front of his people as he spoke to her.

"They called the police and the ambulance already. I see you got rid of the…ah…the things. Thank you. But you should go now, sweetheart," he said kindly. "I can handle things from here." Every eye went back to the body of Mrs. Wesley on the floor, surrounded by her friends.

"What will you say happened?" she asked. Pastor Rod ran a hand through his white hair and exhaled.

"I don't know," he finally said.

"We could tell them the cross fell and broke the table," someone said from the group. Voices agreed in unison.

"That could work," Pastor Rod said. "But honey, you need to go before they find you here," he said.

"I do not need to impress upon you the need to keep what happened here to yourselves," Sammuele addressed them all. Every head nodded, including the Pastor. "Follow your shepherd's lead and all will be well." Sammuele said and turned to stand by Mela's side.

"I'm sorry..." Mela said softly. "I'm sorry I couldn't save her. She was....I liked her a lot." Mela hung her head and turned to go.

"Thank you, Mela," a voice from the group said. Everyone mirrored the sentiment and she turned to look at them again.

"They'll be back, those things. If you see them again, anywhere, you call me," she said.

"Honey, you have to go," Pastor Rod's voice was urgent. The sound of sirens in the distance reminded her of the need to hurry and she turned, pulling her hood over her head.

Mela and Sammuele left the church and walked into the nearest cluster of trees. From the darkness, they watched the blue and red lights from the local police and ambulance drivers approaching the church from the long dirt road. She counted two police cars and more than one ambulance, all pulling to an abrupt stop. Pastor Rod exited the church main doors and ushered them inside.

The parking lot was a beehive of activity now and she was sure the people were safe. For now. Leaning back against the tree, she watched Sammuele. He took in all of the goings-on with interest and she watched his face as he did. Curiosity made him appear more human and he stretched his neck up to see what the inside of the ambulance looked like. The paramedics were opening the doors and unloading a gurney, Mela supposed, to take Mr. DeWight to the hospital.

"Nice sword," she said with a smile. Sammuele looked down at his side and lightly touched the hilt of the silver sword. He turned to her and mimicked her pose, leaning against a tree.

"I do not usually carry one. I did, long ago, when evil was rampant on the earth."

Biting her lower lip, Mela decided to speak her mind at last. "You've changed, Sammuele. So much is different about you now," she said. He nodded. "What made you change?" she asked.

"You," he said at once. "I live surrounded, not by my brethren, but by you and the others. I know I am not particularly well liked among the…among Vashanu, Dektrios, and Theothane, but Wyatt is kind. As are you." Touched, Mela nodded.

"Oy…we ditched the wiry buggers in the woods and covered them with dirt. Good enough, I reckon. What you two doing?" Decker broke in.

"Just watching. Mrs. Wesley died tonight…there," she pointed at the gurney the paramedics pushed out of the main doors and carried down the stairs. The body that they carried was covered in a white sheet. Decker craned his neck to see.

"Wyatt?" Decker asked turning to Mela.

"He's fine. A bit shook up. The creature was coming for him and Mrs. Wesley, the one who died, she jumped in between them to save him." Mela explained.

"That's a damn shame," he said. Which was a fairly sincere response for Decker, Mela thought.

"We should be on our way," Vasha said from the shadows. Sammuele agreed and turned to follow Vasha's voice. Mela stood beside Decker and leaned on his shoulder.

"You okay, kid?" he asked quietly.

"No. Why were they here? Why this church? Why tonight? I'm afraid of what this means," she said. He wrapped an arm around her shoulders.

"No sense in worrying. We'll find out soon enough."

"Mela, who is that?" Theo was at her side, pointing in the opposite direction of the church. Everyone turned to look and sure enough, there was the outline of a cloaked figure standing in the darkness.

She knew immediately it wasn't anyone she'd ever seen before. This person stood in deep shadows while crows flew in circles over its head.

Chapter Eleven

All five stared at the mysterious figure who stood watching, not at the activity at the church, but at them as they hid.

"Who the fuck is that?" Decker called. Vasha shushed him and Theo took Mela's hand.

"Should we go see who it is?" Mela asked. Sammuele said no, as did Theo. Decker and Vasha said yes.

"Your call, Mela," Decker said, turning to her. She watched the crows swoop and glide through the air around the figure's head. Mela stepped forward. There was something familiar about the person standing in the shadows. Something she could feel.

A gust of wind carried a cloud of dead leaves, swirling and dancing through the air. She heard the crows caw and then...the hooded figure was gone.

"Blimey...want us to track him?" Decker asked. Mela shook her head and stepped back into the trees.

"No, let's get home," she said. She turned and looked them all in the eye. "We don't have time for this right now. Whoever that was, obviously doesn't want a fight at the moment. Let's just see what happens." Decker shrugged his shoulders, then turned to climb onto Vasha's back.

"See you at home," Decker called and they were gone. Theo nodded at Mela and Sammuele and shot straight up into the sky until he disappeared into the night.

"Ready to go?" she asked Sammuele. He stood still, watching the ambulance pull away.

"Yes," he finally said. He stepped close to Mela and opened his arms. She wrapped her arms around him and inhaled the scent of rain. He carefully folded his arms around her and pulled her close. She felt him breathe but they didn't move. She looked up into his slender face and frowned.

"Sammuele, are you okay?" she asked. He looked down and his dark eyes met hers. His eyes searched her face and he opened his mouth to say something, but quickly stood straight again.

"I am ready. Close your eyes, Mela," he said. And she did.

She knew they were home before she opened her eyes. She could smell the familiar fragrance of the flowers. Even the rustling of the trees were familiar to her now. Opening her eyes, she saw they returned to the very spot from which they left. Her phone still sat on the porch rail and her clothes lay scattered on the ground.

The rowdy laughter that filled the air announced Vasha and Decker's return. Theo was close behind, quietly landing.

"I'm sure Wyatt will be here in a bit. He'll want to see you," Mela said to Sammuele. He folded his hands in front of him, and seemed to wait for just that. Mela busied herself gathering her discarded clothes from the ground as Decker approached.

"Oy, tell that no good brother of mine he's a liar," Decker commanded as he approached her on the patio. Smiling, Mela raised her eyebrows in question.

"I am not lying, brother. I did." Vasha said.

"Did not!" Decker shot back. Laughing, Mela piled her clothes on the rail beside her phone and waited for an explanation.

"This blue bastard here says he saw your goodies before..." Decker said pointing an accusing finger in Vasha's direction.

"My goodies?"

"Aye. Your wobbly bits. Your uh…" he cupped his hands at his chest and moved them up and down.

"He means your breasts, Little Witch. He made mention that you have nice breasts and I agreed. Having seen them before tonight, I was already privy to the delicate beauty that was bestowed upon you," Vasha purred.

"Yeah, he has," Mela said with a smile. Decker's mouth dropped open and he sputtered but no real words came out.

"We've made him speechless, Little Witch. That is a magick all on its own," Vasha said. Mela laughed. While Decker was demanding to know the reason behind Mela baring her breasts to his baby brother, she saw headlights pull into the front yard.

"That must be Wyatt," Mela said as she let Bear out to join them. Bear bounded out of the house, greeting everyone with a wet nose and a wag of the tail before heading to the front to inspect the newcomer.

Moments later, Bear returned with Wyatt by his side. Mela greeted him with a hug and they held each other tightly. She couldn't imagine living without her most beloved friend. He pulled away and wiped the fresh tears from his face. Mela urged him to sit down and she perched on the rail, joined by Theo. Vasha stood, watching the exchange with a peculiar expression on his face.

Decker let himself in the house and returned immediately with a bottle of wine and glasses.

"It's just wine, Vasha. We deserve it after tonight," he said as he handed everyone a glass. Everyone except Sammuele.

"Sammuele, do you want some?" Mela asked. He stood still, removed from the congregation of friends now pouring wine and reassuring one another. He didn't respond, so she extended her hand and beckoned him to her. "Here, take mine. Decker, go get one more glass please," she said, shooting him a stern look. He glanced at

Sammuele, then back at Mela, then went back and brought another glass, pouring a hefty amount in it for Mela.

"A toast," he called out, holding up his glass. Everyone did the same and waited for him to speak. "To our first family fight. Even though we didn't get to kill anything, more's the pity, our Mela here did a bang up job!" Cries of "Here, here" from the others filled the night.

"And to Sammuele," Mela said. "You were pretty awesome with your silver sword."

"I didn't know he had no sword," Decker said awkwardly. But they all cried, "To Sammuele" and drank again. Wyatt stood and raised his cup up.

"To all of you. You came when we needed you most and saved us..." his voice cracked a little. He cleared his throat and continued. "And to Mrs. Wesley, who died saving me. It could have been me if it weren't for her." A somber silence filled the night and they all looked at one another.

"To Mrs. Wesley," Sammuele said at last. Everyone repeated her name and drank their farewell to the lady in the flowered dresses who died so that Wyatt could live.

"Oy, mate, Did you know Mela showed her goodies to Vasha?" Mela almost snorted wine up her nose but was saved from having to explain by her ringing phone.

"Connie?" she answered right away.

"Well hello, sweet thang. How are you?" she asked.

Mela stepped away for a bit of small talk but Connie quickly came to the reason for her call. "Listen here, sugar, I felt something tonight, something different. I read the cards and they showed me you. Are you safe?"

Sighing heavily, Mela blurted out the events of the night in full, gory detail.

"It was terrifying, Connie. But it wasn't the first time I've seen these things. They were at the hospital where my boyfriend...well, I'm not sure if he's my boyfriend anymore. Anyway, he had trouble and there were a lot of them. Terrifying the patients on the mental ward."

"Now that's something worrisome to be sure. You were able to kill them? With magick?"

"No…I uh, I used my sword."

"Is that right? Well, aren't you full of surprises." Connie laughed heartily and the sound warmed Mela to the core. She missed the quiet confidence of her mentor and friend.

"Decker taught me to fight with the sword. Vasha, he taught me how to fight with sword and magick together."

"Well, it seems you're getting quite the education. When I come to handle my business in your neck of the woods, there's something I'd like to discuss with you…alone." Connie's voice was light, as always, but as with everything about her, there was an undertone of brevity.

"Why don't you come stay? I'd love it if you did. So would everyone else."

"You know, I was hoping you'd say that. I've got some things to finish up here. I don't know if it will be this week or next before I can get away."

"You let me know and the door is always open to you, Connie." They said their goodbyes and just before she was going to hang up, Connie interrupted her.

"And when I get there, I expect to hear the story about why you ain't sure that handsome man isn't your boyfriend anymore." Mela groaned and Connie hung up, chuckling.

"All is well?" Sammuele asked. She joined them on the patio and took a seat on the rail beside Theo again. Mela tossed her phone in the air and caught it.

"Yep. It was Connie. She said she could tell something wasn't right. She could feel them here. She's coming soon. Wants to talk to me about something."

"Connie is coming? Brilliant," Decker said.

"I wonder, should we check on the Keys?" Sammuele asked. Everyone exchanged glances briefly before nodding in unison.

"I'll call Nurse Renee. I have her cell phone number and the number to the nurse's station." Wyatt said.

"Why do you have them?" Mela asked. Wyatt stood and was already scrolling through the list of numbers in his phone and walking away from the group.

"Because I asked her for it," he said quietly as he put the phone to his ear.

"I can go see to the other--"

"No. I need to call Shaun. I haven't checked on Sandra in a long time. I should really do it."

"If anyone needs me, I'll be drinking over here." Decker said as he plopped into his chair and tilted his black bowler hat back.

Mela had Shaun's number saved but hesitated placing the call as she wondered how this conversation would go. Shaun was always a prickly pear, especially if his mother was involved. But she was calling to check on her, that should count for something, right? She hit the call button and waited patiently as the phone rang.

"Hello?" She knew Shaun's voice instantly. His deep baritone accented by a distinct urban lilt made it unmistakable.

"Shaun, hi, it's Mela. Mela Malone." Silence met her on the other end. "I don't know if you remember me but…"

"I remember you. Crazy ass white girl with an angel as her body guard." Frowning harder, Mela exhaled loudly, intentionally showing him she didn't have the patience for the taunts.

"Yeah. That's me. The crazy white girl who is protecting you and your mother. I'm calling to check on her. And you. To make sure nothing is happening there and if y'all are okay." There. A little bit of guilt can go a long way. She heard him breathing and then sigh heavily.

"Shit…nothing ever really okay here, you know. But Momma, she's doing just like she always is. Nothing much has changed except, I think that angel been around here. Momma is always setting out tea and waiting for y'all to come back. Some days…some days she's happy and others she ain't." Stunned, Mela realized that Sammuele had been pulling double duty and spending an exorbitant amount of time caring for the people under her charge.

"Good. I'm glad she's okay. You too. We've had some trouble here, and I just wanted to make sure you were safe."

"Yeah….yeah, we doing alright. Are you?" His question caught her off guard. *No,* she wanted to tell him. *I'm really not. My boyfriend isn't talking to me. My best friend was almost killed. A lady I've known forever was murdered tonight because I didn't get there in time. Creepy Black-Eyed monsters are roaming around. I'm changing too much and I'm terrified.* "I'm as good as can be expected, I guess." She knew it sounded as sad to him as it did to her. But she just didn't care anymore. Her resolve to take care of everyone and every situation was beginning to feel too heavy.

"Hey, baby girl, you can't be Superwoman. I know you got your troubles. We all do." The sage words from Shaun touched her more than she expected.

"Yeah, I know. I've got so many to worry over. Sometimes, I worry…" She blinked and squished up her face. She couldn't cry on the phone with Shaun. She just couldn't.

"Well, you don't have to worry about us here. We all right. But Momma….she's been asking…uh…She wants to come see you. You told her she could, I guess, and she ain't quit talking about it."

"You know, I'd really like that. I'd like you guys to come out here. It might do her wonders, Shaun. To be with Sammuele and the others..." Temporarily speechless, Mela forgot she'd have to explain the others that lived here now.

"The others? Who else you got living with you?"

"Oh, some friends...the kind that would be friends with a Witch and an angel. The not entirely normal kind..."

"Any of them like my Momma?"

"There's one other but she's....she's a child. We visited her. But I don't think she'd be able to come. She's hospitalized." Mela explained.

"Damn. Well...they ain't dangerous, are they? They won't hurt me or my Momma?"

"No. Absolutely not," Mela said, smiling.

"Well, all right then. I got class on Mondays and Wednesdays. I could try and get out of work one weekend. For a day or something like that," he said hesitantly.

"I'd like it if you could. Hey, how is school going?" Mela asked.

"I got all my general classes done this summer semester. Starting my real classes soon. The tuition killing me though."

"Well, you're doing better than I am. I never went to college at all. Just worked."

"Hmm. Alright, I'll give you a holler and let you know when I'm able to take some time. Might have a friend or two with me. They'll want to come since I got to borrow their car."

"I'll let you explain the situation then," Mela said. She didn't want strangers coming around but, if they came around with Shaun, he was responsible for explaining. She couldn't imagine having to do that. However, after tonight, she was certain she'd have to explain herself at some point to more than a few who were at the church. The thought made her stomach hurt.

"What would I be explaining?"

"Oh, you know--angels, part human guys who really don't look human at all, Witches, and a gay guy," Mela said. She dissolved into a burst of giggles. It sounded absurd. So absurd she couldn't stop the laughter that overcame her.

"Damn, girl. You sure you okay?" Shaun asked.

Wiping tears from her eyes and getting control over her laughter, she sighed. "Yeah, it just sounded so funny. Actually saying all of that aloud. But it's the truth."

"I'm sure it is."

"Hey, listen, one more question. Has your mom said anything lately about...well, when I was there she said something about Black-Eyed demons. Has she seen any recently?" She hadn't planned on asking--the thought just sprang into her mind with the memory of Sandra describing their enormous black eyes.

"Uh...sometimes. Not in a while, I don't think. Honestly, Mela, I don't pay no attention when she goes on about that shit."

"Do me a favor, Shaun. Listen to her. If she tells you there are Black-Eyed demons around, she's telling you the truth. They're very dangerous and...well...tonight they killed someone. Someone I've known all my life. I was there but...I wasn't fast enough. If she tells you to run, you run. If she's scared, you call Sammuele's name, he'll come."

"They real?"

"Very real."

"Alright then." After a pause, he asked "Did you get it?"

"Get what?"

"The Black-Eyed demon who killed your friend."

"Yes," Mela took a deep breath and exhaled slowly. "I killed it. I killed them all." Shaun was quiet for a minute.

"You a badass, ain't ya?"

She could tell he was poking fun at her and she smiled.

"You have no idea," she laughed and, for the first time, she heard him laugh on the other end of the phone. It was nice.

"Well, you keep on keeping on. I'll let you know when me and Momma headed your way." They said their goodbyes and she hung up with a smile. The conversation went far better than she'd expected. She saw Wyatt sitting in a chair beside Decker, quietly sipping his wine.

"Wyatt here don't want to get drunk with me," Decker whined.

"All is well with…Sandra Jones?" Sammuele asked. Mela nodded.

"Yeah. Shaun is going to bring her here in a few weeks for a visit. But so far, so good." She turned back to Wyatt. "And Annabelle?" Wyatt sipped his wine and brushed imaginary lint from his pant leg.

"She's asleep. Safe and sound in her dark, lonely hospital room. I want to go back." Wyatt's face was as stern and determined as she'd ever seen it. Mela nodded and patted his knee.

"Sure thing, handsome. You okay?" His beautiful sad eyes met hers.

"I'll be okay. Is it all right if I sleep here tonight?"

"Of course it is," she said softly. He nodded and handed Decker his wine. Decker took it and poured the contents into his glass.

"I'm going to lay down." He hugged Mela and waved to the others before making his way inside.

"Poor bloke. He ain't never seen anyone bite it before," Decker said in between gulps of wine.

"No…it's not just that. Mrs. Wesley was nice to him. He's feeling guilty, I think," Mela said.

"Yes, he is grieving for the woman who died. He is feeling guilt and sorrow. But there are other things there-- he is in pain and conflicted," Theo said.

"I'd be conflicted as all fuck if one of those Black-Eyed bastards came after me and I hadn't a clue about them before. Creepy gits," Decker said.

"I shall retire for the night, unless--" Vasha reached out and caressed Mela's arm. "You will be needing my assistance with anything?" His sly smile reached his eyes, which flicked over to watch Decker's reaction.

"Not tonight, dear. I've got a headache." Mela said, smiling. Vasha threw back his head and laughed. They both turned to see Decker and erupted into more laughter at the look of horror on his face.

Vasha wished them a good night and slowly sauntered to his little home in the shed.

"I shall take the watch tonight. I will alert you if anything is amiss," Theo said. She watched him take to the air with ease, disappearing into the night.

"I'm staying right here...getting drunk. Fuck Vasha and his rules," Decker said. Mela almost felt like joining him. But getting drunk wouldn't lift the heavy burdens from her.

"I'm going for a walk," she announced to Decker and Sammuele.

"I gotta drink alone?" he said to her as she stepped from the porch.

"No, Sammuele has a glass in his hand. You two could use some time together." With that, she turned and walked away. She hadn't planned on a late night stroll into her woods, but as Bear joined her and they walked deeper into the shadows, she knew this was exactly what she needed.

As they walked together through the tall grass, she realized it had been forever since she mowed. The grass had grown up to her knees but she didn't mind. Bear loped along beside her, happy with their moonlight stroll. Carefully avoiding the prickly weeds semi-affectionately known as Sticker Burrs, Mela meandered to the edge of her property line where the wire fence seemed to barely hold the surrounding woods at bay. She remembered the last time she stepped beyond the safety of her manicured backyard.

Without much thought, Mela bent and squeezed through the fence, followed by Bear, and headed in the direction she thought was the one she took before. It didn't matter if it was the same direction; she needed the comfort of silence. A layer of brown, dead leaves covered the ground and she crunched them under each step. Bear happily trotted along beside her, tail wagging all the while. She watched him sniff each tree and mark it as his own. A few times, she thought she heard something in the dark shadows and, when she looked, saw it was an opossum out for its nightly hunt for food.

She lost track of time, listening to the sounds of the woods at night. Seeing a spot that reminded her of the one she visited before, Mela stopped to let the clean, crisp fall air tickle her skin. Bear sat beside her, seeming to wait for her next move. Looking around, Mela realized she missed an opportunity to bring wine and chewed her bottom lip. Too bad really. She would've liked to offer something to Lady Hecate in light of recent events.

Instead, Mela kneeled on the ground and scraped away the dense layer of dead leaves until she felt the cool, moist earth beneath. Carefully, she stacked dead sticks and a few broken tree limbs that were nearby. Much of it was still damp, but that wouldn't matter. She only wanted a little fire to sit beside and think.

Lighting the small stack of sticks brought the shadows out to dance. She adjusted her sword on her hip and sat comfortably on the ground beside her fire. Watching the flames mesmerized her. In them, she could see shapes swaying merrily away. At least, that's what it looked like to her.

"What brings thee out this night, child?" A woman's voice carried through the night. Mela jumped to her feet, hand on her sword, and turned to face the woman who spoke. "Does thou plan to do me harm, girl?"

"My Lady?"

"It is I, but who are thee now?" Hecate asked as she removed the black hood from her raven hair and stepped closer to the fire. Mela smiled and felt the relief wash over her. She'd had enough fighting for one night. And it felt wonderful to see her beloved Lady again.

"It's Mela, Lady Hecate. I'm sorry. I didn't know it was you," Mela stammered.

"I know well who thou are in thine own eyes and who thou are not. I asked thee a question, did I not? Who are thee now?" Hecate's beautiful face tilted to the side but Mela was lost in the starry depth of her eyes.

"I'm...I'm me, same me as always," she said lamely.

"I think not. The face and the name is the same, this is true. However, the light inside has changed. Thou art a killer now," Hecate's words hurt and confused her. With an open mouth, she stared at the woman who was her Lady, the Queen of the Witches, and felt a deep sadness.

"I had to," Mela said meekly. Hecate stepped forward. Mela saw it was the Mother that stood before her with a swollen belly, and smile lines around the corners of her eyes.

"Of course, I know this as well. I have been watching and saw the moment thou changed from a fledgling into a warrior. This I saw because thou art mine. Now I ask again, warrior, who are you now?" Hecate stood very close to Mela and lifted her delicate eyebrows in question. The delicate fragrance of frankincense tickled her nose, the smell reminding her of her first visit with Hecate in these same woods. She was a scared girl then. Now, now she was a warrior and a killer.

"I'm the Elementai, the protector of people, and the daughter of Hecate," Mela said. Hecate smiled.

"That is good. Yes, soon thee will accept the words that have fallen from thy tongue. Accept them and thou will triumph." Hecate looked away from Mela and placed a graceful hand on Bear's head. He stayed sitting but scooched closer to the hem of the Lady's skirts, nudging her hand for more attention. "A loveable beast," Hecate said softly.

"My Lady, I've killed a lot of those creatures. But I don't know what they are or why they're here. Can you tell me? Please?" Mela folded her hands in front of her in an effort to look as submissive as possible. Hecate knelt and touched her nose to Bears, speaking quietly to him in her foreign tongue for a moment, then looked back to Mela.

"They are the Soulless. They have been a plague upon this Earth before, once, long ago. The vermin have crept from the darkest pits of the Ether and have stolen away here. They come to feast on the fears of those who fear. They are not so powerful, as you have seen. But they do much harm and create havoc wherever they go. It is not them thou must fear, child. It is their Masters." Hecate said.

"Why are they here in Trinity Hills? They were at a church, hurting people there. Who are their Masters?" Mela spoke rapidly and Hecate smiled at Bear once more, placed a gentle kiss on his head, then stood.

"Their Masters are the children of Asag. A contemptuous being. The children of Asag are clever and quite powerful, born in secret when all thought Asag was powerless. He shared his power and his knowledge of the Dark Arts with his children, the Asagi. They created the creatures that have vexed thee so of late. They have no name to speak of--they are called The Soulless. Can thy keen mind tell me why that is?" Hecate asked.

"When I look at them, I could tell there was something missing inside. I remember thinking their eyes, when I looked at them, were like voids, just nothing there at all." Mela said.

"Thou has a keen mind and eye. There is nothing there but an empty shell powered by the pain and fear inflicted upon others. Thou did well to rid them from this place you call Trinity Hills."

Mela smiled, not daring to laugh. "Trinity Hills is where we are, where I live. But I wonder what brought them to the church?" Mela said the last part to herself.

"The Soulless go where there is hope and siphon it away until only fear and despair remain."

Mela considered it all and nodded. Her heart and now her body was heavy with fatigue. Hecate wrapped her arms around Mela and pulled her close. Mela did the same, mindful of the swollen belly and smiled knowing there was life in there, the life her Lady would give to others.

"Thank you for coming, my Lady," Mela said softly.

"Thou art a daughter of Hecate and mine to teach when questions remain. Those who fight by your side have done well. Thou art a warrior in spirit, and a warrior's mind you shall have in time. Never forget, thou are to also have a Witch's heart. In all things, keep balance. With every night that brings battle, meet the coming day with peace. You must regain balance and learn from those who will come to you to teach," she said.

Mela smiled. She assumed it was Connie's visit that she was referring to and that made her feel more comfort than a dozen lessons in sword play.

"I will try hard."

"This I know," Hecate released her from her warm embrace and stepped away, placing the hood back over her glorious black hair. Her beautiful moonlight eyes smiling,

Hecate turned and walked until Mela could no longer see her among the dancing shadows.

"Let's go home," she said to Bear, ruffling the fur on his head. His loving brown eyes met hers and he let out a small bark of approval before bouncing off into the darkness.

Chapter Twelve

"Hurry up or we'll be late!" Wyatt called out to Mela. She was rushing around the house, trying to get ready. Mela dug under a pile of laundry, not sure if it was clean or dirty, looking for her other shoe after finding one on the bathroom floor.

"Got it!" she called out triumphantly. Both sneakers in hand, she rushed to the kitchen table to find her phone. Wyatt was standing in the doorway, one foot on the porch with his phone to his ear. She pushed a pile of papers aside and frowned. She was sure her phone was somewhere in the kitchen. She stood with her hands on her hips and heard the chirp of her phone ringing. "Hold it….I hear it…" she said and followed it until she heard it vibrating beneath a dishtowel. Picking it up, she saw Wyatt's number on the screen. "Ha, ha, funny man."

"Let's go, Tootsie Roll. Clock is ticking," he said as he headed to the car. Mela placed a kiss on Bear's nose and scratched behind Kat's ears before walking out and joining him in his car. When she opened the door, she noticed the entire back seat was full of bags and boxes.

"What's all this?" she asked, strapping herself in and gesturing to the stuff in the back. Wyatt backed up and turned the wheel, pointing the car in the right direction before he responded.

"Stuff for Annabelle." He didn't say any more but Mela watched him as he drove. He was quieter than normal and hadn't cracked a joke in days.

"Are you going to Mrs. Wesley's funeral? I saw a notice in the paper about it," Mela asked and watched his face tighten up.

"Yeah, I am. Want to come?"

"You know I don't like funerals. They creep me out. There's a dead body there and people are just sitting around…talking." She shuddered but smiled at Wyatt.

"It's not that bad." He looked over at her for quickly, the first glimmer of a smile brightened his face.

"Yeah, they are. Monday, right? I don't think Claudia would appreciate it if I left work early anyway." Conversation seemed to cheer Wyatt up a bit and they chatted about his and Taylor's plans to meet up again soon. The relationship had been going well, mostly because it was long distance and Wyatt wasn't inconvenienced by someone else's life. It seemed to suit them both actually, and Mela was happy for him.

Her own love life continued to take a serious and seemingly relentless nosedive. Todd hadn't called her in days and she wasn't about to call him after what she saw in the gym. It did surprise her that she thought of calling him the day after Mrs. Wesley was killed. But she was afraid he'd blame her for that as well.

As they slowly rolled up the drive to the hospital, Mela once again noted the abundance of crows everywhere. Mela sat quietly counting them: five, ten, twenty-two….she lost count. Somewhere from her memory she remembered a group of crows was called a murder. That little nugget of information made her even more uncomfortable.

"Here we are!" Wyatt called out in a singsong voice. She smiled, all thoughts of murderous crows leaving at the sound of Wyatt's happy voice. "Help me out with these, will you, Warrior Princess?" She snorted as she reached out to take bags from his hands. He stacked boxes in his muscular arms and hit the button to lock the car. She saw his face over the top of the boxes, straining to see the walkway before him and Mela thought he looked expectant, even excited to return to the gloomy hospital.

When they reached the large front doors, a man in scrubs held it open for them as they entered. Thanking him, Mela followed as fast as she could behind Wyatt, finally catching up to him at the front desk.

Renee greeted them with a million watt smile.

"Hello again, you two. My goodness…you certainly brought a lot with you. That's all for Annabelle?" she asked him. Wyatt nodded and she threw back her regal mane of red hair and laughed.

"Well, come on then. I told her you were coming and she's been ready for hours." Wyatt followed Nurse Renee and Mela followed him through the maze of corridors and smiling patients. Huffing and puffing under the weight of boxes, Wyatt and Mela followed Renee into the sparse hospital room that belonged to Annabelle.

"Annabelle, honey, look who came to see you," Renee said turning to present the visitors. Annabelle stood beside her bed, in the same ill-fitting dress she wore the last time they visited. Her hair was braided once again but this time, a delicate red bow was tied to the end. Mela knew Renee had everything to do with that small kindness.

"Hey there, little princess Annabelle," Wyatt cheerfully said as he placed the load of gifts on her bed. The little girl eyed the bags with curiosity as Mela added to the pile.

"Well, I'll leave you three to your afternoon of fun. Plenty for me to do, never enough time to get it all done," Renee sighed dramatically. She tweaked Annabelle's nose causing the little girl to giggle. Renee gave a wave to the group and left, snapping the door closed behind her.

"Let's get this party started," Wyatt said, clapping his hands together and rubbing his palms together.

"Party?" Annabelle asked.

"Oh yeah. See, Mela and me planned a little afternoon of fun for the three of us. But first," he dug around in the pile of bags and began pulling out items and laying them on the bed. Mela was stunned to see pretty dresses of every color imaginable appearing from the depths of the bags. A beautiful pink dress with brown polka dots had a matching sweater and precious buckle shoes. Another was a white sleeveless dress with clusters of blue flowers and a large blue bow tied around the waist. It reminded Mela of the dresses Mrs. Wesley used to wear.

Shoes, scarves, tights, ribbons, belts, dresses, shorts, and t-shirts with cartoon characters piled high onto the bed. Annabelle cooed and squealed at each new item Wyatt brought forth with a flourish. Nothing pleased Mela more than to see both of them happy, even under the dark cloud that seemed to linger overhead. Wyatt's bags of clothes chased Annabelle's dark shadows away and her face was bright with happiness.

"These are for me?" Annabelle asked over and over in disbelief. Mela began stacking the books (the reason the bags were so heavy) and placed them on the bed for her to see. She noted plenty of stories about princesses and smiled to herself. Wyatt wanted to turn the pretty little girl locked away in the tower into a princess.

"This one," Wyatt said holding up a very fluffy yellow dress with white trim. Annabelle beamed and nodded her consent. While she dressed in the bathroom, Wyatt found the socks with yellow flowers on the sides and shiny white buckle shoes to match.

"I can't believe you did all this," Mela whispered.

"I know. At first, I went to get a couple of things but I ended up buying everything. I couldn't choose." Wyatt smiled sheepishly.

"I think you're amazing," Mela said, giving him half hug. They both turned when the bathroom door opened and Annabelle emerged. She looked like a true princess and Mela couldn't help the smile that came when she watched Annabelle see herself in the mirror for the first time. Wyatt handed Annabelle the socks and shoes, then returned to the mountain of goodies on the bed.

"One more thing," As Annabelle presented herself for inspection, Wyatt presented her with a dainty white purse on a silver chain. "You need the right accessories. Every proper girl needs them."

"Where's your purse, Mela?" she asked. Mela laughed and Wyatt fussed with Annabelle's dress.

"I'm not a proper girl," Mela said, plopping on the edge of the bed. Wyatt nodded and smoothed his pant legs.

"It's true. She's not. I failed and there's no hope for Mela. But you," he grabbed her hands and held her out to see, "are a vision. You make a proper little lady." The words made Annabelle smile.

"I'm hungry," Mela said, biting her nails. Wyatt smacked her hands from her mouth and started organizing piles on the bed.

"So are we. But we have some housework to do before we can eat," Wyatt said. Sure enough, the three of them spent the next hour rearranging Annabelle's room. Mela hung all of the new dresses in her wardrobe while Wyatt and Annabelle worked together putting everything he brought away in its proper place. Books were stacked neatly beside her bed and it took a lot of urging from Wyatt to get her to leave them be. They worked together to spread a beautiful pink blanket, with matching pillows, on her bed. Mela sneaked peeks at Annabelle and saw the delight in her eyes as she followed every direction Wyatt gave her. She smoothed down the corners of the pink blanket, white purse still over her shoulder, and learned how to fluff pillows the proper way.

When everything was as Wyatt felt it should be, Mela gathered the empty bags and stuffed them into the boxes. Wyatt tossed a blanket over his shoulder and held his arm out for Annabelle.

"Mademoiselle, shall we go to lunch?" he asked. Giggling, Annabelle nodded and wrapped her small hand around his arm. "Let's go then," he said to her with a smile. Mela followed behind, closing the door as they left.

The three of them made their way to the cafeteria and Wyatt escorted his princess as if she were true royalty. Annabelle smiled shyly as they walked past people who said hello. Wyatt leaned to whisper something in her ear. She answered him with a delicate shake of her head.

They stood in line, both standing out with their colorful and pristine attire. Mela felt like the country cousin in her blue jeans and gray t-shirt. But she was happy to fade into the background and watch the absolute joy dance in Annabelle's eyes. Wyatt carried both of their trays, the true gentleman he was, and called out for Mela to follow him as he made his way back out of the cafeteria.

"Hey, where are we going now, Prince Charming?" Mela called out. Wyatt laughed and led them out a side door that took them out on hospital grounds.

"I don't think I can come out here," Annabelle said softly.

"Of course you can. Renee said you could. Plus, you're with me and Mela. I promise it's okay." Annabelle nodded but still seemed terrified to be leaving the confines of the hospital.

They walked through the immaculately tended grounds, up a slight hill, and back down a bit until only the top of the hospital was visible. There, Wyatt placed the trays on the ground and spread the blanket on the grass. He sat gracefully on the blanket, helped Annabelle get comfortable, and fussed with her dress once she was beside him. Mela sat, cross-legged beside them and began to eat. Wyatt eyed her and shook his head. He was instructing Annabelle on placing a napkin on her lap, telling her that was how a proper lady eats. Mela snorted and continued to eat the meat-like substance on the tray.

While Wyatt and Annabelle chatted, Mela let their voices fade into background noise. She heard the wind rustle the leaves on the trees and closed her eyes. The sun was shining but the air was crisp. Soon, pumpkins would decorate every window and shop in town. Mela had always loved the fall, short lived as it was in the South. This was the lovely time in Texas when one could spend an entire afternoon outside and not die of a heat stroke. As the wind picked up her hair and made it dance around her head, she heard a worrisome sound. Crows.

Her eyes shot open and she saw every tree was dotted with the black birds. Some were squawking, others were doing whatever it was birds do. Mela focused on one that was larger than the rest. It sat on the branch directly opposite of where she sat and the eerie feeling that it was watching them wiggled its way into her mind. She narrowed her eyes and tilted her head. The bird mirrored her movement and she raised her eyebrows. That wasn't normal, was it?

She did it again to the other side and the crow did the same. Intrigued, Mela lowered her head, sticking her neck out straight. The bird copied that movement as well.

"Whatcha doing?" Wyatt asked with a bemused expression.

"That bird," Mela pointed to it. "It's copying me. Everything I do, he does it too. Watch," Mela tilted her head as far to the right as she could. The crow did the same, much to everyone's amusement.

"What do you think, Princess Annabelle? Is it a magic bird?" Wyatt asked.

"Yes. It is. They belong to him," she said. Both Mela and Wyatt turned to stare at her.

"Him who?" Mela demanded.

"Him," Annabelle pointed over her shoulder to the right and every head turned in that direction. Sure enough, under the shadows of the trees, they saw someone standing still.

"Who is that?" Wyatt said squinting into the distance.

"Oh, you see him? Really? I wasn't sure if you would," Annabelle said innocently.

"Yeah, we see him." Mela said standing. Something about the figure was familiar. From over her shoulder, the large crow gave a loud *caww* and flew over their heads, headed straight for the mystery person in the shadows. Other crows answered the call and followed.

"Mela, should we go back?" Wyatt asked.

"Just stay put," Mela said, and she took a step toward him. This had to be the same person she saw the night of the attack on the church. The last time she saw him at a distance, he disappeared when they made it known they saw him. This time, however, he didn't move. He stood still beside a tree, while crows circled his head. The one large crow that copied Mela sat quietly on his shoulder, watching them.

She slowly walked towards him, hands by her side, but with all senses on high alert. The closer she got, the more the familiar the feel of him was. She stopped when she was no more than fifty feet away. He wasn't wearing a cloak, but a sweater with a hoodie pulled over his head. Carefully, she reached out with her energy, feeling him even more deeply as she did. He was so familiar, comforting even. Then she felt it. His energy was also reaching out for her and the moment they collided, she knew. Not who he was, but what he was. He was a Witch. Not only a Witch, but another Elementai.

She took another step toward him again, and as she did, he stepped from beneath the shadow of the tree and pushed back the hoodie. His face was handsome. There was no denying that. His skin was the color of caramel and his hair a deep, chocolate brown that was tied back in a low ponytail. He wore his beard in a goatee that flattered an already striking face. His eyes were dark.

"Who are you?" Mela asked. She didn't mean for it to come out as demanding as it did but there it was. The man smiled and Mela felt butterflies begin to dance in her stomach.

"Owen," he said softly. "You're Mela. Mela Malone."

"Yes. How'd you know that?" she asked with a frown. He smirked and shrugged his shoulders, but said nothing. "You don't know? Or you won't say?" The large crow on his shoulder let out a loud *caww*, flapping his wings.

"This is Teagan," Owen said, motioning to the crow on his shoulder.

"I asked how you knew my name," Mela said. Owen and Teagan shared a glance, then Owen turned his attention back to Mela. "Should I ask the bird?" she asked. "Will he tell me?" She folded her arms across her chest and waited for an answer. Owen cocked his head to the side but gave her nothing more than a smirk.

"Everything okay?" Mela heard Wyatt call out to her. Shooting Owen a dirty look, she looked over her shoulder and waved. She held out her hands and motioned for them to stay put before she turned back to Owen.

"Boyfriend?" he asked. Mela crossed her arms over her chest again and raised her eyebrows. Clamping her lips shut, she stared at Owen with a stern look on her face. Never mind how sexy his smile was.

"I see," he laughed a little as he looked down at his shoes. He lifted his eyes, coyly smiled at her, and laughed harder at her expression. "Okay, I get it. None of my business. Who's the girl?" he lazily pointed to Annabelle.

Mela's arms fell to her sides and her stance widened. She reached to her side and felt naked without her sword. It didn't matter who or what Owen was,

Annabelle was off limits. Owen looked surprised and he held his hands up to ward off her venomous look.

"Whoa, sorry. Someone important I guess. Whatever." He shrugged and reached up with one finger and scratched under the bird's head. Teagan reacted much like Kat would and leaned his body into Owen's touch. "I was told to come to you," he said.

"Who told you to come?"

"The one I answer to."

"That's not an answer."

"Sure it is. You asked who and I told you." He flashed another roguish smile and chuckled.

"You're being difficult on purpose."

"I am."

"Why?"

"So many questions, Mela Malone. It's like you don't trust people." he said.

"I don't."

"Why not?"

"None of your business."

"Now who isn't answering questions?"

Infuriated, Mela's exasperated sigh came out more like a growl. Owen laughed deeply and she saw the glimmer of white teeth. She tried hard not to focus on his generous lips and the butterflies dancing in her stomach.

"Why are you here? Why were you watching us the other night at the church?" Mela asked. Owen's smile faded and he sucked in air through his teeth.

"That was fucking insane. I caught the tail end. It was enough though. I saw what I came to see."

"Which was?"

"You."

"Me? Why?"

"Because you're Mela Malone. The Elementai with the Avatian friends. You're kind of a big deal lately."

Stunned, Mela didn't say a word. How in the world did he know that? And what did he mean by 'a big deal'?

"How did you hear about me? How do you know about..." she bit her lips and stopped talking. If he didn't know, he did now. She really needed to do better at keeping her mouth shut.

"So it's true? Everything they say, that you're already fighting the war, that's really true?" Shocked into silence again, Mela sputtered and ran her hands through her untamed hair.

"How do you know this shit? If you don't start telling me what I want to know..."

"You'll what? Fight me? Granted," he crossed his arms and leaned against the nearest tree. "I don't have a sword. But I'm pretty good at what I do too."

"Pity, I've never heard of you before. You must not be all that good," Mela smirked back at him as his smile faded.

"I came because I was told to. Not because I wanted to. You've got your own thing going on, I get that. But so do I."

"And what is your thing that you've got going on? What do I need to do to help you so that you'll leave us alone?" she asked. Owen stood up and pulled the hoodie back over his head. Teagan squawked once more and took to the air.

"That will be kind of hard, Mela."

"Why?"

"Because you're the thing I've got going on." Before she could respond, the wind around them gusted, whipping the dead leaves into an all but impenetrable curtain. She covered her head so that she could breathe and turned away.

As quickly as it began, the wind stopped. She turned back to find Owen. He and the crows were gone.

Wondering about what she should do next, she turned back to Wyatt and Annabelle. Wyatt was sitting next to her on the blanket telling her one of his wild tales. She knew he was spinning one of his yarns because she'd seen that expression a dozen times before. The little girl was smiling the biggest, most innocent smile Mela had ever seen. The two, sitting happily in the sunshine together after eating a picnic lunch, reminded Mela of something.

As she walked slowly back towards them, Mela suddenly remembered why the scene before her felt so familiar. It reminded her of the picture in Annabelle's room. The one she said was her favorite the first time they met. She remembered how sad it made her that the little girl's favorite picture was one of a happy family enjoying a picnic in the sunshine. Mela smiled.

Wyatt intentionally recreated the picture on Annabelle's wall. She was able to live the happy scene that decorated the sad hospital room where she lived.

Chapter Thirteen

Since she got home late the night before, Mela planned on spending her Sunday sleeping late. Decker, however, had other plans. Nestled comfortably in her fluffy duvet, Mela could feel someone in the bedroom with her as her eyes fluttered open.

"Mornin'," Decker said. Mela stretched and rolled over onto her side to face him. Decker sat on the floor with his back leaning against the bed.

"Morning. What's up?" she asked, yawning. Decker turned to face her.

"Did you shag my brother?"

Mela blinked a few times, then buried her face in her pillow to stifle her laughter.

"Oy, this ain't funny. It ain't a good idea to…you know…spend naked time with your mates."

His words made Mela laugh harder, tears welling up in her eyes. She waved him off, telling him to wait a minute as she wiped the tears from her face. "Are you serious? You really think I'd do that?" she asked, still chuckling.

"Now, Vasha said he saw your goodies and then you said he did too. Why else would you be showing him your wobbly bits if you weren't…you know…"

"Having naked time?" Mela asked, fighting back another bout of giggles.

"Aye."

Sitting up, Mela pulled the blankets around her waist and wiped the remaining tears from her cheeks. "I'm not sleeping with Vasha. Not having sex with him. Not doing anything with him like that."

"But…"

"Yes. I had to take my shirt off in front of him for the Henna art he painted on my back. Then, when I had to change into my witchy gear, he helped me. Other than that, no naked time spent with Vasha." She gave him what she hoped was a reassuring smile. Decker let out a sigh and sat on the bed.

"That's good to hear, mate. I've seen it before, nothing ruins a team like looking over each other's naughty bits." Another fit of giggles took over Mela but this time, Decker joined in.

After coffee and chatting about Decker's love of eighties rock bands, they were ready to join Theo and Vasha for a morning of training. Mela and Bear ran together, this time joined by Decker. He ran beside her and talked the entire time. He went on and on about how far he had to run once to escape an oncoming attack from foes. He reminded her not to cross her arms in front of her chest as she ran or risk running low on air. He told her he'd once ran beside a moving train, just to see if he could outrun it. According to him, he almost did.

By the time they returned to the back yard, Mela was winded but felt lighter than she'd been in a long time. Seeing Theo nap beneath the nearest tree, Bear decided that he wanted to join him. He curled up beside Theo who reached out and placed a hairy black arm over his massive body.

Mela wished she could take time for a nap. Decker and Vasha thought it was time she learned how to take on multiple assailants, so they happily armed themselves with wooden swords and prepared to attack her. Moving slowly, Decker spoke as he paced closer and closer.

"Don't move your head from side to side. You can keep us both in your sight without flopping your head about." Mela tried to counter a stroke from Vasha but

Decker swooped in and smacked the back of her legs as she did.

"Ouch!"

"Remember what I told you, Little Warrior, use the gifts you have at your disposal," Vasha cooed as he taunted her with another swipe of his sword. Frustrated, and feeling very clumsy, Mela spread her feet apart and sent energy from her body into the ground. The result was a deep hole that opened up, catching Decker completely off guard. Vasha, however, was on able to jump to the other side.

"Bloody balls.....give me a hand outta here!" Decker cried. Vasha reached to rescue his brother but Mela had other plans. Inspired in part by the handsome Witch Owen, she raised her right hand and pushed the air in Vasha's direction. His black hair flew all about and he covered his face with two of his hands. The other two were bracing his impending fall. Feeling a bit smug, Mela turned just as Decker was pulling himself from the hole. Giving Vasha a moment's rest, she hit Decker with a gust of wind so hard that he went tumbling back into the hole.

Quickly, she turned to see Vasha recovered far quicker than she expected. He was charging her, head lowered, and four wooden swords that promised a lot of pain if they made contact. Without overthinking, she did what came most natural to her, and set the ground on fire. Flames jumped from her hands and poured onto the ground like molten lava. The heat kept Vasha from advancing any further. Mela smiled.

"Hey...no fair!" Decker called out from the bottom of his hole as flames surrounded him, keeping him safely inside. Vasha sat back on his hind legs and smiled.

"Nicely done, Mela. Now....take the fire away before someone gets hurt, if you would."

"Only if Decker admits that I win," Mela said with a smile.

"You didn't win shit," he called from below them.

"I would beg to differ, brother," Vasha said.

"Yeah, we beg to differ. Now beg to get out of your little hidey hole," Mela snorted a laugh as Decker began cussing up a storm.

"Must you two torment him so?" Theo softly asked, safely out of reach of the flames.

"Yes," they answered in unison.

Laughing, Mela put the flames out and marveled over how much control she had now. Vasha cautiously approached her, leaving the swords on the ground. Together, they stood over the edge of the hole in the ground and peered in. Decker sat at the bottom with his arms crossed over his chest.

"Oh, don't be like that, Decker. We love you. Come on out." Mela said, fighting back laughter. He refused to look at her but shook his head.

"Come now, Dektrios. Don't be a baby. I'll help you out," Vasha reached down as he spoke but Decker shot him an ugly look.

"Does he refuse to come out now?" Theo said joining them at the edge and peering down at his brother. "You really shouldn't tease him so. His feelings are delicate…."

"I ain't delicate," Decker shot back. Mela had to step away to hide her smile.

"We know perfectly well you are not delicate brother, far from it. Now, grab my hand so I can help you out of there," Vasha said. Mela headed to the house to get a drink of water but when she heard her phone ring, she grabbed it.

"Hello?"

"Hello sweet girl, It's Connie," Pleased, Mela sat down in one of the porch chairs, tucking her feet beneath her.

"Connie! Hi. Are you in town already?" Mela reached for her pack of smokes and lit a cigarette.

"I am, as a matter of fact. I've got some things to tend to, though, before I meet with you."

"Oh? Everything okay?" There was a brief moment of hesitation before Connie answered.

"Yes, everything is fine. I'll explain in better detail when I see you. Which should be later this evening. Mind if I stop by then?"

"Sure. You're staying here though, right?"

"Well, I just don't know…I guess it depends on my other business. I might have to turn right around and go back home."

"Oh no."

"I'm sorry. But we'll talk later on, I got some things to share with you. Spirits have been busy, I can tell you."

"Then I'll see you tonight?"

"Yes, see you soon."

Mela hung up, wondering what business Connie had in the area and what she needed to speak to Mela about. If she was so busy, the things she had to say must be important indeed.

"Shall we go another round?" Vasha said, casually dangling his sword over the porch rail.

"Sure." Mela followed him back to the yard where Decker was swinging his sword back and forth.

"Before you all begin, I have been wondering a few things," Theo said.

"Like why our blue brother is such a prat?" Ducking a backhanded hit from Vasha, Decker laughed.

"No. The man you met, Owen?"

"Yes. What about him?" Mela asked. She was just as curious about him but her mind felt jumbled up when it came to the male Witch. He would come and go with the wind and that made her nervous. The fact that she couldn't think of anything except his chiseled face bothered her even more. Did she still have a boyfriend? Would Owen come back? Those were the thoughts of a girl named Mela, not an Elementai.

"I am perplexed. What did he mean by saying our Mela was what he came for? This bothers me more than a little," Theo said.

Mela watched Decker's face and his eyes shifted from Mela to the ground. "Aye, there's a mystery there."

"You said he was handsome?"

"I said he wasn't bad looking," Mela cut in, giving Vasha a sharp look that promised a few smacks with the sword if he pressed further.

"What he looks like is not the issue. What does he want with Mela? And an even more intriguing question is how did he know about us?"

Mela shrugged her shoulders. She honestly had no clue and apparently, neither did they.

While they stood around tossing out ideas on where the mysterious Owen came from, Bear took off to the front of the house. While Theo and Decker discussed the possibility that he was a threat, Mela felt Vasha's eyes on her. He was watching her carefully and she intentionally did not look back at him. She knew he suspected her rather unexpected attraction to Owen. Thankfully, she didn't have to face that uncomfortable conversation because she heard a car door close.

"It must be Wyatt," Mela said, laying the sword aside. Her desire to fight again was gone with the real troubles that felt particularly heavy at the moment.

"No....that ain't Wyatt's scent," Decker said, raising his head like Bear would do and sniffed the air. Vasha and Theo came to stand beside him and they became uncomfortably quiet.

"I'll go in and see through the window," she said.

"I'm coming too," Decker said, walking beside her to the back door. "You two, keep an eye out," he said as they went inside. Mela heard someone on the front porch walking and saw Bear standing beside the unknown figure, tail wagging and tongue hanging out.

Decker stepped back into the kitchen, hidden by the wall that separated the rooms. Mela opened the front door and was speechless.

"Afternoon Mela," Pastor Rod said. Mela was shocked beyond belief to see him on her doorstep. His hair was a bit disheveled and deep circles from sleepless nights outlined his eyes. Pastor Rod wasn't doing well at all. He fidgeted with the Bible in his hands.

"Pastor Rod....Sorry, this is a surprise. Where are my manners? Come on in," she said. She saw the look on Decker's face and she shooed him back. If Pastor Rod came knocking on her door it must be for a very good reason.

She'd known him all of her life. He was always simply Pastor Rod. He'd been preaching from the same pulpit since she was a little girl. Now, the frail, sickly man standing in her home had none of the pep and energy as the man she once knew. Sad to think she might have had something to do with that.

"I'm sorry to come by unannounced, Mela," he said, still shifting the Bible in his hands. She ushered him into the living room and invited him to sit. At least that way his back was to Decker.

Mela sat down on the ragged recliner and leaned forward. His eyes darted down to her necklace before she could cover it. The lovely silver and wood pentacle necklace given to her by her beloved Pan was something she wore every moment of the day now.

"Is everything okay, Pastor Rod?" Mela asked, hoping to guide the conversation along. She never could abide uncomfortable silences. His head dropped, looking for all the world as though he was in silent prayer. When he raised his eyes, the light blue color of them were drowned in unshed tears.

"There's so much I don't understand, Mela. The Lord gave me unshakable faith all my life," he looked down at his Bible and lovingly caressed the tattered cover. She smiled, thinking of her copy of the Green Book sitting next to her bed, and how much she relied on it for information and comfort as well. "This has always had answers for me. If something was too hard or I felt lost, I knew I only had to open this book and I'd get wisdom. I'd get comfort from the Lord's words." He hung his head again and Mela waited as quiet as she could, nervous about where this conversation was going.

"Did something else happen?"

He set his Bible aside on the couch and ran his hands over his face, resting his elbows on his knees.

"Things just won't stop happening. Ever since that night….when the…"

"They're called The Soulless. Those creatures that came to the church. I still don't know why they came or why they were hurting you, but I know what they are," Mela offered.

"The Soulless…." His voice trailed off as he stared off into space. "And the angel?"

"Sammuele?"

"Was that his name?" His eyes gave the first hint of life with the mention of Sammuele's name.

"Yes, his name is Sammuele and another angel, I forget his name right now, told him to stay and help me with…" she caught herself from saying too much. "He's helping me and my friends do a few things. Some things to keep everyone safe?"

"Like kill those creatures?"

Mela nodded. "Yes. Like kill those creatures. They were at the hospital too, not long ago."

"You killed them as well?"

She nodded again. "They come where there is hope, I was told. They feed off of the death of hope, something like that." She brushed the words away. She could tell he wasn't completely digesting what she was saying anyway.

"When they came that night...They just appeared out of nowhere,"

"Yeah, they do that. They can walk around unseen and either choose to be seen or when they're afraid or injured can't control it anymore."

"Lord have mercy..."

"Not much these days," Mela said and immediately regretted her flippant remark. "Sorry."

"No...I have no one else to discuss this with, Mela. Can you understand that? But I think I agree with you..." Tears fell from his eyes and the look of abject pain was etched into every feature of his face.

"Why do you say that?" She was more than a little worried about the Pastor.

"They came into the Lord's house...they were just there. Everyone was crying and screaming. When they grabbed me....their hands felt like cold, dead things. But they touched me other times and I felt fire... Hell's own fire."

"You might not be far off on that one."

"I prayed, Mela. I prayed for help. They pulled the cross down and I watched it crack when it fell. I think....I keep thinking that my faith cracked right alongside that old cross."

"I don't believe that. You're the most honorable and devout man I've ever known. You and Mrs. Wesley, you two are two of the best people around. Wyatt even says so." Her claim that Wyatt said so was lame but she didn't know what else to say.

"That's kind of you to say. Wyatt is a good man. He's caring and he's been a wonderful addition to the Bible study." Mela's heart swelled with pride both for Wyatt and for the Pastor. He was truly a man who walked in his faith.

"When those things were…when they were hurting me…they told me things..."

"What things?"

"They said it was all a lie, that there was no God. They told me to pray and laughed…laughed when no help came."

"But help did come," Mela said. He nodded and wiped his face.

"Yes, help came. But not the kid I was looking for. I don't know what I was expecting. I was a fool. I wanted the roof to rise and the Heavens to descend down on them."

"But all you got was me and Sammuele."

"That was enough. You weren't in church today, I suppose those days are gone to you now given your…conversion," he gestured to her necklace. "I'm not here to try and convert you back now, don't go getting me wrong. I thought about it and I have a sense that you have a higher purpose that I don't need to meddle in." He looked to Mela for confirmation and she nodded.

"I have a job to do, yes," she answered.

"I thought so. I spoke in the services today about destiny and what God's destiny is for us. It was an old sermon, truth be told, one I'd written years ago. As I spoke today, all I could see was you standing in my church. I had an epiphany. If I wanted answers, all I had to do was to come to you and ask. You were put here to help in this crisis, I see that now. What I need to know is, what am I supposed to do? The dreams won't stop and I've got to be honest, I'm afraid. For the first time in my life, I'm truly afraid of something and it has shaken me to my core. And my faith is leaving me."

Biting her lip, Mela glanced over to Decker. He was standing as still as a statue, watching the back of Pastor Rod's head, deep in thought. The Godly man was obviously in pain and confused, but she felt stunned by the idea that he would come to her for answers.

"Honestly, I don't know what you're supposed to do." She looked back once more to Decker who was now watching her. "You said something about dreams...tell me about them.

"They started right before they came...before the church was attacked. I didn't think anything of them," he waved his arms in the air. "Images of destruction and death...so much death. Then, after the attack on the church, the dreams keep showing me things. Things I know are important but I can't seem to remember them." He ran his hands through his thinning white hair. "Sometimes I see them...the creatures are there...other times, others are there and they're talking to me. But when I wake up, it's all gone." He looked up, his face stricken.

"I've had dreams before. Important ones. I know they mean something. Sometimes they're trying to warn you. Other times help you. But it depends on who 'they' are," Mela said.

"I keep thinking, If I could only remember a little that it would help me. All I see are their eyes blocking everything out...big black eyes."

Chills ran up and down Mela's arms when he said that. A movement from Decker caught her eye. He waved her to him.

"Would you excuse me just a second?" She rose and joined Decker in the kitchen.

"That bloke needs to talk to Vasha," he said in a whisper.

"What? Why?" she whispered back.

"Vasha knows things about dreams and shit...I'll go tell him. You get that sad, tired man ready to meet him." He slipped past her and exited the back door. Mela didn't know what to do. She knew Vasha had a bit of magick, he'd said so himself. She had to trust that Decker knew what he was talking about. *It's like you don't trust people…* Owen's voice echoed in her head. Trust was earned, she told herself. The boys had earned her trust. Owen hadn't.

"Pastor Rod?" He turned at the sound of her voice and she tried to smile. "Listen, there are some things I've got to tell you." She chewed on her lip, trying to choose her words carefully. "The other night at the church, Sammuele wasn't the only other one that came to help. There were three others there as well, ready to…well…they were outside because people would've been terrified to see them, honestly. Wyatt knows them well. It's a long story but…you see…they're not exactly…they're not…"

"Normal?" he said.

"Right. Not all the way human either. Their mothers were but--," she waved the words away. "That's not important right now. What is important is that one of them, his name is Vasha, he knows things about dreams. He can help you. I think. I hope…"

"I gathered that you had some secrets but this, this is unbelievable."

"You have no idea. But I have to warn you, they look very different."

"What do you mean?"

"Yeah, what do you mean?" Decker cut in. Mela smiled at Decker's expression. Pastor Rod stood and looked at Decker with wide eyes. "Hiya, I'm Decker. My brother, the great and illustrious Vashanu, awaits you in his palace," he said, with a flourish and a bow. Mela snorted as Pastor Rod looked to her for reassurance.

"Don't be afraid. They're all right. And Vasha is in the shed, not a palace." She urged Pastor Rod to follow and pushed Decker out of the door in front of her.

"Careful, oh glorious Witch….ouch!" Mela smacked him hard and apologized for his antics. The three walked together toward the shed with Decker in the lead.

"I'll go in with you, do the introductions," Mela said when they got to the door. She crossed her fingers that Vasha was on his best behavior and wondered if there was a way she could delicately convince him to behave appropriately.

She knocked on the door before opening it for Decker to enter first. Pastor Rod hesitated at the threshold, wringing his hands. He craned his neck, trying to see what it was he was walking into.

"It's okay, really. Come on," she said leading the way. Reluctant, he followed and entered the colorful den. Decker placed himself in the corner, perched on the edge of a prettily painted trunk. Vasha looked as docile as a housecat. He was curled up, the position hiding much of his monstrous size. His arms were folded delicately on a bright blue pillow. He smiled, showing the faintest trace of the sharp canines within. Pastor Rod stood transfixed and unable to move. Mela looked back and waved him forward.

"It's okay. I promise." She turned to Vasha, her expression pleading. "Vasha, this is Pastor Rod." Vasha nodded respectfully to the Pastor and extended his hand to offer the man a seat.

"I apologize for the cramped setting for this meeting. However, I find things are less fearful in smaller places," Vasha said kindly. Pastor Rod still stood, mouth open, looking like a cornered rabbit.

"Mela, my lovely one, perhaps you could assist this man of God to a seat?" Vasha was as soft spoken as she'd ever heard. She turned to Pastor Rod and took his hand. Smiling, she pulled him forward and steered him to a large fluffy red pillow stitched with gold thread. Grabbing the nearest pillow, Mela sat and tugged on the dumbfounded Pastor's hand to do the same. Like a terrified child, he complied in silence.

"Pastor Rod, Vasha has had a very long life," she tried smiling to ease his nerves but could see it wasn't working very well. "He's seen a lot and knows a lot too. Vasha thinks he can help you. He helps me all the time." He turned to Mela and nodded silently. Looking back at Vasha, he nodded his greeting. It was a start.

"Greetings," Vasha said. "You are well liked by our beloved Mela. She speaks very highly of you. My brother-- he waved a bejeweled hand in Decker's direction "--says you are having some trouble recalling your dreams. Given the circumstances the other night, I must say this is of the utmost importance. If you, as I suspect, are getting assistance or guidance by way of your dreams, The Darkness will do all it can to thwart it." Mela listened raptly. Vasha, for all of his jokes and sexual declarations, was a deep well of information.

"May...may I ask you a question? Please?" Pastor Rod softly asked. Smiling, Vasha nodded and opened his hands as if to say he welcomed it.

"Are you....do you.... Is there a God you serve?" Mela never thought to ask Vasha such a question. Curious, she looked to him waiting for his answer.

"Do you mean to ask me if I serve the master of Darkness? For that, I think, is what you want to know. What is he called now? Satan? He is also named Lucifer as well, is he not?" Pastor Rod nodded with wide eyes. "No. I do not worship the adversary to your God. Does this please you?" Pastor Rod nodded. "Good."

"Do you serve any God?" Pastor Rod bravely went on. Raising her eyebrows, Mela watched Vasha's reaction. She watched what could only be described as a flicker of annoyance flash across his elegant features, but it was gone as soon as it came.

"I do. Does this surprise you? It does me as well at times. I serve the same Lord as our dear Mela," Vasha smiled and winked at her. Pastor Rod's eyes flicked to her then back to the ethereal creature before him. "He is a loving God of the Wood. God of wine and pleasure…. He is Lord of many things. One of the oldest, did you know?" Pastor Rod shook his head but listened intently. "If you trust Mela, then I am afraid you must trust me as well. As pitiful as that may be for a man of your status, I fear we are what you need at the present moment. Like it or no."

Mela smiled. Yes, that was exactly the right thing to say.

"I understand."

"Excellent. Now, back to your dreams. It is to Morpheus we must turn for this particular quandary. Do you know the name, Leader of Christians?" Pastor Rod frowned and shook his head. "Very well, a lesson is needed before we can precede. It is always important to know the God, or Goddess, you wish to petition before making any requests. Isn't this so, Mela?"

"It is. Very important."

"As she says. Morpheus is the God of dreams. He lives in the Veil. That place we visit in our sleep when one's spirit leaves the body and ventures to worlds beyond this sad existence."

"W-what do I need to do?"

"Accept the help I am giving you, first. Know that we will not let any harm come to you. No harm at all. Mela will make sure of that." Mela nodded. "There, see? You are safe. Your soul is safe as well. No one wishes to harm that part of you either. We wish for you to flourish and be strong so that you may live up to whatever righteous cause The Fates have in store for you. But it seems," he leaned in and looked closely into the man's frightened eyes, "that there are those who wish be a hindrance. But we shall thwart them. We will, together, you and I, walk amidst your dreams and find the truths that are hidden from you. We do this by using a bit of old, yet widely used, magick."

"I don't…I can't do magick."

"No. I suppose you cannot. That is why I must help you. I will be your guide. I've done it many times. We must call to Morpheus-- he is never far off, you see. He waits beyond, amidst the Veil, to bring dreams and messages to those who seek them. Even those who do not. We must cross the River of Forgetfulness in order for you to remember. Then, we will wade through the waters of the River Oblivion. This will open your mind to all that Morpheus wishes you to see. First, however, we must cross the Gates. They are well guarded. But that is my battle, not yours."

"Will it be painful? May I pray before I do this?"

"Of course. You may pray to your God for protection, if it helps you. But this is Morpheus' domain, and it is Morpheus you should request an audience with. I believe he will come, have no fear. He is a curious and unique God with no malicious intent. He is a messenger, if you will."

"How do I...How is this kind of thing done?" Pastor Rod asked.

"Why, when you are asleep of course," he said with a smile. "But you will need to come to me tonight. Can you do that? You will be away from home for many hours, at least. I need to make preparations and we will meet after the sun has set completely."

"I can do that."

"Good. Understand this, Leader of Christians, you must be sure of your decision to petition Morpheus this way. I do not wish to incur the wrath of your God nor do I wish to force you to do something you do not want to do. If you return, it will be because you choose this for yourself. Do you understand?"

"I do."

"Very well. Then, if you still wish to know the answers to your questions, return to me after the sun has set. I will be here ready and waiting," Vasha said. It sounded very much like a dismissal to Mela. It must have to the others as well because Decker hopped from the trunk and made his way out of the shed first. Mela followed with Pastor Rod in her wake.

Once outside in the crisp air, she turned to the man she'd known all her life, hugging her arms around her body to fight off the chill. He walked beside her, silent in thought. Decker was far enough away from them when he spoke softly to her.

"These friends of yours. You trust them?"

"I do. With my life. And you should too," she said confidently.

They continued the walk to the house in silence.

Chapter Fourteen

She watched Pastor Rod drive away, wondering if he would be back. In the distance, flying high above the trees, she saw black specks circling. Before she could ponder if they were crows sent by Owen, her phone chirped that she had a message.

It was a text message from Todd. Her heart began to beat faster. What could he want? Did he want to see her? Did she want to see him? Sitting on the couch, her finger hovered over the button that would show her the message. Before giving in, she headed back outside to light a cigarette. If it was bad, she wanted to be prepared.

Nervous, but slightly pleased, she hit the button and read the message: *I can't get through to Wyatt. Please ask him to call me.* She read and reread the message a few times. Every time she did, it hurt more. He didn't want to talk to her. He only sent her a message because he needed Wyatt for something, not her. More hurt than pissed, she hurled the phone into the grass. She watched it bounce, hoping the screen wouldn't shatter.

"What did it do to you?" Decker asked.

"I don't want to talk about it," she snapped back.

"Well." He bent over to pick up her phone from the ground and wiped away the dirt. "You might be needing this with everything that's happening. Whatever your telephone thing did to piss you off, I'm sure it's sorry," He handed it back to her and she snatched it from him. He was right. But she wasn't going to say that out loud.

Decker pulled his chair forward and sat. He twirled his hat in his hands, pursing his lips together in such a way that she knew he was fighting off the urge to speak.

Theo joined them. "All is well with Vasha and his preparations for tonight. What is it? What has happened?"

"Oy, she's right pissed at her phone. It must've done something awful the way she threw it," Decker said.

"It wasn't the phone. It was the message on the phone."

"You are sad and angry. Who has hurt you?" Theo asked, closing his furry hands around hers. Mela looked down.

"Todd. He doesn't want to see me anymore." Theo looked sad for her.

"He say that?" Decker asked.

"No, not just outright like that. He hasn't contacted me in ages. Then, the other day at the gym, he was working out with this girl, Natalie. They were flirting and…" he voice cracked and she felt the unmistakable sting of tears in her eyes.

"That slimy dick. Want me to go take care of him?" Decker said. She laughed through her tears. Ever since she and Wyatt had become close, she was always thankful for such an amazing friend. She never thought she deserved him in her corner. Now, standing there with both Theo and Decker, ready to comfort her and be squarely on her side, she was once again incredibly thankful.

"No, just leave him alone. It's partly my fault anyway," she said, sitting down in a chair. Theo came to sit beside her, squatting down so that his shoulder rested against hers. He was a lot like Vasha in that he craved physical affection, but he was much less creepy about it.

"We could get drunk if you want," Decker offered.

Laughing, she shook her head. "I can't. Connie is coming and she has things to discuss with me."

"Tonight? Excellent," Decker said, clapping his hands together in a rather ambitious attempt to rally Mela from the dumpy mood she was in.

"Me too. I like it when she is here. She feels nice. She is kind and respectful, even to us," Theo said. Putting her arm around Theo's shoulders, she hugged him tighter.

"Everyone should be respectful to you, Theo. No matter what. And if they're not, they have to deal with me!" She grinned. Theo curled closer to her, making a sound that sounded an awful lot like a cat's purr.

* * *

Connie drove up just as Mela was laying out the food for dinner. She tasked Decker with carrying the table outside on the porch again while Theo was responsible for cleaning the vegetables from the garden. Baked eggplant, chard with cheese, hummus, and a salad was all starting to look very good to her. She was famished after missing lunch with all of the drama in her day. She sighed heavily, missing the days when Sundays were nothing more than sleeping in, watching television, and playing with Bear.

Connie knocked on the door, sending Bear into a tizzy of excitement. Bear loved having all of his pack together, and let Mela know how happy he was that yet another soul he loved was joining them. She called out for Connie to let herself in and smiled as the glowing face of her mentor stepped into the house. Bear wasted no time in his greeting and Connie laughed as she tried to keep him from licking her face.

"Lords above and below, I am tired to my bones," she said as she joined Mela in the kitchen. "It is so good to see you, sweet thing." She embraced Mela lovingly with a smile.

"It's good to see you too. With everything happening so fast, I haven't had time to think about making the trip all the way to Louisiana."

"Oh, don't you worry your pretty little head. I understand how that is, yes I do." She sat down heavily at the kitchen table. Mela brought her a glass of wine and they sat together while Mela waited for the mushrooms to finish roasting.

"Now," she said, wiping a bit of spilled wine off her lip. "Tell me about this man of yours. What in the world happened?"

Mela told her everything. Every painful and regretful detail all the way up to the text message today. "So, that's it. Back to single girl life, I guess," she said with a sad smile.

"Well, I ain't one to get in your business, no ma'am, but can I offer some advice? One single girl to another?"

"Sure," Mela said. Connie's uncanny ability to put things in a new and brighter light always astonished her.

"Forget about him," Connie said waving her hand in dismissal. Shocked at the lack of wise advice or some sort of parable, Mela stared at Connie with an open mouth. "Oh close your trap lest the flies find a new home." Connie reached for the bottle of wine and refilled her glass. "I may not look it now, but I was once quite the looker in my heyday."

"I totally believe that."

"Oh yes. I had the gentlemen callers waiting like starving dogs at a meat market." She laughed at her own joke. "But over the years, after I learned my true calling and more importantly I think, who I was as a person, I learned that love shouldn't be hard. Oh sure, there are hard times, everybody has those. But every day shouldn't be a struggle. Love, I learned, was about the simple times. Just you being you, and him being him, and y'all just being who you are together. No fussin' over who calls who and all that grand standing. Just enjoying each other's company."

Mela turned her glass in circles on the table and frowned. It had felt like a struggle from the get go with Todd. He was so nice and so patient. But she never felt completely at ease with him. She always felt like she was waiting for the other shoe to drop, and that anticipation caused her to hold back quite a bit.

"Well...I guess you're right. Glad I never slept with him,"

"Oh?" Connie sipped her wine with mischief in her eyes. Mela looked away, slightly uncomfortable with herself for blurting out the truth of her sex life.

"Sorry."

"Are you? I would be too if I had that nice hunk of a man and didn't take him for a test drive," Connie winked causing Mela to erupt into a fit of giggles. Reaching for the wine bottle to refill her glass, Mela looked out of the main window and saw a car approaching. Connie followed her gaze. "You expecting more company?" she asked.

"I'm not sure. It could be...yep. It's Wyatt."

"And the other one?" Connie said pointing her wine glass to the window again. Sure enough, Wyatt's flashy sports car was followed by an aging, gray sedan.

"Oh wow, he came," Mela said as she watched Pastor Rod pull to a slow stop behind Wyatt's car. Mela gave Connie the extremely short version of why Pastor Rod was walking up to her doorstep. Connie's eyebrows raised higher and higher with every word.

"I ain't sure how this is gonna work out for you," she said.

Mela sighed. "I know. But he needed help and came to me for it. How could I tell him no?"

"You couldn't. I understand that. But child, you need to be careful," she said, fixing her with a calm, yet stern, expression.

"Yeah, I know. I feel like I'm juggling Jell-O." Mela said as both visitors approached the door.

"Make sure you got a mop handy to clean up the mess."

Laughing a bit, Mela opened the door. "Hi, come on in." She stepped aside as Wyatt entered, followed by a nervous Pastor Rod.

"Hey, Tootsie Pop," Wyatt did a double take and realized Connie was in the room as well. With a squeal to rival any little girl, Wyatt wrapped his arms around the robust woman, and began hopping up and down.

With the silly chant of "Connie is here! Connie is here!" in the background, Mela closed the door.

"You're back," she said to Pastor Rod. He nodded with tight lips and a frown.

"The sun is almost down and ah...he told me to be back when it was dark." She ushered him further inside to offer him a drink. "No, thank you. I don't drink."

"That's unfortunate," she said, taking a big swig from her glass.

"What do you mean you're not staying?" she heard Wyatt exclaim from behind her.

"Now, my sweet boy, I'm here on business. I ain't got time to be drinking and carrying on with you and the good pastor here."

"Forgive me. My name is Pastor Rodrick Jenson." He extended his hand to Connie with an obligatory smile. Connie's eyes squinted and a curious smile made her look slightly disturbing. She looked at his extended hand and took a step closer to him. In wonder, Mela watched as Connie pulled her shoulders back and slowly took his hand in hers.

"My name is Constance. I am Mambo, teacher, protector of the secrets, and facilitator to all who carry the magick." Impressed, Mela couldn't help but stare. Connie in full swing was impressive. "You coming to see that beautiful blue boy, Vashanu?" Pastor Rod nodded while Connie continued to hold his hand. "Good. He's a dear friend of mine, as is Mela. See that you look after her when I can't. See that she's protected from members of your flock that will seek to harm her, and from anyone who would find out about the... unique visitors she has."

"I'm sure I don't know what you're talking about..."

"I'm sure that you do. None have, yet, but they will. You can bet a box full of crosses that'll happen. And when it does, good Pastor," she pulled him so close that his pale face was nearly touching her own dark skin. "I expect you to be the one to speak up for her. After all, you owe our Mela here a great deal. I like the scales to be even. See that they're even, Pastor. Do we understand one another?" Pastor Rodd nodded, wide-eyed and too afraid to move. "Good. It was nice meeting you." Mela and Wyatt stared open mouthed as Connie left the room saying something about needing the facilities.

"Your friend...she's a bit..."

"Serious..." Mela offered.

"I was going to say frightening," he said softly.

"Are you ready to go to Vasha now? The sun is down." Mela watched the last fragile threads of hesitation fall away from him as he looked longingly back at his car through the widow then faced her with a nod. "Okay, let's go."

"I'll be out in a few minutes," Wyatt said, answering his ringing phone. He put it to his ear and walked out the front door again. Mela had forgotten about Todd's message and wondered if it was him. Shaking her head, she tried to forget about it. The night was going to be an interesting one, she was sure of it. She didn't have time to let her shattered relationship distract her from the job she had to do.

Mela took Pastor Rod out through the back door and saw Theo and Decker standing in the dusky new night. The Pastor stopped for a moment when he saw Theo, but hurried to keep up with Mela.

"Who's that?" he said in hushed tones as they made their way to the shed.

"Theo. Decker and Vasha's brother."

"He looks terrifying."

"Funny thing is, Pastor," they reached the shed and she grabbed the latch to open it., "he's the least threatening of all of them." With that, she opened the door and stuck her head inside.

"Did he come?" Vasha asked.

"Yep."

"Then why do you keep him without? Bring him in," Vasha commanded. Mela opened the door and let Pastor Rod enter first. When she made to follow, Vasha held his hand up to tell her to stop. "Not you, my pretty one. Tonight, it is only the Leader of Christians and myself who shall take this journey. You have other matters to tend to this evening."

"I do?"

"Constance, that luscious, dark woman from faraway lands with magick in her voice is here, is she not?"

"You could've just said Connie. Just plain ol' Connie."

"Yet, why shorten what should be drawn out? When one of her stature comes, it is fitting to give her great accolades."

"Umm…okay. So you don't need me?"

"Not at the present, Little Witch. But I do…need you."

"Need me to put my foot up your ass," she said softly.

"What was that?"

"Nothing. I'm going to go visit with Connie. Good luck, Pastor Rod. Behave, Vasha."

"I always do," he said, with a sly grin and a wink. She gave them both a small wave and closed the door. Whatever magick Vasha had planned for the good Pastor tonight, Mela wasn't meant to be a part of it. Although, she was curious about Morpheus. A God that lived in the Veil had to be interesting, if not a little scary. Given her dreams she had when this all started, she did vaguely wonder if he had a hand in them.

Connie was in the backyard when she returned and saw her holding Theo in a warm embrace. Decker was smiling ear from ear, obviously saying something highly inappropriate to her because she playfully smacked his arm.

"Well, the Pastor is settled in with Vasha."

"Good. It's high time you and I had a bit of a powwow," Connie said, gathering her skirts and turned to Decker. "Decker, sweet boy, do me a favor and fetch me the black bag in the back seat of my car." Decker nodded and shot off like a bullet.

"It makes me happy when you are here, Connie. I do hope you return again soon," Theo said.

"Oh you are such a sweet boy. How I wished I could see you all the time. Mela is such a lucky girl," Theo looked down at his hooved feet with a pleased expression.

"Got it." Decker returned carrying a black, leather bag and handed it to Connie.

"Why, thank you darlin'. You're a good boy. Now go, run along, me and Mela got girl stuff to handle tonight."

"Right-o, Constance. While you two paint your nails, I'm gonna enjoy me a drink. Or two. Or three…" he wandered off back to the house, Mela thought, in search of Wyatt.

"Paint our nails…" she shook her head and smiled. "That boy is lucky I got things to do," she laced her arm through Mela's and smiled down at her. "You ready?"

"What are we doing?" Mela asked as Connie led her away into the night.

"What Witches do under the moonlight. We make magick happen." Both women laughed and walked together farther away from the house.

They walked on at an easy pace in silence. Mela always felt comfortable with Connie. Since the first day they met, her quiet strength drew Mela to her. Tonight was no different. They reached the edge of her property and Connie squeezed her expansive body through the fence, followed by Mela.

"Now that we're lost in the shadows of the dark, do you have any idea what I want to discuss with you?" She turned to Mela but in the dark they couldn't quite see one another.

"No. I figured it was something important. The way you sounded on the phone."

"That's for certain," she said and moved to take Mela's hand in order to lead the way.

"Hang on, I can light a fire so we can see…."

"No child. Not tonight. Tonight I want you to walk in the darkness. Sometimes, too much light around you blinds you to what's hiding just out of sight. In order to see everything, sometimes, it's necessary to walk in the dark."

"Okay. Dark it is."

"You've learned quite a bit from your new friends. Those boys," she chuckled. "They're a hoot and half, for sure. An the fighting skills you've learned…ooooh girl, that's gonna be worth its weight in gold, I assure you. However, your skills as a Witch need a bit of, how do I say this? A bit of fine tuning. You went from being a regular, lost soul, to the top of the food chain. Literally overnight. You've missed a few fundamental steps. That's no fault of yours, rest easy. But that's where I come in."

"You're going to teach me?"

"Some. One particular lesson we have to do tonight. But others will come to teach you other things. We'll get to them later. This will do," she said, and stopped.

Mela tried to look around but there was no moonlight to see with. "Well, here we are. In the dark. Ready for my lesson, teacher."

"Ms. Smartypants, you are. Been spending too much time with those boys, I see. Now, come sit while I tell you some things. These things you need to know and you need to remember everything I tell you. You listening?" Connie asked as they sat opposite of one another.

"Yes."

"Good. As I said earlier, sometimes it's necessary for a Witch to walk in darkness. If only to learn what you need to know. You should know how to heal, but also how to harm. You should know how to curse someone and how to break a curse. You should be willing to walk among the living and the dead. You following me?"

"Yes. I am."

"Now, I know I'm crowing to the hen here, but there's trouble of an awful sort coming. Dark things…terrible and dark things are headed this way. And it ain't just you and me who have to deal with them. No ma'am, Witches the world over are coming to the realization that the Veil is lifting and the Darkness is waking up with it."

"Why? Why now?"

"Why not? I learned long ago to not ask unanswerable questions. The more practical question is, What can we do?"

"Okay. What can we do?"

"We fight, Mela. And I'm giving you another weapon to fight with tonight. But let me make this perfectly clear, this, what I'm about to show you, is only for dire situations. Given the recent events, I needed to tell you some things and I thought this would hold your attention while I did. I've got questions about the bug-eyed creatures you've been killing."

"I know what they are," Mela said, happy to contribute. "They're called The Soulless. Created by the children of some dark God or another, I forget his name now."

"Very good. I'm impressed. Yes, The Soulless are a plague. But the ones that created them, they are the ones we need to focus on. When they came the first time, a long, long time ago, they wreaked so much havoc, our foremothers never knew how to look for the ones calling the shots. The creatures, they just follow orders. Their orders are to be a distraction. I want to know where their Masters are. I want to know what they're planning next. Don't you?"

"I do. But how in the world are we supposed to know that?"

"Ah. You said it yourself--how in the world. In this world, there are no answers for such questions. But I gots ways to ask questions of those that aren't in this world. That, my sweet girl, is what I'm going to show you tonight. That and we're gonna get some answers. I'm showing you this because of all the others I know, you've seen more than the rest but had the least teaching. Let this be a lesson tonight."

"I understand. Do you need me to do anything?"

"I need you to sit right there and, no matter what happens or what you hear, don't speak to them."

"Them?"

"Let me get my business straight," Connie opened her bag and reached in to produce a multitude of magickal tools. "Light this candle for me, if you would," she said handing Mela a long, thick candle. Deftly, Mela lit the wick and handed the candle back to her. "No, you hang onto that."

Connie grabbed a long yellow scarf and tied it around her head. It was striking against her dark skin. Next, she opened a drawstring bag and pulled out a necklace that clinked like a tiny wind chime as she lifted it. Reverently, she placed it over her head and flicked her hands three times as if to shake invisible water from them. Next, she unsheathed a knife, her athame, and stood.

"Follow me so I can do this part in the light. These here," she leaned over and drew a large circle on the ground. "are for protection. I put my protection in place with the light shining first." Mela stood over her, watching the knife as she drew the sign. It was simply a line with two other lines coming from it. This she drew four times on the outside of the circle. Next, she outlined the circle with salt poured from her hand as she closed her eyes and beseeched to her Gods for their watchful protection.

"Strong protection, both symbols and salt," Mela stated quietly.

"Yes, we'll need it," Connie reached back into the bag, pulled out an extremely thick black candle, and placed it on the right of the circle. Next, a matching white candle was placed on the left side.

"This cancels out negative energy? Right? I read that in The Green Book once," Mela said.

"That's right. Now, the stage is set. Have a seat, give me that candle now." Mela handed her the tall candle and Connie immediately blew it out. They were once again sitting in darkness.

"What's next?"

"We've got our protection in place. Now that we're prepared, we call to that one we want to speak with."

"What do you mean? Who do we want to speak with?"

"Oh, I don't want to speak with it. No, I do not. But, in times like these, we must do what we must," Connie placed a hand on Mela's head and spoke softly. "Don't be afraid. Nothing can hurt you," She knew the words were meant as a kindness but they only served to enhance her fears.

"Okay," she said softly. Mela could only see a dim outline of Connie as she stood over the circle on the ground, raised her arms and spoke in a loud, booming voice. Her words were in another language. She couldn't understand any of it. But when Connie finished speaking, the black and the white candles lit by themselves.

"Ah, it is a good night for this. You don't know French, but I called to my *Loas* to come and help guide me. I called to the spirits of the dead to step aside and to not interfere. I called to Papa Legba, whose permission I need to complete my task. The candles that lit, that was him granting his permission."

"Does this work with other Gods? Like mine?"

"Yes, same protection, same calls for permission. In your case, Hades might be best. The next step is the hardest for beginners," Connie raised the hand that held the knife and brought it down painfully, slashing her other hand. Blood dripped from the open wound but she simply held her hand over the circle and let it pool on the dirt. Then she got down on her hands and knees. With her knife, she drew a line in the blood. Connie stood upright once more, staring off into the dark night.

"Connie?"

"Hush, child," she said in a whisper. When she spoke next, her voice was loud and packed full of power. "I command those with eyes but cannot see to come to me. Come to me, in all your filth and blood, come to me and accept your chains." Her voice carried in the night. Looking up at her kindly mentor, Mela saw the Voodoo Priestess's eyes were nothing but black holes where her kind, brown eyes were only moments ago. Terrified, Mela waited for what she felt was coming. A potent thumping deep in her soul told her of the evil that was approaching. Her body vibrated as she saw the circle begin to glow. "Ground yourself, Mela. Give the energy somewhere to go, send it back to the Earth."

Mela adjusted her position, sitting cross-legged and sent the energy flooding her body down until it touched the ground beneath her. Immediate relief came from the sensation but the foreboding remained.

The glow within the circle began to grow into a red light. Bigger and bigger the light rose until Mela could feel heat radiate from it. From the red light came fire unlike any Mela had ever seen. The density was like that of black molten rock pouring from the top of a volcano. Each time the fire grew too high, it dropped to the ground, scorching the dirt. Smoke rose as well and Mela waited for whatever it was Connie called to come.

It wasn't a long wait. From the smoke, she began to see the outline of a figure become clearer. It moved with labored steps until she began to see what it was that the fires of the Underworld brought. A creature so vile, so terrifying, Mela felt ill when it emerged. It towered over Connie, dropping its head so that it could peer into the Witch's eyes. Its skin was like stretched leather, marked here and there with open sores that oozed blood, pus, and maggots. The form was long, as were the legs. From all over its body, horns protruded through the leathery skin. With fists clenched so tight it seemed to be fighting the desire to deal a fatal blow, it leaned in closer.

Its head was another horror on its own. Shaped somewhat like a human head, the black, leathery skin had stretched beyond its limits and showed white bones beneath. Small tears seemed to get larger with each movement the creature made. Seeing that it had a short neck, it needed to bend down to look at the one who called it. But Mela had no idea how it saw, as it had no eyes. Black holes with maggots crawling in them served as its eyes. There was no nose, only two holes that leaked green puss. The mouth was open, showing row after row of mangled teeth. Its smell made her want to gag. Dead, rotting, and putrid, it was almost unbearable. She covered her nose with her hand.

"What do you wannnnnt….." it hissed. Its voice made Mela's skin crawl.

"I want answers to my questions. I called upon one who is willing to accept the chains….do you accept them?" The creature made a movement as if to sniff Connie, the closeness of it made Mela extremely nervous.

"Pay tribute to meeeeee….."

"I pay tribute to the Gods, not to abominations such as you. You accept my chains or I call another to the fire. Answer my questions, Demon, and I shall name you and mark you as mine. When I have need of you, I'll call you again." Shaken, Mela watched with wide eyes everything happening in front of her.

"Hungrrrrrry…Soooo…hunnggrryyy…." The creature then turned its head toward Mela and sniffed the air again.

"No!" Like a whip, Connie made a slashing motion through the air. The invisible whip caught the creature on the shoulder and tore a chunk of flesh from it. Maggots fell from the hole to the ground and burned in the fire. "Accept the chains or go."

"Accepppttttt….." Connie nodded and made another slashing motion through the air. This time, a metal chain came from her hand and wrapped itself around the creature's neck. "Hurrrrrtttss…"

"Good." She gave the chain a rough tug and the creature fell to its knees. "Tell me, foul one, what is happening down there? Why have The Soulless left your Underworld?"

"The Sssssoulless….were told to return to terrorize the man flesh. They feeeed on the flesh of little girls…." The creature whipped its head back to Mela, licking its lips with a black tongue. Connie yanked the chain again and the creature cried out but returned its attention to its mistress.

"Will their Masters return with them?"

"They are already herrrre." The creature laughed and licked its lips.

"Already here? What do they want this time? What are they after?"

"You, Witch." The creature bared its teeth and let loose a blood curdling shriek. Mela covered her ears and looked to Connie for reassurance. But the comforting face of her mentor wasn't there. All that was there was a terrifying, eyeless Witch speaking to a horror from the Underworld.

"Me?" Connie laughed. "I don't believe that. Remember what I said about telling me what I need to know. No lies, Demon." The creature stared her down for a few more moments but finally looked away.

"The reign of the Darknessssss will come to alllll corners of the Earth. When it doesss, you will allll die. They will be the new Masters of our world and yourssss. There is nothing standing in their wayyy,"

"Except for me," Connie said in a deadly tone.

"Not muccchhh time leffffft. The Masters are there and will wake the Father…Asag will return!"

"You pitiful creature, Nothing but death and destruction await something as loathsome as you."

"Does my Mistresss have more questionsss….So hungrrrrrryyy…."

"No more questions. I've learned what I need to know. For now."

"Have answered allll the sow's questions. Unchain meeee…"

Connie smiled and pulled the chain tighter. "I don't think so, unclean soul. You're chained to me until I don't have a need for you anymore."

"Then name meeeee….You promisssed." Its voice was scratchy and very deep, made even more pitiful by the desperate plea to be named.

"Have you answered my questions truthfully? Will I have need of you in the future? If I name you, you'll be under my protection."

"Will obeyyy….." It made a movement as if to reach out to her in supplication.

"Very well, filth, your name shall be Damboleth," Connie took her blood stained knife and dug into the cut on her other hand that held the chains. Lifting the fresh blood, she smeared some on Damboleth's forehead. "You are marked as mine now. I release you back into the pits. Come when I call, or your life will be forfeit."

"Yessss……Mistress," Damboleth bent forward in a bow and Mela saw the skin on its back tear away releasing more maggots into the flames. The smoke rose, quickly covering the horrific creature and the flame smothered it until she couldn't see the outline of its body any longer.

"It is done," Connie called into the night. The diminished until there was nothing except for a faint glow left on the ground and the heat left behind. Once the light was gone, the candles went out. Connie reached into her bag and pulled a jar of liquid from the bag.

"What's that?" Mela cautiously asked.

Connie didn't answer right away but unscrewed the lid pouring the liquid on the circle, effectively washing away her blood and the symbols in the dirt.

"It was holy water," she answered, finally looking back at Mela.

"Like, the stuff churches use?"

"In a way. But our holy water is made differently. The light of a full moon will make all water holy." Connie said as she packed her tools away. "Would you be a love and help me, the cut is deep." Hurrying to her side, Mela grabbed the handles to the bag and stood close to her mentor, desperately hoping to see that her eyes had returned to normal.

"Are you okay?" she asked finally,

"Oh yes. Just had to wrap a bandage around this nasty cut. Come along, let's get back to the house. See what sort of trouble those boys found while we were away." She sounded like her old self again. Mela followed closely behind her as they made their way from the darkness of the woods to the fence of her property.

"Were you scared?" Connie asked finally.

"Yes. Honestly, I was terrified,"

"Good. That's good to hear." The women made their way back to the house in silence.

When they arrived at the house, Decker was sitting alone on the back porch drinking straight from the wine bottle. When Decker saw Connie's hand, his eyebrows rose in questions.

"Oh, nothing more than a little cut. Mela dear, would you be so kind as to get me some gauze or something for this?"

"Of course." Mela rushed inside in search of her brand new first aid kit. When she saw it, her heart felt heavy. Todd made this for her after she was injured the last time, telling her he was sure she'd need it one day. He was right.

When she got back outside, Connie was sitting beside Decker telling him a story about her great uncle so-and-so who was the town drunk.

"And Gods be good, one night we were all sleeping just as comfortable as you please, when we heard quite the racket coming from outside. See, my uncle drank a few bottles of wine after a night of carrying on with his friends. He found himself, drunk as a skunk, at the top of one of the trees. We never knew how he got up there neither," Decker let out a barking laugh. "I tell you, I wasn't more than a girl then, but I remember my Daddy telling my Mamma, 'Chere, you let him sleep up there. If he wants down, he'll get down.' It was quite the scandal."

"Did he get down?" Decker asked. Mela, in the meantime, opened the first aid kit and pulled out what she would need to clean Connie's wound.

"He got down alright. Sure did. Come morning, we saw him laying on the ground underneath that big 'ol tree, fast asleep like a happy baby. Woke up with a bunch of bruises, but Daddy was right, he got out that tree all by himself." Everyone laughed, Decker especially, as Mela began cleaning the cut.

"Where's Wyatt?" Mela asked as she wrapped Connie's hand in gauze.

"Oh right. He was acting kinda squirrelly if you ask me. You two took off and he was on the phone. Well, he came back here, told me he had some business to do and to tell you bye," Decker said as he brought the bottle to his lips.

"Who was he talking to on the phone?" Mela asked.

"Hell if I know," he said before he took a long swig from the bottle.

"That looks just nice, Mela. You took care of this real good." Connie said, admiring Mela's handy work. As Mela gathered the trash, Connie began to make preparations to go.

"You can't leave so soon," Decker whined.

"Oh, but I got to. Something wicked this way comes, didn't you know, boy?" She gave him a wink and smile.

Decker raised the bottle to her, flashing his own, toothy smile. "Until next time, Constance. I shall miss you with every breath I take,"

"Oh, hush it now." She waved off his words but her smile grew. "Come along, Mela. Walk me to my car, would you. I got a few more things to tell you before I go." Mela followed, carrying the black case. Connie opened her car door and Mela placed the bag of magickal tools on the back seat.

"Now, I told you I was sending you folks to help. One of them, apparently, you already met," Connie said as she climbed into the driver's seat.

"I have?" She frowned but the realization that she had indeed met someone new made her gasp. "Owen?"

"Yes. A lovely boy. In his own way. A bit of a rascal, but he means well. I told him to come to you. I think you could learn a lot from each other."

"That would've been nice to know before we met. I almost fought him."

"Well, you know what they say, sometimes an enemy at first meeting makes a better friend down the line."

"Who says that?"

"I do. Now," Connie started the car and closed the door. Her window was down, so she leaned her arm outside the window. "I've sent a few more your direction. One, he might be a bit busy for a bit. But I think you will get on with the others just fine. Thank you for having me and I'm sorry I couldn't stay."

"That's okay. Hey, who are the others that are coming? What are their names?" Connie smiled in answer as she put the car in reverse.

"It ain't a name that makes a person known to you. Feel them. When you can meet someone and know who they are by their energy, then you've added another weapon to your bag of tricks. We'll talk soon!" With that said, she backed down the driveway and headed toward town.

Mela stared after her for a long time before she turned to go back to the house. She passed Pastor Rod's car and wondered how his trip to La-La land was going with Vasha. When she got back inside, Mela picked up Kat and snuggled close to him. He purred but the look on his face told her he was already bored with the affection. Bear, however was happy to fill in. As she changed for bed, feeling the weight of everything she'd learned tonight heavy on her mind, Bear crawled in bed next to her. His massive body kept him from being able to snuggle as close as he would've liked, but he did try. She fell asleep wondering about Morpheus and feeling a little put out she didn't have a chance to meet him in her dreams.

Chapter Fifteen

She hadn't dreamed of anything interesting in a long time. As Mela walked beside a river made of a thick, shining substance, she knew she was walking in a vision.

Looking down, she wore the same white dress as she did when she met Pan. Her feet were bejeweled and her hair flowed freely over her shoulders. The water reminded her of liquid mercury, the way it moved and rolled along.

Mela walked on, her feet sinking into the mossy banks as she did. All around her, the air was colorful. Nothing, not even the trees, were the same color from one spot to the next. It was a dazzling display that both confused and delighted her.

She came upon a weeping willow tree unlike any she'd seen before. The trunk of the tree seemed a light purple, then orange, then green. The long, wistful branches swayed in gusts of wind that she could actually see. The pink and aqua-green wind picked up the golden branches and together, a new color was born.

Mela sat on the ground, staring straight across the river of liquid mercury. There were people there. Sitting on a blue rock, Pastor Rod listened as three robed figures spoke to him. Curious, Mela watched the men and wondered what they were saying.

"That is not your dream, little human girl," a voice said in her ear. Turning to the sound of the male voice, she saw a transparent, ghostly shape move from behind the tree.

"Who are you?" her voice seemed so far away and not at all like her own.

"You wanted to see me. You thought it…I crossed your mind just as you were falling asleep." The figure began take shape. First, she saw the outline of a man's body, then the milky white skin, and then his features became clear.

"You're Morpheus. I didn't know what you would look like."

"I appear as I need to appear. From one moment to the next, my visage is as the visionary needs."

"I need you to look this way?"

"Indeed, this is the form I use most often." Mela regarded the God sitting beside her on the soft moss beneath the colorful willow tree. His hair was long, so white and long that it cascaded down his back and touched the green moss on the ground. His lean body was the color of pure marble, not a blemish or mark on his skin. Upon his head, he wore a crown of diamonds that twinkled with a life all their own. She looked into his eyes and saw the vastness of space there. The stars danced in his eyes of black, purple, and gold. "Does this form satisfy you? Or should I take another?"

"I like this just fine. I like to see everyone for who they really are…"

He smiled and caressed her cheek. "A kind human child you are. I do not scare you? No, I suppose when you consort with the Gods, one becomes accustomed to our peculiar ways."

"Why am I here? There, that man," she pointed across the river. "I know him. Who is he with?"

"That is not your dream. It is his and he has chosen to walk a difficult path. Do you care for the mortal man?" Mela thought about it and nodded.

"Yes…I'm supposed to protect him."

"To know one's destiny is a rarity. And in one so young….truly remarkable."

Mela smiled at the God Morpheus. "What about you? Where do you fall in the coming war with The Darkness?"

"Where do I fall? I do not fall on either side, human child. I am ruler of the Dream World. I aid those who ask for it, however. As many have."

"And if I need your help in the future? Will you help me?"

"Cunning and brave...You will do great things. You have a shadow of sadness coming, that I can see. Choices you'll be forced to make as well...your future is...undecided." Morpheus tilted his head and studied Mela some more. "You have visited with me before, do you not remember it?" Mela shook her head. "That is a pity. I brought the Watchtowers to you."

"The Four? It was you?"

"It was. You called for help while asleep and I sent you the help I thought most suitable."

"You were right."

"I usually am."

"Will I remember this when I wake up?"

"If you like."

"Will I see you again?"

"We will meet again in your dreams. I find you interesting." Morpheus stood and walked toward the rolling river of Mercury. She watched his beautiful pure white wings unfold and stretch to the colorful sky. Morpheus turned and smiled. "I must go. So many asleep, so many need the understanding I must show them."

"Morpheus." Mela stood, brushing a wisp of golden leaves from her face. "The man over there--take care of him. Please."

Morpheus nodded his assent, then took to the sky.

* * *

Mela woke up with her alarm, confused. Laying in her bed, she recalled Morpheus and the conversation they had. She decided she liked the winged God even though he was the least human God she'd met so far.

She got ready for work, taking her workout clothes with her in a bag. No matter what, running was on her schedule today so she dug around the mountain of clothes on the floor until she found her old pair of running shoes since her good pair were floating in the creek somewhere. A quick cup of coffee in a to-go cup in hand, Mela stepped out in the predawn morning.

It was cold now. Not just cool, but actually cold. She wrapped her arms around her and jumped in her car. While she waited for the heater to do its job, she saw Pastor Rod's car was gone. Mela really hoped he got the answers he was looking for.

Mondays were a crap shoot at the gym. Sometimes it was really congested with folks who felt guilty about not working out all weekend, or they procrastinated because it was a Monday. She pulled up to work ready to get going.

She started her day with a note from Claudia explaining that she would be gone. Her request was that Mela start to go through the file of applicants for another part-time front desk person. Great.

The day went as smoothly as a Monday could until right after lunch. Mela had just finished her two mile run and was devouring a salad when she saw two police officers walk in the gym. These two she knew from around town. The first officer's name was Clint Feltz. He was a spare, quiet man. His hair was thinning and he had the terrible habit of combing the long strands over from the back to the front. She'd never actually spoken to him before but he and her father knew each one another.

The other officer she did know. Doug Barnhard went to her high school and was a few years ahead of her. He was the football star, the cool jock who would never know someone like her existed. Which was fine, to be honest, as most people called him "Douchebag Doug" behind his back. He had always been an asshole. The years hadn't been kind to Douchebag Doug either. He was extremely overweight with a barrel chest that preceded him by at least two feet. His neck was almost nonexistent now and, when he spoke, his jowls jiggled with every word.

She watched them at the front desk talking to Tracy. Her heart began to race when all three turned to look at her. They could simply be coming in for information, couldn't they? Maybe Douchebag Doug wanted to join the gym? As the officers headed her way, Mela's heart dropped when she saw the smirk on Tracy's face. Whatever the problem was, it wasn't going to be an easy fix.

She placed her food aside and wiped her mouth with the paper napkin just as they reached her door. Douchebag Doug took up the entire doorway with Feltz standing just off to the side.

"Mela Malone?" Douchebag Doug asked, looking at a tiny notebook in his hand.

"Yes. Can I help you with something?" She tried to smile and still her heart but police officers always made her nervous.

"We got a few questions for you," Douchebag Doug drawled. He stepped into her office with his hands on his belt and looked around. With every step he took, his leather belt squeaked under the pressure of his expansive waist. Feltz followed him and stood back, obviously playing second string.

"What kind of questions do you have? Were you looking to join the gym?" Her cheeks immediately reddened. Of course the man wasn't here to join the gym. The grim expression on his face told her that, as did his waistline.

"No, we have a few questions for you, Ms. Malone," he said, looking down at her. Douchebag Doug made a show of looking over his notes in the tiny notepad. Officer Feltz continued his robotic stare in silence.

"What kind of questions? What about? Are my parents okay?" The cold fingers of panic raked her insides. She felt ill with the thought something might have happened to one of them and this was how she was going to find out.

"Your parents are fine." Officer Feltz finally spoke up. Relief made her exhale.

"Can you tell me your whereabouts last night?" Douchebag Doug asked, still flipping through his notebook.

"Last night? I was home."

"Alone?"

"No. Wyatt came over for a little bit and I had some friends over as well."

"Can you give me their names?"

"Why are you asking me this? You still haven't said what this is about," Mela said, trying to contain her anger. It wouldn't do to have her eyes turning into fireballs at the police.

"Just answer the question, Ms. Malone."

"I was with Wyatt, you know who Wyatt is. My friend was passing through town. Her name is Connie."

"And this…Connie…about what time did she arrive at your house?"

"Sometime before the sun went down. Late evening. I don't remember exactly when."

"And Wyatt?" The look on Douchebag Doug's face said it all. He hated everything Wyatt was and didn't mind if everyone around him knew it.

"What about Wyatt?" Mela sounded too defensive, she knew. But she hated the look of disgust he had when he said Wyatt's name.

"What time did Wyatt arrive at your house?"

"A little after Connie did. He…" she stopped herself. Should she tell them Pastor Rod was there? If she did, they might have more questions. If she didn't, they might catch her in a lie.

"He what?"

"He came right at sundown. I remember that because," she took a deep breath. "Pastor Rod, you know who he is? He came with him." Officer Feltz and Douchebag Doug both stared holes into her head. The tension in the room suddenly became palpable.

"You say the good Pastor was at your home around sundown? And that he came with that Wyatt boy?" Douchebag Doug said with a sneer.

"They came in separate cars, but yes. They're in Bible study together." She lifted her chin and felt the warmth of satisfaction at the appalled look on Douchebag Doug's face.

"You hear that? They let him in the Bible study group now." He turned to his partner and they laughed together. Mela counted to ten. Then to twenty. Anything to calm her building rage.

"I'm not sure that was appropriate, Officer Barnhard," she said as calmly as she could.

"He didn't mean anything by it. Just a joke," Officer Feltz said.

"Hmm," Mela said and felt disgusted that these were the men protecting their town.

"Well, speaking of Pastor Rod, funny thing…." Douchebag Doug scratched his head and rested his hands on his squeaking leather belt. "He told his wife that he was coming to talk to you yesterday. Thing is, he hasn't been home and she's real worried."

"He did come over to talk but he left."

"What time did he leave?"

"I don't know, it was really late."

"What did you two talk about?" Officer Feltz broke in. Mela pursed her lips and thought about her options.

There was no version of the truth that would work here. She had to come up with something plausible.

"He knows I left the Church. He wanted to talk to me himself. You know Pastor Rod, always trying to save souls. We talked about religion." She shrugged in what she hoped was a nonchalant way. Douchebag Doug eyed her like a hawk. His beady eyes felt like they were looking into her head and making note of every lie she was telling them.

"Why'd you leave the church, Ms. Malone?"

"That's personal," she said calmly.

"So, you're telling me that the man went missing after visiting with someone who left his church? Is that it? On a Sunday night he had nothing better to do than to hang out with a queer and a…"

"And a what?" Mela asked.

"A lost soul," he said smugly. "You're sweet on that new doctor in town. Right?"

"What?" The change in subject threw her off for a minute. "I was. Not anymore," she said tightly.

"Not anymore, huh?" He made a note in his pad, then slipped it back in his shirt pocket. The radios they wore on their shoulders began to chatter about some thing or another and Feltz stepped out of her office to answer it.

"Is that all?"

"No, that ain't all." Douchebag Doug leaned over her desk, placing his hands on the top and staring into her eyes. "There's something not right with you, girl. You run around with that damn queer boy all the time. You said it yourself, you left the church for Lord knows what. And now, one of the most respected members of this town has gone missing after visiting with you and your friends. Tell me, Ms. Malone, what would you think if you were me?"

"That a lot of that is none of your business," she spat back at him.

"Oh, it's my business all right, girly. You better hope to whatever God you believe in these days that we find the Pastor and he's unharmed. Or I'll be coming to you for answers." With those words, he stood upright and turned to leave her office.

* * *

After that, her day didn't improve. Everyone was talking about it by the time she left for the day. Tracy made it her duty to inform everyone she came in contact with that Mela Malone might have something to do with the disappearance of the good Pastor.

Mela pulled her phone out as she walked toward the doors, feeling every eye on her as she did. Tracy stood at the front desk wearing a shirt that was two sizes too small and a shit-eating grin on her face.

"Bad day?" she asked, inspecting her fresh manicure.

"Fuck you, Tracy."

"Careful, darlin'. Your violent temper might just land you into a heap of trouble one of these days. I'd be careful if I were you."

"You know what?" Mela turned to face her long-time tormentor. "Wyatt was right. Tell me, Tracy, is it drugs? Or did you pick up some venereal disease? Because you look like shit. Everyone says so."

"I don't give a shit what that fag says about me."

"How's your throat? Hurt a little?" Mela smiled at the nervous look on her face. With a little wave over her shoulder, Mela opened the doors and left the building.

When she got in her car, she quickly hit the button to call Wyatt. With shaking hands, she lit a cigarette and waited for him to answer.

"Helloooo, Pumpkin Spice. Have a good day?"

"No. I'll tell you all about it later. But I need to know something, did the police call you or come see you?"

"The police? For fuck's sake, what for?"

"Pastor Rod. They're looking for him. Where are you? We need to talk."

"Well, I'm at home but I can meet you at the house." She hung up, feeling anxious to get to the safety of her own home.

When she pulled up, Bear and Decker were in the front yard playing an interesting game of tug-o-war with, what looked like the pants Wyatt loaned him ages ago. She got out of the car and leaned against the door. She was safe here, no matter what.

"Oy, you little bugger….gimme that." Decker said as Bear got the pants and ran away with them.

"Decker, is Vasha available to talk?" she asked dropping her purse on the porch.

"Uh, yeah. You probably ought to go see him."

"Why? What happened now?"

"Just go." He picked up her purse and slung it over his shoulder, then gave her a nudge away from the porch. "I'll take this inside."

Bear walked by her side to the shed and scratched at the door when they approached the shed. Mela knocked.

"You may enter," Vasha said.

"Hey Vasha. I was coming by to ask you…" all words left her. Sitting on a pillow beside Vasha was Owen. She stepped inside with Bear at her heels. "What are you doing here?" Vasha and Owen shared a look, and a bemused smile that irritated her even more.

"Why hello again, Sister. Connie said she told you about me. Thought I'd come by and say hello."

"Well, you said hello. Now go."

"Mela…" Vasha cut in with a warning look. "Our succulent Connie requested the delightful Owen here to come and help you. It is rude to send him away. Both to your guest and to your mentor," he chided her.

"So, you're here to do what? Annoy me on a daily basis? Great." She plopped down on the pillow farthest from Owen and tried very hard to ignore the fact that he wasn't wearing the hoodie anymore, only a white tank top. His arms were well defined and tan. The tattoos laced around his well-formed biceps made her heart race. That aggravated her even further.

"I'm not here to annoy you. Honest." Owen smiled at her and raised his hand in the air to swear his words.

"Why'd you call me sister? I'm not your sister." She said with a frown, as she bit her fingernails.

"You are my Sister. Not in the regular way of the word but because we're both...I can't believe you don't know this stuff," he said with a cocky smile. Mela simply glared.

"Do not blame our Mela for her ignorance in these matters. The circumstances with which she accepted the tiresome burden of an Elementai came due to an unusual state of affairs," Vasha said, handing the hookah to Owen who readily accepted it.

"Oh? Wanna tell me about it?" Owen asked.

"Nope," Mela said, still chewing on a stubborn bit of nail.

"Well, I for one am glad to have you here now. If you should need anything, my door is always open to you," Vasha said.

"Wait...what do you mean? He's not sticking around." Mela ignored the fact that she sounded like a petulant child.

"Actually, Sister, I am." Owen said with a smile.

"Not here you're not."

"Sure am. Thanks for the smoke, Vasha. It was a pleasure." Owen stood and walked from the shed. Mela watched him, feeling her anger rise, and looked back at

Vasha for an explanation. Vasha simply raised his shoulders and shrugged.

"You...I can't believe this. I don't want him here. I don't know him. I don't trust him. I don't like him."

"Liar." Vasha said with a growing smile.

"You turncoat."

"You sound as droll as my brother. He is a handsome man. He is an Elementai as are you. It is only natural you two should, at the very least, learn what you can from one another."

"But....no one asked me if this was what I wanted."

"Did they not? Hmmm...." Vasha fiddled with a small trinket box. "It seems to me that you trust Connie and because of that, you must trust in Owen. If it bothers you, however, have Theo look into his heart. He will be able to tell you if he has any nefarious intentions. Other than the desire to ravage you, that is."

"I've had about all I can take for one day." She got up and headed to the door. "I'm going to get drunk with Decker." She slammed through the shed doors and ran straight into Owen and his chest full of muscles.

"Whoops," he said, looking down at her with a smirk.

"I thought you left. Why are you skulking around?" she spat as she walked to the house. Owen sped up and matched her stride easily.

"I wanted to talk to you. I know the last time we met I was--"

"An asshole?"

"Sure. Maybe. But I'm really not an asshole. Swear." He smiled at her but she refused to look at him. His inviting lips and dreamy eyes made her want to kiss him them, then beat him over the head with something large and heavy.

"What is it you're supposed to teach me? Connie said you had lessons for me. Maybe if you write them down, I could read them and then we'll be done…"

"No. I'm not just here to catch you up on a few things. I'm here to learn too." Mela turned to face him.

"Learn what exactly?"

"Everything," he said with a smile. "I can hex the shit out of anyone. I can do protective spells, even do a bit of Tarot cards…but you--" his brown eyes locked with hers "--You're a fucking rock star. I want to learn what you know. You're the one who's actually done real shit. You killed those things. You fight with a goddamn sword."

"So….you're here to learn sword fighting from Decker?"

"The dude I met earlier with the hat? Yeah, I guess. But they won't do anything without your permission." That pleased Mela a lot. Owen placed a hand on her shoulder. "Please, Mela. I want to be a kickass fighter like you. I want to help in whatever way I can."

She exhaled loudly. It was true that Connie asked him to come. The fact that he waltzed right in and had a sit down with Vasha irritated her but that was her wounded pride talking. At least he was brave--she had to give him that.

"Fine. You can come around and learn from Decker. And fill me in on whatever I don't know," she turned to keep walking, but he gently caught her arm.

"Wait, could you introduce me to the other brother?"

"How do you know about him?"

"Because Vasha said there were three of them living here." He frowned, obviously confused by her suspicion.

"Sorry. I'm sorry. It's been a really bad day." She ran her hands through her hair and looked around.

"While we wait for the other brother, what's his name?"

"Theo."

"Cool. While we wait for Theo, why don't you tell me about your shitty day?"

"Why?"

"Because maybe I can help. Or just…you know, listen." He shrugged in such a boyish way it almost made her smile. And then she did smile.

"I wouldn't even know where to start."

"Try the beginning. That's always a good place." So she did. Mela told him about what happened at the church and Pastor Rod's subsequent visit. Then she told him about the police coming to her work.

"Oh damn," he said. As she talked, they walked around the backyard. He was a good listener, nodding in all the right places and getting angry at all the right times.

"I don't know where Pastor Rod is. I need to ask Vasha actually."

"Well, let's go ask him now." So they made their way back to the shed. The trip was wasted, however, because Vasha was lounging on the back patio with Decker, Theo and Wyatt.

"Wyatt is here. Come meet him," she said and Owen smiled. Together they joined everyone on the porch and Mela made the introductions.

"Well how-de-do," Wyatt said coyly.

"Wyatt, nice to meet you." Owen extended his hand to Wyatt and they shook hands.

"Isn't this pleasant. A new friend in the mix," Vasha said with a sly grin.

"And this," Mela said, pulling Theo close, "is Theo." She changed her voice into a mock whisper. "He's my favorite." Laughter from Wyatt and Owen mingled with Vasha and Decker's protests.

"Although I know she jests, Mela truly is my favorite," Theo said softly.

"Hello, Theo. It's a pleasure to meet you." Owen said, extending his hand to Theo, who took it hesitantly.

"Well, now that all of the niceties are out of the way...." Vasha said, pouring a glass of wine.

"Mela," Owen said. "You wanted to ask Vasha about the pastor."

"Oh right!" She smacked her forehead. "When did he leave here, Vasha?"

"Oh...sometime in the night. Or the early morning. I do not recall exactly."

"What did you ask me about the police for? Did something happen to him?" Wyatt asked with a worried expression.

"I don't know. I guess he didn't come home last night and his wife sent the police out searching. Since he told her where he was going, I was the first stop on the list. Now, everyone thinks I offed the freaking town's pastor," Mela said glumly, sliding into a chair beside Decker.

"Here you go, you criminal." Decker said, handing her a glass of wine.

"Stop teasing. It's serious. If he doesn't show up... where is he?" Everyone turned to Vasha for an explanation.

"I do not know, loved ones. I assure you, when he left, he was alive and well. Perhaps not well. The dream walk was rather....intense."

"I saw..." Everyone turned to Mela.

"What you mean you saw?" Decker said, scrunching up his face.

"I was asleep and had a dream...I saw pastor Rod talking to people. But they were across the river. I didn't hear anything. But Morpheus said--"

"Wait, you spoke with Morpheus?" Owen broke in.

"Yeah. Not the first time, apparently. He told me that it was Pastor Rod's dream and that he.... That he had chosen a really difficult path or something."

"You had a chat with Morpheus? Seriously. That's so awesome," Owen said.

"Yeah, it was. Do you think we should go looking for him?" Mela asked the group.

"We could tell the angel to do it." Decker said.

"There's an angel here too?" Owen asked.

"Aye. A right pain in the arse he is. Acts all dopey like he don't know what's what or nothing."

"That isn't kind, brother," Theo chided him. "He is lost and alone. He has no one here that cares and is making great attempts to connect with someone." Silence met Theo's words.

"That's fucking depressing. Why's it that half of everything you say is depressing?" Decker asked Theo.

"Enough, brothers. Back to the lost shepherd. Mela, what is your decision?"

"Me?" she looked at everyone but they were all looking back at her expectantly. "I think...This, all of this isn't easy. But we need to make sure he's okay. Yeah, I think asking Sammuele to find him might be best," she finally said with resolution.

"I agree," Vasha said, raising his glass. "Wyatt, would you be a dear and call the winged lost soul and request his assistance?" Wyatt nodded and turned to go inside.

"You're sending a lost soul after a lost shepherd. We'll be lucky if they find their way back at all." Decker said, smacking Vasha on the shoulder.

"How do you call an angel?" Owen whispered in her ear. She tried not to breathe in the delicious smell of him. His scent was intoxicating.

"You have to call their names," she whispered back. He nodded in understanding.

"Want to take another walk?" he whispered in her ear. Looking around, she saw everyone was busy chatting about either the wine or meal plans, so she nodded yes. They both started off the porch when Decker called out.

"Oy! Where you two off to?"

"Witch business," she said over her shoulder. She smiled as they walked away to Decker's complaining about being left behind two nights in a row.

"I like them," Owen said when they were far enough away.

"I do too. They're…they've become my family."

"You're lucky. My family sucks. Dad was a drunk." He picked up a rock and tossed it as hard as he could into the grass. Mela watched the first real moment from Owen since they met. "My Mom was all right. She died a few years ago. Breast cancer."

"I'm sorry."

"I left the day I turned seventeen. Just left. Been on my own since then."

"What do you do?"

"For a job?" she nodded. "Nothing now. I quit the gig I had to come here. I worked for a trucking company changing tires."

"Sounds exhausting." she said and they both laughed.

"Yeah, yeah it was. I did all right. But things change and so do people."

"That's the truth."

"Want to talk about something else? This is getting kind of depressing," he said with a mischievous smile.

"Yes please. No more doom and gloom for me today. I can't handle it." She knew she sounded pitiful but she didn't care. If he wanted to be here as her equal, then he needed to know what it was really like for her.

"I've been wondering something. Want to do an experiment?" he asked.

"What kind of experiment?"

"The magick kind," he said with a devilish grin. "The first day we met, the closer we got, the more I felt things. I want to see what doing magick together is like," he said.

Curious now as well, Mela nodded. "What do you suggest?"

"Take my hand," he said holding his hand out for her. Her hand fit comfortably into his and they stood side by side facing the setting sun. "Now, what's your best element?"

"Fire," she said without hesitation.

"Mine's air, but I guess you knew that. Let's do something different then. Water?" he asked turning to her for confirmation. She nodded.

"On the count of three?" she asked. He nodded and they readied themselves to call the Water, still holding hands. "One…"

"Two…"

"Three…." she said softly. Normally when Mela called Water, it was only a small quantity at a time. The most she'd ever done before was filling the pit she made when she and the boys were sparring.

This time, however, a wall of rushing water circled the both of them. It wrapped around them, roaring, drowning out all other noise. She turned to Owen and he smiled. It was if they were inside a pillar of water and the rest of the world ceased to exist. The orange glow from the sun made the water twinkle and come alive. The smell made her long to touch it. Slowly, she reached out to touch the pillar of water and Owen did the same. Right before their hands touched the wall, they turned to look at one another and shared a smile.

The water was cool and rushing in an up and down motion at an incredible rate. When her hand touched the water, it sprayed her and Owen both. He did the same and she laughed. It felt good.

"WOOOHOOO!" he yelled, throwing his head back. She laughed and stuck her hand in the water so that the spray soaked them both. Still holding hands, Mela looked up and saw the pillar of water went as high as she could see.

"This is amazing!" she yelled.

"Ready to let go?" he yelled in her ear. She didn't want to, not really. But she nodded anyway. The moment their hands stopped touching, the pillar of water fell directly on top of them. The water hit with such force they went tumbling to the ground.

Soaked and laughing, Mela brushed wet strands of hair from her face. Owen wiped water from his eyes and smiled. She watched him pull the strand of leather that kept his long black hair tied back off. He whipped his hair to the side and squeezed the water from it.

"Now that was intense," he said, grinning. Mela agreed. He stood, offered his hand to her for help, and she took it. Owen pulled her to her feet and pulled dead pine needles from her hair. Mela tried hard – very hard – to not focus on his chest that was even more defined by his wet shirt.

"Well, that worked," she said lamely and he smiled. They walked back to the house, laughing in wonder over the power boost they obviously had when they were together. She didn't notice, because Owen's face was mesmerizing when he smiled, that there was an additional person standing on the back patio watching them.

"Hey, who's that?" Owen asked and pointed to the house. Mela turned to look and felt as though she was punched in the stomach. Todd was standing beside Wyatt, watching them.

"Oh no," she said quietly.

"Who's he? Boyfriend?" She turned to look at the Owen and her mood changed again. Todd had no right to be angry. He'd been with Natalie at the gym, she saw them

herself. Besides, she and Owen weren't doing anything...
except magick.

"We were seeing each other. But he got wierded out
by....well, by everything. I guess I better go see what he
wants." She walked on ahead and Owen followed her to
the back porch.

"Look who's here," Wyatt said in an attempt to
break the uncomfortable silence. She could feel everyone
silently watching and waiting for her reaction.

"I see," she said coldly.

"Uh...me and Vasha got to do some stuff," Decker
said before he turned from the group and walked away with
a beaming Vasha.

"I must excuse myself," Theo said and escaped.

"Hi, I'm Todd. Doctor Todd Morgan. You are?"
Mela wanted to roll her eyes at the snobbery that he just
spit out. He was asking Owen but Mela answered.

"That's Owen. What are you doing here, Todd?"

"I texted you. I was trying to get in touch with
Wyatt for his thing. Did you get my message?"

"What thing?" She looked to Wyatt who waved her
off and she understood they would discuss it later. "You
found him," she said, walking past him and reaching for a
cigarette. Owen leaned against the rail and crossed his
muscular arms over his chest. His long hair was sticking to
his neck and back. She had to look away.

"Uh...Wyatt? Would you mind giving us a few
minutes?" Wyatt jumped up and walked past Mela,
touching her shoulder gently as he passed. *Be nice,* she
could hear him saying.

"I'll be inside...eww...you're all wet." He went
inside, wiping his hand on his shirt. Mela stayed sitting
and she noticed Owen stayed right where he was as well.
Todd stared at Owen with a look she couldn't quite define.
It was a mixture of confusion and irritation.

"What do you want, Todd?" Mela asked. He turned to look at her then back at Owen.

"Hey man, you mind giving us a minute?" Todd said. Owen stayed right he was, arms crossed, and shrugged. She knew that side of him and knew how frustrating he could be. However, she wasn't exactly feeling up to recusing Todd from it, so she let the exchange pass without a word.

"Mela…" he beseeched her.

"How's Natalie?" she asked, flicking ashes to the ground. Todd's face tightened.

"That's what this is about? You're angry at me for talking to a friend?"

"If only," she said, sighing heavily. "But I'm not sure what you could want from me. You obviously got to talk to Wyatt. What else could you need?" she said with sarcastic sweetness.

"I came to talk…to see if we could discuss…" He turned back to Owen. "This is a private conversation. I'd appreciate it if you gave us some privacy." Owen simply stared at Todd, then looked at Mela. She knew he was looking to her for ether permission to stay or a request to leave.

"He doesn't have to go anywhere." She tossed her cigarette into the yard.

"Look, I know things have been… difficult. I just think if we talk I can explain how I feel a little better."

"I know how you feel, Todd. You think I'm weird." She held up her hand to quiet his interruption and stood to face him. "I know this is a…unusual situation I live in. But I can't help that. It wasn't this chaotic when I first met you. But it is what it is and I can't change it." She looked to Owen, then back to Todd. "Besides, I don't want it to change. I like my life, Todd. I like all the strange, amazing things happening. It's what I'm supposed to do. If that means I can't have that normal, cookie cutter life, then so be it."

"I never said I wanted a normal, cookie cutter life. I just wanted to spend time with you."

"And I don't have time to sit around at restaurants or go off to the movies. You know this too. Of course, I'd love it if I could. But I can't. I've accepted that. It's time you did too."

"But you have time to play with this one," he said, jerking his thumb in Owen's direction.

"This one plays Mela's kind of games." Owen said softly. Todd glared at the man who towered over him by at least six inches and out- muscled him by a mile.

"Not helping," she said. Owen smirked.

"What happened at the hospital the other night?" Todd asked, throwing her off.

"You know what happened. You were there," she said through clenched teeth.

"I know that something was there and that you and Vasha killed it. Were there more? Because I cleaned up an awful lot of that black stuff. Blood, right?" he asked, anger in his eyes.

"Yes. There were more and we killed them all. We saved your patients' lives. You remember how scared you were when that thing jumped on your back, don't you?" she spit back.

"Yeah, I do, unfortunately. What about at the church? You can't expect me to buy the story going around about the cross falling and Marcus having a heart attack? After everything I've seen, don't treat me like I'm stupid."

Owen coughed and Mela threw him a warning look.

"You're right. There was something more happening there. But they called me. I didn't bring them here." She sounded too defensive, she knew it.

"None of this happened until you started being a…whatever you are."

"What *we* are," Owen whispered in a deadly voice. Todd looked at Owen, then back at Mela.

"I see. He's a…whatever it is you are. I guess you don't need me anymore, then. I get it." Todd pulled his keys from his pocket and turned to go. He took two steps, then turned back around. He went to Mela, and gently kissed her forehead. "I'm here if you need anything," he said softly. And he was gone.

Chapter Sixteen

"Oy, wake up, sleepy head," Mela groaned and rolled over, covering her head with the blankets. "You need to wake up--we can't get the angel here. Wyatt has been trying for hours. No answer. Guess the telephone line to the angel network got turned off." Decker chuckled at his own joke. Mela sat up, hair a mess, crusty gobs of goo in her eyes.

"What?" She yawned and cleared her throat. "What do you mean he won't answer?"

"Either the angel croaked, or is in trouble because he ain't answering. So you got to get up and handle this." He left her side but turned back at the door. "One other thing. We ain't got no meat. No sausage or steaks. I'm hungry. I can't live off rabbit food."

"Let me guess, I need to handle that too?"

"Yep." He closed the door behind him with a snap. Mela rubbed her eyes with the heels of her hands and looked out the window. The sun wasn't out yet. Taking a look at the time, she realized she'd only been asleep a couple of hours. Sighing, she pulled herself out of bed. She felt like she spent the night fighting a bear. She was so exhausted from feeling bad after Todd's visit, she'd drank a bit too much wine. But Mela, Decker, and Owen had a fantastic time. They laughed until their sides hurt. Owen was way more fun once he'd been drinking. Wyatt stayed over as usual but she thought he went to bed early. Apparently, he'd been up a long time trying to get Sammuele. Why she didn't try to help him sooner escaped her. If she really had her shit together, she would've realized there was a problem and dealt with it sooner. But instead, she decided to get drunk. As it was, she was going to work tired and hungover.

As she dressed, she calculated what her grocery bill would be now that there was yet another meat-eating mouth to feed. Decker alone could eat multiple steaks in one sitting. Vasha requested the most obscure, foreign dishes and they were expensive. Her grocery budget had been stretched as far as it could go as it was and now there was another person to feed.

Sighing heavily again, she opened her door and walked into the living room to see Wyatt, Decker, and Owen sitting on the couch.

"Good, you dragged your ass outta bed." Decker said.

"Not yet," Wyatt said with a smile. Mela nodded in thanks to him and made her way to the coffee pot. The black nectar of the gods was still warm. She poured a cup, added sugar and milk, then turned around to address the men in the room.

"No Sammuele?" she asked. Wyatt shook his head with a worried expression.

"First Pastor Rod, now Sammuele. Mela, what's happening?"

"What can I do to help?" Owen asked her. She took a sip of the fragrant brew, then another, while she thought. Calling Sammuele wasn't working. A million different things could've happened to him. She had no idea what to do. She sank into a chair and stared into her coffee cup.

"Didn't you, uh, say yesterday that all you have to do to call an angel was to call their name?" Owen asked her. She nodded, chewing on her lower lip.

"That's basically how it works, yes." Wyatt said.

"Then, do you know any other angels? I mean…their names? You could call another one and ask."

Owen looked around at everyone else to see what they thought.

"I don't know any others," Wyatt said with a sad look.

"We do," Decker said. Everyone turned to look at him. "The day Sammuele came with that other bloke, the one who gave him a talking to about getting you in all this trouble. I don't remember his name though…"

Mela stared at him in disbelief.

"You're right. Oh, what was his name?" she leaned her head on the table and rested her throbbing head on the cool wood. If she stayed like this for much longer, she'd be asleep again in no time.

"Hey, it's ok. Think back to that day and take it one step at a time," Owen's voice of reason broke into her pity party.

"We gotta go get Theo. He remembers shit real good." Decker stood and the others did as well. He and Wyatt headed out first but Owen hung back to walk beside Mela.

"Nice pajamas." He said to her with a wink.

"Thanks," She said and opened the door to go outside. Theo and Wyatt were already filling Theo in on their idea.

"Do you remember his name? The angel that came with Sammuele that day?" she asked when Decker finished speaking. Theo scratched his head and scrunched up his furry face.

"He was kind, he said we were extraordinary,"

"Right, the Watcher had a lot to say. But do you remember when he said his name?" Decker asked, picking dirt from beneath his toenails.

"He was old…his robes were white…" Mela said with her eyes closed. It was easier to remember things when she closed her eyes.

"He approached from there," Theo pointed. Everyone looked to where he pointed. "He said this was a serious matter…said he meant you no harm. He wouldn't call you by your name. I remember that. He said he wanted to see us for himself…"

"It is a freak show around here," Decker said as he pulled his foot to his mouth and bit off a nail.

"Stop it, that's gross," Wyatt told him.

"You, Mela, asked him who he was. He told you his name….Raguel. His name is Raguel," Theo said.

"Brilliant," Decker said, spitting a piece of nail into the grass.

"You're right. Good job, Theo," Mela said. Theo nodded, obviously pleased with himself.

"So…what do we do? Just say his name and click our heels three times?" Owen asked with a grin. Decker let out a barking laugh.

"I'm game to try anything," Mela said. She took one more sip of coffee and stood up. "Raguel…angel Raguel. I think Sammuele is in trouble. We don't know how to find him. Can you help us?" Everyone sat frozen but their eyes moved from side to side, searching for any sign of him.

"Maybe you should've called him sir or something," Decker said. He and Owen giggled like schoolchildren.

"They wouldn't turn their back on Sammuele, would they?" Wyatt asked, looking to Mela to calm his fears.

"I don't know…"

"Of course we would not do such a thing."

Everyone turned at the sound of the voice that spoke. From out of nowhere, two angels approached the back patio like mirror images of each other. Both were tall, lean, brown haired, and wore gray robes. Their demeanors were equally calm.

"Bloody hell. We call one and two show up. I don't like this game." Decker called out. Mela shushed him and stood to face the newcomers.

"Honored Raguel sends his regards and regrets that his duties keep him from coming to your call. He sent us in his stead. We apologize that we are a poor substitute for our respected leader."

"For fuck's sake, you could've just said he was busy and you came instead. Long winded as they are useless," Decker said and turned his attention back to his toenails.

"We've been trying to call Sammuele for hours. He hasn't come and we're worried. Someone else has gone missing too…"

"There is no one else missing. All are where they need to be."

"What the fuck does that mean?" Decker snapped. The angels looked to Decker then back to Mela.

"Have no fear for the one you seek. The Shepherd is alive and well," the one on the right said.

"He is walking with the Lord. The Shepherd is safe," the other said.

"I say again, what the fuck does that mean?" Decker yelled.

"The Shepherd…you're telling us Pastor Rod is okay?" Wyatt asked. Both angels nodded in unison.

"Well, that's a relief," Mela said. "But where's Sammuele? Is he okay?" The angels turned to look at one another, then back at Mela.

"Our brother…"

"Ha! Your brother--you Watchers are pieces of work," Decker said, standing once again. "If he were really your brother, you wouldn't have left him here. He ain't got nobody. He's been mopey and sad here. Stands around and stares at the sky all the damn time. He ain't right for this world and you know it," Decker said, pointing an accusing finger at them. "Mela and Wyatt here are the only folks that care about him and they need your help to find him. And you're gonna help them or so help me…"

"Brother." Vasha approached the two angels with slow, languid steps. "Let us not anger the Messengers, shall we? I'm sure they are under orders, they always are. Tell us what you can of Sammuele's whereabouts, if you please. For we are his friends and comrades in arms. We have all fought The Darkness together, as we all will in the end, and he is a necessary cog in our wheel, if you understand," Vasha said softly.

Something in the way he faced the angels told Mela he didn't care much for them either, except he had a more adept hand at diplomacy. The angels looked at one another again, then back to Vasha.

"Please…we're worried about him. I would consider it a favor if you would tell me where he is and if he's all right." Mela tried her hand at a diplomatic approach too.

"Don't you see? They *can't* tell us, that's why they're standing there all silent and shit. They don't care about nobody, not even their *brother*." Decker spat on the ground and crossed his arms.

"I'm sure My Lady Hecate would consider it a kindness if you told me what I need to know. He is my guide, after all. Raguel himself said he was to help me in all things. Lady Hecate and the Lord Pan told me it was my duty to protect everyone, without discrepancy," Mela said. She watched them watch her. The one on the right tilted his head to the side slightly, then turned to his brother.

They looked into each other's eyes for some time in silence, Mela guessed, having a silent conversation. She glanced at Vasha, who was watching them very carefully. She also noticed that, behind his back, two of the emerald studded swords were in their sheaths and the latch was open, prepared for use at a moment's notice. Wyatt was fretting in silence, whispering to himself. Mela realized he was praying. She turned to Owen, who was watching her. He winked and gave her a nod of approval. Theo watched the angels with interest as they held their silent exchange.

"The Avatian is correct." The one on the left turned to the other as he spoke. "We are aware of him and his duties with you. Sammuele struggled last night with The Darkness. He was wounded but he lives."

"No." Mela felt the all too familiar flare of anger start to take over. "Where is he? How could you just leave him? How could you just watch it all happen and do nothing to help?" she cried.

"Tell us where Sammuele is." Vasha said in a cold, calm tone. Mela stepped forward and she saw Decker move to her right. The angels would soon be completely surrounded.

"We seek no quarrel with you, Elementai," the angel on the right said.

"I might seek one with you, if you don't tell me where he is right now," Mela said in a dangerously low voice.

"You would seek to harm us? To find our brother?" the one on the left asked.

"He isn't your brother anymore. You all left him here. Alone. He's our brother now." Mela said. Nods from everyone all around, surprisingly, even from Decker.

"Very well. Sammuele was with a child and The Soulless attacked him. He was victorious but was wounded in the foray. He is being tended to by the strange child." Mela closed her eyes in an attempt to still her emotions that were spiraling out of control. Wyatt was already frantically tapping numbers on his phone and running inside.

"Thank you. You may go now. We have things to do," Vasha said. The dismissal was curt but Mela supported it nonetheless. They had no more use of the robotic creatures before her. They bowed slightly and turned to walk away. In moments, they were gone.

Mela could hear Wyatt talking on the phone and Decker was cussing up a storm. Vasha looked to Mela and Owen.

"Things are quite exciting these days," he said with a sly smile before he left.

"I'll say," Owen laughed and handed Mela her coffee cup. "Drink up. I have a feeling it's going to be a long day."

"The angels make me sad…they have so many emotions inside. But aren't permitted to express them. It is a painful existence."

"They don't know painful," Mela said darkly and sipped her coffee. Wyatt came out and sank into Decker's chair.

"I just spoke with Renee. She said Annabelle has been more secluded the past few days. I guess we know why. Mela, we need to talk…"

"Oy, who's here now?" Decker cut in. Someone was coming up the driveway. The headlights illuminated the front of the house. Mela could hear the tires crunching on the gravel.

"Later, okay?" Wyatt was disappointed but she couldn't help Annabelle or Sammuele right now. If he was okay and, more importantly Annabelle was, then she'd take that as a win and keep on going.

"You okay?" Owen asked. She exhaled and shook her head.

"No. But I have to be, don't I?" She turned and went into the house to see who this unexpected visitor could be. Owen followed her inside.

"You don't have to be, you know."

"Don't have to be what?" she asked as she watched a small, blue car and the person inside in her driveway.

"Okay. You don't have to do all this on your own," Owen stood close to Mela and looked over her shoulder. "You know, you should consider putting in a gate at your driveway. Keeps the looky-loos out."

"I would if I could afford it. I'm feeding and housing everyone from the supernatural community as it is. No extra money for fancy things like gates. Hey, look at her, you know her?" They both watched a blonde girl about Mela's age pull a large purse from her car, sling it over her shoulder, and head for the door.

"Nope. But I'm not into blondes so..." Mela snorted as the unknown visitor knocked on the door. She turned to look at Owen who motioned that it was her door and that she should open it.

Putting down the cold cup of coffee, Mela was already irritated. Whoever this girl was, she was about to get a rude answer. Who comes knocking on a stranger's door at this hour? Mela grabbed the doorknob and took a deep breath. She opened it and came face to face with the unexpected visitor.

She was slightly taller than Mela with bright blonde hair that fell in soft curls past her shoulders. Her face was plump, with bright blue eyes and pouty lips. She was what Wyatt would call fluffy, not fat and not skinny. The girl smiled and laughed.

"Mela!" she lunged at Mela and wrapped her arms around her neck. "I'm so happy to finally meet you. I had a hard time finding your house. It didn't show up on the GPS." She let go of Mela smiled brightly. "But I'm here now. Whew. Hi," she said to Owen. "Sorry, didn't see you there." Her words came out quick and excited. The unknown blonde was peppy and full of smiles and hugs. She had Owen in a tight embrace as he looked at Mela over the girl's head with a bemused smile. "I'm just so happy to be here."

"Sorry…but, who are you?" Mela finally said. The blonde girl, still smiling, tilted her bouncing head of curls to the side and put her hands on her hips.

"Oh, silly, I'm Layla. Layla Moon. Well, my Momma named me LauraLynn. But everyone just calls me Layla." Her smile widened and she nodded as if to tell Mela that what she said was the absolute truth.

"I don't know you," Mela said.

"Oh pooey. I know that. Connie told me to come. She said she told you I'd be dropping in," Layla's hands fell from her hips and her face immediately fell into an adorable pout. "She didn't tell you? She called me just yesterday, asking me when I was coming. She said someone else was already here. You?" she asked turning to Owen.

"You're not a Witch," Owen said, eyeing her carefully.

"No?" Layla asked. All of a sudden the room was filled with an incredible energy unlike any Mela, or Owen, had ever felt. It was a profound vibration that made Mela think of the deepest parts of the ocean. Mela let lose her own energy, feeling more secure surrounded by the warmth of her power. Owen was doing the same. She felt his energy which was familiar to her now. Together, they felt wave after wave of Layla's rhythmic essence and were stunned at what they discovered.

"You're another… you're another Elementai?" Mela finally asked. Layla smiled like the cat who ate the canary.

"Why didn't we feel you? When you were coming, we should've felt you," Owen said. He looked terribly annoyed that he wasn't able to tell she was one of them.

"Well, that's because I shield my energy. Almost all the time. If I let it out, sometimes things go all wonky," she laughed at her joke and looked around. "Oh, a kitty," she walked past them and rubbed Kat on the head. He tolerated the affection for a moment then sat up to inspect the newcomer. "Well, aren't you adorable, yes, you are..." Kat had enough and hopped down from the couch headed to Mela's bedroom.

"He's not real affectionate."

"What's his name?"

"Kat," Mela said.

"Kat? Just...Kat? Hmmm...What about you? Do you have a name?" she turned to Owen with a smile.

"Yeah. I'm Owen."

"Well, it's nice to meet you, Owen."

"Mela? Everything okay?" Wyatt called out. All three Witches turned as he entered the room. "Oh, hello," he said kindly.

"Hello to you, too. I'm Layla. New Witch in town." She laughed a little. "You're not a Witch. So you must be a friend of Mela's. Well, any friend of Mela's is a friend of mine." She smiled again as did Wyatt.

"Well, thanks. It's getting crowded around here." Wyatt said.

"Layla, sorry, but I really didn't know you were coming today. Connie said she was sending people here but failed to tell me anything about you," Mela tried to explain. Layla nodded and placed her purse on the edge of the couch.

"Yes, I know. She wanted to see if you could figure it out without me telling you. There are ways. Energy work is one of my specialties, so don't go getting all upset that you couldn't tell me right off. But I can teach you and in no time you'll be as good as me. Well, better most likely-- the way I hear it, you're one tough cookie," she said with a smile and a friendly pat on the shoulder.

"That's our Mela. The toughest cookie in town," Wyatt said.

"That's good to hear. Say," she turned to Mela and Owen. "Are they here?"

"Who?" Mela asked a bit too harshly. She really didn't want to hear of more people coming to her house.

"The Avatians, silly. Connie went on and on about how wonderful they are. Told me all about what they looked like and that they've been alive for over two thousand years. Gosh, the things they must've seen. I think it's wonderful."

"Oh, right. The boys. You want to meet them?" Mela waved her hand for Layla to follow her and she took her outside.

"You've got such a cute house. I love it. The way it sits way out here, all tucked into the trees all cozy like. Just wonderful." Mela looked back at Layla and smiled her thanks. Her eyes caught Wyatt's and he made a face as he tried to contain his laughter. Owen followed behind with a scowl.

"Theo." He was the only one in the backyard and he turned at the sound of his name. "Theo, meet Layla. She's another Elementai. She wanted to meet you." Mela stepped back. "Layla, this is Theothane. He likes short names so he goes by Theo."

Layla, with one hand on her chest approached Theo with wonder in her eyes. She smiled so warmly at him, Mela released a breath she didn't know she'd been holding.

"Oh, Theo, it's such a pleasure to meet you." She reached out and wrapped her arms around him in a hug much like the one she forced on Mela and Owen. Theo reciprocated the hug, however, with much more grace than either of them.

"It is a pleasure to meet another like our Mela."

"Thank you so much." She released Theo and stepped back "I've got lots to learn, I know. But I'm here to work hard and learn everything I can. I'll teach you anything you want to learn, Mela. And you too, Owen."

"Thanks, Layla." Mela said. She sneaked a look at Wyatt, who was smiling ear to ear.

"What's all the commotion?" Decker called out. Decker came with Vasha from the direction of the shed. However, the closer the got, the shock on Decker's face was evident.

"Layla, these are Theo's brothers. That gorgeous, blue beast there is Vashanu. But you can call him Vasha." Vasha bowed with all four arms extended in greeting. His eyes raked over her body as he smiled.

"It is a pleasure, Layla." His voice dropped into what Mela knew was his sexy voice.

"Where are my manners?" she looked around, horrified at herself and bounced off the patio to greet him properly. "It's lovely to meet you." She smiled up at Vasha and wrapped her arms around his waist. Vasha looked down, wrapped his arms around her, and smiled. His hands caressed her bouncing curls and one hand dared to venture farther down than was decent.

"Behave, Vasha," Mela warned him.

"My apologies. However, how am I to control myself when such a woman falls into my arms so willingly?" Layla giggled and stepped out of his grip.

"And that," Mela said, pointing, "is Dektrios. He goes by Decker now." Layla smiled and turned to Decker. Curiously, Decker's face looked like he'd seen a ghost. Without speaking, he yanked his hat from his head and nodded politely. Mela raised her eyebrows in question to Wyatt who was just as captivated by his actions.

"I'm Layla," she said to him. Decker looked down at his feet. "Oh, you're a shy one. Come here." She wrapped her arms around Decker's neck and squeezed. Decker carefully patted her back and then dropped his hands. Confused by Decker's behavior, Mela looked to Theo for answers.

Theo was watching the exchange with as much interest as everyone else.

"Oh, now I get it…" Wyatt said to himself.

"Get what?" Mela asked him in a whisper.

"I'll explain later. Long story. But shit is about to get really interesting." Wyatt's cryptic words frustrated her but she didn't have time to punch it out of him. Layla was speaking to Vasha and they were coming to Mela.

"So you will be with us here for some time then?" Vasha was asking.

"Yes, if it's all right with Mela that I stick around." Everyone turned to Mela and she saw the hopeful look in Layla's eyes, the barely contained glee in Vasha's, the curiosity in Theo's, and the strange bewilderment in Decker's. Resigned, Mela shrugged her shoulders.

"Sure. I have an extra room if you need it," If it were possible, Layla's smile got larger and she clapped her hands.

"Thank you so much, Mela. It'll be so much fun. I promise. Hey, it'll be like a slumber party every night!"

Wyatt, half-jokingly, clapped his hands too and offered to take Layla inside to show her her new room. Vasha watched her walk away with more than a little appreciation in his eyes.

"Hands off," Mela warned him.

"She grabbed me, I want that noted."

"It's noted. Now no more touchy feely." Vasha laughed and turned to go back to his shed. Decker stood in the same spot and stared at the ground. Theo approached him to whisper something in his ear. Decker nodded, then turned with Theo to walk away.

"What's with him?" Owen asked.

"I have no idea. He's acting strange."

"Well, looks like you've got another mouth to feed." Mela looked up at Owen and sighed.

"Seems so. Good thing I have a job that I'm really late for now. Let's all hope I don't get fired. Everyone would starve." Mela went back inside to get ready for work and call Claudia with her apologies for being late.

Chapter Seventeen

Luckily, Claudia was running late herself and the two women pulled up at the same time. Claudia was all business, waving off Mela's apologies at being late.

"It happens, Mela. Let's move on," Claudia said as they walked in together. "Have you had a chance to look over the applications I left for you? None of them are really inspiring, I know. But we've got to get someone up at the front desk who's cheerful and good with people." An idea started to grow in Mela's mind but she held her tongue until Claudia was finished. Her boss was going on about how the front desk employees were lazy and rude to the clients. Something she couldn't allow to continue. "Any prospects?" she finally asked.

"Yes, actually," Mela sat at her desk and pretended to rummage through the papers. "I'm looking for it....there's this girl, her name is Layla. Just as happy and cheerful as you could want. Smart as a whip too..." Claudia went through her mail while she listened.

"Great. Set up an interview once you find her phone number." Claudia tossed a stack of junk mail and grabbed the rest.

"I'll set it up for today, if that's okay?" Mela called out.

"Sounds good," Claudia said. "Say," Claudia came back out of her office frowning. "What's going on with this Pastor Rod business? I heard about Barney Fife coming here to question you. They don't think something happened to him, do they? And why in the world would they be coming to you about it all?" Mela explained why she was on the list of information stops and Claudia nodded her head in understanding. "That makes more sense. The way Tracy tells it, you would've thought they found blood and hair samples in your car."

"No, nothing like that. They're just worried. But I'm sure he's fine. The business at the church upset him a lot," Mela confided.

"I heard about that. Wyatt was there, wasn't he?" Mela nodded. "What happened? Folks are going on and on about that too. Of course, I know rumors are like shit in a bucket. Stinks to high hell and gets worse over time."

"From what I understand, it was just one of those freak accidents, you know? Cross falls, breaks the table, scares everyone...I guess that's how that guy had a heart attack. Then Ms. Wesley..."

"That poor woman. Nobody knew she had the cancer. I heard tell her heart stopped too, just gave up."

"I don't know exactly what did it."

"Yes, from what I hear, she saw Marcus drop and her poor heart just couldn't take it and she passed away right then and there. Horrible."

"It was. So, Wyatt says."

"But why did the Pastor come to you? I mean, I love the hell out of you, Mela, but it is kind of odd that he came looking to you for help." Claudia's eyes narrowed, scrutinizing Mela's face.

"Well, it is weird. But Wyatt brought him to me because he...well...he was trying to bring me back to the church. You know, recruit me for Bible study or something." Mela gave an exaggerated shrug and Claudia rolled her eyes.

"Ugh. These people and their religion. Don't do it, Mela! Don't drink the Kool-Aid. If you turn into one of those, I'll fire you," she said dramatically.

"No worries about that," Mela laughed.

"Good. Now, bring me this peppy Layla gal, would you? Lord knows we all could use a bit of pep." And with that, she went to her office.

Feeling much more relieved, and consequently more open to the idea of Layla, she dialed Wyatt's number and explained the situation. In just moments, the breathless voice of Layla filled her ear.

"Hiya, roomie!" she said. Mela laughed.

"Hi Layla. Listen, everything happened so fast this morning, I never got a chance to explain a few things. First off, given the recent rash of attacks," she whispered into the phone. "None of us should ever be alone if we can help it."

"Oh, okay. Good thinking."

"Yeah so…Since I happen to be alone here, I was thinking you could come. For a job."

"A job? Really?" She sounded much too enthused about the prospect. "Where do you work?"

"At the gym. The only gym in town."

"Oh. I don't know. I'm not real good at physical activity." she said, for the first time sounding down.

"No need to worry. It's for a front desk position. Part-time and Claudia, my boss, says she wants someone friendly and helpful at the desk. I immediately thought of you."

"Aren't you so sweet! You really thought of me? Thank you. That sounds perfect. I just love working with people. I think that would suit me just fine."

"Great. Wyatt will give you directions. Can you come today?"

"Yep. Will do. I'll just freshen up and race right over." They said their goodbyes and Mela hung up. Chuckling a bit to herself, she had to admit that Layla really was a breath of fresh air. It was one thing to be serious and down to earth. But Mela's life was a continuing spiral down a dark and depressing road. Layla seemed to be the patch of sunshine everyone needed.

In less than an hour, Layla bounced into the gym flashing her million watt smile. Tracy, unfortunately, was working at the front desk, looking every bit like she had been rode hard and put up wet. Her one redeeming quality were her good looks, at least, as an employee goes. But now, even that was suffering.

Tracy escorted Layla to Mela's office and rudely waved her hand for her to go inside. Turning on her heels, she left the two without a word.

"Well, she's not friendly at all," Layla said, watching Tracy walk away.

"Nope. She's a real bitch. She hates me, by the way, so get ready to hear all about how much I suck," Mela said.

"I can't imagine why she would think that. Poor thing. She's suffering." Layla continued to watch Tracy.

"Not enough. Come on, have a seat." Layla shrugged off the concerns she had for Tracy and sat in the small chair opposite Mela's desk.

"Did you curse her?" Layla asked.

"Me? No. Of course not. Not worth my time. To business now…" Mela shuffled papers around until she found what she was looking for. "Here," she handed Layla a blank application. "I said you already filled one out. So do that real quick and then I'll let Claudia know you're here." With one last look at Tracy, Layla got to work filling out the paperwork.

"Hey, I don't have an address…" Layla said.

"You have mine. But let's not put that on there yet. Just write that you're still looking or something. We'll let her know we're roommates after you're hired."

"Good idea." Layla hurriedly filled out the rest of the information and handed it to Mela.

"Great. Hey, can I ask you something?"

"Sure. Anything."

"Did you just pack up and leave when Connie asked you to come here? I mean, what did you tell people?" Layla had to have family and a ton of friends wherever she was from.

"It was real hard. I had to tell my family I was going on a retreat. It's horrible to lie to them, I know." She looked positively miserable about it. "But they can't know the truth. I said goodbye to my friends and tossed what I could in my car and came here," she said with a gloomy expression.

"I'm sorry. It must be hard. Did you have a job there?"

"Yes. I'm from a little town outside of El Paso. Not much there but it was home and I loved it. I was just starting out as a real estate agent, actually. But…things changed." Mela felt sorry for the happy girl sitting alone in her office who had given so much to come and help.

"Well, you're with friends now. Just sit tight, I'll be right back." Mela scooted off to Claudia's office and in no time, Layla was in there charming the pants off Claudia.

It came as no surprise that Claudia hired her on the spot. Mela spent the rest of the day showing Layla around, introducing her to everyone. Layla charmed everyone she met – except Tracy – who loathed her on sight. Maybe it was her fresh beauty or her obvious friendship with Mela, but Mela saw Tracy zero in on her new friend and warned her when they were alone.

"Be careful. She's vicious and nasty. She'll say whatever she needs to in order to hurt you or make you angry." Layla's face changed from her happy visage to something completely different.

"I can handle girls like that. Flies, that's what my momma calls them. Girls like that are flies. They're attracted to the stink of everyone's poop. No matter how many times you try and shoo them away, they always come back. You gotta smack 'em," she brought her hand down so hard on the table that Mela jumped. "People take my kindness for weakness. Their mistake." Impressed, Mela started to like Layla a lot more than she did before.

As the girls prepared to leave for the day, Mela informed Claudia that Layla would be rooming with her and requested their schedules be the same as much as possible. Claudia readily agreed, anxious to please the new employee, if for no other reason than to keep her around.

Pleased, they left work, exhausted but very happy. Layla chatted on and on about ways Mela can start exercising her abilities, even at work.

"When you're close to someone, reach out with your energy and feel them out," she explained.

"Sounds kind of rude. Like I'm invading their privacy or something."

"Oh, you are. But as long as they're not a threat, you shouldn't have to dive too deep. But you can feel their emotions, and from that, you'll get a better sense of their intent. And we both know that intent is everything."

Mela smiled and nodded but, as she drove home, she felt a little lost. There was so much she didn't understand and, at some point, she'd have to sit down and have Layla start from the very beginning to see just how much of the basics she was really lacking.

When they arrived, Mela entertained thoughts of a big dinner, a glass of wine, and her comfortable bed. However, the Universe had other plans, as the Universe was want to do.

Wyatt was still there. She found that a bit odd since it was in the middle of the week and he normally had a job to do. No one was in the house when they arrived, so Mela and Layla went searching for them. They found the small crowd of friends on the back porch, with Sammuele at the center. He stopped talking when they arrived.

"Sammuele, I'm so glad you're back," she said, approaching him with caution. She put her hand on his arm and inspected his face. There were cuts across his cheek and his lip was bruised. "What happened?"

"They came to…" he looked at Owen and Layla.

"The place where Anabelle is?" Mela offered.

"Precisely. They came and there were many. I did not have time to come and retrieve you. There were so many."

"Is Annabelle okay?" Mela looked back to Wyatt who nodded with a strange look on his face.

"She is. But they were not after the child. They came for me," he said.

"For you? Why?"

"We think it's payback for the little scuffle at the church," Decker offered up.

"Indeed. I believe it is so. Annabelle was able to hide with the help of the…lost souls that inhabit the building. They took her to a place to hide and I stayed."

"Did you kill them?" she asked.

"Every last one." Sammuele said.

Relieved, Mela wrapped her arms around Sammuele and hugged him. She knew it was out of character for her and uncomfortable for him, but she wanted to tell him how happy and proud she was. Sometimes, where words fail, the only other option is to convey it with touch.

"We are happy to have you back with us in one piece, Sammuele," Vasha said kindly. Theo nodded his agreement as did Wyatt.

"It's really dangerous here, isn't it?" Layla asked with fear in her eyes.

"It is dangerous everywhere, little sunflower. However, we shall do our parts to protect the innocent and defeat the wicked," Vasha said.

"Mela, how much do your new companions know of your…duty?" Sammuele asked. She looked around at the newcomers and shook her head.

"Nothing. I haven't had a chance to fill them in. I guess it's time to do that." So she did. Starting from the beginning, Mela told them her story with the help of the others. At times, Decker chimed in, followed by a comment or two from Theo. Vasha simply nodded along, listening and watching. She told them everything from the day she bought The Green Book to the police coming to question her.

Owen asked a few important questions and they did their best to answer him. He was most concerned for the wellbeing of Annabelle and Sandra. Layla was more concerned with the dark creatures roaming around.

"I'll be able to see them?" she asked again. Mela and Owen both assured her that she would and that seemed to satisfy her.

"There's one more thing happening. Sorry, doll face, you've been so busy and I haven't had time to tell you," Wyatt looked down at his hands and she could hear the tears in his voice. "When we went to see little Annabelle, we were both horrified by the conditions she's living in. She doesn't deserve to be stuck in the place like that. Nurse Renee agrees. So…" he exhaled in an attempt to control the tears that threatened to fall. "I've been talking to Renee and she's been helping me. I've petitioned the courts on Annabelle's behalf. I'm going to be her legal guardian and get her out of there."

"You're what?" Mela was shocked and blurted the question out without thinking. "You're adopting her?"

"Not yet." He shook his head sadly. "It's hard because… well…you know."

"I don't. Why not?" Decker asked brusquely.

"The state of Texas doesn't allow me to adopt without some serious red tape. I know I probably could, but with the current social climate being what it is these days, it would go faster if I was just her guardian. Being a single man, I could do it but since she's a ward of the State, it's really subjective to whoever the Judge is. So, Renee is helping me. So is Todd," he looked at Mela apologetically. "He's agreed to speak on my behalf and also, to be Annabelle's primary care provider. Pastor Rod has agreed to help too."

"It is fitting to call yourself her guardian rather than her parent. I think it rather poetic." Vasha smiled.

"And," Wyatt continued, "I thought it was best to go for the more expedient option."

"I think it's an amazing idea!" Mela cried. "You're going to be someone's Dad!" She covered her mouth and laughed. She knew, without a doubt, Wyatt would be the best possible parent to Annabelle.

"Congratulations, mate!" Decker said, smacking Wyatt's arm.

"Ow!" he laughed and visibly relaxed. "Mela, you're a character witness for me. We'll go in front of the judge soon. Like, really soon. Renee has been busting her ass getting this to move quick."

"I don't know if I'm the best character witness for you." Her heart dropped in her chest when she said it. "I mean, they suspect me of having something to do with Pastor Rod's disappearance."

"Nah." He waved her words off. "That's just Douchebag Doug being a douche bag. It'll blow over." Everyone agreed but Mela stayed silent. He hadn't seen the look of pure, unadulterated hate in Douchebag Doug's face. She didn't hold out much hope that he'd drop his interest in her unless the good pastor showed up soon.

"Mela, a word?" Sammuele requested. Nodding, she followed him into the backyard and they walked, side by side, until they were out of range from the others.

"Was it bad?" she finally asked him.

"No more so than what you have endured. My wounds will heal." He sounded tired, if an angel could be tired. "I want to thank you, Mela."

"Thank me? For what? I feel kind of guilty, to be honest."

"Do not feel guilt on my behalf. No, in truth, I am grateful. I had two visitors while I was recovering."

"Oh? The winged, oddly androgynous kind?" she laughed at his confused expression. "Sorry, go on."

"Two of my brethren who, I suspect, you met with in order know to my whereabouts." He looked to her for confirmation and she nodded.

"Yep. We were worried. So, we put our heads together until we remembered that angel's name. Still can't remember it…"

"Raguel…"

"That's it," she pointed at him and laughed. "They weren't very helpful so I kind of had to persuade them," she confessed.

"I see. That you would go to such lengths to assist me, it is much appreciated." He stopped and turned to her. "I know I do not have a place here among you all." He looked back to the group gathered on the back porch. "But your kindness and acceptance of me has been both reassuring and a pleasant reprieve from what I've become accustomed to."

"Sammuele." She put her hand on his arm and smiled. "You do have a place here with us. I know Decker gives you a hard time, but it's not personal. He just has a general dislike for anyone of the winged persuasion. But I'll confess a secret to you." She stepped closer and lowered her voice. "He was ready to fight the angels in order to find out what they knew. So was Vasha. They were right there beside me, ready to pound their feathers into the dirt." Sammuele stood silently searching her eyes for any hint of a lie. "They do care about you, Sammuele. In their own way. Me, Wyatt, and Theo care a whole bunch too. You have a place here."

"I do not deserve such kindness from you. But I will accept it with a grateful heart."

"Good." She laced her arm through his and guided him back to the house.

"While we are celebrating, perhaps it is a good time to discuss speeding up the search for the next Key. Time is running short," Sammuele said.

"Not yet. Let me go a few days without something crazy happening. I don't think I can take much more excitement right now."

"Very well. Let us celebrate the good news Wyatt has shared. We can revisit this at another time." Relieved he wasn't going to push the issue, they returned to the group of friends on the back porch. Decker was throwing a tantrum because Mela hadn't grocery shopped yet. Even with the pressures of caring for her vagabond crew, she was thankful for the calm that surrounded them. In the back of her mind, a voice cautioned her against tempting the Fates like that. She shoved those thoughts aside, enjoying the moment instead.

Chapter Eighteen

Mela and Layla left for work early in the morning. That was when Mela found out Layla was definitely not a morning person. She had to pound on her door to wake her and even then, Layla was slow to get up. She stayed in the shower too long too. Mela cringed at what her water bill would look like with yet another person in the house. Layla drank coffee like she was taking shots of Vodka before she cracked her first smile.

Sadly, she had to leave Layla in Tracy's clutches for training while she went about her own work. She heard her phone going off in her purse but was too busy to pay much attention to it. She felt guilty because she figured it was her parents checking in. She was avoiding the inevitable question of, "How's it going with Todd?" She knew she'd have to tell them their hopes of her marrying a doctor were gone for good. She just wasn't up for being the disappointing daughter today.

It was sometime after lunch when the normal, everyday grind, came to an abrupt halt. Mela was at her desk when she saw them enter the gym. Both Officer Feltz and Douchebag Doug went to the front desk and spoke with Layla. Mela watched as the color drained from Layla's face and she turned to look at Mela.

Something bad was happening, something very bad. Layla picked up the phone as Mela watched her speak into it. In moments, Claudia was at the front desk with the two officers. Layla was backing away slowly, Mela could tell, hoping they wouldn't notice. She rushed into Mela's office, pale faced and breathing heavily.

"Mela go, just go." She couldn't catch her breath. "They're here to arrest you, I think. They said they need to speak with you and need to you to leave with them."

"What?" A cold grip of terror knotted her stomach and she almost doubled over in pain. "What?" she said again.

"Listen, I'll call Wyatt and tell him what's happening. We'll help you." She looked behind her and saw the three from the front desk approaching. "Stay strong and don't do anything stupid. If it gets too bad, just go. Use your magick and leave." She whispered the last part and turned when the officers entered the office.

"I want it noted that I think this is horseshit. Mela doesn't have anything to do with this nonsense and I'll bet my ass you don't have any clue what happened to that man, so you're grasping at straws smaller than your dicks," Claudia barked.

"Ma'am, unless you want to get arrested for obstruction, I suggest you get out of my way and be quiet," Douchebag Doug snarled.

"Mela, I'll call Tom Clark," she focused on the two officers as she continued. "The *best* lawyer in town. When these yokels figure out their ass from their brains, we'll sue the both of them."

"Ms. Malone," Douchebag Doug spoke over Claudia. "We'd like you to come with us. We've got to have a little chat." His oversized gut hung low over his black leather belt. His hands rested on what would've been his hips, if he had any. The satisfied glint in his eye told Mela she was in serious trouble.

"What for?" she asked. Her heart was racing in her chest and her palms were beginning to sweat. She saw Layla slip out of the office and dart to the front desk.

"As you know, we're investigating the disappearance of Pastor Rodrick Jenson. Otherwise known to us fine Christian folks as Pastor Rod."

"Yeah, so?" Mela belligerently remained seated and glared at him.

"We're bringing you in for a few questions about his disappearance. You see, you were the last person to see him and his last known whereabouts was at your house. That makes you a material witness, missy."

"This is against the law," Claudia spat at him.

"Naw, Ms. Sherman, it ain't. We've got probable cause. Ms. Malone, could you gather your belongings and come with us please?" He backed out of her way, creating an opening to the door. Taking a deep breath, Mela grabbed her purse and stepped from behind her desk.

"I'll take that," Claudia said, grabbing her purse from her hands. "We don't want anything happening to it. I'll just hang onto it for you in my office."

"This way, Ms. Malone." Officer Feltz said. She noted he did not look directly at her.

"It'll be okay." Layla whispered as she passed her. Humiliated beyond belief, Mela walked with her two police escorts from the gym as everyone watched. She fought the urge to vomit as they stepped outside into the gloomy afternoon. Light raindrops fell on her as they walked to the waiting car as if the sky was crying for her and all her troubles.

Silently, Officer Feltz ushered her into the backseat of the cruiser and shut the door. They remained outside of the car talking together for a few moments before they loaded in and started toward the police station. She watched her small town slide by. They passed the bowling alley, the grocery store, and the park she used to play in as a child. Raindrops slid like silent tears down the glass as she tried to make sense of what was happening.

They pulled into the small two story police station, parking under an awning to avoid getting wet. She would've preferred walking in the rain. At least she could feel refreshed if she were soaked with the calming energy from the rain.

No such luck. Officer Feltz opened the back door and placed his hand lightly on her elbow. They followed in the wake of Douchebag Doug who opened the double doors. Every head turned when she walked in. Thankfully, she wasn't in handcuffs. That was a small mercy.

Officer Feltz took her through a long hallway, through another set of double doors, then through a room full of desks littered with policemen. Gently, he showed her a room to the left that had a table and three chairs set up inside.

"You can have a seat, we'll be right with you." He closed the door, leaving her alone. The table was made of wood but had so many coats of paint on it, it looked like it was padded. The chairs were metal with no cushions. She guessed comfort wasn't high on their priority list here. She couldn't sit but paced around the room, going over everything she was and wasn't going to say. She felt panic taking control over her so she tried to control her breathing.

The only thing in the room was a clock. She watched it tick and focused on the second hand as it made its way around the clock face over and over again. She toyed with the idea of calling Sammuele to her. But he couldn't help her out of this. It was best not to complicate matters further with an invisible angel.

Just about the time Mela wanted to start pounding on the door and screaming for anyone to come and talk to her, she heard voices on the other side. She strained to hear their conversation and realized it was Douchebag Doug and another unknown officer talking about the local football game. With fantasies of sticking a sword in his expansive belly, Mela crossed her arms over her chest and stood still, waiting for them to enter.

When they did, they were laughing at something someone said without a care in the world. Mela felt the all too familiar flames of rage start to bubble inside her. Douchebag Doug entered, followed by Officer Feltz, and another unnamed officer. Without a word, they closed the door behind them and took two of the three seats. Of course, Douchebag Doug sat, as did Officer Feltz. The other officer leaned against the wall with his arms crossed over his chest.

Douchebag Doug placed a file folder on the table and opened it up. Without looking at her, he waved his had in her directions and spoke. "Come have a set," he said imperiously. Weighing her options, she could either tell him to fuck off, inflict some sort of bodily harm and strut out, or comply with his demand. In the spirit of being normal, which she was fully aware that she was not, she decided to comply – for now.

Allowing herself to accept her decision calmed her down a degree. She sat in the lone chair opposite of the officers and folded her hands in her lap. Douchebag Doug picked at something between his teeth as he read through the papers in his file. Mela watched him and was disgusted. How could any self-respecting police officer allow himself to be such a slob?

"Now, Ms. Malone," he said, breaking the silence. "As I said before, we want to know exactly what you know about Pastor Rod's disappearance. His wife has filed a Missing Person's report." He waved a piece of paper at her. "She's real concerned about her husband, rightfully so." He folded his hands over the paperwork. She watched his fat cheeks shake from so much use.

"I already told you everything," she said quietly.

"Now I don't believe you did. But for the sake of understanding, we'd like you to tell us again. Let's go back to last Sunday. What were you doing all day?"

"Hanging out with my friends. Went for a run...dinner." She shrugged. "The usual."

"The usual…" he repeated her words and she wondered what it would feel like to slap his fat face. "Does the usual usually involve Pastor Rod coming to visit you?" he asked.

"Nope. That was unusual." She gave him a sarcastic smile.

"So tell us what happened when he came. You claim he showed up with…." He checked his notes. She knew he remembered exactly who she said he showed up with. "Your friend Wyatt. That correct?" he asked, looking up at her with the hint of a smile on his face.

"Yes."

"And he was coming to you to do what?"

"He came with Wyatt because they were trying to talk me into joining their Bible study group," she said evenly.

"And you didn't want to?"

"Nope."

"Why not?"

"Sometimes fine Christian folks aren't as fine or Christian as they like to think they are." She smiled sweetly when she spoke. "I know of a few people who claim to be fine Christian folks," she leaned in to whisper loudly. "Most of them are as shitty as the rest." She leaned back in her chair and stared at their stunned faces. She was particularly pleased by the red blotches appearing on Douchebag Doug's cheeks.

"So, you didn't care for Pastor Rod?"

"Oh, he's all right. He can't answer for the shortcomings of all of his flock though."

"Christian people make you mad?"

"No more than any other people."

"But you have a particular aversion to those who walk the Christian path?"

"No. I have an aversion to those who *pretend* to walk the Christian path. There's a distinct difference." She pointed at him to emphasize her words.

"I won't have you slandering the Lord in here, Ms. Malone." Douchebag Doug shook with anger. Mela shrugged dramatically.

"I wasn't slandering your Lord, Officer, I was slandering some of the people who follow him. Again, a big difference."

"You're a real smarty pants, aren't you?" he sneered.

"Just answering your questions." She looked away in order to get control of the rage that was bubbling up with each passing minute.

"Now, according to Mrs. Jenson, the good Pastor left a note saying he needed to talk to you and that you could help him through this difficult time. What was he referring to?" Stunned, Mela looked at all three of the officers.

"I honestly don't know," she said. She could make plenty of sense out of that note, to be sure, but they couldn't know that she could, so playing ignorant was best.

"Do you have any guesses? Did he say anything to you about any troubles he was having?"

Mela chewed on her lip. "He mentioned how upset he was by what happened at the church the other night."

"Yes, the night Mrs. Wesley died and others sustained either injuries or health emergencies. Your friend Wyatt was there that night too, wasn't he?" She didn't like the way he said that but she nodded anyway. "What else did he say?"

"He went on about Church-type stuff. Wyatt wanted me to come to the Bible study too, so I guess they were ambushing me in a way."

"So, you're the victim of a religious intervention, is that right?"

"No. Just the victim of unexpected guests."

"You see, we can accept what you're saying as true up until the time you say he left. You told me you don't remember what time he left, that right?"

"Right. It was late, I now that."

"Late, huh? You all talked about his church for that long?" he waved his hands in the air in a state of confusion.

"No, we talked about other stuff. Family, friends, dreams…"

"Dreams…. Funny you should mention that. Mrs. Jenson told me her husband had been suffering recently from nightmares. Did he mention anything about those?"

"No."

"You sure?"

"Yes."

"Now, why don't I believe you?" He leaned back and regarded her with his beady eyes. Mela sat as still as she dared, fighting the urge to let her anger take control.

"We're in quite a pickle, Mela," Officer Feltz finally spoke up. "You see, Pastor Rod has been missing now for over forty-eight hours. In his own words he said he was going to your house where you say he did, in fact, show up. Then, after your house, things get murky. In my line of work, this usually means one of two things," he held his hand up and counted on his fingers. "One, there was some sort of foul play somewhere. Or two, he's been kidnapped and forcibly held against his will. The latter," he said, leaning forward, "would require we bring in the FBI to investigate. We'd get to search warrants for your house, your property, and your car. But any way we look at this, all roads lead to you."

"And to your friend, Wyatt," Douchebag Doug added.

"Pastor Rod left my house. I really don't know where he is. He got in his car and drove off Sunday night."

There, that much was the truth and she sounded convincing, she thought.

"In your opinion," Douchebag Doug went on. "Does your friend Wyatt have a violent streak in him? Any grudges against the people of this town? The pastor of the church maybe?"

"No, of course not."

"Tell me, Ms. Malone, you claim Pastor Rod left your house late Sunday night, right? Did Wyatt leave at the same time?" Mela really didn't like the direction this was going.

"No, he stayed."

"So, the two people who saw the good pastor are yourself and a photographer?" The sadistic sneer returned to his face when he said the last word. Mela stared into his eyes and decided that if push came to shove, she really could do serious harm to this man.

Looking away from Douchebag Doug and eyeing Officer Feltz, as well as the other officer in the room, Mela realized how frail they really were. It would only take her a few minutes to rid the world of their hateful, bigoted, slovenly souls. As they stared back at her, she allowed the reality of her position in the world to sink in. She could kill them with a flick of her hand. She could hurt them and make them suffer on a whim. The fact that she could do it made it easier for her not to do it. For some peculiar reason, this realization calmed her. The deadly rage was there, it was always there, hibernating just below the surface. But the rage monster was no longer forcibly chained, but tamed.

Her thoughts were interrupted by a knock at the door. The unnamed officer pushed himself from the wall and opened the door a crack. After a few whispers were exchanged, he opened the door wider.

"You're serious?" he asked the person at the door.

"Excuse us a minute, Ms. Malone." Officer Feltz said and he tapped Douchebag Doug on the shoulder for him to follow. With a click, the door shut behind them.

Calmer now, Mela relaxed in the chair waiting to see what would happen next. Whatever it was, she knew she would be okay. Sure, if Pastor Rod came up dead, she, or Wyatt, could be charged with murder. Of that she was certain. But she had no intention of letting that happen. They would disappear and no one would ever find them. It was a sad thought, yet a comforting thought all the same.

From the other side of the door, Mela heard raised voices. Someone was very angry and it made her smile. She hoped it was Douchebag Doug.

Sure enough, he came barreling through the door a moment later, his cheeks fiery and his face covered in sweat. Behind him came Officer Feltz, followed by none other than Pastor Rod.

Mela stood and covered her mouth to muffle the gasp that came out. Douchebag Doug glared at Mela but didn't say a word.

"Are you all right, Mela?" Pastor Rod asked.

"Yes. Are you?" He wrapped his arm around her shoulders. Turning to the officers, she saw the first hint of anger in his face.

"As you can see, I'm just fine. Mela would never hurt me, neither would Wyatt. I'm appalled you could even think such a thing. If you don't mind, gentlemen, I'm going to take Mela home." All of the officers stepped out of their way with the exception of Douchebag Doug.

"You owe us an explanation, Pastor."

"I owe you nothing. It is to the Lord that I answer to, not you and your--" he looked the repulsive man up and down-- "badge. Come along, Mela." Pastor Rod stepped in front of her, leaving just Mela and Douchebag Doug alone in the room. She got to the doorway and turned to face the officer who obviously wanted nothing more than for her to pay for the crime of being different.

"I won't forget this, Doug," she said, glancing over her shoulder to make sure no one was listening. "I suggest, in the future, you keep your distance from me," She dug down deep and stroked the tame rage monster. It was so easy now, like turning on a switch. "If you don't, you will regret it." She let the flames show in her eyes for only an instant. But an instant was all that was needed. Douchebag Doug's mouth fell open and he backed away from her, tripping over one of the metal chairs. Both he and the chair hit the floor with an awful racket.

As he picked himself up, his face went from beet red to a sickening shade of white. His mouth opened and closed but no words came out. He pointed at her and looked around for someone to help him.

"Doug, you okay?" the unnamed officer asked from the doorway.

"She…her…look at her!" he stammered. Mela turned to the unnamed officer with a puzzled expression.

"You should go, Ms. Malone." He turned to Doug and spoke quietly with him for a minute. Mela waited a moment, in a mock show of concern. "It's all right, man. You're just a little tired. Come on, I'll get you some coffee."

Mela turned and hurried to catch up with Pastor Rod in the lobby. Together, they walked from the Trinity Hills police station.

Chapter Nineteen

Mela decided to go home after Pastor Rod dropped her off at her car. He promised her that they would talk soon but he needed to get home to his wife. It was late in the evening and she didn't have the emotional fortitude to walk into the gym again today. Pastor Rod strolled into the building for her, as calm as can be, and retrieved Mela's purse from Claudia's office. She called her boss as she headed home and was reminded why she loved and respected her so much. After calling Douchebag Doug every name she could come up with, Claudia simply growled and spat random curse words into the phone.

"You want to sue their asses, Mela?" she asked for the third time. Fighting back tears of gratitude but laughing at the same time, Mela told her no.

"I think he'll keep his distance from now on. Pastor Rod really tore into him." Claudia made her retell that part of the story again and this time she didn't interrupt.

"You want to take a day or two off?" she offered.

"No ma'am. I'm not hiding from anyone. I'll just go home today and I'll be back in the morning with Layla. How was her first day? Other than me being hauled into the police station for questioning?" They laughed and Claudia said Layla was going to work out just fine. She was pleased as punch that she showed such strength and loyalty to Mela.

"I'm telling you, I thought she was a complete pushover. But Tracy was being Tracy and talked her pretty little head off about you and Layla, well, Layla came unglued. Mela, I thought she was going to hit her!" They gossiped about Tracy for a few minutes with Claudia laughing but apologizing all the while for not being a proper boss.

"Oh, don't worry about it. You wouldn't be normal if you didn't bitch about Tracy every once in a while," Mela laughed. Claudia told her again how happy she was her ordeal was over and they said their goodbyes.

A few minutes later, she pulled into her driveway. As she got out of her car, the front door exploded open and Layla, Wyatt, Owen, Decker, Sammuele, and Bear poured out. Theo and Vasha came from the back and she was surrounded by her friends as they each hugged her in turn and asked if she was okay.

"Give the jailbird some room," Decker said loudly as he shoved everyone aside and ushered her into the house. "I was gonna smuggle you a nail file but Owen said that don't work no more." Everyone laughed as Mela collapsed onto the couch with Bear on her heels. He sat by her side and leaned against her legs. Even Kat woke up to see what all the fuss was about.

"What happened at the police station, Mela?" Wyatt asked. She could tell he'd been crying and she grabbed his hand and pulled him close.

"Douchebag Doug was being his same old self. He hinted that you and I had something to do with Pastor Rod's mysterious disappearance."

"I was a suspect?" he screeched.

"You and me, kid. We were almost wanted felons. They questioned me about Sunday night, why he was here and all that. Oh, by the way, if anyone ever asks, you two were trying to get me to join your Bible study group."

"Got it. Then what happened?" he asked.

"Well, that's when Pastor Rod showed up. He was so mad." She looked around at everyone. "But he was awesome. Shamed them from here to Mexico and back again. And then…." She stopped, a bit hesitant to tell them what she did to Douchebag Doug. "Well, I had to send

Douchebag Doug a message to leave me—us--alone from now on."

"What did you do?" Owen asked smiling.

"I told him to stay away and I might have let a little fire into my eyes when I said it." Decker thought it was the most hilarious thing he'd ever heard. Owen shook his head and laughed. Layla covered her mouth and said "Oh no!"

"See, what'd I tell you, toughest cookie in town," Wyatt said and hugged his best friend.

* * *

It was a big day around Mela's house on Friday. As Mela and Layla prepared to go to work, there was an air of nervous excitement already hanging over everyone. Wyatt would be picking up Annabelle that afternoon and bringing her to his home to live.

Wyatt, Mela, Layla, and Owen spent the previous night decorating the spare bedroom in Wyatt's townhouse in vibrant shades of pink and purple. Owen fought with the canopied bedposts, cussing up a storm, while Layla hung clothes and Mela played assistant to Wyatt, hanging a large painting on the wall. He insisted on everything being done to his specifications and they worked tirelessly until the perfect princess room was missing only one thing – the princess.

Wyatt would go to the courthouse with Nurse Renee, and together finalize the paperwork. He was as nervous as any new father could be. Although Mela understood the reasons for it, she still wished he would reconsider filing formal adoption papers. However, he said he and Nurse Renee had spoken on the subject at length and this was what would free Annabelle from the hospital the quickest.

When she and Layla, exhausted but excited for the day, pulled out of the driveway, Mela saw Owen sitting some distance away from the house in the tall grass.

"What is he doing?" Mela asked. "It's cold outside and he's just sitting there." She turned to Layla who was smiling ear to ear.

"Oh, silly goose, Owen is meditating. It's a wonderful practice to meditate as the sun rises, the energy is strong and lasts all day. Did you know that there are Yogis out there who say they don't even need food because they practice meditation called 'Sun Gazing'?"

"Oh really? Well, that'll be nice. Maybe we can get everyone to start sun gazing." Layla laughed, but Mela really wasn't kidding. She'd put off the large grocery shopping trip until this weekend when she was paid again. Decker was a very unhappy man.

"Do you like him?" Layla asked, eying Mela as she drove.

"Who? Owen?"

"Mmhmm."

"Yeah, sure. He's all right." She felt a blush creeping into her cheeks. Despite feeling like hell when Todd walked away, she knew it really was for the best. For now anyway. That didn't make the ache any less. But Owen, he was on the same level as Mela on almost every way. He was nice to look at and fun to be with. But Mela knew what Decker would say, 'No naked time with your mates!' The thought made her smile.

"Oooh. You're smiling. You like him." She started chanting. "Mela and Owen sitting in a tree…."

"How old are you?" Mela laughed along with Layla.

"Old enough to know that hunka hunka man has the hots for you."

"Oh, stop it." He was flirtatious but it always seemed as though that was simply his personality. She'd known men like that before. They would flirt but it meant nothing. Did she hope that was the case with Owen? She really wasn't sure.

"I have to work with Tracy again. Gods above and below, I want to hex that girl until her face turns into oatmeal."

"Whoa! Those are some strong words," Mela laughed.

"I know. But she's just so darn mean. I can't tell if all the negative energy is really all hers or if there's something else happening."

"Oh, it's all hers. She has always been this way. Since we were in school. She used to get her friends to humiliate me in the lunchroom when we were kids. Everyone would laugh and point. She loved to torment a few of us."

"That's awful."

"She's awful. If she's struggling with something, it's because of something deep and rotten inside. I really don't care."

"Hmm. Okay, if you say so." They rode on in silence and arrived at work right on time. Together, the girls walked in, saying goodbye to one another before heading in different directions.

Mela watched Layla in her black shorts and bright pink top. She'd tied a pink ribbon in her blonde hair and Mela had to admit, she was adorable. The smile never left her face, even when Tracy was right beside her.

The day went as normal as any day. The phone rang, she answered it, she created accounts, she closed accounts. She found comfort in the monotony of her job.

Right after lunch, Mela checked her phone to see if Wyatt had called. The message wasn't from Wyatt but from Shaun, asking her if it was still okay that he bring his mom over this Saturday. After thinking about it, she decided it was the perfect idea. Sandra and Annabelle were both Keys. They craved the time when they would all be together. They should get to know one another.

So, she called him back and left him a message saying that it was a wonderful idea and she was anxious to see them both. She left her address and told him to come as early as they liked. Just as she hung up from that phone call, her cell rang.

"It's done! I'm on my way to get her now!" She heard the pure joy in Wyatt's voice. Mela smiled. No one in the world, as far as she was concerned, deserved the happiness of parenthood more than him. His loving and all-encompassing acceptance of everyone was the perfect recipe for an exceptional father.

"I'm so excited. Are you nervous?"

"No--just ready to get my little princess and take her out of there. I can't believe it went so well. Renee is now and forever on my Christmas card list." They laughed and chatted for a few minutes. She filled him in on the plans for Saturday and he too thought it was a wonderful idea.

"That is, if it's okay with you, Dad." Mela teased.

"It is." She heard the smile in his voice. "I mean, the girl played with ghosts in a mental hospital, I don't think our brand of weird will be too much for her."

By the time Layla and Mela left work, they were giggling like school girls. On the way home, they decided to stop by the grocery store and pick up a small cake for the big day.

While Layla oohed and ahhed over the pink roses and colorful confetti, Mela eyed the chocolate cake behind the glass. It had been forever since she'd indulged in a moist, milk chocolate dessert. She was so wrapped up dreaming about the decadent chocolate, she didn't notice Marcus DeWight standing right behind her. He cleared his throat and she jumped before turning around.

"Mr. DeWight! Sorry, you scared me." She attempted a smile but knew it didn't come across as bright and sincere as Layla's.

"I didn't think anything scared you," he said.

"You'd be surprised. How are you doing? I heard about your...ah...medical problems." There wasn't an easy way to ask a person if their heart was better after almost giving up because he was attacked by evil, Black-Eyed creatures.

"Well, the doctors all say I'm recovering well and should be back to work real soon," he nodded and pressed his lips together as he looked down at the floor. "Mela," he said looking back at her. "Those things...everything that happened that night," he looked around again and stepped closer to her. "I ain't sleeping so good. I can't help but think they're gonna come back."

"Mr. DeWight..."

"Marcus, please. You call me Marcus."

"Alright," Mela nodded. "Marcus, I'm sorry to say they probably will. But," she leaned in close and whispered the rest. "I'll be here too. Don't you worry about anything. If you're having trouble, go talk to Pastor Rod. He knows a lot more now."

Marcus nodded and gave her a teary-eyed smile.

"I sure do appreciate what you did. I feel it's only right that I say thank you. We're all alive because of you, well, almost all of us. Don't you forget it." He gave her a gentle pat on the shoulder and walked away.

"Who was that?" Layla asked, bouncing up to Mela's side.

"His name is Marcus. He was one of the people there the night the church was attacked."

"Oh." She watched the man walk slowly away. "What did he say?"

"He said thank you."

"Oh, Mela, that's wonderful! How sweet of him to take the time to do that." Mela nodded and quickly changed the subject to the cake. They chose a pink and white one and had the nice ladies behind the counter write in purple icing, *'Welcome to the family, Annabelle'* across the top.

When they pulled up to Mela's house, she could see the inside was a beehive of activity. They carried the cake inside and saw that everyone had been extremely busy while they were gone.

The house was covered in streamers of every color, taped haphazardly to random surfaces with no real order at all. Balloons were piled on the floor with Kat sitting like a king among them. There were party hats, colorful horns Mela remembered playing with as a child, and confetti bombs.

"What's all this?" she asked.

"Just hold still!" she heard Owen say. "We're back...hold still, damnit. Back here."

She tracked the sound of Owen's voice, followed by a smiling Layla, to the bathroom. She turned to enter and stopped in her tracks. Decker was sitting on the toilet with Owen standing over him holding one of Mela's good towels.

The makeup on Decker's face made him look like a drunk hooker. Bright shades of blue circled his eyes accented by some sort of decoration in what looked like permanent marker. A perfectly drawn red circle adorned each cheek. His lips were completely caked over with red lipstick. There was even a black dot over his lip that was, apparently, supposed to be a beauty mark.

"What in the world?" she exclaimed, fighting back the laughter that was almost too much to control. Layla stood beside her, hand over her mouth, making noises that sounded suspiciously like giggling.

"I don't even know where to start! It's been a long day." Owen continued to rub the colorful mess from Decker's face but he wasn't having much luck.

"Decker, what did you do?"

"Me? Me? You think I'd do this to myself, do you?" he asked, horrified.

"Who did this to him? How?" Mela couldn't fight it anymore and she doubled over with laughter. Layla was right behind her doing the same thing.

"Having fun, are you?" Decker's sour expression helped her gain a little control.

"Oh Decker," she entered the bathroom and checked the towel Owen was using. "This won't come off with water...here." She reached under the cabinet and found an old jar of Vaseline. Reaching into the jar, she scooped out a liberal amount and smeared it all over his face.

"Well, while you two were gone, I thought it'd be a good idea to decorate for the big day," Owen said. "This one here--" he handed the towel to Mela to start wiping the mess from Decker's face--"decided it was a good idea to get tanked. Dude drank almost a whole bottle of whiskey."

"I can hold my drink just fine," Decker snapped.

"Go on." Mela said, wiping tears from her eyes.

"Well, I can't believe he did it..." Owen sat on the edge of the tub and started laughing.

"I'm gonna get him back, I swear to that."

"Who?" Layla asked.

"Sammuele." Owen doubled over laughing and Mela lost it again. Eventually, the whole story came out, although with difficulty.

After consuming too much whiskey, Decker passed out on his chair on the back porch. Apparently, after some prodding from Vasha, Sammuele decided he would pull a prank he learned from Annabelle on Decker. He confessed to Owen that he and Annabelle would make a regular habit of sneaking into other patients' rooms and playing this particular prank on them.

A half an hour later, very little of the makeup remained on Decker's face. The permanent marker, however, was going to be there for a while. Mela and Owen cleaned up the bathroom while Layla took Decker for a walk to cool off.

"Have you heard from Wyatt yet?" he asked.

"Not yet. I hope he's on his way."

"Well, I have something I'd like to talk to you about." Mela looked at Owen and noticed he looked different. Nervous.

"Okay. What's going on?"

"Let's go outside and find Vasha first." He grabbed her hand and pulled her from the bathroom. They stepped outside to find Theo, Bear, and Vasha on the patio, which was decorated in the same manner as the house. Mela guessed drunk Decker hung all of the streamers.

"Oh good, you're here," Vasha said

"I heard I missed quite the afternoon," she said, giggling. "Where's Sammuele?"

"It was delicious revenge for him. I truly do not know if he meant it to be so, but it was. I do like this new and improved Sammuele. Unpredictable." Vasha said with a smile as he fondled a pair of balloons.

"It was very humorous." Theo said quietly. He took a few steps into the night and took flight.

"Our prankster is with Annabelle and Wyatt," Vasha answered.

"What did you need to talk to me about?" she asked Owen.

"Well, I know you've been stressed lately," he said sitting down across from her in a chair. "I also know how much of a burden we all are to you."

"No, you're okay…"

"My dear one, please do not lie to us. I was unaware of the financial strain we were putting on you until Owen here came and enlightened us." Mela turned to Owen then back to Vasha.

"Look, we all want to be here, together. But we can't put all the burden on you." He leaned forward, elbows on his knees, and forced her to look him in the eye.

"Are you leaving?" she asked. She was surprised how much the thought of any of them leaving hurt her deeply.

"No." He flashed his incredibly white teeth. "But we did fix the money problem."

"How?"

"That's where I come in, sweet one. As you know, I have many things worth more money than one lifetime could spend."

"No…you didn't." Mela was horrified. Vasha held up his hand and Owen reached out to hold her hands between his.

"Vasha donated a few things and Decker and I went and pawned them. Got a great price too. We have plenty of money to donate to the family pot." He held her hand firmly and she felt his thumb lightly rub the top of it.

"I don't know what to say. I wish you didn't have to sell your things, Vasha," she said , looking at him sadly. "But thank you."

"Think nothing of it. I have much and more where that came from. A mere drop in a large bucket."

"One less worry." Owen said, looking at her steadily. She nodded, more thankful than she was willing to admit aloud.

"They have arrived," Theo swept from the sky and landed lightly on the grass. "They will be here in moments."

"You are positively breathless, Brother. I have not seen you so excited since you found that kitten when we were little. Do you remember it?" Vasha asked as he pulled his massive form from the floor and stood.

"I do. I loved that kitten."

"Hey, maybe you could get another one," Owen offered, winking at Mela. "What's one more these days, right Mela?"

"We will await the honored guest here. Bring her when you think she is ready." Vasha said imperiously.

"I hope we do not frighten her. I do love children so." Theo fretted.

Mela and Owen went inside to find Layla and Decker having a quiet conversation.

"Theo said they were almost here. What's up?" Mela asked. She immediately got the feeling they walked in on something private.

"Oh good, I can't wait," Layla said quickly and hopped up.

"I'll just go out with the others," Decker said and he too jumped up to leave.

"You don't have to," Mela said.

"Aye, I do. I'll be with my brothers."

The headlights of Wyatt's car illuminated the front window and Layla squealed with glee. Grabbing Mela's arm, she jumped up and down like a child on Christmas. Mela was nervous and excited as well. She didn't feel free enough to squeal and jump as Layla did but she sure envied the girl's ability to do so. Owen stood back, as he always did, and took everything in in silence.

They heard Wyatt talking on the other side of the door before he opened it with the biggest smile Mela had ever seen on his face. Following behind him was his little princess Annabelle. She wore the white dress with blue bouquets on it she remembered hanging for her in the sad hospital room that was once her home. Now, she wore the beautiful dress with a shy smile.

Wyatt held her hand and guided her into the house. Bear sniffed her excitedly, making her giggle. Annabelle stared at the new people, then up at Wyatt. He graced her with a loving smile and gently smoothed her hair.

"Sweetheart, you remember Mela?" Annabelle nodded silently. "That guy over there is Owen. And that very pretty blonde girl, her name is Layla. They all live here at Mela's house." Annabelle eyed everyone carefully.

"Oh, I'm just tickled pink you're here, Annabelle. We're going to have so much fun." Layla rushed over to her and wrapped her in a warm hug. Annabelle looked to Wyatt who continued to smile until Layla released her grip. "You're just so pretty. I love your dress. I had one like it when I was little," Layla gushed.

"Let her breathe, Layla." Owen said from across the room.

"Come on, munchkin. Do you want to have a look around Mela's house?" Wyatt asked. Annabelle stood still, getting the feel of the place.

"This house is very old. Spirits are here…shadowy …but I can feel them." Annabelle said to a silent room.

"This was my grandparents' house," Mela said in answer to her unasked question. Annabelle nodded as if that explained a lot to her.

"Are they here?" she asked Wyatt.

"Who? Her grandparents?" he asked. She shook her head.

"No. The ones you told me about. The three brothers who look like monsters but aren't really monsters. I want to see what a nice monster looks like," she insisted. Wyatt looked to Mela and she shrugged. He was right, she thought. If the little girl spent most of her time with the dead in a mental hospital, the three amigos on the back porch were a cakewalk.

They headed for the back porch, single file, with Mela in the lead. She walked out to the waiting brothers and stood between Vasha and Theo. Layla stood beside Decker with Owen on the other side. Mela looked and saw Sammuele standing off to the side, eyeing a grumpy looking Decker. She waved him closer and he hesitantly stood beside Theo. Wyatt and Annabelle stood together facing the small crowd.

"Annabelle, this is Theo," Mela said pointing to him on her left. Theo stepped forward and crouched down like he did when he perched in high places. His black, leathery wings trailed the ground behind him and he did his best to look as nonthreatening as possible. Annabelle stepped forward, releasing her grip on Wyatt. Her small hand reached out and gently touched Theo's head.

"Hello, Theo. You're very soft," she said. He looked into her eyes and the little girl smiled.

"Hello, Annabelle. I should like to be your friend."

"Okay." Her soft voice carried in the silent night. Theo turned to Mela with a happy expression.

"Annabelle, this is Vasha." Mela said, urging him from her side. He towered over her as he approached. She looked up at him with wonder and little bit of fear. Gracefully, he folded himself into what Mela called his cat pose. His legs were tucked neatly under his body and his hands folded calmly in front.

"Greetings, little one. I have heard much of the Princess Annabelle, as Wyatt calls you. We are pleased you have come to be part of our family," he said kindly.

"You're very pretty. But you don't have any fur." She looked slightly disappointed by that and everyone tried not to laugh.

"And over there is Decker." Mela said pointing to him. Layla said something in his ear and he grudgingly took a step forward. Slowly, they approached one another and Annabelle eyed him suspiciously.

"You're not a monster at all. I thought you'd look like them," she said, pointing at Theo and Vasha. "But you look really normal."

"That's the nicest thing anyone has ever said upon meeting me. I thank you kindly." He took off his hat and bowed low. He stood and went back to stand beside Layla.

"Well, who wants cake?" Mela asked. A chorus of voices replied that they did and Layla went inside to retrieve the treats. Owen pulled out colorful plates and napkins and started handing them out.

Wyatt couldn't stop smiling. Neither could Mela.

Chapter Twenty

There were no workouts scheduled for Saturday morning. There was a lot of preparing to do to get ready for yet another party. Shaun was bringing Sandra and another friend to spend time with them today and Wyatt would be bringing Annabelle back after they spent a quiet morning together at home.

As Mela and Layla drained their coffee cups, Owen was cutting the grass in the front yard. She couldn't keep her eyes from straying out of the window every time he passed. He wore a pair of brown shorts with holes in them. Somehow, men could get away with such a thing and still look good. The part that kept getting her attention was the fact that he wasn't wearing a shirt. Regardless of the cool fall air, his caramel skin was soaking up the morning sunlight creating a glossy sheen all over his muscular torso. She liked the colorful tattoos on his back, and how they snaked down his arm.

After Mela's turn in the shower, she heard Owen coming to do the same so she quickly shut her bedroom door. Taking her time, she pulled out all of the clothes she thought would be appropriate for this afternoon gathering. Nothing seemed to look or feel right. She was happy to note that her jeans were a little loser and her arms looked fantastic in the strapless shirt. But nothing felt comfortable when she put it on.

Until her eyes found her black Witch cloak. Pulling it from under the pile of clothes on the floor, she ran the soft, water-like material through her fingers. She had no idea what it was made of, but whatever it was, Vasha had amazing skill. The little red rubies dotted the hem of the cloak made it feel heavy in her hands.

She rummaged around until she found the top and pants. Sliding the cool cloth over her skin, she felt good – comfortable. It took some finagling to get the top right, but she managed to tie it shut. Standing in front of her mirror, Mela finally felt the outside matched what was inside. She felt beautiful. She felt powerful. She felt like herself.

Deciding to go all the way, Mela pulled out the lovely beaded feet jewelry Vasha made for her birthday and put them on after fighting with the tiny strings. She brushed her hair straight and let it hang past her shoulders wild and free. After applying a touch of mascara, her reflection told her she was done. Grabbing her cloak and tossing it over her arm, she left the only room in the house that afforded her any privacy these days.

Everyone was outside, so she went to join them. When she did, everyone turned to look at her.

"You are a vision, my little Witch," Vasha purred.

"Mela! Oh my goodness, you look fabulous. I couldn't pull off an outfit like that but you look great. Wow." Layla came over to inspect her getup and Mela informed her Vasha made the whole thing for her. Vasha and Layla quickly got lost in a conversation about making her something similar to Mela's. Except that she wanted it in blue.

"You do look good," Owen said behind her. Turning around quickly, she came face to face with his muscular chest. He looked down at her with a smile and wiggled his eyebrows up and down. "Or should I say, *we* look good?" Mela was having such a hard time tearing her eyes away from his flirtatious smile that she almost missed the obvious.

He held his arms out to his side and backed up a step. He wore pants exactly the same as hers except they were gray. The belt he wore was studded with jewels of every color with a gold buckle that nestled neatly against his darker skin. Fighting to bring her eyes back up to meet his, she saw he also wore a cloak – but no shirt. Owen looked delicious. From the trees, Teagan let out a mighty *caww* in appreciation.

"No fair!" Layla cried in mock irritation to Vasha who assured her she was next in line.

"Yeah, yeah, everybody looks good. Where's the wine?" Decker asked, elbowing his way through everyone and looking quite a bit better himself after a shower of his own.

"What, no whiskey today?" Mela teased.

"Nope. Gotta pace myself, see." They laughed but Theo interrupted them with the announcement that someone new was arriving. While Decker handed out the wine, even though it was barely lunchtime, Mela went inside. Owen was on her heels as they looked to see who had come.

"It's Wyatt and Annabelle." Mela said with a quick glance. She turned to face Owen and caught him staring at her with the oddest expression. When he realized she was watching him, he flashed a smile. Wyatt came in then with Annabelle in tow. Both of them looked as though they stepped from the pages of a catalog. Wyatt looked as fresh and dapper as ever. He even smelled amazing. Annabelle followed him in in a pink dress that had purple trim and a white lace flower on her belt.

"Annabelle, you look gorgeous," Mela told her. Annabelle smiled and looked around the room before turning to Wyatt.

"Can I go?" she asked him.

"Sure, munchkin. Go ahead," With a small wave, Annabelle made a beeline for the back door. "It's Theo. Can't stop talking about him and couldn't wait to get here to play with him. She even said she missed Sammuele too."

"Well, Sammuele was the one with her day after day when she was… at the hospital."

"Look at you..." he took her hands and held them out, looking her over. "Meow," he said with a wink. "Oh, look, Owen has new clothes too." He dropped her hands and went to inspect Owen in all his half-dressed glory. Ridiculously, Owen started striking poses, flexing his arms and wiggling his eyebrows for Wyatt who clapped his hands like a cheerleader.

"Someone else is here," Layla said, coming in and eyeballing Owen who continued to delight Wyatt with his physique. The girls shared a secret smile, then watched a long blue car pull into the driveway. It reminded Mela of a car her grandparents had when she was growing up. It was just a really big car, especially sitting next to Wyatt's sports car.

"Is that... Who is that?" Layla asked. Mela saw Shaun and another man get out of the front seats of the car. She forgot how handsome he was, with his ebony skin and long braids swinging. He could have been a poster boy for African royalty.

"That's Shaun there, with the long hair," Mela said, pointing through the window. "That's his friend with a car. I don't know him. Oh look," she said, pointing again. "There's Sandra." Sandra Jones was helped from the backseat by her loving and protective son. Mela remembered the first time they met--she was new to everything supernatural then. She showed up at their house with hope for Sandra and Shaun met her with suspicion. He was terrified she was with the State, come to take his beloved mother away. No matter how difficult, or strange Sandra Jones was, her son refused to leave her.

"He's good looking." Layla said.

"Who is?" Wyatt interrupted and pushed his way to the window and oogled the men as they looked around Mela's front yard. Mela only had eyes for Sandra. Her first successful connection to the supernatural world, Mela had a genuine fondness for the confused woman. Her hair was properly tended and the faded dress she wore looked as though it had seen better days. But she wore the biggest smile as her son escorted her to the door. Mela opened the door for them with a smile.

"Look, Shaun….she's on fire. It's so pretty….she's just so pretty…" Sandra stepped inside and hugged Mela tightly. "It's been so long….such a pretty girl…" her eyes found Layla and she covered her mouth with her hand. "Oh Lord…just like the waves of the ocean rolling off you…it's so nice and peaceful. Look, Shaun. Look at how nice she looks." Layla smiled and hugged Sandra tightly. Mela turned to Shaun and his friend and told them to come inside.

"Hi Shaun," she said. Mela wasn't the hugging type. She guessed he wasn't really either.

"You got a nice house. This is my boy, Ronnie," He inclined his head to his friend. Ronnie had no hair and the most gorgeous long eyelashes she'd ever seen. "Ronnie, this here is Mela. The one I told you about." He nodded to her in greeting.

"Nice to meet you. Please," she said showing them the way. "Come on outside. That's where everyone is." She turned to lead them but stopped in her tracks. Turning back to Shaun she gave him a questioning look. *Did you prepare your friend?*

"Well, I can't wait. Is the angel here? Sammuele? You know he and me spend lots of time together. Just chattin' and laughing. But mostly we sing…." Sandra happily sang her way with Layla on her arm out of the backdoor.

"What's the hold up?" Wyatt asked as he followed the ladies out. Owen stayed behind with Mela, back to his quiet ways.

"Is everything okay?" she asked Shaun, darting her eyes at his friend, then looking back at his with a pointed expression.

"Yeah. I told him he'd see some crazy shit here. What do you expect when you go to visit a white girl?" He laughed and elbowed her. "I'm just playing. Yeah, we cool, right, Ronnie?"

"Yeah." He said. Mela tried feeling his energy. It didn't take long to feel his fear. He was afraid of her.

"Don't worry, Ronnie. No matter what you see, everyone here is your friend. Come on," she grabbed Shaun's elbow and tugged him to the door. "The little girl I told you about? She's here." Mela explained the rest as they walked outside.

"Where'd Momma go?" Shaun asked as they stepped outside. She watched the shock on his face when he saw his mother hugging Sammuele. "That's him, right? That angel?" Mela nodded. Ronnie and Shaun whispered together for a minute while Mela watched Sammuele cradle Sandra against him. With her eyes closed, she wore a smile that broke Mela's heart. This was something she should have done long before now. Seeing the joy in Sandra made her feel guilty for not making time for this sooner.

Theo approached with Annabelle's hand clasped firmly in his. She skipped along at his side as though she was having the time of her life. Mela suspected that she was. Wyatt tried to get her to eat something but she refused once she saw Sandra.

While everyone watched, Sandra opened her eyes and focused on the pretty little girl in the pink dress. Sammuele whispered something to her and she nodded.

"I know who you is. Do you know who I am, little girl?" Sandra asked Annabelle. Annabelle nodded her head and smiled.

"Only a part...we're halfway there now..." Annabelle's voice, so full of innocence, spoke to the part of Sandra that lived alone in the shadows. The woman nodded, dropped down to her knees, and opened her arms to the only soul she'd ever known who spoke the language she understood.

Annabelle ran to her new friend and hugged her tightly around the neck. Sandra softly ran her hand over and over again through Annabelle's hair, rocking her gently like a baby.

"Well, this ain't weird at all," Decker broke in and started pouring wine. He'd obviously had some already, but he poured more into wine glasses and passed them out. Mela noted that he handed one to Sammuele, who took it with thanks. That was an improvement.

Decker made great attempts to get the two newcomers to start talking by plying them with wine and dirty jokes that had them laughing boisterously. Vasha was still nowhere to be found but she suspected he would make an appearance when he was ready. Wyatt was introducing himself to Sandra and the three of them went to visit with Sammuele. Mela crossed her arms and surveyed the people in her life. So much to be thankful for and so much to protect.

"Great party," Owen said, sneaking up behind her.

"There you are. Where'd you go?" she asked. He shrugged and took a sip of wine as Teagan flew down to perch on the railing to beg for food.

* * *

Lunch was a chaotic affair. Everywhere, there were hands grabbing sandwiches, plates, wine, people laughing, talking, even singing. Mela's house was too small for too many people to fit in comfortably, so everyone stayed outside, sitting in chairs, or simply standing around.

"A word?" Sammuele came to Mela, wine in hand, looking far too serious for such an occasion.

"What did Decker do?" she asked.

"He has done nothing...yet. I shall keep vigil constantly for his revenge. However, that is not what I need to discuss with you."

"What's wrong ?" Of course, Mela thought, it was too good to be true. It was a quiet happy time after all. Something had to go wrong.

"I am concerned with the presence of two Keys in the same location. After the attack at the hospital..."

"Relax, feather-brain. There ain't a safer place to be than right here." Decker interrupted.

"I disagree."

"I disagree," Decker imitated Sammuele's logical, no-nonsense tone.

"Mocking me is not necessary..."

"Mocking me is not necessary..."

"Stop it," Mela warned. "I think he's right though. This is better than any of us being alone. Besides, it's only for one afternoon. Relax and try to have a little fun, Sammuele."

Wyatt, Annabelle, and Theo sat on the edge of the porch with Bear at their feet, begging for scraps. Layla sat beside Sandra, talking quietly while Sammuele prowled, watchful.

"Where are the boys?" Mela asked, looking around.

"Try Vasha's place. I saw Decker head that way a minute ago," Wyatt said over his shoulder.

She slipped from the patio headed for the shed to find the boys. With each step, her toes sank into the cool, moist grass. It was a pleasant feeling, one that she didn't indulge in enough. When she reached the shed door, she heard a voice speaking, then rowdy laughter. She pushed on the door to find Vasha, Shaun, Ronnie, Decker, and Owen sitting around the smoke-filled room laughing hysterically.

"Come…Come in, little one. I do apologize for not making my introductions. I was otherwise preoccupied." Vasha said, wiping tears of laughter from his eyes.

"Do I want to know what's going on?" she asked.

"Probably not," Owen said, still laughing.

"Everyone doing okay?" she asked, raising her eyebrows to Shaun.

"Oh yeah…" Shaun said, reaching for the metal pipe attached to Vasha's hookah.

"Man, you weren't playing when you said there was some crazy shit happening here. Damn," Ronnie said, shaking his head and taking the pipe from Shaun.

"Glad to see you're all getting along so well. I'm going to go back. I don't want to interrupt," Mela said, turning to leave the boys to their fun.

"Mom's doing okay? I can come back and sit with her," Shaun made to get up but she shooed him away.

"No, she's just fine. You have fun and we'll keep her busy. She's having a good time." Shaun's face looked softer. Perhaps it was the dim lighting in the shed, or whatever he was smoking, but his demeanor took on a much less aggressive look.

When she made her way back to the house, Sammuele was sitting with Layla and Sandra, deep in conversation. Annabelle sat in the grass flanked by Theo and Bear far away from the house. She looked for Wyatt but didn't see him anywhere. Assuming he was inside, she sat on the porch steps for a moment of quiet.

That was when they started to scream.

Mela and Layla jumped to their feet and watched both Annabelle and Sandra throw their heads back and scream. Panicked, Layla tried to comfort Sandra but Mela looked back and forth between the two Keys and knew in her soul that she had been wrong – Sammuele had been right all along.

"Ms. Sandra…calm down…it's okay…" Layla tried to sooth the woman as her body went rigid. The screams wouldn't stop. Wyatt came rushing from inside the house, sleeves rolled up from doing dishes, terror in his eyes.

"Mela!" Sammuele cried, pointing. She turned to see, her heart pounding. A horde of The Soulless were closing on Theo, Bear, and Annabelle.

"Get her inside!" Mela screamed to Sammuele and Layla. As she ran from the porch, she knew she wouldn't get to the three in the yard in time before the creatures were on them. There were so many, too many to fight. The Soulless seemed to come from everywhere, and they were moving too fast. Theo stood over Annabelle, who no longer screamed, but cowered on the ground beside him. His wings popped up and she heard his deep roar as he bared his teeth.

Mela ran as fast as she could, but felt herself slow with the realization that she didn't have a sword. She let out an involuntary howl of "*Nooo*" as the horde closed in on the three she loved, knowing they would soon be overwhelmed. Bear barked frantically, turning this way and that, snapping his teeth at the creatures as they reached for them. Theo's massive hands grabbed the nearest creature and brought it to his mouth. His feline teeth sank into the gray flesh and he twisted his head back and forth until the creature went limp in his hands. Black blood sprayed them all and, with another roar, he threw the dead body into the encroaching horde.

From behind her, Mela heard someone coming. Their footsteps pounded the earth quicker than she was running. Looked over her shoulder, she saw Vasha and Decker closing in fast. Owen ran with them but was a bit further behind. As Decker passed her, he tossed a sword her way. With her right hand, she caught the hilt and instantly felt herself. Now she was ready.

From somewhere far behind her in the direction of the house, Mela thought she heard Wyatt's scream something. But she had to keep going, she had to trust that Sammuele and Layla could manage things there without her.

The first few creatures she killed swiftly without a second thought. She simply sliced through them and kept on. From the center of the host, she saw Theo throwing Black-Eyed creatures like little toys into the air. She heard Bear barking savagely but she couldn't see him anymore. She swung her sword at anything that came her way, yelling as she did. Some she made contact with, others jumped out of her way.

"Go right!" Decker yelled at her, pointing as he did. She nodded and cut through where the creatures were thickest. One jumped on her back and brought her down to her knees. It clung to her with a strength she never imagined it could have. She struggled with it for a moment before a thought sparked in her mind.

She closed her eyes and exhaled deeply. Moments later, her entire body was engulfed with flames. She held out her arms and heard the creature shrieking as it burned. It fell to the ground with a thud, still ablaze, but she got up to continue on. She was closer to Theo now and, she hoped, Bear and Annabelle as well.

However, the creatures had crowded around them so tightly that, every time she cut one down, another two took its place. She could open up the ground to swallow them all if she knew where Annabelle and Bear were. If she did that, would she kill the little girl and her familiar? No, she couldn't risk it. She kept fighting.

"I'm here," Owen said breathlessly. She turned to see him standing by her side, eyes burning a light shade of gray, like flames in a black and white photograph. She knew her eyes burned with orange fire, she felt the rage and, for the first time, let it come completely unchained.

Tucking her sword safely in her waistband, she called the fire to her once again and let it pour from her hands onto the ground in front of her. She burned everything that moved. What she didn't burn, Owen caught with a jet of wind so incredibly fast, it twisted their frail bodies into something unrecognizable.

With every step, she killed an enemy. She and Owen moved closer to the center of the host until she saw Theo grappling with two creatures in an attempt to keep them from Annabelle, who was on the ground with her hands over her head. He ripped the arm from one and a chunk of flesh from another before they fell back and were replaced by two others. From the other side, Vasha and Decker were making their way to the center, slashing and ripping The Soulless to pieces as they went.

In all the chaos, Mela found Bear. He had a creature by the throat, and ran toward her with it as if it were a trophy. His eyes were locked onto hers as he ran with the dying creature. It flailed about weakly, but its insides trailed behind it like black, wet streamers.

When Bear reached her, he dropped the thing from his mouth. He leaned against her leg, letting out a small whine of worry for his friends still in the center of the fight. But he bravely stepped forward by her side as she closed in on the last line of creatures that surrounded Annabelle and Theo. First one, then two, then three…all fell to the sword in her hands. It wasn't really her sword, but one of Decker's. It was heavier than her own, but she liked it because it sank so easily into the creature's flesh.

Finally, she stood over Annabelle and said Theo's name.

Without looking away from the creatures that were facing off with him, he spoke. "Take the girl to safety."

"I'm not leaving you." She stood over Annabelle, Bear by her side, and looked for Owen.

He was standing further back, having a great time twisting the creatures on a whim into the most absurd shapes in the air before letting their bodies fall, broken, to the ground. Decker was telling him something but she couldn't hear it from where she was standing.

By now, they had significantly culled the horde of creatures to a more manageable size. She could see through them, at least, and that was an improvement. To keep them at bay from behind her, Mela opened up a deep cavern in the ground to protect their rear. It was enough to keep the attacks from coming from all sides, and for that, she and Theo were thankful. She concentrated on the creatures approaching from the right and Theo lashed out at anything that came too close from all directions.

Whether they saw what she did and made a plan, or it simply worked out that way, she wasn't sure. But when Owen came from the right and Decker from the left, she knew they would survive. Vasha was running, constantly running, catching whatever he could and ripping them apart as he went. Bear, seeing Vasha run, backed up and started doing the same on the right side. Mela waited for him to herd the creatures close and she dropped them all with fire and her sword.

From behind them, a sound so loud she thought it was gunfire, made her duck down. When she looked, she saw Layla coming fast, her eyes burning bright as sapphires. Mela saw her raise her hand and bring it down in a whipping motion. From her hand, a bolt of lightning tore through the air and hit the nearest creature. It split as though it was chopped straight down the middle.

"Oy, heads up!" Decker yelled as he leaped into the air and landed beside Theo. He slipped a bit when he landed and needed to hold onto Mela to stand upright again. He was sweaty, dirty, covered in black blood, but grinning from ear to ear. "Turned out to be quite a party."

He let out a hoot of laughter and jumped back into the fray, slashing as he went.

"Give me Annabelle. You go help," Layla said Mela nodded and helped get Annabelle to her feet. "Just close your eyes, honey. Close your eyes and hold my hand while we run," Layla said and took off back to the house with the terrified little girl in tow.

Mela watched them for as long as she dared. When she felt they were at a safe enough distance, she turned her attention back to the fight. Knowing Annabelle was safer away from the fight, no one held back any longer. Theo lunged at the creatures near him, and let out a breathtaking roar. The spindly creatures tried to fight back but were soon ripped from where they stood and broken at the hands of the most gentle soul she'd ever known.

Owen came to stand beside her with Bear pacing behind them, watching the fight. Even Teagan got in on the action by flying at The Soulless and picking at their eyes. Vasha was to Theo's left, four blades out and at the ready. The emerald studded blades had obviously been used because they dripped with black blood. Decker stalked the creatures from behind before letting out a whistle that was, apparently, a signal of some sort.

"My darling Little Witch. You stay here. We shall coral them together. Keep their attention focused on you." He ran to the left and Owen bolted to the right. Theo bent his knees and took off to the sky, leaving Mela and Bear standing alone.

They faced more than twenty creatures. The Soulless tripped over bodies of their fallen comrades as they searched for their next victim. Bear stayed at her side, growling his warning to the crowd of creatures before him. She took a deep breath, exhaled, and then let the flames take over her body once more.

She was a human torch that never stopped burning. She felt the warm tickle of the flames dance across her flesh but there was no pain. Every bottomless black eye turned to her as she took a step toward them. They hissed and growled but stepped away from her as they did. From above, Theo swept down and snatched two creatures from the middle of the group. Moments later, their lifeless bodies fell to the ground with a wet noise.

"Now!" Decker yelled. All three charged the dense circle of creatures from all sides. Mela, only after seeing them charge, moved forward, sword in hand, to take care of those who were trying to get away. She cut through them easily, only suffering scratches on her arms as they fought for their lives. Bear snapped and pulled the feet from under the nearest creature, then pounced on it with a snarl. His strong jaws clamped down in the thin neck and he swung his head from side to side until Mela heard a *snap* when its neck broke.

The next thing she knew, there were no more creatures left standing. Putting out the flames, she looked around and saw everyone covered in black blood. But they were alive.

"Oy, you little shit, why won't you die?" Decker called out irritably as he struggled with his sword. Everyone watched while he tried to pull his sword from the body of a squirming Black-Eyed Creature. He'd brought it down with such force, the blade was lodged deep in the ground. The creature lay on the ground, impaled by Decker's sword, but still very much alive. "Son of a bitch…hold still, you little shit…"

"Let me, brother," Vasha said, approaching them.

"No, no…this one's mine…" Too late. Vasha brought the curved blade of one of the Emerald Studded swords down into the skull of the last living creature that day. "You're a right prat, you know that? I called it…that there was mine to kill. You don't go around stealing a man's kill…"

"My apologies, Dektrios. But I grew tired of watching you struggle with your sword." Vasha winked and turned away, only to get hit in the back with the dismembered leg of one of the creatures.

"You deserved that." Decker said pointing at Vasha, then yanked once more on his sword before finally releasing it.

"That was amazing." Owen said breathlessly.

Mela turned to him. "If you think that was..."

He cut her off by grabbing her around the waist and pulling her into a kiss. He smelled of sweat and tasted like wine but his kiss was slow and deep. He let her go before she had the opportunity to protest.

"Figured now was as good a time as any," he said with a shrug and turned to walk away. Stunned, Mela stood still and watched him walk around, looking at the dead bodies that littered the yard.

"I don't know about you," Vasha purred in her ear. "But after a fight there is nothing I want to do more than partake in the pleasures of life."

Feeling the blush creeping up into her cheeks, Mela went to the house with Bear at her side sniffing all of the fallen. On the porch, Sammuele stood in front of Sandra, Shaun, Ronnie, Wyatt, Annabelle, and Layla.

"Is everyone okay?" Layla's shaky voice called out. Decker walked quickly to the porch and flashed a toothy smile.

"Never better." Layla smiled at him, tears of relief in her eyes.

"What in the hell?" Shaun asked over and over, surveying the carnage.

"Aye. We sent them to hell, that's for sure. I'm hungry." Decker hopped onto the porch, looking for something to eat.

"Are they gone?" Annabelle asked Mela.

"Yes. All gone." She looked up at Wyatt to see his tear-stained face. "I'm sorry, I didn't know they would come."

"It's not your fault," Owen said from behind her.

"No…that's how evil works, child," Sandra said. "They come when you happy and suck it right away. It's their way…their dark evil ways but they got those big black eyes…like mirrors into the pits of hell…"

"They'll be back for us. More are coming," Annabelle announced.

"Not today," Decker said as he plopped into his chair and took a hefty swig of wine.

"I do not see any more nearby." Theo said as he swooped down onto the porch. Annabelle yanked away from Wyatt and ran to Theo. Her little arms couldn't reach his waist, so she satisfied herself with wrapping her arms around his leg and held him tightly.

"You saved me, Theo. You saved me from the monsters," she said softly. He reached down and gently patted her head.

"I would never let any harm come to you," he promised her.

"Damn right. We'll just kill 'em all." Decker laughed at himself.

"You cannot defeat us." A voice behind them said. Everyone turned to see an intruder. The being that stood in Mela's backyard was unlike The Soulless. It stood taller than the bug like creatures and wore robes of shimmering red. Its skin was gray but appeared like that of a reptile. Its body was much more defined and humanoid in shape. The face made Mela's insides go cold. There were four horns growing from its head, two pointed up, and two pointed down its back. The eyes were white lights that glowed even in the afternoon sun. It spoke to them again as it stepped closer. "You will all die…" Its raspy voice crept into the hearts of each one there and they felt the dread in each word.

Furious with her fear and for the unwelcome visitor's appearance, Mela hurled a ball of flame toward it. It laughed as the fire went straight through it, only to hit one of the dead bodies on the ground.

"What is it?" Layla asked anyone who could answer.

"We are legion, Mage. We are conquerors. We have come with our children to put an end to you," it rasped.

"A child of Asag," Sammuele whispered.

"How do we kill it?" Mela asked.

The creature laughed again. "Your pitiful magick cannot kill us. Nothing from this world can kill us. We will kill you instead…in time." The Child of Asag vanished, leaving everyone staring at its absence.

"That's not good," Owen said.

"Sure ain't," Decker agreed.

"We have a lot of work to do before that thing comes back," Layla said as steadily as she could manage.

"I think Sandra should go home now," Sammuele said, pointedly looking at Mela.

"I agree." Mela turned to Shaun who was still staring at the carnage in her backyard. "Can you guys get home okay? I'd rather you were safe at home. I'm sorry I put you in so much danger." Feeling the familiar grasp of guilt twist her insides, she waited for a response from Shaun.

"Nah, ain't your fault. If they woulda come to my house…Hell, I don't think I could do what you did," Shaun said weakly.

"Sure you could, mate. A little training, you could fight with the best of 'em," Decker said over his shoulder. Shaun eyed Decker for a moment and turned to escort his mother away.

"Goodbye, little girl…I'll see you soon, real soon." Sandra waved to Annabelle, who waved sadly back. Ronnie, Shaun, and Sandra left without another word.

"I should be with them. Just in case," Sammuele said and he disappeared as well.

Mela sat on the porch and Bear came to nuzzle her hand. She scratched behind his ears and he sank to the floor, rolling over for a belly rub. Theo and Vasha were already piling the dead bodies as Owen started a large burn pile in which to expedite the cleanup. Layla sat beside Decker. Both were surprisingly quiet as they watched the cleanup.

The fight that was coming was bigger, and more dangerous, than she previously could have imagined. But they survived today. For that she was thankful. As Bear wagged his tail and licked her hand, she smiled. No sense in worrying about the inevitable. What was coming was ancient and deadly. Looking at Layla and Owen, Mela realized they were from a line of something just as ancient and just as deadly. Evil had been beaten once. It could be again – as long as they stayed together.

Epilogue

Halloween night was a rowdy affair at Mela's house. She'd never celebrated the holiday as a Witch but it was the most amazing time for her kind, Layla told her. The Veil between the living and the dead was thin and, as legend told it, the dead walk about on All Hallows Eve.

Of course, there was a party at Mela's house. While Wyatt and Annabelle decorated the back porch with pumpkins and plastic skeletons, Vasha was inspecting the wine goblets Wyatt brought for the occasion. They were goblets that looked like a human skull, made of heavy wood and painted to look incredibly lifelike.

"Come on, it's dark and we've got to hurry," Layla called to Mela and Owen. Together the three Witches moved from the back porch into the darkness of the night. "Now, Mela," Layla asked, "Do you remember why we're doing this? Tell me so I know you remember."

"We're leaving offerings to our ancestors and to the Gods for…for…"

"For a blessing. And," she continued with a smile, "because the Gods like to get special attention. It's their way, after all. Like my Lady, the glorious Goddess Athena. She likes to be given beautiful things. So, I'm leaving her flowers and lots of little sparkly trinkets."

"What did you bring, Owen?" Mela turned to ask him. He gave her a half smile and a shrug as he held up a plastic bag weighted down with whatever was inside.

"The Lady Morrigan, she prefers flesh." He swung the bag as he walked on.

"Mela, what did you bring for Lady Hecate?" Layla asked.

"Wine and honey. Bitter and sweet, just like her." They laughed as they continued on until they were on the far edges of the property.

Layla instructed them on leaving their offerings for the Gods in a pleasing way. Owen rolled his eyes as she chattered about arranging the flowers and small treats for Lady Athena. Mela cleared a small circle of dead leaves and pine needles. She pulled out a small wooden bowl and poured wine inside. She arranged the honey in another bowl but thought something was missing. Looking around, she plucked a small bunch of flowers and arranged them around the offerings, all the while giving thanks to Hecate for her new life.

Finished, they turned to Owen who still stood with his plastic bag of flesh. He stepped forward and dumped the bloody carcass on the ground. Blood and chunks of whatever it was slopped to the earth. He shook the bag free of what remained and turned back to them.

"What?" he asked when they continued to stare.

"That's it? Dump a dead…whatever on the ground?" Layla asked, scandalized by his meager offering.

"Hey, you appease your Goddess of love and beauty however you need. I'll appease the Lady Morrigan the way I need. Trust me," he said, looking back at the pile of blood and flesh. "This is what she wants."

Only partly satisfied, Layla turned to go. Mela and Owen shared a smile behind her back. Layla was who she was, regardless of how different she was from them. They'd all grown accustomed to her cheerful ways. Even Decker, Mela thought as they made their way back to the porch. He seemed happier, less sour, now that she was here. That was an incredible development.

"Oh good, you're back. Come here," Decker said as giddy as they'd ever seen him. He ushered them to the porch with barely contained excitement. "Stand right there…yep, right there. Now…come on, feather-brain. You promised."

Everyone looked around for Sammuele but he was nowhere to be seen.

"I don't think Sammuele likes the costume you picked out for him." Annabelle chided Decker with the air of a grown-up.

"I like your costume, Annabelle." Mela smiled at her. The little girl was a true princess tonight, complete with a tiara and puffy blue dress. She caught the sides of her skirts with the dainty white gloves she wore and gave a graceful curtsy to Mela.

"Thank you, my Lady," she said.

"Oy, feather-brain! If you don't come out right damn now, the truce is off!" Decker yelled.

"What's his costume?" Mela whispered to Owen, who shrugged.

"While we await his arrival, I have a gift for our newest Little Witch." Vasha announced.

Layla squealed and bounded to Vasha's side. "For me? Really? What is it? Oh, please give it to me…" she cried much to Vasha's delight. He handed her a package wrapped in brown paper, tied with a blue bow. Layla hugged Vasha quickly, then sat in the nearest chair to open it. Decker stood close by watching her every move.

In silence, everyone observed as she pulled a dark blue dress from the package. It was made from the same material as Mela and Owen's clothes. The fabric flowed like water. But Layla's was very different. It was a full length dress with long, flowing sleeves. Instead of a separate cloak, the hood was attached to the dress itself. Mela had to admit it was beautiful. Layla stood and held the garment to her body with an expression of pure adoration. The sparkles at the hem of the gown told of the hidden stones sewn into the dress. From where she stood, Mela thought they were diamonds.

"Oh Vasha," Layla sighed, overwhelmed. "Oh, it's just lovely."

"Not as lovely as you are, little one. Would you like to try it on?" Vasha asked, reaching for her.

"She don't need no help dressing." Decker barked at his brother.

"I'll be right back. Thank you so much." She wrapped her arms around his waist briefly again, then darted into the house.

"You got five seconds, feather-brain, then it's game over for you!" Decker called out.

"I am here," Sammuele said calmly. Everyone turned to see Sammuele standing in the shadows of the trees.

"What in the world?" Mela said. Owen doubled over in laughter as did Decker. Sammuele approached them in, what can only be described as, a Devil costume. Instead of his blue robes, he wore a red one made of cheap material. It was the tail and horns on his head that made the first bubbles of laughter start to rise in her. When he produced the forked staff, Owen and Decker lost it completely and rolled on the ground laughing.

"Sammuele...why?" Mela asked, struggling not to join them.

"I am paying penance for the jest on Dektrios. He said that if I wore this we would be...I do not remember the phrase..." he looked around, confused.

"Square...I said we'd be square," Decker said from the floor, between gasps for air.

"Yes. That means that he will no longer hold ill will toward me for the trick."

"Yep. That's what it means." She couldn't hold it in anymore and joined the boys in their laughter.

Sammuele watched them for a moment before the corners of his mouth began to twitch. Decker jumped up and tossed an arm around his shoulders.

"It's all right to laugh, feather-brain. It's a good look for you." He pulled Sammuele to the table and handed him a skull goblet full of wine.

"Annabelle, I have grape juice for you," Wyatt called out. "And wine for me," he said with a smile to Mela as he poured a hefty goblet full. They stood together watching Annabelle taste her grape juice from the only bedazzled goblet at the party when Layla made her entrance.

Whistles from the guys and applause from Mela and Wyatt made her blush. She looked stunning in her gown of blue and diamonds. She joined them with a goblet of wine and a big smile.

"A toast!" Decker called out.

"Happy Halloween everyone!" Wyatt said.

"Aye, it's All Hallows Eve," Decker stood on a chair and raised his glass. "A night when the spirits dance and gay boys prance." He raised his cup to Wyatt, who bowed dramatically. "When Witches gather in blue, black, and gray, to watch over us and keep evil at bay." The three Witches raised their cups. "To friends and brothers," he turned to the rest. "Who make us laugh and make us cry, dear Gods above and below...don't ever let us die. For this merry group is dear to me and we'll stick together through thick and thin. My friends, the feather-brain, and my kin." Everyone applauded and cheered.

It was a magickal night.

READ A PREVIEW OF THE FIRST COMPANION NOVEL TO THE EARTH'S MAGICK SERIES

DECKER

Now available

Chapter One

The light from the fire made the back of Mela's house dance with shadows. Decker sat on the back porch smoking a cigarette while he stared off into the night. He took a drag and tilted his head back to exhale the smoke. His ever-present black bowler hat sat on one knee, the other leg stretched out before him.

He righted his head, tilting it slightly to the side as Wyatt approached. His yellow catlike eyes never moved as they searched the darkness. He could hear Wyatt's steps but it was his smell that shouted his presence in the darkness. Decker knew everyone's smells the way others knew the sound of a voice.

"Oy, what you doing out here?" Decker quietly asked. Everyone had gone to sleep, or so he thought.

"Hey there, Decker. I was wondering," Wyatt grabbed a patio chair and noisily moved it until it sat right next to Decker's. "I was wondering if we could talk."

"Talk? What for? About what?" Confused, he faced Wyatt and frowned. "What'd I do?"

"Nothing," Wyatt laughed. "I had an idea and I wanted to run it past you. You know, see what you think." Decker's eyes narrowed and he nodded his head for Wyatt to continue. "I think this is a fantastic idea. I want you and the others to tell me your stories. You know, like dictate your memoirs to me. I take good notes, and I also want to record it, to make sure I get it right. What do you think?"

"Why?" Decker growled.

"Because, you brute, you're fascinating! The history and the stories you could tell are like nothing we've ever heard before." Wyatt's charming smile never withered under Decker's glare.

"Why don't you ask Vasha? He likes to talk about things like feelings and he's better at remembering stuff. Why you asking me?"

"Well, you're the most important one, aren't you? Shhh…don't tell anyone I said that, though." He brought his voice down to a whisper. Decker fidgeted in his chair for a moment and wrestled with the desire to tell Wyatt to go to hell. He didn't want to talk about the past. The past was better left alone to fade into nothingness. But there were things he knew that would not only be interesting but possibly helpful as well.

"What kind of questions?" he asked finally as he tossed his cigarette into the yard.

"Easy ones. I ask the questions and you just talk till you can't talk anymore."

Decker shrugged and waved his hand for Wyatt to go ahead. He eyed Wyatt as he lit another cigarette, silently watching him produce a small recorder from his back pocket, and a pad of paper.

"This is Wyatt recording the life and times of Dektrios, otherwise known as Decker to his friends." He cleared his throat a few times and flipped through his notebook until he found the page he was looking for. Decker's eyebrows raised but he said nothing. "Decker, how old are you? When and where were you born?"

"That's three questions in one, mate. I've got a general idea, but not exact. A long time ago, I was able to figure it pretty close. We didn't keep records the way your lot does now." He gestured toward the recorder in Wyatt's hand. "We told stories over and over until we remembered them and then passed them along to other people. That's how my people worked."

"What were you able to figure out?"

"I'm trying to tell you, if you give me a moment, thank you very much. I was able to do some simple arithmetic once and came up with my approximate age of two thousand three hundred years."

"Seriously? You were born before Jesus?" Wyatt's hazel eyes were wide with excitement.

"Bugger it all….yes. I was born before your Jesus. Now, back to me. My tribe, well, it wasn't really mine, was it? We never belonged to that bunch of ingrates. But, for the sake of this conversation, our people were from the Arabian tribal lands. Now, it's the country of Saudi Arabia. Fuck, things were different then. Really different." He took another drag from his cigarette and slowly blew the smoke into the air. "Basra. The nearest place that would show on a map was Basra. There was a market there where merchants brought their goods to trade."

"Did you ever go?"

"Yeah. Yeah, I went a few times with…with my sisters, Akasma and Aydan. We would go to the markets for things we needed. Material for clothes, food, incense too. There was a huge area in the market just for incense. The smell was lovely. Sometimes, Mela will light some of her incense sticks and I remember things…"

"Smells always make me remember things too. That's common for people, I think." Wyatt's voice trailed off and he gave Decker a small smile. "Sorry. Go on."

"Bah, it was such a long time ago. Why you want me to go back this far? I could tell you about my time as a soldier of Rome." Wyatt waved him off and shook his head.

"Nope. I want the whole story. No cheating, Decker. I ask and you answer, that's what we agreed on."

"Camels."

"What?" Wyatt asked, taken off guard.

"Camels. There were a lot of camels everywhere. People used them for traveling and for carrying their stuff. Smelly and noisy creatures, to be sure. When we went go to market, Akasma would borrow camels from a family in the village who were kind. Not many were, mind you. Even less then than now, I think." Decker sat back and stared off into the night again as he continued.

"We would walk through the market streets, the girls all wrapped up in their scarves. I did the same then but we men only wore one on our head to keep the sun off. I was there to protect them, see. My sisters were beautiful and I had to protect them..."

"Did anyone ever notice that you were...different?" Decker sat for a moment, lost in his deep well of memories, when suddenly he let out a bark of laughter.

"Oh sure." He chuckled again. "Oh yeah. Once, when we were leaving the market, a group of men came up behind us. They said how lovely the sky was and how lovely the views were. Then, they said there were two lovely maidens there that made it all the better. My sisters didn't react, they simply kept going forward. But me, I listened well to them while they discussed my sisters with their filthy mouths and their stinking bodies that craved them. They smelled like stale wine and camel shit. It didn't take long for them to overstep their bounds neither. They rode up beside us and tried to grab the reigns of Akasma's camel. They paid me no mind because I was smaller then, but stronger than they were, even young as I was."

"Oh my God, did you kill them?" Wyatt couldn't help but ask. Decker seemed to enjoy the question and he smiled.

"The man pleaded with my sisters to stop and to sit with them on their camels. When they said no, the men surrounded us and stood in our way. What else could I do? It was my duty to watch over the girls. They brought me along to protect them, after all. The one that grabbed Akasma's reins lost an arm. With one slice from my sword, it plopped right to the ground." He laughed at the memory.

"Yuck. You and chopping off body parts."

Decker howled with laughter. "It was bloody glorious." He stood up and held his arm as if he were the wounded man and made a terrible grimace of pain. "My arm! My arm! You cut it off!" he mimicked. "It was beautiful. The other men drew short swords on me and thought they could rush me."

"They couldn't take you, could they?" Wyatt asked, enthralled by the tale.

"Hell no, they couldn't. But it didn't even come to that. My sisters sat like statues on their camels and I hopped off mine to the howling man with one arm. I picked up his bloody stump and hit him with it." Wyatt made a face of disgust and Decker laughed again. "It made a wet noise when it hit his face. I beat the man with his own arm. That's a beautiful, and rare thing, make no mistake. The others, seeing a crazy, wild boy wielding a severed arm as a weapon, decided to turn around and leave."

"Smart of them," Wyatt sat with his hand almost covering his mouth.

"Yeah. Real smart. I turned to the man on the ground and pointed his own hand at his face. I told him, 'Sir, you have no honor and for that, you have lost an arm. Follow us no more or you will lose the other one!'" He sat back down and searched for his pack of cigarettes. "The one-armed man sat on the ground and nodded his head, begging me to spare his life. I did. See, I can be very merciful."

"Full of mercy."

"Judge not, Wyatt. Those were the times we lived in then. Had I not been there, the girls would have been raped and their throats slit open. No one travelled alone in those days." Decker lit another cigarette and smiled.

"I'm not judging, Decker. It's just gross that you like to cut off body parts all the time."

Decker stretched his legs in front of him and took a drag from his cigarette. His yellow eyes focused again on the darkness beyond the firelight. Wyatt wanted him to talk more but the expression on his face forced him keep his silence. Decker wasn't seeing the trees or the fire, but people from very long ago. He was remembering their faces. He was remembering how they spoke. He was remembering they were all dead.

"The girls loved it," Decker's voice was almost a whisper. "They loved to go to the markets and see all of the people and the stacked pottery. I don't know why they bought that stuff. We lived in a cave that was full of dust and bugs. But they would spend all day cleaning up the dirt and moving rugs here to there..." His voice trailed off.

"It sounds like they were trying to make a home for you and your brothers." Wyatt said softly. Decker nodded, still lost in his memories. Wyatt cleared his throat to try and bring him back.

"What else you want know?" Wyatt smiled and checked his papers. He made a quick notation on the paper and looked back at Decker. "Well...I was wondering if you could tell me about....Him. The man that came to take you and your brothers away. Sammuele called him The Darkness in human form. Can you tell me a little about that time?"

Decker stared at him for a long moment and considered the question.

"We were older by that time. Azul was almost to his full size." He pointed his cigarette at Wyatt. "An impressive size, mind you. As tall as this house. I remember Azul spent many nights alone then. He was too big to be left in the cave all the time. Azul needed to fly."

"Wait. Azul...the scary one...he flies?" Fear made Wyatt's face pale. Lately he has seen many things but everyone spoke of Azul as something to fear with a level of seriousness that frightened him.

"Aye, he flies. He would hunt and come back before sunrise. I remember...he changed then. He stopped speaking to us and slept all day. When the sun fell below the horizon, he would get up and swoop right out the cave without a word. The girls, they would worry and try to make him happy when he returned. They would make him things, hang a new garland of flowers for him but he stopped caring." Decker tossed his cigarette into the yard and crossed his arms over his chest.

"That's when you knew something was going on?"

"No. Not me. I just figured he was tired of being cooped up. We all were. But it was when he asked Vasha, Theo and I to come with him that I knew something was different. He'd never done that before. The girls knew but pretended not to notice us leaving the cave together one night. I rode on Azul's back while Vasha and Theo, who got longer legs than me, kept pace with him. He took us to the little river that flowed next to our cave. I remember seeing the stars in the sky and the moon was waxing that night."

"Was He there?"

"Usually I can sense stuff, I can smell others around. But this one, he had no smell. He came from behind a tree and smiled at us."

"What did he look like?" Wyatt's curiosity got the better of him.

"He wore the same sort of robes those in the village wore. His hair was brown and he wore sandals on his feet. Nothing made him special except…"

"Except what?" Wyatt didn't have the patience to keep quiet any longer.

"His damned eyes. They were black and bigger than they should've been. You see my eyes, Wyatt?" Decker leaned into Wyatt's face and stared with his yellow catlike eyes. Wyatt nodded. "Mine are like an animal's eyes but his…his eyes weren't natural. You get my meaning?" Wyatt nodded again and then shook his head. Decker sighed heavily and leaned back in his chair.

"Wyatt, he wasn't natural so his eyes and his smell were all wrong. He isn't alive like you and me. The man standing there was a…a glamour or some kind of thing. But you can't glamour a smell or the eyes. You can always tell by the eyes."

"What did he say?"

"That's the thing, Wyatt, I can't remember. I remember a fire appeared outta nowhere and we were sitting there listening to him. But I don't know if he really said anything or if he just…thought it and we heard him." Decker shook his head and ran his hand through his long locks.

"That's interesting. Was every meeting like that?" Wyatt was scribbling away in his notepad as he spoke.

"I don't know. I don't remember much about our meeting with The Dark One. Every night Azul would take us out there and every night blended with the next. Before I knew anything was happening…everything changed." He said the last words softly.

"Your sisters found out then, right?"

"Yes. We were…I was confused. They tried to make us stay in the cave one night. They blocked the door and scolded us. Said we were doing things that were bad and that we had to stay inside and away from the dark. I thought then that they were trying to keep us out of the dark of the night. I think they meant a different dark…"

"Sounds like it to me." Wyatt whispered.

"Well, one evening my sisters weren't in the cave. It wasn't yet full night so Azul couldn't go out. Theo was worried about them because that's what Theo does, he worries. I didn't know it then but they were down by the river waiting for Him. I don't know what happened. When the sun went down, we left the cave and found Him there. I remember he was angry. He was angry we hadn't told him about our sisters." He sighed heavily and spun his hat on his finger.

"That's when he said they were dangerous, right?" Decker nodded his head. "When you went back to the cave that morning, were they there?"

"No. They were gone. Theo cried and sulked for ages. Azul flew out every night looking for them but never found them. I tracked them to a nearby field but from there their smell was gone. Vasha, he stayed quiet and mourned in his own way. One night, Azul simply never came back. We waited for him but he left us as well."

"Oh, I bet Theo took that so hard." Wyatt said. Decker smiled a tight, painful smile.

"We all did. He was our eldest brother. Our protector. One morning when I woke up, Vasha was gone too. With him, every piece of jewelry and rug that had made it a home was gone with him. Me and Theo were all that was left."

"Did they leave to find the girls?" Wyatt asked.

"I don't know. I know when I left...I left so I wouldn't be sad anymore."

About the author:

Mel Massey is the author of the *Earth's Magick* series and other paranormal stories. Her husband is an active duty soldier in the United States Army, which keeps Mel's family moving around constantly. Mel is a practicing Pagan and an avid bibliophile.

Visit www.melmassey.com for book news and visit the forums to chat with other *Earth's Magick* readers.

www.ingramcontent.com/pod-product-compliance
Lightning Source LLC
Chambersburg PA
CBHW060950030726
47503CB00003B/813